GUESS WHO

CHRIS McGEORGE

GUESS WHO

A NOVEL

HANOVER
SQUARE
PRESS

**HANOVER
SQUARE
PRESS**

Recycling programs
for this product may
not exist in your area.

ISBN-13: 978-1-335-65282-9
ISBN-13: 978-1-335-00713-1 (International Trade Paperback Edition)

Guess Who

Library of Congress Cataloging-in-Publication Data has been applied for

HanoverSqPress.com
BookClubbish.com

Printed in U.S.A.

For my grandfather John Board

The school is quiet by the time I get back. My mum always used to say I was scatterbrained when I forgot stuff, but she never got round to telling me exactly what it meant. Looks like I've been scatterbrained again though. I knew it the second I looked in my bag, halfway home—I'd left it in the Maths room. My notebook, with tonight's homework on it. I don't want to let Mr. Jefferies down, so here I am.

I slip back across the field and into the main entrance. There's something really creepy about school after dark—when all of us have gone. Usually it's loud and busy, but now the corridors are quiet and my footsteps sound like elephants stomping because they echo up and down, up and down. I don't see anyone but a man dressed in green overalls, using that weird machine to clean the hall floor. He looks like he's the most unhappy man in the world. Dad says if I don't study, this is the kind of thing that'll happen to me. I feel sorry for the man, and then I feel sorry that I feel sorry because pity isn't nice.

I start walking quicker and get to the Maths room. The door is half open. Mum always taught me to be polite, so I knock anyway. The door squeaks like a mouse as it opens.

I don't see him straight away. The door gets stuck on the papers and exercise books all over the floor. I recognize one and bend down to pick it up. Mine. Mr. Jefferies had collected them in at the end of class.

I realize that something is very wrong, and I look up to see him. Mr. Jefferies, the Maths teacher, my Maths teacher. My friend. He's hanging in the center of the room with a belt around his neck. His face looks a strange color and his eyes are so big he looks like a cartoon.

But he's not. He's real. And it takes me too long to realize what it really is that I'm looking at—too long to see that this isn't some kind of horrible joke.

But as I look, there he is. Mr. Jefferies. Dead.

And at some point, I start to scream.

1

Twenty-five years later...

A sharp, undulating tone—drilling into his brain. But as he focused on it, it separated into ringing. In his head or out there—in the world, somewhere else. Somewhere that couldn't possibly be here.

Brring, brring, brring.

Brring, brring, brring.

It was real—coming from beside him.

Eyes open. Everything fuzzy—dark. What was happening? The sound of heavy breathing—taking him a second longer than it should have to realize it was his own. His senses flickering on like the lights in a hospital corridor. And then, yes—he could feel his chest rising and falling, and the rush of air through his nostrils. It didn't seem to be enough. He opened his mouth for more, and found it to be incredibly dry—his tongue rolling round in a prison of sandpaper.

Was it silent? No, the *brring, brring, brring* was still there. He had just got used to it. A phone.

He tried to move his arms and couldn't. They were above his head—elevated—slowly vibrating with the threat of pins and needles. He could feel a ring of cold around both of his wrists—something cold and strong. Metal? Yes, it felt like it. Metal around his wrists—handcuffs? He tried to move his limp hands to see what he was attached to. A central bar running down his back. And he was handcuffed to it?

Both arms were throbbing at the elbow—both bent at odd angles as he tried to maneuver himself. He was sitting up against this thing, whatever it was. But he was sitting on something soft—and felt his current unease was most likely because he had slipped down a bit. He was half sitting and half lying down—an uncomfortable arrangement.

He braced himself, digging his feet into the surface and pushed himself up. His foot slipped, unable to keep any type of grip (shoes, he was wearing shoes, had to remember that), but it was enough. His bottom shuffled back so the strain on his arms was released. With the lack of pain focusing his mind, the blurs around him began to come into focus.

The objects to his left were the first to appear—the closest. He saw a table, between whatever he was sitting on and a white wall. On the table, a black paneled cylinder with red digital numbers on it. A clock. Flashing 03:00:00. Three o'clock? But no—he watched it and it didn't change, illuminated by the light of a lamp next to it.

It hurt his eyes to focus on the light, making him realize the room was rather dark. He found himself blinking away sunspots and looking up at the white wall. There was a picture there, framed. A painting of a distant farmhouse across a field of corn. But that wasn't what drew him to it. The farmhouse was on fire, red paint licking at the blue sky. And in the foreground there was a crude representation of a scarecrow smiling. And the more he looked at it, the more the scarecrow's smile seemed to broaden.

He looked away, unsure why he felt so unsettled by the picture. Now, in front of him he saw his legs and feet—black trousers, black shoes—stretched out over a large bed. The plump duvet had slid down and he had been scrabbling against the bunched-up sheets. Assorted dress cushions were scattered around him.

In front of him was a familiar scene—would have been to anyone. Desk, small flat-screen TV, kettle, bowl full of coffee and tea sachets, a leather menu standing open on its side. There he finally saw the phone—far and away out of reach. He moved his head slightly to see a walk-in wardrobe to the front left. To the front right, a window—curtains drawn with the ghost of light creeping through.

Unmistakable. This was a hotel room. And he was handcuffed to the bed.

And it was all wrong.

Three sharp tones, drilling into his brain. Brring, brring, brring.

This was all wrong.

2

He didn't know how long he sat there, listening to the ringing. Forever and no time at all. But eventually there was a new sound. A voice. A female voice. Slightly robotic.

"Hello, Mr. Sheppard. Welcome to the illustrious Great Hotel. For over sixty years, we have prided ourselves on our excellent hospitality and vast range of unique comforts that you can sample while staying in your luxurious surroundings. For information on our room service menu, please press 1, for information on our newly refurbished gym and spa, please press 2, for room services such as an early wake-up call, please press 3…"

Mr. Sheppard? Well, at least it was his name. They knew his name? Had it happened again?

"…information on live performance in our bar area, please press 4…"

Had he had too much, *done* too much? Twenty years of using and drinking, and using *and* drinking, he had started to think that *too much* was a concept that didn't apply to him. But it had happened before. A grand blackout where he woke up somewhere else entirely. A rollercoaster of a fugue state, where he'd bought the ticket.

"…information on the local area, such as booking shows, and transport options, please press 5…"

But he knew how those situations had felt. And this wasn't that.

Because— It still wasn't there. Where had he been? Before. Where— The last time he remembered. Now, a hotel room, and then—a figure danced around on the edges of his memory. A woman.

He swallowed dry and ran his tongue over his teeth. There was something in them—the gray and rotting aftertaste of wine along with something chemical.

"…for early checkout, please press 6, if you would like to hear your options again please press 7."

This was wrong. He shouldn't be here.

And the phone—the phone had gone silent. For some reason, no voice felt worse. If he could hear her, could she hear him? *It's a robot, just a robot.* But the line could still be open. Worth a shot.

"If you would like to hear your options again, please press 7."

He tried again to move his hands, to get some feeling back into them. He made quick fists with his palms. And when he had enough control, he braced himself and moved his wrists quickly against the central metal bar. The center of the cuffs clanged against it. The sound was loud, but not loud enough. *You're wasting your time. Just a robot.*

"If you would like to hear your options again, please press 7."

He opened his mouth, his lips ripping apart as though they hadn't been open in years. He tried to say something, not knowing what. All that came out was a hoarse grunt. "If you would like to hear your options again, please press 7." Silence.

He opened his mouth. And what came out was something like a "Help." *Just a robot.* Still not loud enough.

Silence.

And then the robot on the phone laughed. *Not a robot.* "Okay, Mr. Sheppard, have it your way. But you're going to have to start talking soon. Can't wait to see what you do next."

What? He didn't have to time to think about the words because there came a terrible sound. The dull tone of a dead phone line. The woman was gone.

He tried to calm down—his heart was racing in his chest. This wasn't happening—couldn't be happening. And maybe it wasn't. Maybe it was just some bad dream, or some kind of new bad trip. He had been hitting it pretty hard lately. But as he thought it, he couldn't believe it.

It felt too real.

Someone would come. Someone had to come. Because the staff obviously knew he was here, which meant the whole hotel knew he was here. And he couldn't have handcuffed himself to the bed, so…

Can't wait to see what you do next.

What was the point of the call? That's the thing about a phone—you could pretty much be whoever you wanted to be and there was no way of knowing for real. Why would this woman *robot/not a robot* be calling him? He couldn't reach the phone. So, this woman could be the one—the one who'd handcuffed him to the bed. The one who was playing some sick joke. And if she wasn't a staff member, maybe that meant no one would come.

No. This was a hotel. Of course someone would come.

Eventually.

He shut his eyes. And tried to slow his breathing enough to listen for anything outside of the room. Any thundering past, any suitcases rolling. But there was nothing. Silence.

Except that wasn't quite true.

He felt it before he heard it. That prickling on the back of his neck. And then, very softly, the sound of breathing.

He wasn't alone.

3

He realized that it had always been there—such a natural sound that he didn't register it. But, as he held his own breath, it became louder. Breathing. Almost silent—like the breaths of a specter. But it was there. Soft, shallow breaths.

And the more he focused, the more he heard. It was all around him. Not just one person. How many? He couldn't know. People—plural—in the room with him.

He knew he had to open his eyes, but they refused. His brain was starting to connect dots that weren't there—trying, fruitlessly, to make sense of it all. Was this some kind of PR stunt? His agent had warned him about stuff like this—the tabloids paying for a scandal. What more of a scandal than some kind of hotel room orgy?

But it didn't sit exactly right. Would they really abduct him, cuff him to a bed, just for a story? Not their style. And besides, he was fully clothed. The most disappointing orgy ever.

Against all odds, he almost laughed. He was going crazy now too. Add it to the long list of things that needed addressing.

But first—he wrenched his eyes open again. The hotel room

looked back at him. The breathing was still there. He had to look. He shifted left as far as he could with his wrists bound. The ice-cold cuffs bit into his skin, but he tried to block it out. His body leaned left, and he tilted his head so he could see over the edge of the bed.

He expected—*hoped?*—to see nothing but the carpet. Instead, he saw something he couldn't quite define. Until he realized he was looking at the back of a person, dressed in a gray suit, lying facedown on the carpet. As the thought clicked in his head, he hurriedly rocked back on his wrists and shuffled back to the center of the bed.

A person. A real person. Facedown on the floor.

Silence again—the breathing still there. But now began something else. A skittering sound, like mice nibbling on cardboard.

He forced himself to look over the right side of the bed, straining on the cuffs again. There was no one there. The carpet was a muted purple. Looking down at the slice of floor he could see, however, he noticed something. A small trail of something yellow toward where the bed ended. It looked too fine to be string, and as he looked it started to twitch. Hair. It was hair.

He returned to the center of the bed. Hair? God.

He looked straight ahead, into the black mirror of the television. Couldn't see anything in it—not even himself. And he was glad. He didn't want to know how pathetic he looked. The blackness calmed him—the nothing. He would focus on the television until someone came to rescue him. He would refuse to accept any of this.

And even as he told himself that, he found his eyes drawn downward to the edge of the bed, past the shine of his shoes, as something rose up. One finger. And then two. And then a whole hand gripping the duvet.

His heart sank. The shuffling grew louder and the breathing did too—all around him. And now— They were waking up.

4

A face at the end of the bed. Blonde. A girl—twenties. Looking like he felt—confused and pale, her eyes filled with panic. She looked around first, her head rocking around on her neck, and then she saw him, rapidly ducking down again in surprise.

"H-hey," he tried to say. His voice was cracking in all the wrong places, making it sound like more of a threat than a greeting. He tried again. "Hey." A bit better that time.

The girl surfaced—just her eyes. They flitted to his handcuffs. They looked even more confused. But hey, he wasn't going anywhere, so maybe that helped her stick her head up again.

"What—? What's happening? Where am I?" Her voice was small and scared. "What did you do to me?"

He looked at her, shocked. "I woke up here, just like you." He clanged the handcuffs to corroborate. It worked. There was something new in her face—understanding. For a moment, they were locked in each other's gaze, sharing their fear.

There was more stirring around her on the floor, and her eyes drifted down. He couldn't see. But whatever she saw made her jump up and back. Her hip collided with the desk and the room-service menu toppled over. She gave a small, curt squeal.

He could see her more clearly now. Jeans. Light yellow hoodie. Just your average girl. As he looked, he saw that there was something on her left breast. A sticker of some kind. "More people," she said, gasping. "There's more people."

"I know." Speaking was becoming easier, like an engine rolling over and starting up. "How many?"

"I don't... I can't..."

"I need to know how many." Why? Why was it important? Maybe because every extra person would make this so much worse.

Upon hearing his voice—his full voice—something must have sparked in her mind. She looked at him—her eyes wide and full. That look he saw nearly every day.

"Wait a minute," she said. "Aren't you—? Don't I—?"

Don't I know you? This was only going to delay things. He always existed on the fringe—he wasn't recognizable at a glance but a double take would do the job.

"You're..."

"Yes, yes." He usually would have loved it. But not now. "How many?"

"Oh God... There's four people. A girl. Two men. And a woman. I don't know if they're..."

"Are they breathing?"

"I think so. They're moving—the woman and the girl anyway. I don't want to check."

"No, no, you need to get to the door, okay?" He was losing her again—she was shaking her head. Hysteria—the enemy of progress. He took in a deep breath. "Just get out of here. Go and get help. You need to go and get help, okay?"

"What is this?" she said, her eyes darting around the floor. He was glad he couldn't see what was there.

"I don't know—but please, the door." He was almost pleading. What had he been reduced to already?

Can't wait to see what you do next.

The girl kept her eyes up, not looking at the floor. She made her way across his vision, toward the alcove. She must've been able to see the door. He was right about where it was. Of course. The girl made two exaggerated movements, side to side. She was dodging bodies. He didn't have to be able to see them to know. She disappeared from view into the alcove.

He leaned on the cuffs, forward this time, and craned his neck, but he couldn't see her. He heard her try the door, fumbling with the handle. The shake of it. But he didn't hear the door open. Why did the door not open?

"It's locked," she said. "It's... The key-card light's red. I can't..."

Another sound. Another scraping. The girl was trying the lock—the physical one.

"It's...it's stuck. It's locked." How could it be locked?

"Do you see anywhere the key card could be? Like a holder on the wall to activate the lights?"

"No, there's nothing. There's..."

"Look through the peephole," he said, "someone might pass by. There may be..." *Someone. Anyone.*

A beat. And then, "I just see the corridor." Banging. She was banging on the door. Bang. Bang. Bang. She kept at it, louder and louder, until it sounded like she was punching the door. "Hey. We're trapped in here. Someone! We can't get out."

And above the banging, he heard and felt something else. Another presence. A mumbling. As if someone was whispering by his right ear. He turned and looked into the eyes of an old woman with blankets of long black hair. They looked at each other, and he wished he was able to block his ears, as she began to scream.

5

It felt like his ears erupted as the old woman emitted the shrill, coarse sound that seemed so loud it could alert everyone in the building. She jumped up and backed herself into the corner nearest to him, so it was hard for him to see her—his blind spot.

The banging stopped, or at least he thought it did. His ears were ringing. He looked across the room, to the alcove the girl had disappeared into, but he faltered along the way. There were faces—two new faces. Just like the girl had said.

A young girl—younger than the one at the door—at the end of the bed. Maybe she was seventeen at most, and she was wearing some sort of black sweater. She had a large pair of purple headphones around her neck, a wire snaking down into her jeans pocket. She tried to stand up, but her legs gave way and she dropped out of sight again.

A young man, slightly to Sheppard's left, fared better. He was slowly becoming conscious, but as soon as he opened his eyes, he snapped to alertness. He was wearing some kind of jumpsuit, pure white. There was something on him, a sticker, matching that of the girl's. Some writing. Impossible to read across the distance. He looked around, with more of a sense of wonder than confusion. When he saw Sheppard, he just stared at him.

The girl, the man, the woman—how many had the blonde girl said? Four. One more. The old man. The man he had seen when he looked over the left side of the bed.

The blonde girl appeared from the alcove, a look of dejection and shock on her face to mix with the panic.

The screaming woman must have seen her too, as she shot toward the girl, moving around the bed with a speed unreasonable for someone so delirious. The teenage girl darted out of the way of the woman, and Sheppard saw her decide to shuffle under the desk, wrapping her arms around her legs. A good but ultimately futile defense.

The black-haired woman grabbed the blonde girl by her arms and shook her, finally stopping screaming to utter, "What is this place? Is this it—the consequence, the punishment? I must endure it." She pushed past the girl and ran into the alcove, then a loud BANG, as if she had just collided full-pelt into the door.

The blonde girl, discarded by the woman, lost her balance and collided with the young man, who in turn toppled over, into something—or someone—new. There was a grizzly "Ouch" from a new mouth.

The two responsible scrabbled up and away from the new voice. Sheppard knew the look—apologetic toward authority. He had seen it worn many times. They both made their way around to the right side of the bed, as though they were using Sheppard as a blockade to whatever was coming.

As the blonde girl came closer, Sheppard could see what was on her sticker now—the sticker they all seemed to be wearing. It was white, with a red bar on the top—one of those stickers one would see on a team-building exercise at work.

HELLO MY NAME IS... on the red.

And then scrawled in black felt tip on the white—Amanda.

Sheppard looked at it, and then, by instinct, looked down at his own chest. It was the first time he had looked down and he was a little surprised to see he was wearing a white shirt, a dress shirt, and on his breast, his own sticker.

HELLO MY NAME IS… Morgan.

A fresh bout of "What the hells?" burst in his mind.

He looked back up. The blonde, Amanda, was looking too. She looked down at her own sticker, and then they both looked at the young man's.

HELLO MY NAME IS… Ryan.

"That right?" Sheppard said, nodding to her sticker.

"Yes," she said. "How do they know my name?"

"Amanda."

"Yes. But people call me Mandy. Mandy Phillips."

"Yes," the young man said, "Ryan Quinn." He pointed to his sticker on his—yes, it was a jumpsuit—and a rather strange one at that.

"Morgan Sheppard," Sheppard said, but Ryan just nodded.

"I know. I've seen you on…"

"How is the door locked?" Mandy interrupted, thank God. "Is this some kind of reality thing?"

"What?" Sheppard said. Reality thing?

Technically, everything's a reality thing.

Against everything, he almost laughed. But Mandy had meant a reality show and hadn't he thought the same thing? And then it clicked. Why she'd calmed down when she realized who he was.

"Where're the cameras?" she said, looking around.

He frowned and Ryan looked at her, not quite getting what she was talking about. Mandy thought it was all some kind of stunt too. His TV studio was indeed pure evil, there was no doubt about that, but even they wouldn't stoop to kidnapping and, most likely, drugging. "I'm sorry, Amanda—Mandy, but this is real. I woke up here, just like you." An age where reality television was all but fantasy. Why not believe it? But this was real. He could feel it. And as he caught her gaze, he realized that, really, she knew it too. She could see it, but that didn't mean she wanted to. Her smile dipped. "No…"

He was going to lose her again. He needed her. Her and Ryan. He couldn't move, which meant they had to be his eyes.

"Mandy. Ryan. I need you to keep calm. And try to keep everyone else calm. You need to see if you can get me out of these." He nodded upward to the cuffs. His hands were almost totally numb now—limbs just along for the ride.

"A key," Mandy said.

"Yes—a key. See if there's a key around."

There was little chance of it just lying around. Whoever had handcuffed him, handcuffed him for a reason. For a… Wait. A new question. A new big question. Why was he the only one handcuffed? They had chained up the famous guy—but no one else?

Mandy went around Ryan and started searching. But Ryan was still. He was looking at Sheppard, trying to puzzle out whatever was in his head. He seemed calm though, which was good.

As if to prove how he should be acting, the woman with the long black hair reappeared, only to charge into the alcove again. A slamming sound. She was going to hurt herself. "Is sorry not enough?" in her shrill voice. "This is Hell. Hell."

Sheppard knew better than that. Not hell. Hell wasn't a place. Hell was inside, deep inside. He had found it a long time ago.

"Hell. Hell. Hell," the woman shouted, almost singing it. "And you're all here with me. Why might that be, I wonder?" She slammed against the door again, and cackled. Insane. They were locked in here with an insane person.

Sheppard looked back at Ryan. He appeared to be wrestling with something, and the longer it took to come out, the worse Sheppard thought it was.

"Ryan."

He almost jumped at his name.

Ryan leaned in and whispered in his ear, "I need to tell you something."

A clearing of the throat. Ryan and Sheppard looked at each other—the noise didn't come from them. They both looked around to see the old man steadying himself precariously against the wall and the bed, trying to get up. When he finally managed, his face changed to anger. "What on earth is going on here?" Sheppard felt Ryan step back. "Anyone? Tell me. Now."

He was a smart man in an old-fashioned way, wearing a gray suit and a dulled tie. His dark skin was illustrated with a weathered way of worldliness and the flecks of a pepper-pot goatee. His hair was black, obviously dyed, with patches of gray showing through. His face seemed to rest comfortably in a scowl and his round glasses were slightly askew. On his chest, above his left pocket, his very own sticker—HELLO MY NAME IS… Alan.

All eyes in the room were on him. Mandy had stopped what she was doing to look at the new arrival. Even the teenager under the desk was staring at him with wide eyes. It was clear that this man commanded attention.

"I—I…" Even Sheppard felt himself back down. He didn't usually do that. He usually stood strong against anyone. But the compromising position…

"What is everyone looking at?" Alan barked, and looked down. "What?" He ripped his sticker off and crumpled it up. He smoothed the patch of his suit down. "You can't stick things on this. It'll leave a bloody residue." He threw the sticker into the corner and glanced around again. "Well?"

Sheppard decided to be honest. "I don't know."

"You don't know?" Alan said. "You don't know? Of course you don't. What is this, some kind of new TV show? Some Channel 4 rubbish. Dear God, tell me it's not Channel 5. Well, looks like you've included the wrong arsehole. I'm a barrister, idiot. I know my rights and the rights of everyone in this room. Look around. That's five lawsuits staring you in the face."

"For the last time," Sheppard said, out of frustration, "this is not a television program."

"Of course it isn't." Alan looked up to the ceiling. "I want out now please. And I want everyone's name involved in this sham." When no one answered, Alan stepped toward Sheppard again. "I'm a real person, unlike you. I do important things. Like…" He looked at his expensive watch. "Dear Christ, the MacArthur case. I have to be in Southwark by two."

Sheppard's blank look only seemed to rile Alan more. Everyone else was quiet, not wanting to incur any wrath themselves.

"The biggest case of my career and you people have put me here. Well, you are going to learn the harshness of the law when I get out of here. And I'm not talking about your studio, or your company. You. Sheppard. You." Alan enunciated these points with jabs at the air.

Realization by denial, by mania, by acceptance, by anger and, Sheppard saw out of the corner of his eye, by mere disapproval. The teenager, whose sticker was unreadable without his glasses, watched Alan while taking her headphones from around her neck and putting them over her ears. Sheppard suddenly felt a strong kinship to her, as she shuffled farther under the desk— clearly trying to disappear into it.

"I'm sorry," Sheppard said, although he didn't know why.

"Nonsense. Utter nonsense."

Sheppard felt movement beside him. Alan seemed distracted too. Sheppard looked around. Ryan was moving over to the window. He realized what the young man was about to do. Ryan grabbed at the curtains, clutching them tightly, and with one swift movement, he flung them open.

There was a flash of sunlight, instantly stinging his eyes.

After the relative darkness of the room, the light felt too much. He blinked once, twice, trying to blink the multicolored spots away. He looked to the window, looking outside. Buildings. Tall and thin. They were high up. The buildings were familiar, the backdrop he could so easily trace with his mind. He was looking out at Central London. But why did that feel so wrong? Why did it all feel...

And then he remembered.

6

Four hours earlier...

They barreled into the room in each other's arms. She was kissing him, deep and strong. A passion he hadn't felt in a long time. He managed to reach out and slot his key card into the light slot, and the lights turned on. They were back in his hotel room, upstairs from where he had met her—in the hotel bar. She pulled him back in and he was lost in her, and the night.

"*Pas maintenant, monsieur television. Not now.*"

She regularly lapsed into French. Drunk. Which only made her so much hotter.

She hadn't known who he was at first, and he found that endearing. He bought her a drink, and she spent the rest of the night Googling him on her phone, wondering why people were talking to him all the time. The Art Opening being held in the hotel function room eventually thinned out, and they were left at the bar with each other, talking into her phone. Foreign Siri didn't recognize his London accent.

She pushed him down onto the bed and crawled on top of him, hungry, nipping at his neck with her lips—sliding up him.

"Mind the tux." He laughed.

"Vissez le costume!"

"You understand I have no idea what you're saying, right?"

She straightened up and got off him. "Got anything to drink?" she said.

He gestured to the minibar. There were a few things left in there at least.

Her head disappeared into the fridge and she pulled out one small bottle of white wine and one of bourbon. They had known each other for all of two hours and she already knew his drink of choice. Was this what finding "the one" felt like?

"Avez-vous de la glace?"

"One more time," he said, laughing.

"Sorry," she said, adjusting her language. "Er...do you have any ice?"

He gestured to the desk, where he had put the ice bucket, already knowing it had all melted. She picked it up, looked inside and smiled. "I'll go and get some then." She lunged at him and kissed him rabidly—the ice bucket remnants sloshing onto his trousers. He didn't care. This woman was something else—something new.

She pulled back. *"Je reviens."* And she rushed out of the room with the bucket under her arm, slamming the door behind her.

"Okay," he called after her. He got up from the bed. "I should have paid more attention in French class," he muttered under his breath.

He walked over to the mirror and took off his bow tie, undone and hooked around his neck. He took his suit jacket off and put it on the desk chair. He stepped forward and checked his eyes. The paranoia had set in a month ago. It had started when he had had to do a segment on liver cirrhosis on the show. The liver had the power to regenerate. A night of heavy drinking, and afterwards the liver works back to what it was before. But heavy drinkers (over years) damaged the liver so much that it would just give up. Therefore the damage would stick. Early signs included abdominal pain (which would have been dulled by the painkillers, even if he did have it); advanced signs included the whites of the eyes turning yellow. (At least, all of this was what he gleamed from the internet when he was curious after the show.) He had never considered himself a hypochondriac but…

You're not a hypochondriac if it's justified. Said every hypochondriac ever.

He was just being cautious of his health. Anyway, he was fine. He was making something out of nothing.

"Je…mappale Sheppard. Mapelle?" He stepped back and smiled at himself. He only remembered one phrase from school. *"Je voudrais un torchon s'il vous plait."* Meant "I would like a towel please." Wouldn't get him very far. *Merde.*

He went over to the window and drew the curtains open. The city looked back at him. He loved just watching the skyline, no matter where he was. There was something about staring out at a city, high up, making you think you're the king of the world. Seeing all the streets and the roads and the alleys and the highways all working together, becoming one organism. He had never been here before, to this city. But it was the same feeling. The Eiffel Tower was lit up, a beacon around which everything else emanated. He had been up there yesterday, lamenting the way he had decided to be a tourist. He was meant to go to the Louvre tomorrow with Douglas (his agent, who was staying somewhere *"a little more appropriate to an agent's salary"*), but now he was thinking he might have other plans.

After a late morning, and morning sex, he would probably just rest. Maybe get in a swim. Spend the day in the bar. Maybe she could do it with him.

This was the first real holiday he had had in years. *Resident Detective* had made him a household name, but at a cost—the intense filming schedule was crazy. When your series was on every weekday, you had to pump out ridiculous amounts of content, ridiculous amounts of lives he meddled in: affairs, stolen money, illegitimate children, misguided domestic lawsuits, more affairs—he had seen them all in the Real Life segment of the show. That was his favorite bit. That was the bit where he could really have some fun.

When you filmed five episodes a day, it was hard to remember specific cases. They all seemed to blend into one. And of course, he couldn't remember names. One time, he caught a *Resident Detective* episode and watched himself on screen as if he were someone else. He couldn't remember doing any of it. Part of it was because he didn't care. Part of it was because he was "overworked." Overworked and high all the time, he supposed.

Douglas had suggested the holiday. A chance to recharge the batteries. Come back a bigger and better Morgan Sheppard. Sheppard hadn't been so convinced but one day, backstage, he had heard Douglas and the programming controller of the station having an argument. The PC said Sheppard was burnt-out—heavily implying it was because of the substance abuse. The plan was for Sheppard to take fourteen days, slow down a bit and come back "refreshed."

Sheppard didn't tell Douglas he'd overheard the conversation. He just agreed—and after that, he set about convincing himself. Maybe this was a good idea and maybe he had been hitting it a little hard lately. Douglas was overjoyed—so overjoyed he came too (which was probably why he was so into the idea all along).

So he'd come to Paris five days ago. And so far he felt great. Even more so now he had met this crazy hot woman. *Who seems to be taking some time?*

He turned from the window and flopped down on the bed.

Scrabbling around so he was finally lying down properly, his head between the two pillows. It was comfortable. He closed his eyes. He didn't realize how tired he was.

What time was it? He hadn't worn his watch either. He was on holiday—what would be the point? Now was for relaxing. But he didn't want to be asleep when she came back. He would probably ruin it if he was. And she was so hot. And it had been unreasonably long since the last time. But he was so tired. And his eyes remained shut. And there was a soothing sound. Almost a hissing. He hadn't heard it before, but maybe it had always been there. And the more he listened, the faster he seemed to fall.

His thoughts fell away. And he was gone.

7

How could this be real? How could this be possible? How could he be in Paris one moment and London the next? The woman. Had the woman done this to him? He hadn't just moved rooms, he had moved countries. How could you move countries without knowing it? He wouldn't call it impossible but not entirely possible either. It was in the gray area in between.

How long had it been? How long could he have been out? The red room. And here. How long between those two points? It could've been no time at all, could've been an eternity. But— no. He had his own personal way of knowing.

His last drink had been in the red room with the woman. Red room. Wine and bourbon. The stuff he had tasted in his teeth. And now, his throat and brain were dry. But there wasn't that gnawing feeling. That little scrambling on the edges of his brain matter, like something fizzing, whenever he didn't take his pills. So, all dried up but dosed enough. If he had to guess—six hours at the least but no more than twelve. That coupled with the fact that it was day—morning. Ten hours was a reasonable estimate. Ten hours all gone.

He looked away from London. Just in time to see Alan grunt in disapproval. He was walking over to the window. "I'm supposed to be across the river for Christ's sake."

"Oh shut up," Ryan said. Alan looked taken aback and stepped away, crossing his arms and frowning at no one in particular. Ryan was looking out the window, his eyes darting around the scene outside. "We're near Leicester Square. Facing south." He looked to everyone else, as if for approval. Sheppard just looked at him in amazement for figuring it out so quickly. Ryan looked back at the window. "We're in Bank," he said again, like he was confirming it.

"Try to open the window," Sheppard said, stretching his arms, although Ryan was already reaching for the latch.

It was a sliding window, one that looked like it would only open an inch due to how high up they were. Ryan unlatched the window and pushed. Nothing. He made a confused grunt and then tried again, putting his full weight on the handle. Nothing. Ryan continued to try, until his hand slipped from the handle and he fell to the floor. Alan just watched him get back up, not bothering to try to help. Ryan righted himself and tried one last time.

"It's locked," he said. "Won't even open an inch."

"Then let's try this," Alan said, and before anyone could stop him, he picked up the chair which Headphones had pushed out from under the desk. Alan brandished the chair and thrust it full force into the window. The chair, and Alan behind it, bounced off the window like it was the wall of a bouncy castle. He was thrown to the floor and the chair flew into the center of the room. Mandy, who was looking through one of the drawers of the desk, narrowly dodged it.

Ryan held his hand out to Alan. "You couldn't break these windows. They're thick and antishatter." Specific. Alan's eyes narrowed, as Sheppard's did. That was very specific.

"And even so, where would you go?" Mandy said, looking up from the drawers.

Alan chose not to accept Ryan's hand, reaching out for the desk to help him up. "Well, I apologize for trying. You all seem to have made yourselves at home here. Ms. Looney Bin might actually be the only sane one amongst you." He looked around, catching sight of Headphones. "What's your story?"

Headphones just looked at him, her eyes wide. Alan peered at her sticker.

"Rhona, what are you up to, Rhona? Just listening to some tunes, waiting for the world to end. You teenagers are all bloody imbeciles."

"Lay off," Sheppard said, rattling the cuffs. A new pain and a glance upward confirmed what he thought—his wrists were red raw, the cuffs digging into his flesh.

"Oh, don't you start." Alan rounded on him. "You're a walking, talking embarrassment. I read the papers. I know all about your addictions. But this is the worst addiction of all, isn't it— the lust for attention. Well, congratulations, you've got everyone looking at you. And now you've got us all stuck here with you."

"For the last time, I don't know why we're here."

"Bollocks. You television types always know when some idiocy is going on. Is this about the MacArthur case? You want me out of the way or something?"

"This isn't about your stupid case," Mandy said, still rifling through drawers.

Alan laughed, looking from Sheppard to Mandy and back. "Stupid. That's the word we're going with, is it? *Stupid?* Do any of you watch the news?"

"Let's not lose our heads," Ryan said, "we're all in this together." He put a hand on Alan's shoulder—an act that wasn't entirely favored.

Alan shrugged him off. "Yes, but some of us are more in it

than others." He nodded to Sheppard. "Why are you hand-cuffed, and no one else is?"

The same question he'd asked himself—Alan was just a bit behind him.

Sheppard gritted his teeth—shut his eyes and took a breath. "I don't know." Losing his temper wasn't going to help anything.

Mandy had finished searching the drawers but hadn't found a key. Now, she was just standing there, growing paler and paler. She had something in her hands. She put it down on the bed, and Sheppard saw the words glistening in the light. The Holy Bible. A hotel room's only constant. "I need to…wash my face." It looked like she was going to faint. She stumbled out of view, and Sheppard heard a new door open. The bathroom. How had no one thought to check the bathroom?

As Sheppard looked toward the alcove, he saw the woman with the black hair emerge from it. On her chest—HELLO MY NAME IS… Constance. Sheppard watched her, wondering what she was thinking about.

"What I'm saying is this man may be dangerous. Maybe he's handcuffed for a reason," Alan was saying. "And I sure as hell know I need to be across London."

Sheppard kept watching Constance. Her silence unnerved him. Her large, almost cartoonish eyes, accentuated by her panda mascara, fell to the bed and she snatched the Bible up, clutching it to her chest.

"Religious terms must not be taken in vain," Constance said, in a low guttural tone, which probably escaped everyone else's hearing.

The situation was slipping from bad to dire in front of Sheppard's eyes—and he couldn't even move.

"Let's all just keep calm," Ryan said.

"No, let's not. Let's not keep calm. This is not about keeping calm," Alan said.

"Hell. Hell. Hell. Hell. Hell," Constance said. Headphones, mouth screwed up, looked at each in turn. And then—a scream. A high-pitched desolate scream.

One that seemed to bounce around the room, piercing everyone in the heart.

Sheppard glanced at Constance. But he already knew it wasn't her.

It was Mandy. In the bathroom. And, just like that, things got worse.

8

The scream seemed to go on forever, but at some point it was over and then there was silence. And somehow the silence seemed much worse. No one moved—Alan and Ryan frozen in their conversation, Headphones peeking round the desk and Constance looking toward the bathroom.

Sheppard's first reaction was to jolt forward at the sound. The handcuffs ground into his wrists and he yelped in pain. His flight response was overwhelming. He was not a man who wore panic and fear well. Even the moments when he woke up in a cold sweat, his heart beating three times too fast, and thinking that maybe he had finally overdone it, he always secretly knew he would pull through. But here, in this room, he was scared—genuinely scared.

There was a crashing sound as Mandy reentered his field of vision, backing away from the alcove and bumping into Constance.

Constance pushed her away selfishly, like she was diseased.

Mandy looked to Sheppard. Her eyes were glassy reflections of themselves as tears streamed down her face.

She was a pale white color and her skin was slick with sweat. "What? What is it?" Sheppard said.

Ryan saw it before anyone else, and rushed to Mandy just as she was about to collapse. He caught her just in time.

"There's... In the bath..." Her voice was small.

"What?" Sheppard said, leaning forward as far as he could.

"A man. I think...a dead man."

Sheppard felt the bed drop out from under him—free-falling through nothingness. But, of course, he wasn't.

A snort of derision. Not exactly the response he expected, but Alan seemed to be chuckling to himself. "A dead man. A body in the bathtub. We've all been through a lot. We're all jumpy—we need to keep our cool here. The mind is a fragile thing." He went over to Mandy and tapped her on the arm—a curt attempt at comforting her. Through tears, Mandy looked at him. "There is. A man. A man in a brown suit."

"Well, if there is a man, who's to say he's not sleeping like we all were."

Mandy gritted her teeth. "You're more than welcome to take a look."

Alan frowned. He straightened one of his cufflinks absent-mindedly and cleared his throat. "Very well then." Sheppard watched Mandy as Alan disappeared around the corner. The girl was silently weeping and turned around to bury her face in Ryan's shoulder. Sheppard believed her completely. "Alan, don't go in there."

But it was too late. He heard the bathroom door open.

Sheppard's eyes drifted as he tried to focus his hearing on what was happening in the bathroom. He couldn't move more than two inches, and now the situation had changed. He found himself looking at the TV and had to look for a few seconds before he realized what was different. It was on—the TV was on. The last time he had looked at it, it had been blank. But sometime between then and now, it had started showing a gold mantra in the center of the screen.

We hope you enjoy your stay! in a loopy, almost illegible, scrawl.

And there was something else in the corner. A little blue bar with white numbers, like something you would see when you connected a very old VCR. Sheppard had to screw up his eyes to see it. "YOUR PAY-PER-VIEW STARTS IN: 00:00:57." Counting down—less than a minute. How did the TV turn on? And what was the pay-per-view?

Sheppard opened his mouth to tell someone—anyone. But at that moment, the bathroom door opened and Alan reappeared. His face mirrored Mandy's almost perfectly. He took off his glasses and wiped them with a cloth he took out of his upper pocket.

"It appears the situation is slightly graver than I first thought."

Ryan detached himself from Mandy and started forward.

Alan put up a hand. "Save yourself some sleepless nights, son."

Ryan took a beat, and nodded.

"He's facedown, so I couldn't tell much, but there's blood— a lot of blood. Around the torso," Alan said, plainly. Sheppard wondered if that was the tone of voice he used in court. "No one else goes in there. Believe me, you don't want any part in this."

Sheppard didn't know what to say, so a question slipped out. "Did you recognize him?"

Alan's eyes snapped to him. "Now that's an interesting question to ask."

"There has to be a reason we're all here. I just…"

"What are you hiding, Mr. Sheppard? I'm supposing you know all of this already. I'm supposing this is all some kind of sick game and I'm supposing we've all been roped into it against our will. Anything to say for yourself?"

Sheppard stared at him, walking the line between anger and

fear. And he only half noticed the fact that the TV screen had changed.

And a new voice cut in. Slightly muffled. Coming through the TV speakers. "No. Yes and yes." Every face in the room turned toward the TV. A profile on the TV screen, but Sheppard's brain had to catch up to puzzle out who. It was a man, but his face was concealed behind a garish and colorful cartoon horse mask—like something you would see on Halloween. The eye holes were cut out, so this cartoon had big green human eyes. It was unsettling—gross, and Sheppard felt a shiver of disgust and fear.

The man on the TV laughed. "Glad to see we're all getting along."

9

"Hello, everyone," the horse man said. His voice was slick and smooth and the bad speakers on the TV gave it a detached, otherworldly cadence. "Hello, Morgan."

Someone yelped. Constance—Sheppard thought it was Constance, although he couldn't really tell. His full attention was on the horse mask. He didn't know why, but he just knew. They were all in serious trouble, and he couldn't shake the feeling that he was worst of all.

"What is this?" Alan said, stepping forward to the TV. "Who are you?"

Was this a conversation? Or a recording?

The horse mask reacted. A conversation then. "You don't know me, not yet at least. But I know you. I know all of you. Especially you, Morgan Sheppard. I have been following your work very closely. It's hard not to."

Eyes on him, like always. Was this a fan—a deranged, obsessed fan? Sheppard had had his fair share of oddball supporters over the years, and he had heard horror stories about others.

"What's happening?" Sheppard heard himself say. "What do

you want?" Something was very wrong here—more than it had ever been in his life.

The mask heard him. That meant there was a microphone. Maybe a camera. Somewhere—most likely watching since they woke up.

"How the mighty have fallen," the horse mask said. Enjoying this—the sick bastard was enjoying this. "Cuffed to a bed, with your mind racing to every eventuality—every possible way you could get out of this. With your instincts, I'm surprised you haven't bitten off your own hands and gone barreling through the front door by now."

Sheppard faltered. He hadn't exactly done that, but he had ripped at his wrists. "What did you do to us?"

The horse mask ignored him. "Do you ever look at yourself, Morgan Sheppard? Do you ever look in the mirror and see the drug-addled insipid attention whore you've become? A life governed by television contracts and YouTube comments. Stepping all over other people."

"You put us here?" Trying to regain the conversation.

Not wanting to hear any more.

"And yet some still call you 'Detective.' Even after everything. You're the bastard child of a Conan Doyle nightmare. You're not fit for the word."

"You put us here." *Stop, please stop.*

"Of course I did, you idiot." The horse mask twisted as the man crooked his neck. "You see, I'm here to see if you can live up to your supposed reputation. Or more accurately, your self-proclaimed one. *Resident Detective*, rather gauche."

"What is it talking about?" Mandy said, shooting Sheppard an unsure look.

Sheppard didn't hear. Thoughts, too many thoughts, swimming in a dead sea.

The horse man cleared his throat, although he already had all the attention. "As you probably know by now, you have been checked into a hotel room. The Great Hotel in Central London, to be exact. You are on the forty-fourth floor. It's not a luxury room but my people have made a few modifications.

"Firstly, they sealed the doors, the ducts and the window. There is no way out of the room, unless under my express orders. You cannot escape, unless I want you to. In the event of a fire, well…" He stopped to make a guttural chuckle. "Secondly, they did some DIY and covered the room in soundproofing. You've already managed to make quite a noise with the screaming and the banging, but rest assured that no one will hear and no one will come. You could make the loudest noise in the world and not a soul on the other side of that wall would hear.

"It took a lot to get you all here. More than a few trips in luggage containers. Luckily none of you woke up. The point is the staff think that there is a very exclusive party going on in this room and have been asked to leave you alone. If for any reason you manage to contact the front desk, it'll be the woman you have probably already heard."

"The woman?" Ryan said, looking to Sheppard.

Sheppard took a moment. "There…was a woman on the phone. I thought she was one of those automated things, but… She… That's how I woke up."

"She's one of my people. Of course she is. And now she has disabled all calls going in or out of this room…"

"She said something about next. *Can't wait to see what you do next.* What's happening next?"

The horse mask stopped. No way he could tell, but he imagined a look of disdain. "Today, we are going to be playing a little game of Murder. You've already found that one of your fellow guests is no longer with us. In fact, he has been brutally murdered by one of my associates. And here's the snap: that associate—the murderer—is in the room with you right now. One of these people is a murderer. The others are not—red herrings, McGuffins, whatever you want to call them."

What? The killer—of the man in the bathtub. The killer was in the room?

"Take a look around you, Morgan. Five people. Five suspects. One killer. One of these things is not like the other."

Sheppard wasn't the only one glancing around. The others were too, and now they were slowly separating—eyes darting as they moved into their own safe space.

He knew where this was going.

"So here's the deal, Morgan Sheppard. Seems you are the actual definition of *resident detective* in this room. I'll give you three hours. Three hours to solve the murder, to find out which of your fellow guests has killed a man in cold blood."

"Why are you doing this? Why should I do this?" *It's my fault. It's all my fault everyone's here.*

The horse mask made that chuckle again—low and humorless. "You never are a man to do something pro bono. Boring people need reason to do unboring things. There's always got to be something to incentivize. Well, how's this? When it begins, a timer will start. The timer on the table next to you." Sheppard looked down at it and then back to the horse mask. "And there's no way to stop it until it ticks all the way down to zero."

Sheppard was silent. The mask was silent.

And finally, Mandy's voice came up. "What happens at zero?"

"If Morgan Sheppard doesn't correctly identify the murderer in three hours, then you all die. And not just everyone in the room. Everyone in the hotel. My people have placed explosives around the structure of the building. I press a button and The Great Hotel becomes a Great Mess."

Various cries of disgust rang out. Who from—everyone? He didn't know. He wasn't in the room anymore. He was somewhere else—a blank place with only him and the man on the TV.

"It's school holidays, Morgan. How many tourists do you think are staying here? How many young families—how many kids who just want to see *Wicked* and go to Hamleys? All going boom."

"You're sick," Alan said. "Depraved."

The mask twisted round again. "Three hours. One murder. Should be easy for the good Sheppard. Really it would be a relief to have a few hundred deaths off my conscience. But rules are rules. And just like promises, they must be stuck to. Otherwise, there would be chaos. Although I suppose this time there's chaos either way."

He could use a drink right now. Some of his pills. Things were too real, and they always helped with that.

"Speaking of rules, there's a rule book in the bedside drawer, should you forget anything. But it's really quite simple. Three hours. Get the wrong answer, I blow up the building. Refuse to cooperate, I blow up the building. Cause too much of a headache, I blow up the building. You step one foot out of line—I. Blow. Up. The. Building. Got it?"

A sudden movement. Ryan pelted for the door. He disappeared around the corner and Sheppard heard him banging.

"Let us out. Let us out now," Ryan shouted.

"Someone clearly wasn't listening," the mask said.

"Hey. Let us out now." More banging. "Please, someone," said Ryan. "Let us out—now."

The mask resumed, eyes front, talking to Sheppard directly. "You can't do an investigation in chains. Forgive me for even handcuffing you in the first place. You're just a little…unpredictable. Addicts always are."

That word. Addict. Not a good word.

"Besides, thought you might find a use for some handcuffs."

Ryan reappeared.

"You're crazy," Sheppard said. "Insane."

"Means a lot coming from you." Sarcasm now? Impossible to tell in the mask's monotone. "You'll find a key in the rule book beside you. They'll unlock the cuffs. And then we can get this show on the road."

"Please, let us go. Just let us go." Straining on the cuffs. Thrashing out with his body. Until the real question came out. "Who are you?"

The mask studied him for so long, he didn't think he was getting a response.

"I'll give you two minutes grace period before the games begin. Because I'm a good guy."

The TV went black.

10

This wasn't real—it couldn't be. And yet it was.

In turn, they all faced him, looking like he had answers. The room seemed bigger now. They had all claimed their own place in it. They had been thrust together and then torn apart. Suspicion was etched on every face.

"What—?"

"I don't—?"

"But—?"

Voices running together. He couldn't focus. He had to focus. He shut his eyes, and took a deep breath. When he opened them again, Ryan was making his way down the left side of the bed. He opened the top drawer and took out a folder marked "Rules." He opened it. Sure enough, he took out a small key. He put the folder on the bed, and shrugged at Sheppard.

The key had been so close. Yet so far.

Sheppard gave him a sad smile, as the young man reached up.

"Now wait a second."

Ryan stopped. *No, no, no.* He looked around.

Alan was watching them both with his familiar scowl.

"Maybe it would be in our best interests not to let this man loose."

"C'mon," Sheppard shouted.

"Why?" Ryan said.

"I'm just saying," Alan said, "there's no reason why we should believe everything we're hearing. What if this man is behind everything? What did you…" He looked around to Mandy. "Blonde, what did you say before?"

"What?"

"You thought this was all some setup, some publicity stunt? Well, why not?"

"You went into the bathroom," Mandy said. "You saw that… man."

Alan shrugged. "I'm just saying, what if the only dangerous person in this room is already in cuffs?"

Sheppard groaned. He needed to be free. "Are you serious? You heard what the TV said? You need to let me go now." *And then what? I can't do this. I just can't.*

"We don't *need* to do any such thing," Alan said. "This whole thing is your fault, no matter which way you slice it. You television types are all the same. If this mask man is telling the truth, then you're the only one who can save us? Give me strength!"

"And what do you think is going to happen in three hours?" Ryan said, turning back toward Sheppard. *Yes. Just use the key. Use the key.*

"Empty threats," Alan said. He actually believed every word coming out of his own mouth. "We're supposed to take a man in a horse mask on his word?"

"It's all we have right now," Sheppard said. "He put us here. He put us *all* here, and if you're all the same as me, here is goddamn surely not where I want to be."

"God—" Constance started.

"Sorry," Sheppard said. "Who's to say his threats aren't real?"

Ryan nodded at him. "That's good enough for me."

"You're making a mistake," Alan said, even as Ryan reached up to the cuffs again. *Yes. Thank you God.*

Ryan fiddled for a moment and Sheppard thought, for a horrifying moment, that maybe it was the wrong key. Maybe the mask was just toying with them. But then there was a *click* and Sheppard's limp arms fell down to his sides. Sliding down the bed, he took a moment to right himself.

He stretched his arms, getting the blood back into them. Peeking out from his shirt sleeves, he saw his raw, red wrists, crusted over with dried blood. They stung to the touch.

"Thanks," Sheppard said, and Ryan nodded.

He tried to scrabble off the bed, fighting with the duvet, putting his legs over the side. He stood up too quickly. The world swirled around him. He put a hand on the wall to keep himself from falling.

The room corrected. Everything seemed smaller from higher up—the people less intimidating. He put a hand up to his chin and he found prickly stubble, longer than he remembered it.

They were watching him. He knew that. He needed a plan. *We need to get out of here.*

He turned slowly. Didn't want to upset his eyes again.

The bedside table. The clock. Still on 03:00:00. Hadn't started yet. The two minutes. How much time had passed? The binder saying "Rules" was on the bed where Ryan had put it. It was large—a lot of pages. Ryan had only looked at the first one. He reached for it.

It was heavy—packed with pages. It would take over three hours to read it all.

But this thought was eradicated the moment he opened the folder. On the first page were four simple words—LISTEN TO THE HORSE. And then—nothing. He rifled through quickly.

Blank page after blank page. Nothing. No more rules. A joke.
Except one last sentence on the last page.

THE BOY LIED.

What the hell was that supposed to mean? Sheppard threw
down the folder in disgust—it hit the bed and bounced off onto
the floor with a thud.

"There's nothing—there's nothing else." What was he expecting?

"What now?" Ryan said.

Back to the room. All the lost faces, even Headphones, watching him. How much had she heard with those headphones
cupped on her ears?

Sheppard didn't answer. He pushed past Ryan, and toward
the alcove. The head of the room was just as he imagined it.
There was the main door, a closet on the right sitting open with
bare coat hangers, extra blankets and a small safe and there was
a door to the left which must lead to the bathroom. *Don't think
about what's in there. Just don't.* A dead body—he couldn't face a
dead body. Not until he knew he absolutely had to.

He ignored the bathroom and went to the main door—first
seeing the fire-escape information plastered on it, the rendezvous
point of Floor 44. The door handle had a hooked message, Do
Not Disturb or Please Clean My Room, whatever your prefer-
ence. He tried the handle, relishing how cold the steel felt on
his hands. To feel something again. He pulled. Nothing. Pulled
again. Nothing.

Mandy was right. The key-card light was red. Could it be
overridden? Had the masked man hacked it somehow? He looked
around. There was indeed a place to put the card to activate the
lights, but it wasn't there. On a whim, Sheppard flicked the light
switch. The lights came on. *What?* He turned them off again.
That didn't make any sense.

He looked at the door again. It would be impossible to break down. It was a fire door and it opened inward not outward. He ran his finger across the edge of the door. He thought he felt the draft from outside—the corridor—but he could have been imagining it.

He looked through the peephole out into a hotel corridor in a fisheye lens. Muted carpet, nothing but more doors and doors left and right. Across from him, a door labeled 4402. He put his hand into a fist, and it made it halfway to the door before he stopped. There was no point hammering. It had already been tried and deemed pointless.

Claustrophobia crept in. No matter how big the room was, it felt suddenly very small. A drink would be great right about now and maybe a pill or two. He needed to get out—why was his mind on the minibar?

He wheeled around. All eyes were still on him, watching him with interest. No one looked like they could help—even Alan had nothing to say. He went over to the window and they parted for him. Maybe they were hoping he knew the way out. He had been in many hotels in his time and he had never entered or exited any way other than the main door.

He put his hands on the windowsill, looking out to the London skyline—a sunny day. The London Eye peeking up from the tops of buildings, Waterloo off to the left, Westminster to the right. They were high up enough that all these landmarks were framed by the window.

He wondered if they could get a signal to someone. A tall building was in the center of the frame, running vertically against their own building, blocking out most of the sunlight. It looked like an office building. He screwed up his eyes to try and see in the windows. There was no one in the office—in fact, it looked all packed up. There was no one there.

Next... What was next? The main door was a no go. The window was impossible. The vents? Maybe the vents?

He looked to the bed and the wall above it. It took a few moments to locate it as someone had painted the vent the same shade of cream, but he saw it.

He climbed onto the bed steadily, hoping he wouldn't fall. His wrists protested as they rubbed against his cuffs but he maintained his balance and then went to the wall. The vent was large enough for someone to crawl through, it looked like. He managed to loop his fingers around the central bar of the grille and pull. No give. He looked at the edges. Flatbed screws on all of them. He tried getting a hold of them, but there was no way they were budging.

He turned. "Does anyone have anything in their pockets?" Sheppard said. "Like a penny? Some change?" Everyone checked. They were in their own little worlds. After a few seconds, they returned blank faces—turned up nothing.

Trust was gone. And it wasn't coming back.

"Here, try this," Ryan said, and reached up and handed him the handcuff key.

Sheppard turned back, trying to work the key into the slots of the screws. It was too thick and he quickly lost grip.

Nothing. Door. Window. Grate. No way out.

There had to be something else—something he hadn't tried. Short of banging on the walls, he couldn't think of anything. He scanned the room, tossing the key back to Ryan. No other exit. Just a normal hotel room.

But it wasn't quite. It had stopped being normal a long time ago. Ever since the horse mask had decided to play a little game. But if the horse mask knew anything, he would know Sheppard couldn't do what he asked. Sheppard hadn't been a real detective in a long time. He was just a front man. A man who talked about things that didn't matter, made bold predictions about *things that didn't matter.*

He wants to see you fail.

So what was he to do? Curl up in the corner and prepare to die? Because as Sheppard looked around, he didn't see a hotel room. He saw a coffin.

11

His life had gone too quickly. A blink of an eye and he was here, in this room. Fame rushed by, and now, for the first time ever, he wished he wasn't famous anymore. Even though that's all he had ever wanted. He had been fourteen when he met his agent for the first time. Three years, his parents had tried to keep him away from the limelight and that only made him want it more.

"Hey, little guy," the man said. Decades ago. But very close.

Was it his fault—the man he would come to know as Douglas, the man who he considered his only friend? Was it his parents' fault? Or was it he, himself?

Douglas had taken him out for ice cream. He had asked if he was too old for ice cream but being fourteen years old didn't make ice cream taste any worse. People stared, they must have seen him on TV, people were still talking about what he did—it was awesome.

"What do you want most in the world, Morgan?"

"I want to be famous."

"You already are, son. What you did a few years back—that boggles the mind. You want fame? You got it. Now, staying famous—well, that's something I might be able to help you with."

And Morgan smiled. He always smiled.

Years later, in this room, and Sheppard thought he might never smile again. Fame? Wash it all away. Be done with it. The show, the book, the newspaper articles. *Just never let me end up here.* Because now he would be famous for a whole new reason. For killing people.

A sharp beeping noise pulled him out of his self-pity. Beeping somewhere in the room. Sheppard got off the bed and looked around, locating the noise—the bedside table. The cylindrical digital clock had started counting down. 03:00:00 had turned to 02:59:54. Six seconds. More—already gone. Slipping away in front of his eyes. The beeping stopped. The countdown didn't.

Three hours to solve a murder.

Sheppard looked around. Ryan was watching him intently, a dangerous look of hope in his eyes. He was probably thinking that Sheppard looked like this a lot on his TV show, but Ryan was mistaking blankness (reading the autocue) for thoughtfulness. The autocue was always Sheppard's best friend—behind the little black box was a team of people, the real brains. That's all television was. Smoke and mirrors.

"You can do it, right?" Ryan said. "You can get us out?" All that was behind Ryan was the others. And he could see that hope was infecting them all. Even Alan looked slightly less furious. Mandy was worst of all—she looked almost certain.

I can't get anyone out. There is no way out.

The murderer—in this room.

None of them looked capable of murder—but one was.

Sheppard looked down at his hands, unable to look at the others anymore. His hands were ever so slightly shaking—his body and his mind aching for a drink and some pills. His shoulders ached in response. But that wasn't his biggest problem, was it?

You can't do it.

His one real victory was twenty-five years ago. A lot could happen in twenty-five years, and a lot had. But as he thought back, not a lot happened of much consequence. Was his really a wasted life—only half lived? Maybe this was to be a fitting end.

He thought back to all the rookie books he'd read—books on how to be a detective. Most information gleamed from TV dramas and novels. A murder investigation was a big thing. Not for one person. There was such a thing as a Sherlock Holmes, a Miss Marple, a Hercule Poirot, but that wasn't the real world.

The hero saves the day. Every single time. Rubbish. *But then—* What if he could actually do it? The odds weren't in his favor but—three hours. Five people. One dead man. That couldn't be impossible, right? Unlikely, but not impossible.

That's what I like about you, Morgan. You're a bastard. Douglas had said that once, and he had never truly understood it until now. The masked man was giving him a chance to become more than he ever could on his own. The chance to truly be a hero.

Sheppard looked up. The hope wasn't rotting people's faces anymore because he felt it too. He remembered a quote from some book he had read long ago: *"Murder isn't the greatest crime anyone can ever commit. But at least it gives you a good place to start."* He had laughed at it at the time—but it was true. He had to do it—go into the bathroom and confront what he knew was in there.

He pushed past Ryan and rounded the corner into the alcove. He paused in front of the bathroom door. He put his hand on the door handle and took a deep breath.

"What are you doing?" Mandy said.

Time was escaping from the room. They were standing in an hourglass, with hands out trying to catch the sand. "I'm going to solve a murder," he said, and found that he had one last smile in him.

12

The bathroom was dazzlingly bright compared to the murky bedroom. Sheppard put up an arm to shield his eyes as he shut the door behind him and glimpsed under his elbow. As his eyes adjusted, he saw the marble sink, the pristine toilet, the towels hanging on the heated rail, with more stacked up above it. He had been here before, many times, all over the world. He didn't have to look to his right to see the bath that could double as a shower, with containers of shower gel and shampoo clasped to the wall. But he didn't see any of that—the transparent cream shower curtain was pulled across it.

He didn't want to think about what was in the bath yet, so he found himself staring at his own reflection in the mirror above the sink. He stepped forward, reaching up to his face to confirm what he saw. He looked older than the last time he had seen himself. He had deep black bags under his eyes like shadows. His hair looked duller and his patchy stubble shrouded half his face. There were a lot more wrinkles, around his eyes, his mouth, his brow. A stranger wearing his face.

As he rested on the sink, his hand crunched something. He

looked down to the little bars of soap and tubes of toothpaste, but those weren't what he felt. He lifted his hand to find a pair of glasses.

His stomach dropped as he picked them up and turned them over in his hands. From any angle it was unmistakable—these glasses were his. He was shortsighted, and he didn't wear them nearly as much as he should. He never wore them in public. Never. No one knew he needed glasses, not even Douglas.

He looked up to meet his own eyes.

Who is doing this?

He shook off the thought. Not now. He had a job to do. Just be grateful he had them. He put the glasses on. He always thought he looked stupid in them. Never mind that now.

He rolled up his shirt sleeves, revealing the real damage the handcuffs had done. It looked like he was wearing two jagged scarlet bracelets.

He turned the tap on and put his left wrist under the stream of cold water.

An "ah" escaped him. It stung. He put his right wrist under.

When he was finished, he reached down to the toilet paper. The end was folded into a triangle, just as he knew it would be. He dabbed at his wrists and the paper came away red.

He turned to the bath. He took a deep breath—there was really no escaping it now. It was large and the base was pure white, except there was a small line trickling down to the floor. It had only got halfway before drying up. It was red, a color to match his wrists. Blood.

There was no blood on the shower curtain at least, but as Sheppard stepped toward it, he saw an ominous shape through it—a black mass, distorted by the curtain.

His nose picked up the unmistakable smell—dark and metallic.

Before he could stop himself, he reached up and grabbed the

curtain. Counting in his head—one, two, three. One quick motion, and he drew it across the bath.

The smell intensified as he forced his eyes down into the bath—and he saw. God, he saw. And he knew why Mandy screamed as he stifled one himself.

A man in a brown suit, lying face down in the drained bath. He looked uncomfortable, but you could be forgiven for thinking he was sleeping—if not for the blood. All the blood. It was pooling around his torso, snaking out from underneath him—frozen as the liquid hit the cool air. There was so much—too much. It seemed to have made its way around the length of the tub, giving the illusion that this man was bathing in scarlet.

All that blood. *Focus on something else.*

The man was gray-haired and balding—clumps of gray and white stuck out of his head at odd angles and Sheppard could see the scalp beneath. The man's hands were by his sides, flecked with blood and wrinkled. Sheppard tried not to think about what he had to do next—he bent down and reached into the bath, slowly, trying to stay as far away from the blood as possible. He pressed a finger to the old man's ice-cold wrist. He waited thirty seconds. No pulse. Had he really expected anything?

An old man. Dead. But how?

The wound was in the front—Sheppard had to turn him over. He felt sick just thinking it but it had to be done. He awkwardly got to his knees using the side of the bath to steady himself. As he reached the floor, he lost his balance and his hand slid into the bath. He lurched forward and felt the cold thickness of blood.

He withdrew his hand in disgust. Before he could stop himself, he wiped his hand on his shirt, a smear of red down his chest, regretting it instantly as the smell traveled up from the smear, promising to stay with him.

He recovered. How was he going to do this? He reached both hands into the bath, one gripping the man's nearest side, the other reaching over to the farthest. *Do it quickly. Do it quickly. Do it quickly.*

In one quick motion, he pushed with his knees, lifting the man. Then pulled with his hands. He used the slope of the bath to leverage the weight. And the man slid down, resting faceup.

Don't look at the face. He couldn't bring himself to do it. The half-congealed blood squelched as the body came to rest on the bottom of the tub.

He focused on the man's torso, thinking back to all the crime scene photographs he had seen on the show. Always still images. Taken in the past. Taken a long way away. Never right in front of him. Never there to smell and touch.

The man's suit lay open to reveal a light green shirt and a blue tie. At least he thought. The colors were all stained with red. The suit ruined. Hard to tell where the blood was actually coming from. Too much of it. But it seemed to be most around the lower area of the torso.

Looking closer, the shirt was ripped, lower left. Peering into the tub, as close as he dared, he could see the wound. Two wounds, two deep wounds above the waistband of the man's trousers. Gashes, so deep they probably hit some internal organ. Intestines, maybe? Sheppard didn't know. Straight gashes. Narrow. Stab wounds. Maybe a knife?

Two. Someone had buried a knife in this man, pulled it out, and buried it again. Schup. Schup. Once for safety. Probably aiming for the same place. A hell of a strong attack for so much blood.

That was it. That was all he could assume. A knife attack. Would a better person know? Know from this exactly who killed him? Who, out there, had the right MO? As he thought, he found his eyes drifting up the man's chest. His old dusty suit. Clashing tie and shirt. To his face. His white stubble. His eyes shut. His— Sheppard jumped back from the bath, slamming into

the heated towel rail and falling on his ass with a great *thwack*.
It was a pain he didn't even feel. He scrabbled with his limbs
and found his way to the corner, squashing himself next to the
toilet. He let out a long, drawn-out gasp.

No…

13

Before…

He was dropped off at the foot of the drive. They got out of there as quick as they could, speeding away as though they'd just dumped a broken washing machine. They didn't even look him in the eye anymore like he was possessed by something.

The house looked nice—big. The nice side of London. Not what he wanted when he grew up, but nice. A quiet neighborhood.

He made his way up the gravel drive, making sure to crunch all the way. The front door opened before he even got there. Like the man on the other side was waiting.

He was old—wrinkly. He looked like he dyed his hair as some gray was creeping through the brown. His eyes were kind and green and framed by a round pair of glasses. He looked like the kind of man who read the paper every morning, grumbled at the weather and saw doing his taxes as an adventure. But he looked nice enough. A nice man, for a nice house, for a nice place. How boring.

"You must be Morgan," he said, as Morgan came to a stop on the doorstep.

He didn't say anything.

"Was that your parents in the car? I had hoped to talk to them."

He was welcome to them.

"No matter, I'll catch them some other time." The man looked down at him.

"You're a quack?" he said.

The man laughed. "I am a therapist, yes."

"They said I needed to see a quack. That was the deal."

"Well, sometimes we all need to talk through our problems. But I won't push you to talk about anything you don't want to. When you've been through something like you have, sometimes it's good to have an avenue to explore it."

Morgan just looked at him.

The man seemed to visibly convulse. "Silly me, I haven't introduced myself." He held out a wrinkled hand. "I'm Simon Winter."

Morgan took it. The texture of a used tea bag. But he shook it nonetheless. And when he was asked inside, he went.

14

No…

How long had it been? Five years? Six? Simon Winter lay in the bath tub—dead.

How was this possible? How was this happening?

Sheppard couldn't breathe. It couldn't be him. It just couldn't. He crawled over to the bath, fighting instinct all the way. He peered over the edge. Simon Winter. Unmistakable. Lying there, his life streaming out his gut.

Sheppard's vision blurred as tears gushed down his face. He gave out a sound that could easily be a dying animal. *No. No. No. Not him.* How did this happen—how was Winter here, in this room?

Questions—too many questions—but in front of his eyes, there was a constant fact. Simon Winter, his old psychologist, was dead. This had to be more than just a body—this had to be a message. The man in the horse mask knew him and knew what Winter had meant to him.

Sheppard covered his mouth with his trembling hand as a fresh whimper came out. Winter must have been so scared—dying all alone. He took off his glasses and wiped his eyes.

He looked at Winter again. A message—a message that the horse mask didn't just know Sheppard. He knew him well—almost too well. The speech, the glasses no one knew he had and now Simon Winter, served up for him. The tears just kept coming. No one knew he had seen Simon Winter for the better part of his life. But here the old man was. And Winter had almost certainly died because of Sheppard. When was the last time he had seen Winter alive? What were the last words they had said to each other? All he could remember was that they weren't kind.

The old man had his part to play. Every murder mystery needed a corpse. And every corpse was a fresh mystery. Would Winter still be alive if…?

No. *Can't think like that, Morgan.* Almost like Winter was speaking to him. *Think like that, and you're as dead as I am.*

Sheppard brushed his eyes, and reached down to check Winter's pockets, forcing himself to remember the time limit. He reached into the left pocket, which was soaked in blood. It felt like he was pressing his hand into the wound itself.

He felt sick.

There was nothing in the pocket, so he pulled his hand free, trying to ignore the resistance from the sticky, congealed blood.

Right pocket. Wallet. He took it out, looked through it. The usual cards—Oyster card, bank card, some reward card for a bookstore. Nothing to tell him what he didn't know already. Dr. Simon Winter, sixty-five years old.

He put the wallet back and then paused, remembering something he couldn't quite put his finger on. Instinctively, he took two fingers and clutched at the left side of the suit, lifting it up. The inside pocket. He reached inside with his free hand, to find what he had thought would be there.

He pulled out a small pocket notebook. After all these years, he still kept it in the same place. During their sessions, Winter would reach into his jacket to pull out the notebook, write a few words, and then replace it. It became a quirk that delighted and frustrated Sheppard in equal measure—why didn't Winter just keep it out if he was going to write in it every few minutes?

The notebook was relatively untouched with blood, although it did seem very shabby and old. Without a second thought, he opened it up and flicked through it expecting to find brand-new notes. Instead, he found faded writing that looked years old. He flicked through notes on various patients, until he turned a page to find his name.

Morgan Sheppard. *Wait, what?* He hadn't seen Simon Winter in years, but he was carrying a notebook with notes from one of his sessions. The notebook had to be years old.

Sheppard glanced down at the notes—feeling as though he was violating some kind of privacy. The notes were dated 06/06/1997 and they detailed one session with him. Winter seemed to have written down standard things—Sheppard's mood, temperament, what he said. But somehow, in stronger pen strokes, certain words were underlined—dotted all over the page. "Aggressive. Muddled. A new dream about…"

The words seemed to be underlined with no real purpose. Why underline "A new dream about—" and then not under-line what the dream was about? He was asking questions that were decades old. What was more important was why Winter had this notebook with him now? Was it another message from the man in the horse mask? Had he already tampered with the body. How could Sheppard trust anything in this room? How could he trust anything at all?

Sheppard slipped the notebook into his pocket, not being able to think straight while his dead therapist was staring at him. Winter had been more than that though—Winter had been his friend. A friend when he couldn't rely on anyone else, not even his parents. Did Winter remember Sheppard fondly? Or did all that happened cloud his perception? Because after all, Sheppard had taken him for granted. Just as he always did. Winter didn't look in pain—at least there was that.

"I'm sorry," Sheppard said, choking on a fresh bout of tears.

15

Sheppard crashed out of the bathroom, losing his balance and almost going tumbling into the closet. The image of Simon Winter lying in that bath was imprinted on his vision—a photo negative seared into a life.

Sheppard. This puzzle was all based around Sheppard, and all he could think of were impossible questions with impossible answers. Winter, blood, sunlight, London, Paris, handcuffs, glasses and a horse mask—all swirling around in his head. A mess. And he had three hours to straighten it out—no, less than three.

Sheppard remembered something the French woman had said in the red room. She had called him a good man, and she had meant it.

A good man. But she hadn't known him—not even slightly.

Had she been in on it? Had she been tasked to get him into that room? What he'd felt for her had been real—or as real as he could manage nowadays—but was she stringing him along? He had made it easy for her—falling for it hook, line and arsehole.

Sheppard shut the bathroom door as though it might contain the horror within. But no, it was too late. He looked up to see it had infected the whole room—everyone a little paler and a little less alive.

Constance was sitting on the desk chair, silently clutching the Bible like her life depended on it, Headphones was still under the desk, Alan and Ryan were standing by the window talking in hushed breaths—Mandy was the only one to look at him as he came back into the room, waiting for him to come out.

"You saw him?"

Someone in here killed Simon Winter. Someone in here with him.

"Yes," Sheppard said, his voice catching. "I saw him."

Was Winter killed in the bathtub—surely he had to be with all the blood? But there hadn't looked like any scuffle. Did that mean the killer had been standing in the bathtub too? That didn't make any sense. The blood was dry—how long did that mean it had been there? Was Winter killed before or after Sheppard was taken? He couldn't do much without a timeline—something to measure everything against.

Someone laughed—a breezy chuckling. Sheppard and Mandy looked around to see Constance spinning around in the desk chair and laughing.

"Shut up," Sheppard said.

Everyone could hear everything in the room. Sheppard could pick out what Alan and Ryan were saying. They were talking about the logistics of breaking the window, and what that would actually do for an escape attempt. No secrets. The room was an amphitheater—you could hear every single word uttered from every corner.

"Mandy," Sheppard lowered his voice as much as possible while taking Mandy aside, although he knew everyone could still hear. "Do you know anything about that woman?"

"Her?" Mandy said. "The crazy one?"

"Yeah." He didn't expect much but Mandy nodded. "Well..."

yeah," she said, in a tone as though it were obvious, "she's pretty famous. I mean, not like you famous, but still… You've never seen *Rain on Elmore Street*?"

A twinge of familiarity but nothing concrete.

"It's a musical on the West End. The Lyceum, I think. That's Constance Ahearn—she's the lead."

Vague recollection of passing the theater, the grand awnings, the sign lit up in the darkness while people queued around the block. *Rain on Elmore Street.*

Constance's laughing punctuated the memory. Sheppard guessed her acting was the flamboyant kind.

"I need you to go and try to keep her quiet."

Mandy frowned. "I suppose…"

"Please. I need to think."

Mandy gave a curt nod. She went over to Constance and put an arm around her. She whispered something into Constance's ear. The woman stopped laughing, got up and followed Mandy around to the right side of the bed. They sat down, with their backs to everyone else. Mandy was good at this.

"You saw the body?"

Sheppard jumped at Ryan's voice. Ryan and Alan had turned their attention to him. "Yes. I had to see it—him. I had to see him."

You're not telling them. Why are you not telling them? Is it for them, or is it for you?

What would it accomplish—other than more needless speculation that would get in the way of actually escaping? "It looks like he died of a knife wound. Well, two knife wounds—in his gut."

Ryan looked at him. "Who is he?"

And there it was. The choice—two paths, two possibilities. "I don't know," Sheppard said. *God, help me.* "I—I'm still working out what to do here."

"But I might know the guy," Ryan said.

And Sheppard raised an eyebrow, as Alan clapped a hand on Ryan's shoulder.

As if he was summoned by the scent of unjustness, Alan cut in between Ryan and Sheppard. "Wait, son. Usually my opinions cost seven hundred an hour but this one's a freebie. Don't talk. Or do talk—I'm not your father. We are in a highly volatile situation, and anything uttered in this room is suspect. I'm sure Mr. Sheppard knows that that means anything said here will not stand up in a court of law."

"I just want to help," Ryan said.

"Get that window open, that's what would help."

"How would that help?" Sheppard said.

"We need to get a message to the outside world. If we break the window, maybe someone'll see it. Call the police."

"Forty-four stories up, no one in the building across from us, and someone'll see it?" Sheppard said.

Alan snorted. "Better than anything you're doing. What are you doing anyway?"

"I... I'm working things out." Sheppard hoped that sounded a little less pathetic to Alan.

"Yeah, that's what I thought," Alan said, smiling. "You see, I know people like you. I see them every single day. Difference is they're usually handcuffed in a box instead of on a bed." Wrists stinging to punctuate this. "Everyone's a liar—to the world, to other people, to themselves. But you put yourself up on a TV screen and spread your own lies out into the world, just to make it a little more insufferable. You're the definition of a joke, Mr. Sheppard. And your big detective act is not going to fly here. You can't even save yourself. Why the hell would you be able to save anyone else? And maybe, as that clock runs down, you should remember that. Remember that you are the reason we're here."

He could suddenly feel every inch of his skin, slick and sticky.

Obviously worse than he thought. Drowning in sweat. What he wouldn't give for a drink right now—even half a pill. It felt as if the strength was pouring out of him. "I have to try," he said, his voice weak, and hitching.

Suddenly he felt a buzzing in his head, in his cheeks—weak, tired. He needed to sit down. He needed water.

"I know," Alan said, shimmering in front of him, and pulled Sheppard close to whisper in his ear, "and watching you bumbling around this room searching for answers like an idiot will be the last bit of enjoyment I get from this sad mess of an existence."

Alan released him. He rocked back on his legs. They felt impossibly thin, not enough to hold him up.

Faces turned to look at him.

And then the floor came up to say hello.

16

Before…

He stared at himself in the mirror. There was something about viewing himself like this, with his stage makeup on looking almost impossibly young—the wrinkles papered over, the pot-holes under the eyes filled in. Looking like a cartoon version of himself. But under studio lights, he would look perfect. The immaculate man.

Not the tired, bored man he usually was. "Why are you here, Douglas?"

Douglas sat in the far corner of the room, reading the pamphlet all the audience members got before the show. The rule book. He threw it aside. "What, I can't visit my favorite client?"

Sheppard smiled. Couldn't help it. "Mmhmm." A kind of *cut to the chase.*

"Look," Douglas said, jumping up and pacing in the mirror, "I just wanted to make sure you were okay after our last conversation."

"I feel fine."

"Good, good—that's great." A thumbs-up reflected to him. "Because you were kind of saying some crazy stuff."

"I'm not going to quit, Douglas. If that's what you want to hear."

"I want to hear that you're happy," Douglas said. "You don't look happy."

"I'm fine."

The door opened behind him. The assistant stuck her head around it. "Three minutes, Mr. Sheppard."

He nodded and she left.

Sheppard stood up, fiddling with his cufflinks. Douglas stepped forward, and gripped him by the shoulders.

"You've really got something here, Morgan. You've built something for yourself."

Sheppard smiled. "I know." Reached into his suit and brought out his hip flask. He took a swig.

"That's my boy." Douglas beamed. "How's your shoulder? You taking the medication?"

"Yes, boss," Sheppard said.

"Knock 'em dead out there."

Sheppard nodded, laughed and left the room.

Walking through the back corridors of a TV studio was a lot like walking through the trenches. He walked the narrow line. People stopped when they saw him, wished him good luck. He smiled back at them. But he was thinking.

He'd got drunk. Told Douglas he wanted out. Douglas called it cold feet. He'd only been doing this six months. The show was a hit. But it was too much. It wasn't what he had thought it would be. It was too…too something. Too raw?

He'd fallen on the stairs going out of the club. Where all their business meetings took place. Slammed his shoulder something terrible. Douglas recommended a doctor. Who recommended the pills.

He took the little capsule out of his pocket and popped two out. He took them. Made the pain go away. Maybe a little too well.

He made his way around the back of the stage. It was dark. But he saw the assistant with a headset on, holding up a hand. Behind her, the light. She smiled at him, her fingers counting down from four.

Four.

Three. He felt the booze and the pills kick in, helping his mouth form that trademark grin. Already felt like he'd done this forever. And forever would.

Two. And that was okay, wasn't it? One.

He skipped out onto the stage. The light drowning out anything past the set. An audience of rabid fans back there, silent. Just wanting to see him do their favorite dance. And who was he to deny them?

"Camera one," he heard the director say, in his earpiece. He turned his gaze to the camera on a crane contraption, sweeping overhead. "Today on *Resident Detective*: Is international pop sensation Maria Bonnevart sneaking around with Red Lions' lead singer, Matt Harkfold, while being pregnant with *FastWatch*'s Chris Michael's child? I'll be reviewing the evidence later in the show. Also, we head over to the Real Crime Board to see how police in South London are reacting to the latest spree of robberies where perpetrators only seem interested in nicking industrial radiators. Let's hope the trail hasn't gone cold on that one." Pause for laughter. Plenty. *Christ.* "But first, in our Real Life segment, we meet Sarah who has reason to believe her husband, Sean, of five years, has been seeing their babysitter behind her back. Let's see if I can shed some light on the situation. I'm Morgan Sheppard. This is *Resident Detective*." Applause. The kind you can only describe as rapturous.

Sheppard stepped aside as a TV screen lowered from the ceiling and the title sequence started to play, and then was followed by a short VT about Sarah and Sean. This was only for the live audience of course. For people at home, the video was spliced with the live footage in the control room upstairs. Sheppard didn't pay attention to the video. He had seen it all before—his producer made him watch every VT before the show.

It was hard not to see these things as all the same. A wife, a husband, sexual intercourse—sometimes not with the right person. His team did some rooting around and told him whether the guy was guilty or not.

At least, that was the deal. But what had prompted that drunken desire to get the hell out? Sheppard had found that nine times out of ten, what his team told him was guesswork. Fifty-fifty.

They didn't do lie detectors like other shows did because Sheppard's reputation meant he "didn't need them."

Was Sean guilty? The cue cards in Sheppard's hands said yes.

Is Sean really guilty?

The VT ended and the TV rose up to the ceiling. Giving way to a row of chairs that the production crew put on during the VT. Silence.

Well…

He looked out to the crowd. Invisible shapes in the darkness.

Choose what you become.

"Sheppard," the director said. "Snap out of it."

"Well let's…" Sheppard said. "Okay. Let's welcome Sarah onto the stage. Everybody give her a big hand." He raised a hand as a woman walked out onto the stage.

Applause.

"Jesus Christ, Sheppard. You want to give me a heart attack?" In his ear.

The woman sat down in the center seat. As she was told, probably. Young, pale and sad. Not made for the limelight. A girl who worked in the behind-the-scenes of the world. She gave a small wave to the audience.

Sheppard sat next to her as the applause died down. "Now, Sarah, how are you?" Sheppard said. Conversing with her, projecting pretty much everywhere but. "I'm okay," Sarah said. Voice small and timid.

"Now, Sarah, you contacted me—" *the show* "—and told me about this, and I've—" *the team* "—been out investigating this for some time now. It seems like a bad situation." *War is bad, death is bad—this is busywork.* "Could you maybe just tell the audience your story in your own words?"

Sarah started talking, basically repeating the entire story that had just been told on the VT. Repetition was a key part of the show—didn't want anyone getting lost, and that way the team didn't have to think up too much content.

"…and that's when I confronted him about the text messages…" The text messages already. He needed to slow her down.

"Unbelievable," Sheppard said. "So you found text messages on his phone from this babysitter and confronted him about it?"

"Uh…yes," Sarah said. Like she'd just said that. Because she'd just said that.

"And what did these text messages actually say?" Talking slowly.

Sarah put her head in her hands, muffling the microphone clipped onto the collar of her top.

"I know it's hard, Sarah. But I'm here for you. All these guys are here for you, aren't you?"

The audience gave out something that sounded like a sympathetic whoop prompted by the guy holding up the sign at the side of the stage. This had all been rehearsed in the preshow. Now the crowd was eager. Chomping at the bit.

Sarah looked up at Sheppard again, her eyes streaming. "They were organizing meetups. At hotels, at bars, everywhere… Holi-day Inns, Premier Inns, you know the cheapest places."

Crap. Did she really have to say the names? "Lock it down, Sheppard," the director said, "we can't have anyone on our ass."

"Cheap hotels in the center of London," Sheppard said. Com-panies didn't like to be referenced on the show. Negative con-notations. Say the name of a place, and people will associate it with affairs. "Now was there anything about Sean and this girl's relationship in these texts?"

Sarah looked at the audience. "He said that she was the love of his life." A collective gasp. "He said that he loved her like he'd never loved anyone before and one day they would run away together and take the child too."

Another gasp. Parrots echoing each other. His adoring pub-lic. Was this really what he wanted? But the little boy he once was spoke up. *Are you kidding? This is what you've always wanted. This is what we've been working for all along.*

Sheppard looked at Sarah. A real woman. With real problems. He thought he had the solutions. Not a team of white-collared idiots backstage. Him.

Sarah looked at him. Really looked at him. *Are you the per-son you say you are?*

"SHEPPARD!" the director shouted, making Sheppard jump. "Jesus fu—"

"Well…um…" Sheppard stumbled, looking from Sarah to the crowd, "he sounds like a complete idiot, but let's not take my word for it. Shall we bring him out, ladies and gentlemen?" The audience cheered with the severity of a lynching mob.

Sheppard stood up and strode out to the edge of the stage, turning his back on the young man, who was walking out from behind the right side. The audience booed ferociously, and he waited until they'd calmed down to spin around on the heels of his shiny pointed shoes.

Sean looked like a lost puppy in the middle of the A1. He sat down slowly, as though the seat may be booby-trapped. He wore a grubby white T-shirt and ripped jeans. Probably dressed by the production team. He had a snake tattoo peeking out of his V-neck and licking up his neck. He looked as though he should be intimidating, but all pretense of that had gone from his face. He was clean-shaven, but had missed patches. He seemed rather jittery. Not drug jittery, but a sleepless night jittery. But was this just nerves or was Sean really guilty?

He's guilty. They said so, didn't they?

Mouth open. On autopilot. "Sean, welcome to the show." Pause but no applause. This audience had already forged their conclusion. "Sean, you've been hearing the accusations from backstage, what do you have to say for yourself?"

"They're not true," Sean said. Thick Manchester accent. Eyes flitting—Sheppard, audience, Sheppard, audience. "I would never cheat on Sarah. We have a baby together." He wrenched himself around to look at his girlfriend. "I love you. I love you, Sarah. I thought you knew that."

"I don't know anything," Sarah said. "I'm stupid for believing you."

You know where this is going… Morgan said in his mind. *It's your favorite bit. And don't lie and say it's not.* It was time to ramp it up. This was what they wanted.

This was what he wanted.

"Sean, mate, what about these texts on your phone? Sarah found these texts, I've seen these texts." Enunciating every point. "You going to call her a liar, Sean? Are you going to call me a liar?"

Sean shuffled. "No."

"So you're going to explain it away? I suppose those texts were for your mother, right?"

Laughs. Sheppard looked down at his cue card.

GUILTY.

This is what I've always wanted. The hundreds of people in the audience, invisible beyond the lights, and then the hundreds of thousands beyond the camera lens.

"Those texts were for Sarah," Sean said, not making any sense. Maybe he actually was guilty? Fifty-fifty, right? *DO IT.*

Sheppard paced back and forth, and then turned to face Sean directly. He walked toward him. "Those texts were for your girlfriend? Hmmph. That doesn't fly, Sean. That doesn't fly. You do not come onto this stage and lie to my face, Sean. Look behind me, you're lying to everyone in this room. You're lying to everyone watching this show, Sean." Sheppard got in close, his face centimeters from Sean's. The audience liked when he did this—it all seemed so primal. A hundred pairs of eyes trained on him. And beyond them, infinity. *Always.* "You know the worst thing, though? You're lying to that little lady sitting next to you, right there. And you're jeopardizing a relationship where a child is involved for some little fling with a babysitter? Think carefully before you answer that, Sean. Remember who you're dealing with—" *YES* "—because now you're dealing with Morgan Sheppard, and you know what?"

Sheppard smiled in Sean's face before backing off. The audience erupted, nailing their cue. "Nothing gets past him!"

And it all fell away. Sean—Sarah—the set.

Just Sheppard and his audience—loved. And that was when he knew that he could never walk away.

Sign away his soul. Because he didn't want to be saved.

17

He didn't know where he'd gone, but he'd managed to convince himself it had all been a bad dream. So, when he opened his eyes to see the five faces of the people trapped in the room with him, his heart freshly broke. Strangers who almost felt like home—Mandy, Alan, Ryan, Constance and Headphones. A bizarre family.

The lights seemed too bright and his body ached with longing. Pills, drink—if he didn't get one or both soon he was going to crash. Hard. And he wouldn't be useful to anyone when that happened.

How long had he been out?

He tried to get up but couldn't. Mandy held out a hand. He grabbed it, and she pulled him upright with surprising strength. The others took a step back as if he were contagious.

"Are you okay?" Mandy said.

"I don't suppose anyone here is a doctor or a nurse?" Sheppard rubbed the back of his head. He was getting a headache, especially where he'd hit it on the way down.

The room was silent, except Ms. Ahearn, who was muttering something under her breath.

"You have a fever? Sit down," Mandy said, gesturing to the bed.

Sheppard shook his head. "I don't have time. I just passed out. It happens."

"The rock 'n' roll lifestyle, huh?" Alan said.

Sheppard couldn't manage a retort. His body was shutting down…no, not shutting down. More like, going into SAFE MODE.

Where was he? Winter was dead and now what? He knew nothing of these people, but that would have to change. Right now, it was entirely possible that anyone in the room murdered Winter. Five people. Five suspects. A one in five chance of being the murderer. The fact that he had thought it was probably a man didn't mean anything—at least not yet. He was no expert. Everyone was guilty until proven innocent.

You still haven't told them…

He would have to. Winter's identity was the only real clue he had. But at least, he could do it one by one, reduce the fallout. Maybe these people knew Dr. Winter too.

He looked across the room to the bedside table. The rule book was gone. Glancing around, he saw that Ryan was looking through it. Then back to the table. The timer. He had passed out for almost five minutes.

Five fewer minutes…

When the wheels started turning, five minutes could be the difference between life and death.

He needed to start talking. But with no evidence and no clarification, anyone could say anything. They could've all been lying to him already.

The woman still lurked in the background, in the red room. In Paris. As though, if he turned his head quick enough, he might catch her. To be back there, with all this just a bad dream. It was almost too much—to hope.

The others went back to what they were doing. Alan was still staring at the window. Constance was muttering and looking down at her Bible. Ryan was reading the rules. Headphones was in her own little world. Only Mandy remained looking at him, concerned.

Sheppard took her aside, into the alcove by the door. "I have to start interviewing people. Talking. Seeing if I can find anything that might give me a clue to who…who killed him. See if we can work out why we're all here."

"Interviews?"

"Yes. We should really do them in private, but—" Sheppard's eyes skirted the bathroom door "—I think over here will have to do."

"Okay," Mandy said.

"I need to start thinking about identities, possible motives, time frames." All things he had learned reading his crime books. "Everyone else should stay on the right side of the room. I need to try and make it so no one else can hear." Even as he said it, he knew it was impossible. Alan's ears were twitching on the other side of the room, and he wasn't even facing them. Every single word any person said in the room could easily be heard by others—discounting Constance, who was spouting illegible nonsense.

"Okay. Who do you want to talk to first?"

"You?"

Mandy looked at him, and gave a smile. It was the same kind of nervous smile he saw on everyone who came on his television show. A smile that always looked like the smiler had something to hide. Under the spotlight though, everyone did.

Sheppard smiled too. And at that moment, he knew he was really going to try. He was a sham—a terrible excuse of a detective, hell, a terrible excuse of a man. But he was really going to do all he could to try to save them. To save the innocent ones.

Because they were the ones who didn't deserve this.

And, if he had the time, he might even try to save himself.

18

"I never usually come into Central London, at least this side of the river, not if I can help it. When you just come here for a holiday, that's all you want to see, right? But the second I moved here, it seemed like the last place I wanted to go. All those people just rushing around but not really looking like they're doing anything—just there to get in your way. I hate it."

Sheppard knew what she meant. It was always impossibly busy. He remembered going to Oxford Street for the first time as a child, when he didn't even know there were that many people in the world. "You used to live somewhere else?"

"Manchester. It was much quieter. Even though I still lived in the city. I moved here for university and never moved back."

"London's expensive, how do you get by?"

"I have a job as a barista in a coffee shop in Waterloo. I'm trying to get into the television business. My degree was in journalism, so not like you—I'm trying for behind the camera. My job supports me, mostly. Also, my brother gave me some money and well, I had a wealthy aunt who liked me," Mandy said.

She put enough emphasis on the *had* for Sheppard to discern what happened.

"Still, the money is running out, and if nothing happens soon I'm probably going to have to move back up north. To have some fraction of savings left. Not that I want to move back. The center horrifies me, but I love the quieter parts of London. The atmosphere of it, you know. Like anything's possible."

Sheppard nodded. "Where do you live?"

"Islington. A shared flat. I live with a struggling actor and a professional drug addict. Only one of them is great at what they do. I'm sure you can probably guess which. Times are tough, but we get by."

"So what about today? Can you walk me through what happened?"

Mandy thought for a moment. He wondered if it was the same for her—like trying to recall a dream. The moment you thought you had it, it slipped through your fingers.

"It was pretty much the same as any other day. Number seventy-three bus to Waterloo at some stupid time. It was about eight, but at this time of the year, it might as well be the middle of the night, you know. I work at the CoffeeCorps just inside the station. It's like a little kiosk on its own. If you've seen that film with Matt Damon, he runs right past it. What's it called?"

"Mandy," Sheppard said, constantly aware of the timer over on the bedside table. He had a lot to get through.

"Sorry," she said. "So, it's a horrible little kiosk and it's really cramped in there. There's really only space for two people in the kiosk, but management always puts on three, because of first aid or something. Anyway, it was fine—as busy as you would expect—and it got to my morning break. I've always had this routine where, on my break, I walk down to the South Bank. It's nice. People are a little slower down there because it's just nice to be there. Looking out at the Thames, seeing the London

Eye, seeing the rest of the city. Close but far enough for me. I go to this coffee place called Nancy's—small place, independent. I get the irony of that, but I really hate CoffeeCorps. I'm not a big small-business warrior—I just don't like the coffee."

"The South Bank's not far from here," Sheppard said, more to himself than Mandy.

"No, it's not. In fact I remember looking at The Great Hotel building. I never thought…" She trailed off.

"So this coffee shop?"

"Yeah, sorry. I went into Nancy's as usual, and the guy who runs it has recognized me for a while so he knows my order and starts making it up for me. The place is always really quiet, which makes me sad. It's a small café—nice though. There's a few sit-in tables but they're never usually full. I remember a few people were there this morning, but not many.

"While the guy's making my coffee, I go in to use the toilet in the back. It's a hot day, so I wanted to wash my face. I locked the door, put the toilet seat down and looked in the mirror. My hair was messed up in the heat, so I wanted to try and fix it. I propped my bag against the sink and was looking for a clip when…when something happened."

"Something?" Sheppard prompted.

Mandy looked at him. She seemed to be rolling it through in her mind seeing if it made any sense before she said it. Sheppard could empathize, but wouldn't really care either way. Nothing made much sense yet. "It was a smell—a weird smell. I started picking it up and I looked around to see… I don't know…if I could locate it, I guess. It grew stronger. I remember it burning my nostrils. It was a chemical smell I think. And then my vision started going fuzzy. And then—I don't remember anything after that. Not until I saw you cuffed to the bed." Sheppard nodded. That was exactly in line with what he experienced. A chemical smell, a burning sensation, passing out. "This sounds like you were gassed. Like *we* were gassed."

"The same for you?" Mandy said.

"Yes. But why gas? It doesn't make much sense. Were they just waiting for someone to use that toilet and gas them? Or if they really wanted you, why didn't they just drug your coffee? Gassing someone is a hell of a lot more work."

"The horse mask said we were random. Maybe I was just unlucky?"

"Maybe," Sheppard said. "I'm not entirely sure he was telling the truth though. At this point nothing's certain. You said you go to that coffee shop a lot?"

"Yes. Three or four times a week at about the same time. Ten thirty."

"People know you go there? Can identify you?"

"The guy knows my order."

Sheppard sighed. Gas—in a public place. How would they get her body out of there? How would they get past the people in the café—let alone the people outside on the South Bank? Back up a truck to the shop maybe? But that would draw attention? This made no sense. "We both experienced the same thing. This sounds like a plan, not random. They could've gassed you through the vents, like they did to me. I think someone knew you were going to be there."

Mandy looked puzzled. "But even I didn't know I was going to use the bathroom. I've never once used it before."

It didn't make *any* sense at all. "You had ordered coffee."

"Yes."

"And who else was in the café? Do you remember anyone?"

"There was hardly anyone in there, like I said. There was just one guy."

"Had you seen him before?"

"The guy? No."

"What did he look like?"

"I don't know? Normal I suppose."

Mandy taken. Mere miles from The Great Hotel. Sheppard had to have already been taken at that point. The night before all this. So where was he as this was happening? A shiver. Not something he really wanted to know.

"Was there anything out of the ordinary?"

"There was something, I suppose. But it could be nothing."

"I'll take what I can get at the moment."

"From the moment I stepped in there, I felt eyes on me. You know that feeling when you're convinced you're being watched? Yeah, it was like that. And I didn't really place it until I passed the guy sitting down on my way to the toilet. As I passed the guy, I saw that his eyes were almost locked onto me. He sort of smiled when I looked at him and I smiled back—like an automatic response during work hours. But he was creepy. I don't know what it was—I can't put my finger on it. Anyway, I just passed him and that was that. I didn't really feel it at the time, but looking back...it was kind of weird."

"Can you describe him?"

"Like I said, he was just—normal. Um...he was thin, wiry. He had short brown hair. Wore these thin glasses. He was a looker, pretty handsome. Probably about your age. He was wearing a black suit, with a red tie. He looked like some kind of banker or something."

"It could be nothing," Sheppard said. *Or it could be everything.* "You said you were on your break? So people would know when you don't come back?"

"Yeah, definitely. And I'm not the kind of girl who slacks off—I've never missed a day in my life and I'm proud of it."

Mandy was now officially missing. But a young girl disappearing in her break wouldn't be any cause for any real panic. There would be no calling the police or sending out a search party. Not at this stage anyway. People would just think she had decided to play truant. It was a lovely day after all.

Mandy seemed to have come to the same conclusion. "The girls I was on shift with will think it's weird I'm gone. But they'll probably cover for me. We're friends. I'd do the same for them."

No. There would be no rescue party. And even if the police did become involved, they would have no idea where to look.

Sheppard lowered his voice. Scanned the room to see no one watching. But how many of them were listening? "You've seen the body, right?"

Mandy seemed to take his cue. Lowering her voice too. "Yes. But only from the back. And I don't want to see it again."

"No, you don't have to. Even from the back, did you think you recognized the man?"

"No."

Sheppard frowned. He took out Winter's wallet, flipped to his driver's license and held it up to Mandy. "Do you recognize him now?"

Mandy looked at the picture for a long time. "Simon Winter," she said. Barely audible. "No, I don't recognize him. But…"

"But what?"

"I work with an Abby Winter."

Sheppard's brain turned over. Abby Winter. He hadn't heard that name in a long time. Simon's daughter. Around the same age as Sheppard. Sheppard remembered the first time he'd seen her. After a session. He left Winter's office. They were kids— just kids. She was sitting on the stairs.

"I know you," she had said.

Little Morgan had smiled and sat down next to her.

"Sheppard?" Mandy said.

Abby. Now she was an orphan—because of him. "I… Do you know this Abby at all?"

"She's— I like her, but she's a bit of a mess. I think she's an addict of something—I don't know what—but she shakes a lot and she gets like that weird kind of slick sweat over her face. You know?"

Sheppard nodded. He did. More than she knew. But he was only half hearing her. His mind was on Abby—a girl he had cared about once. Now she was a drug addict, working a dead-end job. How long had it been since he saw her last? He remembered her as a bubbly, fun person, with one hell of a smile. And now—

"It's kind of sad—you know. She's a nice enough person, but she has her demons. I think our manager only keeps her on because he feels sorry for her... Are you okay?"

Sheppard nodded again. "Okay," he said, changing the subject, "now what about the masked man? The horse mask? Did you recognize his voice?"

"No, not at all. Although..."

"Although?"

"I don't know, it's just—I might be wrong but the mask looked familiar."

"The mask?"

"Yeah. I don't know why but I think I've seen it somewhere bef..." Her eyes searching and then... Something snapped into place. "The theater. The show. *Rain on Elmore Street.*"

"Constance Ahearn's play?" Sheppard said, looking into the room. Constance had backed herself into a corner again, and was silent. Her eyes met Sheppard's and he looked back to Mandy. "Are you sure?"

"No...not sure exactly. I saw it like a year ago."

"Okay," Sheppard said. "Now I need you to think about that coffee shop—think of everything that happened this morning. If you think of anything else weird or out of place, you have to come and tell me straight away. I also need you to try and keep everyone calm—I need someone I can count on to try and keep the peace."

"I can try," Mandy said, and smiled that small sweet smile again. Almost too sweet.

There was something behind her words—something in the shadows. Sheppard thought it was fear, but what if it was something else—something with a slightly more ill intent?

"Thanks," Sheppard settled on. He really couldn't trust anyone. But one thing he did trust was Mandy's scream when she first saw the body. It sounded so incredibly scared. That would be hard to pull off if it wasn't genuine.

"What are you going to do?"

Sheppard sighed again, and turned to the rest of the room. "Looks like I'm going to have to talk to Ms. Ahearn next."

19

Mandy moved away from Sheppard, awkwardly moving around the bed, passing Alan and Ryan to sit down next to Constance. Constance shuffled closer to her and Mandy put her arm around her and whispered something in her ear. Alan and Ryan were both watching him now. He wondered how much they had heard. Everyone being in such close proximity was terrible. He could feel the fear seeping out of everyone else.

"You understand we can hear everything you say," Alan said.

"I know this isn't ideal…" Sheppard started.

Alan scoffed. "Ideal? That's the word you're going with? This is a waking nightmare."

Alan started toward Sheppard.

"I need to talk to Ms. Ahearn next."

"No," Alan said, "you'll talk to me."

"No, I will talk to Ms. Ahearn."

"No, Mr. Sheppard. I personally think I am more equipped to deal with this investigation. You are a floozy, a human-sized bag of hot air. And you can only blow into bags so much before they pop."

"Sit down, Alan."

"You will talk to me next."

"Yes. After Ms. Ahearn."

"You have no authority here," Alan said, spitting vowels at him. "The mask says this is all on you, so why even give you the time of day? Who's to say that you didn't kill that man in there? In fact, that makes perfect sense." Alan's eyes sparkled with something Sheppard couldn't quite place. Had he heard Mandy talking? Or did he recognize the body?

Sheppard opened his mouth to say something to this effect, but…

"Stop it." They both looked around. Ryan had stood up, the folder still in his hands. "I'm going next."

"And why's that?" Alan said.

"Because I've got something I need to tell Mr. Sheppard. Something I should have said before."

"Well speak up, son. There's no secrets here," Alan said.

"I heard you talking to Mandy. I need to tell you some things. Can we go into the bathroom?"

"Now wait a second…" Alan said.

Sheppard couldn't think. He didn't want to go back in there.

"You better think fast about what you're saying, son, because it's starting to sound like you're a murderer."

"Shut up, Alan. I need to…"

"I didn't lie. I didn't," Ryan said quickly.

Ryan held up the last page of the rule binder. THE BOY LIED.

"Someone tell me what is going on," Alan said.

"Shut up, Alan."

"No, you shut up. Son, what the hell are you talking about?"

"Why don't you butt out and let me do my job?" Sheppard rounded on Alan again.

"Your job?" Alan laughed. "Your job?"

He needed drink. Needed pills. Needed to not have a stupid old man telling him what to do. "I am listening to you, okay. I am taking all your concerns on board. But right now, if you hadn't noticed, we're almost half an hour down and so far I'm coming up empty on the ideas front. So I'm going to do things my way."

Alan stepped forward. "You're only a detective because people like to label things. What you did however many years ago doesn't mean a damn thing."

"Guys," Ryan tried.

"You know what I'm detecting right now? I'm thinking that the only person who would actually want to delay me in this investigation is the murderer. Did you murder the man in the bathtub?"

"Guys."

"No, I didn't. Did you?"

Ryan stepped between them, pushing them apart as they continued to fight, and shouted over them, "I work here."

This did the trick. Silence.

"Now please," Ryan said, "can we go into the bathroom?"

20

Sheppard went in first, and drew the shower curtain over the bathtub. He tried not to look, he really tried. But Winter was still there. Dead. With that look of sadness upon his face. It made him feel sick. He turned to the sink and splashed his face again.

Ryan took a tentative look toward the bathtub as he came in. Then focused his eyes on Sheppard.

"Start talking," Sheppard said. The dull ache behind his eyes. That feeling at the back of his throat. That rumble in his chest. His hands were starting to shake. Why hadn't he checked the minibar yet?

"I'm sorry, I should have told you sooner," Ryan said. "I tried to tell you at the start."

Sheppard vaguely remembered. "Who are you?"

"Ryan Quinn. Like I said. I'm not lying."

"You work here?"

"Yes. As a cleaner. That's why I'm wearing this." Ryan gestured down to his white jumpsuit. Sheppard took a closer look at the young man. Black hair, short. Clean-shaven, didn't look like he could even grow a beard. Midtwenties, probably. The young man towered though. Was almost taller than Sheppard. "It's not my ideal job. But I do it. I come into the rooms, clean them, make the beds, give fresh towels, do that triangle thing on the toilet paper."

Sheppard was thinking. "That's how you knew where we were so fast. Between Bank and Leicester Square."

Ryan nodded, sadly.

"Seems like a big thing to keep back from us," Sheppard said. "Where were you when we were trying to escape?"

"I told you, didn't I? There is no way out."

Ryan and Alan talking at the window. Ryan convincing him that there was no way to escape.

"So you're a cleaner for The Great Hotel?"

"Yes. I have been for about a year now. Things are hard for my family. My mother and father moved here from Hong Kong just before I was born. They run a dry-cleaning business in Soho, but it's not enough to support them. I have to help them with their bills. I hate this job. But it's the only way I can keep our heads above water.

"I'm in the fourth quadrant with two other guys. That's three floors, this floor and the two below. There are thirty-five rooms on each floor."

"That's a lot of cleaning."

"Hotel this big has a lot of manpower. We start at nine in the morning and end by three. Then I have to go and clean the communal areas."

"So you were cleaning this morning?"

Ryan seemed to visibly back away—his gaze slipped from Sheppard's.

"Ryan."

"Don't freak out."

"Ryan, where were you?"

"I…" Ryan said, trying to find the words. "I think I was here."

And that was that—why Ryan hadn't come forward.

Simple. "Christ, Ryan."

The young man put his hands up in defense. "It's not what you think. Nothing was wrong with this room, when I was in here before. The window was open. The door wasn't deadlocked. There sure as hell wasn't a body…" He looked toward the bath. "Everything was fine. You have to believe me."

Sheppard didn't know what to think—except now Ryan was the prime suspect, like it or not. "You were in here?"

"Yes," Ryan said. "I came into the bathroom to change the towels and clean the toilet. I looked in the bath…and there was no one. There was nothing in it. You have to understand, I had nothing to do with this."

"Tell me exactly what you did in here." Trying to slip him up or rooting for him, he wasn't totally sure.

"Towels. Toilet. Bath. I even wiped it down and replaced the shower gel in the holder. Then I wiped down the mirror. And mopped the floor. And put a new toilet paper in the holder. That was all, I swear."

"Does that mean someone was staying here?"

"Yes."

"Who?"

"I don't know. I don't usually see many people when I'm cleaning. They're usually out for the day by the time I come around. Sometimes I see people at the start. But this room is toward the end of my quadrant, so there's even less chance of them still being around."

"Was there anything lying around? Anything that gave you a clue to who this person was?"

Ryan thought for a moment. "No, it was all very clean. In fact, the bed didn't look like it had been slept in. There was no mess anywhere. But there was a suitcase next to the wardrobe. So I knew someone was staying here."

"There's no way you could've heard this guest's name in passing or anything? Any way you could have seen him in the corridor?"

"Well, yeah, I guess it's possible," Ryan said.

"Okay." Knowing what needed to be done. But Ryan knew too. That's why they were in here, wasn't it? With the smell of blood and the thing looming behind the curtain. "I need to show you the body now." He could just show Winter's driving license, but he needed to see how the young man reacted to the body.

That's mean. Maybe so, but necessary. Ryan steeled himself and nodded.

Sheppard gripped the shower curtain. He didn't want to see again. He didn't want to have to look at Winter's face. But it had to be done. He drew back the curtain fast, before his brain could stop him.

Winter lay there. The blood grew stronger in the air.

Don't look down. Not at all the blood and the...

Sheppard looked at Ryan instead.

He was clenching and unclenching his fists. In a calming technique that wasn't working. Ryan looked shocked, pale. But he didn't look away from the body. He stared at it, taking shallow breaths.

"His name is Simon Winter," said Sheppard, his voice quieter than before. The stench. God, the stench.

Ryan looked at Sheppard, then back to the body. "Out there. Out there, it is hard to believe. It is easy to think that this is all some kind of joke. But this...this is real. This poor man."

"Do you recognize him—or his name? Was he staying here?" Sheppard said, a little too pushily. The image of Simon Winter was making him uncomfortable.

"I don't..." Ryan trailed off. He was thinking hard.

Looking at Winter's face.

The young man was a wreck. There was no way he could have killed someone. Was there? If this was the reaction...

"I saw him," Ryan said, in a whisper hard to catch. "What?" Sheppard said.

"I saw this man."

"This morning?"

Ryan shook his head slowly. "No, not today. I... I suppose it was about a month ago."

"What?"

"Here, in the hotel. It has been a long time. I can't say for sure where, but every room is the same. The same furniture, the same dimensions, the same contents. I think it might have even been this floor." Ryan looked like he was about to break out in cold sweats.

"A month ago?" It seemed very strange that Winter would be in this very hotel a month ago and then turn up dead in one of their rooms—hijacked by a maniac.

Unless it's a big coincidence. Or you've all been in cold storage a hell of a long time.

There was something almost comic about that. The situation overwhelmed him and he didn't know if he was going to laugh or cry.

Ryan peered further into the bath, as if for answers. "Yes. I remember."

"Remember what?"

"This man... Winter, you said? Winter was here. And he was acting...strange."

"Strange?"

Ryan tore his eyes from the body, back to Sheppard. "I didn't remember before. It's a hotel. People act weirdly all the time. Especially the small amount of people who are still in their rooms when you come around to clean. They act like you're invading their space, when it was never theirs to begin with."

"How was Winter acting?"

"It was toward the end of my shift. That's how I know it was this floor, even if it wasn't this room. Everything had gone fine with the other rooms, I was ahead of time. I thought I might even be able to get off early. I knocked on the door of the room as I always do. But there was no reply. So I just went in.

"That's when I saw this man. He was pacing around the room. He had a notebook in his hand and he was writing stuff down. He had something as well, some sort of bright yellow thing. It looked like he was... It sounds stupid, but it looked like he was..."

"Like he was what?"

"Like he was measuring."

Sheppard was caught off guard. What—measuring?

Why would he be...? Too many thoughts at once.

"I think that thing was a tape measure. And he was properly pacing, one foot in front of the other. And every step, he stopped to write something down. Maybe he was doing something else. Rehearsing for a speech, or mapping something out...but from the door, that's what it looked like."

"Why would he be measuring a hotel room?" Sheppard said. More to himself.

"The moment he saw me, he quickly threw down the note-book and the yellow thing, and tried to step in front of it all. He was acting like he'd been caught doing something bad. For about five seconds. But it seemed longer. We were just staring at each other. I didn't know what to do. Then he came to his senses and apologized and just let me clean the room."

"What did he do while you were cleaning?"

"He gathered up his things and left. I didn't see him again. It was definitely this man."

Sheppard couldn't not look down at Winter. The man now seemed to be hiding something behind his expression. What was going on? "Did you report it?"

"Report what? I didn't even know what I saw and it wasn't as if it was particularly suspicious. I forgot about it the moment I finished my shift. Until now." Ryan's voice hitched. He put his hand up to his mouth. Took a few moments. Lowered it again. "Sorry, the smell. And the blood."

Sheppard nodded. "I... You can go if you want."

"You don't need anything else?"

Too much already. What was Winter doing in this hotel... maybe even this room, a month ago? What could he have possibly been doing? "No. Just anything else you can think of, let me know." Now, he couldn't take his eyes away. What was Winter hiding? The bathroom door opened and shut. He was alone with Winter again.

Sheppard took out Winter's notebook, and flipped through it again—not sure what he was looking for. He looked down at the old man. Measuring the hotel room? Why would he be measuring a hotel room. Unless... Did it mean that Winter was in on whatever plan this was? Was Winter in on the whole thing? But what led to him ending up dead in the bathtub? Surely that had not been part of the plan...

"What were you up to?"

Winter didn't answer.

21

Nausea washed over Sheppard as he returned to the room—he had to put his hand out to the wall to steady himself. Dizziness—the cold, hard crash was getting closer. How long had it been without pills? His hand shook violently, the dull throb of his head, the smell lingering in his nostrils and the itch—everywhere. A cocktail of awful—the usual symptoms.

"What's wrong with you now?"

He looked up. Alan had been waiting for him to come out. *Great.* The man was standing right in front of him, arms still crossed. His voice didn't sound caring—more irritated.

"Nothing, I'm fine," Sheppard said.

Alan looked him up and down. "Whatever, I'll keep this short and sweet. Not to mention loud," he turned to the room and back, "as I have nothing to hide."

Sheppard looked over his shoulder to see the rest of the room, much as it was. Mandy and Constance were sitting with their backs to everyone. Ryan was pacing back and forth. And Headphones was watching them, with her ears still covered.

"I've heard all the questions you were asking Mandy—hard

not to—and I assume you asked the same of Ryan. So I'll give you the complete rundown of what happened to me. I was in my office when I was drugged by the same gas as everyone else. We all talked while you were in the bathroom—even Crazy Irish and Generic Teen. We were all gassed. I didn't only smell it, but I saw it pouring through the vents. It was some kind of colorless smoky gas, dissipating around the room very quickly. I tried to cover the vent, but it seemed like I'd already inhaled too much. I didn't even have time to call for help. I collapsed and then I woke up here.

"I was preparing, as I said, for the MacArthur case. A biggie. The kind of case to make or break a career. Of course, my career was 'made' a long time ago, but it's always nice to have another notch in your belt."

Sheppard was trying to keep up. "Must be interesting for you to…"

Alan got him instantly. Could read him so easily. How did he do that? "You're alluding to the fact I am black. Yes, Mr. Sheppard, I am a black man. I worked damn hard to get where I am, and yes, I fought some opposition along the way. You know how many black lawyers are in London? We make up one point two percent of them. So yes, to answer your question, it is 'interesting.'"

Sheppard nodded. Alan didn't seem like the type of person to let anything get to him. Sheppard wondered how old he was. Wrinkles under his eyes—tracing around to his cheeks. The wrinkles on his forehead seemed to be chiseled into a permanent scowl, making the man look more sinister. Fifties? Late fifties, maybe?

"Of course, none of this makes any difference. Because I'm here now. And that means the MacArthur case is ruined. Thank you for that, by the way."

Sheppard frowned. "Right." Couldn't even be bothered to retort.

"I suppose you want to know about my connection with the body," Alan said, nodding to the door.

"What?"

"You see I lied a little before. I did recognize that man. There was no point explaining it at the time—but now here we are. I see a lot of people in my line of work, so I pick up on all the details I can. My peers joke that I can recognize people by the backs of their heads—I guess I just proved that right. That coupled with the fact that I saw that man yesterday wearing the same suit—that made me sure. You showed something to Mandy, I assume it was his wallet. Anyway, that man's name is Simon Winter. He is a private psychologist operating out of his home in East London. The psychologist to my client, Hamish MacArthur. Winter is a key witness. That's all I can disclose."

Sheppard was speechless and Alan seemed to relish that.

"You're wondering why I'm offering all of this up so easily," Alan said, failing to hide a smile. "You know how many clients I see try and hide the facts, even from someone who's trying to help them—just because they're scared of the outcome? It's pitiful and it's weak. Don't confuse this with me being cooperative.

"Now I believe I've answered everything from your stellar line of questioning. Shall I see myself back to my window?"

"Wait…" Sheppard said. How could this man be so defiant, even in the face of death? That was the kind of person who was dangerous, the kind of person who found control in chaos. But still…

"Try to keep up, Mr. Sheppard. Yes, I know Simon Winter. I haven't really ever talked to him," Alan said.

"Because," Sheppard said, "he's not your witness."

Alan scowled. "No. I was rather looking forward to grilling the bastard in court."

"What is this case?"

"I can't disclose any details of the case, Mr. Sheppard. Much speculation has been made in the media. Maybe you could ring down to room service for a newspaper."

Sheppard rubbed his eyes. "If Simon Winter is here, is it possible that the person behind this is connected to the case?"

"Of course," Alan said. "That's why I thought it best to be as aboveboard as possible. There is a possibility that this revolves around the MacArthur case."

"But you still won't tell me anything about it."

"No, Mr. Sheppard. I won't. Because I think that I might be able to figure this out a lot better than you. I'm keeping my cards close to my chest, sure, but I'm doing what needs to be done. If that makes me more suspicious, so be it."

Sheppard shook his head. "Of course this makes you more suspicious. How could I take it any other way?"

"It doesn't matter," Alan said, "I am already a prime suspect. You want a motive, Mr. Sheppard? Well, I've got a hell of a one. That man in there has been a thorn in my side for the past year. I have dreamed of gutting him like a fish, slicing him up into a million little pieces. But that doesn't mean I would. It is clear what's happening here. The horse mask is trying to pin this murder on me. And if you take the bait, then you'll kill us all."

"Pretty big ego, even when defending yourself against a murder."

"My ego is not the one on trial here."

A lot of information, buried in not much at all. Alan was presenting an account that surely the murderer would want to hide. If it was true. Still, Alan did have motive. And he knew how to play the game.

"So the MacArthur case was supposed to be today?"

"Yes. But none of the other details matter. They are not related to this…this case, although calling this a case is charitable to say the least."

"Not related? Or you just won't tell me?"

"As a lawyer, I am bound by my station to keep certain things between me and my client."

"MacArthur?"

"Yes."

Sheppard could see Alan was not going to budge. How could he compete with a lawyer? Alan was really doing what Sheppard pretended to do every day. "Two people involved with this case in the same hotel room. That can't be a coincidence," he said, more to himself than Alan. Was there some way that Sheppard and the MacArthur case were connected? The horse mask seemed to have had only Sheppard in his sights, but maybe he had Alan too.

"No."

"I really need that information, Alan."

Alan smiled. "You really are terrible at this, you know." Alan was prepared to die for what he believed in. Morgan knew people like that—so honorable they would fall on their own sword. He wasn't one of those people and didn't understand those who were.

"You're a very successful man, Mr. Hughes, I can see that," he said, picking his words carefully. "You like being the leader of the pack, like all the attention…"

"Please spare me the psychoanalysis. You're embarrassing yourself."

Sheppard held up a hand. "You're a winner. You muscled your way into your business, didn't take no for an answer. You've won. Is this really how it ends? If the horse mask is correct, we all die."

"You're asking me if I want to die? Of course I don't. But if I am to die, I will do it with dignity."

"You don't want to die. You think we have nothing in common. But *that*—we have *that* in common. You don't want to die, and you're scared. Just like everyone else in this room. Just like me. I'm terrified. And when I look at you, I can see somewhere in there that you are too. Whether you like it or not, we're the same type of person, Mr. Hughes. The kind of guy who busies himself and mouths off to forget his problems. But this problem, we can't walk away from."

"No," Alan said.

"The thing I keep thinking is that we were all put here for a reason. But I haven't worked out quite why yet. Until you. You might be the key to the puzzle."

"I was gassed in my office. I was alone. Yes, I may well have been targeted for my involvement with the case. But you're asking the wrong questions, Sheppard. You should be asking what connects all these other people, not me."

Alan Hughes, the defense lawyer who conveniently disappears the morning of the trial. A key witness who disappears as well.

This had to be connected. Maybe the horse mask wanted to know who had killed Simon Winter. And Alan looked like the prime suspect.

Was the horse mask Hamish MacArthur? But Sheppard had never heard of him before. And MacArthur would have had to know Sheppard too well. And that theory discounted how involved Winter might be? Why was Simon Winter here? Maybe he was more than just the victim. His mind circled as though he were chasing his own tail. Too many loose ends...unable to be tied up. A good idea. But a wrong one.

"Kidnapping six people. To make a murder puzzle. What are we missing?" To himself. He was surprised at an answer.

"Kidnapping five people. We have to assume the murderer and victim were already here," Alan said.

Ryan. Ryan was here. But, that look when he'd seen Winter. That kind of look you couldn't fake.

"I think the horse mask wanted Simon Winter dead, so he enlisted one of us to do it."

"So, how do I find the murderer?" Sheppard asked, before he could stop himself. Weak. Weak. He was acting weak.

"Maybe it's just a question of simplicity. Maybe the murderer is the one with the simplest story. Murderers don't tend to be great storytellers."

"Your story seems simple enough."

Alan chuckled. "Yes, I guess it does. That is all I have for you, Sheppard."

"Okay," Sheppard said. It had to be him. It had to. But he had two more people to interview and already too much to think about. He had to get everyone's story first. "If you think of anything else, please tell me."

"I will," Alan said, not sounding very convincing.

"And, Mr. Hughes, since you've been honest with me, I'll be honest with you. You're my prime suspect."

The lawyer laughed again. A gruff, joyless laugh. "And I'll be honest with you, Sheppard. You're mine." He smiled and winked, before moving away. A glint in his eye. Easy to miss. Knowing.

A chill ran through him, that smugness. Alan had to know of Sheppard's link with Winter. Somehow, he knew. And he didn't know why, but that scared him more than anything else.

22

Two left. He looked at the clock. 02:14:00. Where was the time going? How could forty-five minutes have gone already?

He cleared his throat, trying to get attention. No one looked at him—they were all gone to their thoughts.

"Ms. Ahearn?"

Slowly, Constance looked around. Mandy whispered to her and she stood up. She was wearing a black flowing dress that matched her hair. It was baggy, and Sheppard couldn't see her body underneath. She looked like a ghost, floating around and wailing. She was still clutching the hotel Bible, and as she made her way toward Sheppard, he could see the whites of her knuckles. On her face, her makeup had run so dramatically she looked like a mixed paint pallet. She looked old, but wore the years well.

Constance tucked one curtain of hair behind an ear, and Sheppard saw a fresh scratch down her left cheek. Must have done it to herself, with her long, clear manicured nails.

Sheppard guided her to the alcove. Not much point but the illusion of privacy at least. They were all, at least, pretending not to listen.

"I'm sorry we have to do this here. Limited space," Sheppard said. Taking Constance into the bathroom would be a mistake. She was bad enough out here. "Maybe it's best if you just focus on me. Forget about everyone else, forget where we are."

Constance looked at him and opened her mouth. He expected lunacy. But coherence came out. "Yes." Black hair, dislodged, cascaded down her face again. Like something from a horror film.

"I have to ask you a few questions. It'll all be stuff I need to know for the case. I need to know all about everyone in the room. I won't ask anything I don't need to know. You see?"

Constance peered at him, one eye out, one eye through hair. "Yes."

"Good." Where to start? He'd only thought this far. He looked down. "You're religious?"

Constance laughed. He thought he might have lost her. But then, "Yes, Mr. Sheppard. And now we are in Hell. And we are being punished. Not just you. All of us. We all must atone."

"And what do you need to atone for?" Sheppard said.

Constance frowned at him. Looked to the floor.

Needed to be softer. "Okay, let's start a little simpler. Do you remember where you were, before you came here?"

"I was…" Constance thought. "I was in my dressing room, I think." Sharp voice. One built for singing. And projecting.

"Your dressing room? At the theater? I understand you're the lead actress in a play?"

Constance looked angry. "A musical. It's a musical. *Rain on Elmore Street*. Three years. Never missed a show. Eight times a week."

"What were you doing there this morning?"

"A rehearsal. The male lead's off sick, so we had to run through some scenes with the understudy. Amateurs, both of them." Constance stopped. Stuck her nose up, like a dog. "Is that blood? I don't want to stand here."

"Sorry, I'll make this quick. So you were on your own in your dressing room?"

"I have my own dressing room, but no one is truly alone."

"Excuse me," Sheppard said.

"I am receptive, Mr. Sheppard. I am one of the few who can see those lost on their way to the next life. I see through people. I see their auras."

Suppressing a sigh. "Ah," he made do with. "Okay then." She was crazy then. That proved it. Ghosts and auras.

"Your aura is very troubled, Mr. Sheppard. Light and dark mixing all together. Tell me, do you think you are a good man?"

Sheppard fumbled. "What?"

"I cannot tell yet, that is all."

Tell me, do you think you are a good man?

One of the last things Simon Winter ever said to him. "You're a Catholic. Devout, by the looks of it. But you believe in all of this stuff?" Sheppard asked. *Get away from the question. Get away.*

"There are more things in Heaven and Earth than can be dreamt of in your philosophy," Constance said. "Besides, I did not pick to become what I am. It just happened to me."

"You can see everyone's colors, can you see the murderer in this room?"

Constance smiled, baring her teeth in an animal way. "It doesn't work like that."

"Of course it doesn't." Before he could stop himself.

"You can choose not to believe, Mr. Sheppard. That doesn't make it not real."

Back on track. "You were in your dressing room. And then?"

"I was getting ready. Mainly going through my lines. They had to change them a little bit for the understudy. In my line of work, performing is like breathing. You don't notice when you're doing it. Shows slip away with the days, and the weeks, and the months. I know my lines back to front, and then they went and changed them. Fully knowing that I would have to overwrite my instincts. They knew, but they still did it. All because of that bastard and his bastard cancer scare. I can't learn new lines in a day. I just can't. I won't, Mr. Sheppard."

"Okay?" Sheppard tried.

"I was livid. I threatened to quit, you know. I threatened to quit five times over. But I didn't. Because they want to replace me anyway. They want someone younger. So I stayed. And then I went back to my room to learn my lines. Like a good girl. And then I heard something. A…hissing. And then a bad smell."

"Yes. A smell." Sheppard was finding it hard to follow Constance's rambling. But seized on the bits he could discern. "It seems that's how we were all knocked out and brought here." New question. Was the murderer gassed as well? Or did they just pretend? Whoever would've done that would've had to be a good actor. And Constance was definitely skittish enough to fit the murderer's MO. She could even hide her nerves behind fake ones.

"Yes. Gas. That makes sense," the woman said. "I don't remember anything else until…I woke up here."

"You think we're in Hell, but you accept we're still alive."

Constance chuckled. A clucking sound. "There is more than one Hell. This is a Hell on Earth. We must atone."

"And you still won't tell me what you need to atone for?"

"No, Mr. Sheppard," Constance said, "the bigger question you should be asking is what you need to atone for?" Sheppard suddenly felt itchy, like something sliding under his skin. How did she do that? Manage to get to him. Past all his defenses. "Ms. Ahearn."

"No. I won't hear any more. I did not kill whoever is in that bathroom. I can't even stand next to the door without feeling like I'm going to vomit—that should tell you all you need to know. What makes you think I could kill a man? Just because I won't talk about my private life with you, a stranger?" Every word lavish. As though she was reciting Shakespeare.

A dead end. Sheppard knew she wouldn't budge. Constance was persistent. He took out Winter's wallet and waited for her to calm down. He showed her Winter's driver's license. "Do you know this man?"

Constance looked at it. For too long. "I don't think so. I never forget a face."

"His name is Simon Winter. Ring any bells?"

"Never heard of him."

"Are you sure?"

"Yes, I'm…" Constance's eyes flitted back to the driver's license. Another long pause. "I've seen this man."

"What, where?"

"I… I'm trying to remember," Constance said. She really was. "I saw him at the theater bar after a show. A few weeks ago, I think. I go out to the bar after the show once a week to sign autographs. There's a lot of people usually. It was crowded."

"What makes you remember Simon Winter then?"

"It wasn't him I remember specifically. It was the man he was with."

"What?"

"They were talking at the bar. I don't know what they were saying. It was so noisy and people were rushing up to me. But, every once in a while, when the crowd parted, I saw them. This man was with a younger man, in a suit, red tie, with rectangle glasses. He had the darkest aura I've ever seen. I couldn't stop looking. This man was evil, Mr. Sheppard."

A man. Red tie. Glasses. The same man that Mandy saw. Was this him? Was this the man behind the horse mask?

"Can you remember anything else? Did you hear anything, anything at all?"

"No. But I kept watching. They were deep in conversation. They looked like they didn't belong there. This...Winter was doing most of the talking, and the evil man was listening. The Winter man handed the evil man something. Something like a notebook, or a pocket book. They weren't drinking anything, so I wondered why they were even there. I got distracted signing autographs for a few minutes, and I thought that when I looked back they would be gone. I *hoped* they would be gone. But when I looked back, they were still there. And..." Constance gulped at air.

"And what?"

"They were staring right at me, Mr. Sheppard. The Winter man and the evil man. Staring right at me. Like they knew I'd been watching them. The evil man's eyes. They looked so...like they were on fire...they looked so hot. I've never seen anything like it. I felt so scared. Like a little child. But for some reason, I couldn't look away. Until my assistant came and took me back to my dressing room. And all that time, he was looking at me."

A shiver fluttered on Sheppard's spine. If this was the horse mask, this solidified that Winter was in on it. This plot, this plan. Winter knew. And was working with the horse mask. The evil man. *Handed him a notebook.* The notebook that Ryan saw him writing in? It was all getting clearer.

"I tried not to think of the man after that. I tried to forget the whole thing. But for the last few weeks, I haven't been able to sleep. Because when I shut my eyes, all I can see is him."

"Do you think he's the one doing this to us?" A man in a suit and a red tie. Constance's "evil man." He seemed to be a thread connecting them together. Sheppard thought—had he ever seen anyone that fit this description? Maybe—he saw lots of people in suits. There was no way someone like that would stand out to him. Also, most of the time he wasn't exactly on "high alert"—he was usually a little "washy." He hadn't seen anyone who had seemed particularly "evil."

Constance looked up at him, sadly. "Of course he is, Mr. Sheppard. Because that man wasn't just evil. That man knew what I'd done, just like he knows everyone else in this room. He knows you. He knows what you're hiding. He is the Devil."

Constance took a few steps backwards. Moving away. Sheppard couldn't move. The way Constance put it, this man did seem evil. And he was talking to Winter. Constance had stared into the eyes of their captor. It had to be.

Sheppard almost forgot. Grateful to change the subject. "The mask the man is using? Do you recognize it? Maybe from your show?"

"No. I don't... Maybe. We did use horse masks for a dream sequence once. Is it important?"

No idea. "I don't know."

"We have a prop department that makes everything in-house."

"So it would not be possible to acquire one elsewhere?"

"Why do you care about this? We have been put here by the Devil."

"I..." No good answer, except he had to stay grounded. Would be all too easy to get swept away, with Constance.

And not be any use to anyone.

"Please hurry, Mr. Sheppard. That man, he's coming. And he's coming for you," Constance said, and stepped away.

Sheppard let her go. His breath caught in his throat. The evil man, behind the horse mask. The man who knew him all too well. The glasses, the show, the psychologist dead in the bath. The evil man knew him better than he knew himself.

And he's coming for you.

The devil didn't exist.

Why didn't that make him feel any better?

Constance found her way back to Mandy's side, while Sheppard stared out at the room. Her words still ringing in his ears.

Tell me, do you think you are a good man?

He had no idea.

23

Headphones was watching him. He didn't know if he'd seen her blink yet which was slightly disconcerting. Sheppard wanted a break—to do as the others were doing, a period of silent reflection. But he couldn't. He had to move on. He beckoned to Headphones.

On her black hoodie, the sticker HELLO MY NAME IS... Rhona. *Headphones* stuck in his mind though. She looked at him for a moment longer and then shuffled out from under the desk. She got up and made her way over to Sheppard, keeping her purple headphones clamped to her ears.

They looked at each other, the silence unnerving, till Sheppard dared to speak.

"Hi."

Headphones said nothing. "Rhona? Is it?"

Standing still like a statue. "What are you listening to?"

She just stared at him. Maybe she couldn't hear. But there was something in her eyes. A glint of understanding.

"What are you listening to?" he tried again. Nothing.

Sheppard was suddenly very annoyed—everything suddenly

peaking. "Okay, we'll just stand here for the next two hours. I wonder what exploding feels like." He regretted it as he said it. It was all taking its toll on him, but that was no way to go about talking to a defenseless kid.

Headphones frowned, opened her mouth and closed it again. She looked around, probably to make sure no one else in the room was looking, and slipped her headphones off, hooking them around her neck.

"You're rude," she said, her voice younger than she looked and softer than her expression implied.

"I'm not the biggest fan of talking," she said. "I'm listening to the Stones. Greatest Hits. Volume Two."

"Ah, the Stones. What's your favorite song?"

"People like 'Paint It, Black,' but I prefer '2000 Light Years from Home.'"

Sheppard smiled. "Unconventional choice, but I can definitely agree with that decision right now." The evil man. Winter. And a hotel room full of truth or lies. He felt two thousand light years from home too. "You're a bit young to be listening to the Stones."

"I'm seventeen," she said. Defensive. As though she'd had to say that many times before. "I also have taste."

"Undoubtedly," Sheppard said. "I don't suppose that thing you're listening to can connect to the internet or make a call or anything."

Headphones's mouth twitched at the edges. She pulled the device from the pocket of her hoodie—an old retro Discman. "You're welcome to try and call someone on it if you want." Kids her age would usually have an iPhone or something, and she must have seen his look because she added, "Better audio quality."

Sheppard looked from the device to her. "Why are you not

more freaked out by this situation? Have you heard anything that's been going on?"

"I heard the TV. When you were still cuffed to the bed. I heard there's a dead man in the bath. I heard there's a murderer here. Otherwise, I don't really care what these people have to say. I don't need to hear anymore. If I'm going to die, I want to sit in a corner and listen to my music. I can't think of a better way to go. At least not with the options available."

"That's..." Sheppard struggled for the word. The more he thought about it, the more he thought it was the sanest thing he'd heard in the room so far. "That's very grown-up," he settled with.

Headphones's face screwed up at *grown-up*. "My dad taught me to prepare for the worst. Anything else is a pleasant surprise."

"He sounds great at parties," Sheppard said. "But you know that I can't just sit in a corner and wait to die." *Although that sounds enticing.* "I'm not going to let anyone else get hurt, not if I can help it." *Keep telling yourself that.* "So I need to ask you a few questions." Sheppard knew the type of girl Headphones was. A girl who hadn't seen the good in the world so just assumed the darkest parts were normal. Sheppard had seen his fair share of terrible but he knew that there was good out there, like the good he thought he saw in Dr. Winter. Even if he didn't always feel that that good was inside himself. "First off, do you remember where you were before you got here?"

"I was at home," Headphones said, "in my room on my laptop. My dad and some of his friends were downstairs, watching football. I try and drown it out with music but I can always still hear them cheering. Idiots. So instead of my stereo, I used my headphones. It works a little better. Then I heard them go to the pub after the match, as usual."

"Do you live with anyone else?"

"You mean like a mother? Nope, I don't have one of those."

"Everyone has a mother." A flash of his own. A dreadfully insufferable woman.

"There was a woman. But she left."

"Okay," Sheppard said. Giving up. He scratched his chin. The backs of his hands were itching with want. "So you just blacked out? And then you woke up here? Did you maybe smell something?"

A flash of recognition came across Headphones's face. "Yes. There was. I smelled something weird, something chemical. And my head got all swimmy, you know. I couldn't focus on anything. And then I was here."

"The same as everyone else."

"Yes. I remember. But why did I forget?"

"It'll be the drugs. Making it all feel like a dream."

"Right."

"I need you to remember—I need to know if you were alone in that room."

"Of course I was—it was my bedroom."

"And you were alone in the house?"

"Yes," Headphones said, like she were talking to a toddler.

"And you were sure everyone had gone out? You know these people?"

"Yes. My dad. His friend Bill and his friend Matthew. Although I have to call them Mr. Michael and Mr. Cline to their faces."

"But how well do you know them?"

"I don't know them really, not very well at least. My dad does though. He's known them for years. They all work at an estate agency in Angel."

"Do either of them wear glasses?"

"What the hell are you talking about?" Headphones said. "No, neither of them."

Stupid really. These people didn't sound important.

But you never knew...

Sheppard had a picture in his mind. The evil man. Rectangle glasses. Red tie. Straight suit. The man that Constance described. The man that Mandy might have seen this morning. So he couldn't be in two places at once, right?

"It's always the same on a Friday. My dad and his friends get a half day. Isn't it weird how no one high-up seems to work on Friday afternoons? Anyway, they always come back to our house and watch whatever sports are on, then they go to the pub. I go to college, go to therapy and then I come home."

Sheppard froze. "What?"

"I go to college. St Martin's. I'm doing a Foundation in Art and Design."

"No. You go to therapy?"

Headphones narrowed her eyes. "Yeah. What's wrong with that? Jennifer Lawrence went to therapy."

"No. It's..." *Pick your words carefully.*

"I go mainly because of unresolved family issues. I also have claustrophobia, which I thought was getting better...until I got locked in a hotel room with five other people and a dead man."

That explained Headphones's conduct a little more. Why she had squashed herself under the desk, closed her eyes and kept her headphones on.

He decided not to press the issue. "Did you see your therapist today?"

"No, I went around his house as usual, but no one was home. It was weird, Dr. Winter's never missed an appointment before. I guess it must have been serious."

"Dr. Winter." *Of course, it's him. That's how everyone's connected, isn't it?* Surprised. Why was he surprised?

"Yes." Headphones obviously saw something in his face. Maybe it was as pale as he thought. "What?" She hadn't heard. She was listening to the Stones. She had no idea.

Sheppard took a shaking hand, got out Winter's wallet and opened it. Held it up to Headphones.

"Is this him?"

Headphones, confused, looked at the driver's license. "Yes. How did you…" She stopped. Her brain making connections it didn't want to make. She looked up at Sheppard with big eyes. And before he could stop her, she rushed into the bathroom.

Sheppard was taken off guard and rushed after her.

He was used to the bathroom now—the bright lights and the smell, but it was still revolting. Headphones had pulled back the curtain to see into the bathtub. When she saw Winter lying dead, she dropped to her knees, her hands gripping the side of the tub.

"What…" Headphones croaked. "No…"

Sheppard stood behind her, not knowing quite what to do.

Headphones didn't cry. She just sat there on her knees and looked.

Any question that Headphones had murdered this man was immediately wiped from his mind.

Sheppard made his way around her and sat down in front of her… *No, the blood. No closer…*

Headphones looked down at Dr. Winter as though he were someone very close. A father figure. Sheppard hadn't expected such emotion would appear on her face.

They sat there for a while. Until he knew he had to move her on.

"I'm sorry," Sheppard said.

"Who did this?" Headphones said.

"That's what I'm going to find out."

"I'll kill them," Headphones said. And he believed her. "I'll make it worse for them. Why would they do this to Dr. Winter? He never did anything to anyone. He just tried to help."

He didn't do anything. He was good and kind. And naïve.

"How long have you known him?"

Headphones dragged her gaze from Winter to look at him. "I've been in therapy for five years."

We could've bumped into each other. "Do you mind me asking why?"

"I had social anxiety. Really bad stuff. That's why I don't participate much. I've got a lot better but it's still there. Dr. Winter helped me. Showed me how to cope with it. He is…was…a good man."

Tell me, are you a good man? The pangs of pain in his head accentuated with every word. He mentally swatted at the air trying to get them to disappear.

A jolt of confusion on Headphones's face. And Sheppard realized he had actually swatted the air. *Keep it together.*

"When's the last time you saw him?"

Her eyes back on Winter. "A week ago. My normal session. He was telling me that I really didn't need him anymore. But I did… I do. He says I'm better. But I'm not. I need him."

"Was there anything weird about the session? Maybe something he said?" *Maybe something he was planning.* Sheppard still couldn't comprehend Winter being involved in all of this.

Headphones wiped her eyes, although she wasn't crying. "He cut the session short. I usually see him for an hour and about halfway through, there was a knock at the front door. His office is at the front of the house, so he looked through the window. He didn't waste any time after that. He told me something had come up and I had to leave. He was really apologetic. He said we'd make the time up this week. I didn't mind. He ushered me out the back way, into his living room. Then he shut the door to his office and I heard him opening the front door to the next person. And that was that."

"Did you hear or see who was at the door?"

"No, I just assumed it was another one of his friends…" *He called them friends because "patients" was too clinical, too cold,* Sheppard remembered. "Anyway, I thought, maybe someone needed to see him urgently. So I didn't mind."

"But you were still in his house?" *He has an entrance door and an exit door. You know that?*

"Yes. Usually I go out the kitchen door and leave. The back door. But... I don't know why, this time I stuck around. I feel safe in his house. And my dad wasn't expecting me home, so I just sat down. I knew Dr. Winter wouldn't mind. I was there about ten minutes. Just sitting. And then..."

"Then what?"

"I'm not a nosy person," Headphones said defensively. In that way someone said something before saying another thing directly to the contrary. "I don't know what came over me. But... after about ten minutes, the printer on a desk at the far side of the room started spitting out stuff. Maybe it was just instinct. But I got up. And I went over to it."

"What was coming out?"

"Pages and pages of stuff. Loads of text. I didn't really read any of it. It looked like someone was faxing it over. I thought it was never going to stop. But then the last page came out or the first page I guess... I picked it up. It was a diagram of something. Filled with boxes, and measurements, and even coordinates I think. Then I looked at the second page. It was a deed to some land somewhere. I remember being confused, like why Winter would want any of this. I thought maybe it was a mistake, but on the first page at the top, someone had handwritten 'TO WINTER.' It was signed 'C.' I didn't understand any of it."

Sheppard said nothing. A diagram. With measurements. Could it have been a diagram of this room? There was no question about it. Winter was deep into this. But what else had Headphones said? A land deed? What the hell did that have to do with anything?

"I just put the paper back. And I turned around. And I

jumped. He was standing there. Dr. Winter. He must have heard the printer or something. I thought I was going to get into real big trouble. But the strangest thing happened."

"What?"

Headphones was silent for a moment, looking down at her dead doctor. "He started to cry. Really. He rushed over to me, and was blubbering words I didn't understand. He saw what I was looking at. He saw it. And I saw it. Just some stupid document, but he was going crazy, saying something like 'No, not you.' To me. I was still so shocked that I didn't know what to do. So I got my bag and I got out of there. As fast as I could. And I looked back, and he was there. Bawling. Sinking to the floor. And that was the last time I saw him...until now."

Headphones bit her lip.

Sheppard didn't know what to say. Still thinking about what she'd seen. She made the connection before he could.

"Do you think that's why I'm here?"

Still not getting it. "What?"

"Because I saw those things. He said 'No, not you.' Like he wanted to protect me, but couldn't. I ran out of there, when I should have helped him. Like he always helped me."

"We don't know anything for sure yet," Sheppard said. But it fit. Headphones saw the plans. Constance locked eyes with the evil man. Alan stirred the wrong pot. Ryan walked in on Winter. Mandy worked with Winter's daughter.

The evil man had used Winter. To get information on the hotel room. And now, to be the murderee in a game of Cluedo. But who did it? Who killed him? Assuming it wasn't the evil man himself...that meant someone in the room was lying.

Sheppard got to his feet and held a hand out to Headphones. "C'mon, you don't need to keep looking at him. It won't do any good."

Headphones took a moment, then accepted it. He pulled her up and drew the curtain again.

"I can't quite believe it," Headphones said. She seemed lost. "I can't believe he's dead." She gravitated toward the door—no real sense of purpose.

She turned back. "I'm scared now. I'm really scared." And with that, she was gone.

24

He was alone in the bathroom once again. He turned to the mirror to see that he looked far worse than before. His skin seemed to be covered in some kind of slick liquid. His vision was blurred.

He tried to focus on his reflection but he was fuzzy around the edges. Cold jolts of electricity pulsed through him—his heart going three times too fast—enough to power an aircraft. He ducked down to the toilet as the urge to vomit rose up inside him. Opening the lid just in time, he threw up the entire contents of his stomach—a purple-tinged liquid mixed with small chunks of what was once food. It burned his throat and he choked as more came out. Three lurches of his stomach and it was done. The leavings floated on the top of the water. It stank of iron—of acid and The End.

He rested his head on the toilet bowl, blindly searching with his hand for the flush. He pressed it and the vomit swirled away. The smell stayed, mixing with the smell of blood. He closed his eyes and thought of how easy it would be to stay here, to just go to sleep.

His throat was on fire.

Somehow he pulled himself back up to the sink. He turned the cold water on full blast and cupped a full handful of water into his mouth. He slurped it up and it slid down his throat, feeling better. A few more cups and he swilled the water around his mouth this time, spitting it out to get out the last bits of vomit. He turned on the hot tap, and after a few seconds, warm steam rose from the bowl. He closed his eyes, taking pleasure in the heat on his face.

He didn't know how long he stood there, sipping water from the cold tap and steaming himself from the hot. But he knew it was too long. He was feeling better—just had had to clear some space in his belly. But the Crash was still coming. He needed a drink, or pills, or both. The Crash would be worse than this.

Alan. Mandy. Constance. Ryan. And Headphones. *One of these is not like the other.* Who was the murderer? They had all given him reasonable stories. They all seemed genuine. No one had hidden the fact that they were connected to Winter. They were all linked together, in ways they didn't know.

Alan still seemed the most likely. He had a strong motive—even admitted it himself. But Alan didn't seem like a man to do something so brash. He was a terrible person, but he was also clever. Killing a witness would be irrational, stupid. But if it was all in service of some bigger plan…

Constance could've done it. She was an actress, so could've easily made him believe her story. And she was crazy, volatile. Who knew what she was capable of? He bet that getting her to murder someone wouldn't take too much. But there was something about her face when she was describing the evil man. He had seen something in her eyes.

Ryan worked here—in this building. He could've been a useful person to have on the inside of a plan like this. He knew things about the rooms that normal people wouldn't. And he also seemed to desperately need money to help his family. He was athletic, probably quite strong. Was it really too far a leap to think he could be responsible?

That left Headphones and Mandy. He couldn't see it. Headphones's reaction to Dr. Winter—she saw the old man as a father figure. They were friends. And Mandy—there was one thing he kept coming back to with her. That first time she saw Winter. That first scream. When she had come into the bathroom. It was so loud, so scared, so devoid of hope. It was real. There was no way. Surely.

They're the least likely. So maybe they're the most. A strange thought, but he couldn't entirely dismiss it. After all, he was an entertainer, and on his television show producers regularly employed that tactic. They deflected suspicion from the actual perpetrator to make it a bigger shock when it finally came out. Maybe the man in the horse mask knew this. But still, Headphones? Mandy? Really? He still couldn't imagine they would be capable of such a thing.

Are you capable of such a thing? A strange thought, a sickening thought, but not unwarranted. After all, he was suffering some memory loss. But could he do such a thing? Especially to Dr. Winter?

Winter and the evil man had been planning this for a long time. Did Winter really hate Sheppard that much? To condemn hundreds of innocent lives. Was this what Sheppard did to people? He didn't mean to. Whatever Sheppard had done…he didn't mean it. *Maybe this is why you killed Winter. You found out what he was up to.* With a sickening feeling in his gut, Sheppard realized he couldn't rule himself out.

Could he totally blame Winter though? Sheppard knew he had probably meant to do whatever he did to make Winter hate him so much. The old Sheppard wouldn't have. The old Sheppard who thought that maybe things had gone too far. The old

Sheppard that was going to quit his show, shrug off all the attention and go back to being nobody.

But he wasn't that man anymore. He was governed by the little kid he once was. The kid who wanted attention more than anything else. The kid that wanted "it" so much, and reached out and got it. And then vowed never to be an unknown again.

Tell me, do you think you are a good man?

Things had happened too fast. The drinking and the drugs. Making it easier to move. Forward. Always forward. He had grown into something terrible. And he hadn't even cared.

Self-pity gushed over him. He couldn't even look at himself. The bloodshot eyes, the slick skin, the look of disdain. He was broken. A shadow of the illusion that appeared on television. The man behind the mask.

The mirror was fogging up. His face disappearing in the mist.

He was not that man. Not now, not in this terrible bathroom. He was just another man with too many questions and no answers. He had ducked and dived all his life, trouble finding it hard to catch him. How had he not known something like this was coming? How one day the mouse would fall into the trap?

Was it enough to be sorry?

He turned the taps off to see the last of the steam swirl up and settle in the room, mixing in with the smell of blood and vomit.

At the door, he glanced around. The shadow of Dr. Winter behind the curtain. He drew it back once more.

Tell me…

"I'm not a good man. I never was." Finally answering him. After twenty years.

And Winter's face was cold—letting him know that it wasn't enough.

25

Before…

Brickwork was buzzing by the time he got there. He got out of the back of the limo and waved to the large queue of people waiting to get in. They waved back and a number of them screamed at him happily. He chuckled and nodded to the bouncer as he passed. The big burly man smiled and unhooked the cordon.

Sheppard made his way down the steps slowly. He'd already had a lot to drink, and had taken one too many pills. His limbs felt comfortably numb, as though they could float, and there was that familiar fluffy feeling in his brain. He was seeing the world through a cloud, but the drink was yanking him back down to earth. That was the coolness of the combo. He existed in the in-between. The new reality. Unfortunately, in the reality he had left behind, he could walk straight. He grasped the banister as he almost slipped on the carpeted steps. His heart fluttered. Stairs were the enemy of the drunk.

He prevailed eventually and emerged into the large open area of the club. It was incredibly dark, lit up incrementally by flashing strobe lights. The area was a fantastically crowded dance floor with a raised bar to the side and booths placed around at the edges. The dance floor was already packed with people, jumping up and down to some pop track.

He smiled and started to make his way across the dance floor. As people saw him, they moved out of the way. Some people tried to talk to him, or grab him. He just smiled at them. In the light, he couldn't see anyone, pick out any distinguishing features, so he had no idea who anyone was. They were ghosts. And for that, he was almost glad. He didn't have time for real people.

He looked around the edges. For the VIP area. Found it by the bar. Familiar faces behind the barrier. The security guard spotted him and smiled.

"Mr. Sheppard." His mouth made the movements. "Good to see you."

He opened the barrier and let him through. Sheppard smiled back at him, slapping him on the back and covertly handing him three twenty-pound notes.

The code for *No interruptions*.

The VIP area was slightly offset from the rest of the club. An alcove, small but long enough to channel the music coming from the rest of the room. Changing it. Making it quieter. It was also lighter, from small bulb lights embedded in the brick ceiling. The area was a round of comfy seats and Sheppard could actually see the faces of the people sitting there. It was largely empty but Sheppard saw his publicist, who was absorbed in conversation with two glamorous women who looked like identical twins, his director and PA, who were not so enraptured in talking with each other and Douglas Perry, who was very obviously waiting for Sheppard to arrive while sipping on a strange-looking colorful drink, topped with a slice of orange and a small pink umbrella.

On the circular table, there were mountains of empty glasses, and as he looked, a pretty young waitress came along to clean up. The table was slick with alcohol and he thought he detected her grimace as she picked up the first glass to put on her tray.

As Sheppard slid down into a chair, happy to be able to stop worrying about falling over, Douglas looked up from his phone. With a straw hanging from the side of his mouth, he gave a great guffaw. Sheppard wondered how far gone he was. The agent had a penchant for cocaine and was rarely seen off it. He had even got Sheppard to try it a few times, and although it wasn't unpleasant, Sheppard didn't like the aftereffects of it. He much preferred pills. "Here he is, the man of the hour. Or should I say, the man of the year."

Everyone in the area looked around at this bold statement, and saw Sheppard. They all turned, smiling and clapping. The girls talking to his publicist seemed to want to ditch him for Sheppard, although the publicist was so locked in conversation, they couldn't get away.

"Come on, what are you having? I'm buying."

"It's an open bar, Doug," Sheppard said, already slurring his words.

"Exactly. That's why I'm buying," Douglas said, and laughed heartily. He raised a hand and waved over a woman in a short red dress. She was pretty, with long legs. Sheppard slowly looked her up and down as Douglas ordered him a bourbon and another monstrously colorful concoction for himself.

Once she had gone, Douglas returned his attention to Sheppard. Sheppard grabbed at one of the baggies of white powder and started setting up a line.

"So how are you, old mate?" Douglas always had the cadence of an older gentleman, one who might have seen wartime. In reality, he was fifty and as spineless as they came.

"I'm great," Sheppard said, shuffling in his seat. Already thinking he could use another pill. He never felt sated by them—

never content. He existed in one of two camps—too much or too little. He didn't know which one was worse.

"You look a little weathered, if you don't mind me saying, mate."

Sheppard smiled at him as the woman came to give him his drink. He took it and downed it in one. A shiver through his brain, a jolt of energy. Better already.

"That better?"

He replaced the glass on the waitress's tray and asked for another. She nodded and left.

"HA. Well I guess you deserve it. You alone are putting my children through college, you know that."

"Don't mention it."

"Honestly, Sheppard, this is fantastic. Absolutely fantastic. Your numbers are going through the roof. The show is doing better than anything that has ever been in the morning slot. Have you seen the numbers? Did Zoe give you the numbers?"

"I've seen the numbers. She gave me the numbers."

"I haven't seen Zoe here yet. When she comes, she'll give you the numbers."

"Doug," Sheppard said, laughing, "I've seen the numbers."

Douglas stopped talking and laughed too. "I'm sorry, mate. It's just so fantastic. YOU are bloody fantastic. You remember when I took you on? You were—"

"Fourteen. Yes I know. I was there."

"—fourteen. I never thought you'd get this far. I mean, I don't want to speak ill of the dead, but thank God that Maths teacher was murdered when he was."

Sheppard didn't know how to respond. So just smiled. Douglas could always find the most tactless way to say something—it was his talent. It was why he had two ex-wives and four children who despised him.

Through his foggy mind, he thought of Mr. Jefferies. The

kind, rotund Maths teacher who had always helped him with his homework. The teacher who'd been found hanging from the ceiling.

"What did you want to talk to me about, Doug?" Sheppard said, as the woman with the legs came back with another drink and Doug's cocktail. This time Sheppard took his and held it up to the light. The crisp brown liquid looked inviting, silky. His life fuel. He took a sip and said to the woman, "Don't let my glass get empty, yeah?"

The woman nodded. She looked dazed, excited. She was obviously a fan. Women did that weird fluttering thing with their eyes whenever they recognized him. He couldn't tell if they wanted to sleep with him or murder him. Either way, they looked invitingly dangerous.

Douglas took his new drink. "I wanted to talk to you about new opportunities."

"Sounds ominous," Sheppard said. The drink wrapping round him, like a warm blanket on a cold evening.

"I've been approached by a number of parties about the possibility of you writing a book."

"A book?"

"Yes, those things with words in."

"Very funny, Doug. What would I write a book about?"

"Well, anything. Anything you like. As interesting or as dumb as you want. To be honest, it doesn't really matter. People will buy it because it'll have your name on it. Books are just like television. It's all about the man behind the glass."

"I don't know how to write a book."

"People will help you. Hell, people will write it for you, if you want. You just need to be the name on the cover. What do you say?"

Sheppard laughed. "Easy as that, huh?"

"Think about what the book could be though. The Resi-

dent Detective Morgan Sheppard tells of his struggles solving
the murder of his own teacher, when he was just eleven years
old. I mean Christ, Morgan, that's a surefire hit. That's *Times*
bestseller list stuff."

"It does sound enticing," Sheppard said, swirling the bourbon
around in his glass. He could almost see it. The book in the front
window of Waterstones. A tasteful artsy cover maybe. His face
on the back of the jacket, smiling out of thousands of copies. A
nice thick volume, filled with the accounts of the child detective.

"So?"

"I don't very often say no, Doug," Sheppard said, "so it would
be rather pointless to start now."

Douglas almost jumped out of his seat. "HA. Yes, sir, you
are fantastic, Sheppard. We're going to be kings of the world.
You and I. Morgan Sheppard at the top of every chart. You're a
brand. And we're going to make millions. I've already got pub-
lishers willing to pay out the ass for the first one."

"The first one? Let's not get carried away, Doug."

"Let's not get carried away," Douglas mimicked. "That sounds
like a Sheppard without enough booze inside of him. Waitress."
And he waved over the woman for another round.

The rest of the night was lost in a toxic fume of poisonous
substances. Sheppard and Douglas talked a while longer about
nothing in particular as they became steadily worse for wear.
Many times, small groups of mainly girls came up to the VIP
rope and asked Sheppard for an autograph. Although this was
meant to be a TV company party, he didn't recognize any of
them. Douglas insisted that he sign every single one and Sheppard didn't complain.

At some point, the music got louder and the lights got lower,
so Sheppard could hardly see Douglas in front of him, let alone
hear him. The two shouted to each other, but didn't get much
of what the other was saying. Sheppard decided that he would

have to cross the vast expanse of the dance floor to find somewhere to urinate. He gestured to Douglas, and somehow the
drunken man got the right end of the stick.

Sheppard stood up, the world around him rocking. It was the
world that was unsteady, not him. He was the greatest he had ever
felt. Child Detective. TV Presenter. And now Author. He found
his way out of the VIP area, patting the guard on the shoulder
more for support than friendliness. The dance floor looked bigger than it was before. It swelled and pulsated in front of him.
The people all morphed together in his mind, so he was just
looking at one dark mass. He kept his head down and walked
through them.

A weird part of being famous was that people always seemed
to want to touch you. It was rather bizarre. People didn't seem
content with just seeing you—they had to make sure you were
real. As he was crossing the dance floor, Sheppard experienced
this phenomenon in full force. People tapped him, shook his
hand and even hugged him. And Sheppard was drunk enough
to let it happen.

It felt like an age before he finally got free of the dance floor
and looked up to see a neon sign saying "John" and an arrow
pointing down a narrow corridor. John? Well, it was a male
name he guessed, so he followed it and finally found the toilets.

It was another half an hour before he finally got back to the
VIP area. As he sat down, he noticed that Douglas had made
his way through three more glasses of multicolored sludge. The
groups had converged and Douglas was talking animatedly to
the twins while the producer and the publicist were having a
heated discussion. His PA, Rogers, was looking pale…like he
might pass out or throw up or do both at any moment.

The others looked round as the waitress came up to Sheppard
with another bourbon.

"Thank you," Sheppard said, and downed it without a second thought. "Another please."

The woman smiled and nodded.

Douglas laughed. Gesturing to Sheppard. "Now this mate really knows how to party," he said to the girls.

Sheppard smiled back. "Just a little."

"You alright, mate? You were a long time."

"Ha, let's just say next time I want to take a piss, I might start out fifteen minutes early. You know what I think we need? I think we need to get far more drunk."

Perry smiled. "Well, I guess I better drink to that."

As if on cue, and horrifically fast, the woman came back with another bourbon for Sheppard. He'd lost count of them—he remembered a time when he used to keep track. Now he didn't bother. Sheppard touched glasses with Douglas and the girls, just as PA Rogers finally passed out. The man's face hit the table and he collapsed on the floor.

The whole VIP area erupted into uncontrollable laughter.

Sheppard got up onto the table and the music dimmed as the DJ noticed something was going on.

"Three cheers for dopey Rogers," he shouted.

And the entire club joined in in a round of hip-hip-hoorahs. Half of the people there probably had no idea why, but they joined in nonetheless.

Sheppard waved his drink around, sloshing it everywhere, before collapsing back into his seat.

That was when he lost the night.

26

Sheppard left the bathroom so fast that he crashed into Mandy, who was staring at the wall beside the bed. They almost toppled over together, but Mandy grabbed and steadied him. The commotion drew everyone else's gaze before they went back to whatever it was they were doing.

"What is it?" Mandy said. She must have seen it in his eyes.

Sheppard opened his mouth, and thought better of it. He didn't know what to say. He was a fish gasping for air. Something about his admittance to Winter—*"I'm not a good man. I never was."*—seemed to draw a line under everything. And the feeling that the evil man knew Sheppard's inadequacies better than he knew them himself. "What are you doing?" he said.

"I'm looking at this picture. It's really weird, don't you think?" The painting of a farmhouse burning and a scarecrow smiling had almost smugly caught his attention when he'd first woken up but he hadn't thought about it since. "Why the hell is this in a hotel room?"

"I don't know," Sheppard said. He remembered thinking exactly the same thing.

Mandy reached up and ran her hand over the paint of the farmhouse. "It's sad, isn't it? I like art, puzzling over what it all means. This painting freaks me out. Somehow I just know there's a family in that house, children burning. And that scarecrow with those eyes. They remind me of the eyes of the guy in the café."

"What?"

"There have to be people in that house, right?"

"No, the other thing. About the eyes."

"Oh," Mandy said, putting her hand down, "I remembered something. That man in the café who was looking at me? I know now what freaked me out so much. It was his eyes. They just looked like the eyes of a man who was up to no good. Like the scarecrow's."

Sheppard looked up at the painting. The scarecrow's eyes looked oddly human. As he stared, they seemed to move and look at him. *No, just an illusion.* But this lined up with what Constance had said. Mandy had met the same man.

Which meant...

Sheppard put his arm on the wall to steady himself, as a pulse of dizziness threatened to topple him. "We have to get out of here."

Mandy's face was losing color. "But..."

You can't do it.

"I can't do it."

All the interviewing, all that time lost, when he should have been doing the right thing. Trying to escape.

Alan's voice, far off. "Well nice to know he's on the same page as the rest of us."

"Shut up, Alan." Ryan.

Who was lying? Someone had to be? But all the stories fit together. They all had run in with Winter or Constance's evil man.

They all ended up here because of it. But who was lying? Someone with more skill could tell. They could see it in their eyes.

Sheppard looked from Mandy to the timer. Under two hours to go. Too much time. If the evil man knew that Sheppard couldn't do it, why not just kill him straight off? Not place him here. In death's waiting room.

"Sheppard, what's wrong?" Mandy again. Scared this time.

Sheppard looked at her. And pushed past her. Ignoring her follow-up query.

There was only one thing for it now. One way to stave off the shakes, and the cold, hard crash. Take the edge off imminent death. Although maybe it would be the evil man's last laugh for it to be empty.

Sheppard almost fell to his knees in front of the television. The others were talking to him. Instead he found himself on Headphones's level. She had her headphones on again, and had shuffled back under the desk. He looked at her and she looked back. Running his hands over the cupboard underneath the desk in search of a handle, he hoped to God that he was right.

It was indeed the minibar. And even in the relative light of the room, the manufactured flickering of the fridge bulb was comforting. However, what was inside was not.

The minibar was almost entirely empty, just as he feared. It looked pathetic, in the way barren fridges often do. There were only two items, on the top shelf—airplane miniature bottles. His favorite brand of bourbon.

It was almost worse than nothing.

Sheppard picked up one bottle—barely the size of his forefinger. One swig of alcohol, maybe two—barely enough to get a taste.

His favorite brand—best not to think about the implications of that.

Sheppard slipped one bottle into his pocket and took the other. He stood up and looked around, bottle in hand.

Alan was looking at him with something like confused disgust. The others were just confused.

"I don't think it's really time for a piss–up, Sheppard," the lawyer said. An acid tone that could melt through skin.

"It's two bottles, Alan," Sheppard said.

"I knew it. I knew the papers were correct," Alan said. "Shaky hands. Sweating like a pig. You're coming down with a nice case of withdrawal."

Sheppard launched himself at Alan, grabbing him by the lapels of his suit and slamming him into the window. Alan let out an exasperated grunt, snarling at Sheppard.

"There he is," Alan said, "our real hero."

"Can you shut your mouth for two goddamn seconds?" Sheppard said. "It's two bottles." Too close. He could feel the hatred running out of the old man. Almost burned him.

"Sheppard?" Mandy said, uneasy.

She was staring inside the minibar. Ryan was looking too. Sheppard let Alan go, the lawyer readjusting his tie and dusting his lapels as if Sheppard was unclean.

Sheppard stepped back toward the minibar.

Mandy knelt down and reached into the small fridge, bringing out a small white box that was slotted into the lowest shelf. He hadn't noticed it before as it perfectly fit the dimensions of the fridge and was suitably camouflaged. She held the box up to Sheppard.

It looked like a first aid box. But written in black marker, in the same handwriting as the rule book, was "With regards, The Great Hotel."

He turned it over, but nothing was written on the bottom. The box rattled. It was heavy.

A first aid kit? Was this another one of Sheppard's cravings? If the evil man knew Sheppard's favorite bourbon, surely he knew what else was needed. Maybe this box was a present.

Sheppard put the other bottle of bourbon in his pocket, and grasped the box with both hands, sliding the locks to open so it flipped open.

It wasn't what he wanted. And it wasn't food or water or sustenance. But even still, Sheppard couldn't quite believe it.

"What is it?" Ryan said, and Mandy echoed him. Sheppard looked up at them, and emptied the box.

They all looked down at the contents strewn out across the bed. Six mobile phones.

27

Mobile phones—what?

Sheppard looked around at everyone—they looked as confused as he felt. Even Constance had looked around from her seat on the bed and Headphones had stuck her head up from beneath the desk.

He looked down again—he couldn't see his own phone. "What is this?" Ryan said.

Sheppard randomly grabbed one—a thin smartphone—and tapped the screen. It lit up with a wallpaper of a dog wearing antlers. It had a passcode. No matter. Sheppard saw what he needed. No signal.

Who would he call? The police? Never called the police before. Was it like on television?

999. What is your emergency?

We've been trapped in a room by a guy in a horse mask. I've got to solve a murder in the next hour and forty-five minutes or he's going to blow up the building. No wait—don't hang up.

Sheppard went to put the smartphone down and someone whimpered. He looked around—Headphones was staring at it.

He held it up, the picture of the dog looking out to her. She nodded, and Sheppard gave it to her.

"Do you all see your own?" Sheppard said, but no one moved. So he picked up a flip-top phone that lit up as he opened it. Plain blue background. Old style. And in the corner—no signal.

Phone companies are really doing God's work.

He put the phone down, and Ryan picked it up. "It's mine," Ryan said, opening it.

Alan started forward into his view and snatched one of the phones up. "Finally, I can tell Jenkins to prep my report."

"I think we'll call the police first, yeah?" Mandy said, picking another one up. Hers had some kind of dongle thing hanging off it.

Two phones left. A BlackBerry and a smartphone. Neither one his. He picked up the smartphone. Slightly older than the last and cracked in one corner. Wallpaper—a young woman with a baby in her arms. Corner—no signal.

Wait.

Three phones with no signal. Looking around at Alan's and Mandy's faces, maybe more than three.

"How is that possible?" Ryan said, realizing what Sheppard had already realized, holding his phone high in the air. Mandy too—whatever was hanging from her phone was swinging in the air.

"Goddamn it."

There was a groan from Constance, as she digested the words. "God doesn't need a phone tower."

"Oh put a sock in it, Jesus-freak," Alan spat. Sheppard ignored them. "Has anyone got anything?" Blank faces all around.

"No signal," Mandy said, "but we're in the center of London."

"Bastard must be blocking it somehow," Alan said. "The reception. He's playing us like a damn flute. Getting our hopes up and then dashing them."

"What are you talking about?" Ryan said.

"I see this all the time, son," Alan told him. "This is how you break people."

Constance shuffled up the bed and gestured to Sheppard. He handed her the smartphone. She took it and recoiled, slinking back to her former position.

One phone left. The BlackBerry. One of the models that had an entire keyboard on it, with impossibly small keys for each letter. But whose was it?

He picked it up and pressed one of the keys at random. The screen lit up. On the screen, behind all the icons were two faces. A wife and a daughter. Younger than they would be now.

The drink and the drugs, they fogged him. They obscured the past. Made him live in nowhere but the present. They made it harder to remember, but it was still there. He just had to be helped in jogging his memory. Looking into Winter's daughter's eyes was more than enough. And he remembered how he had hurt them all. And now Winter was dead and they might never know. He shielded the screen from the others, as though he might contain what he had done.

Mandy faltered slightly. "Is that yours?" she said, with a smile. Evidently this phone didn't look like Sheppard's style. Which was true.

"Um…yeah," Sheppard said, looking up. "No signal." He put it in his pocket, next to the bottles of bourbon.

Lies can ruin a man, Winter had said—in one of his last sessions. *They can rot him from the inside out.*

Evidently he hadn't learned.

28

They fanned out to all corners of the room, holding up their phones, looking for any chance of a single bar. Sheppard watched them, knowing it would be no use. No point in putting on a show.

Because Alan was right. The evil man was toying with them, making them waste time.

There's more to it than that. Right? There had to be some reason why.

His phone wasn't in the box. Did that mean something? Had he had his phone on him in his pocket in his room in Paris? He couldn't remember.

So maybe—? Sheppard made sure everyone else was preoccupied with their own devices and took out Winter's Black-Berry again. It didn't have a passcode, so he was free to select whatever he wanted. He went to the messages to see none. They must have been deleted. He scoured through the rest of the applications on the home screen, to find much the same. No emails. No alerts. No notes.

Until he came to the calendar. The day was blocked out with

a big yellow bar. A bar that kept on running. According to the phone, Winter was busy from now until...

He tapped the bar and it expanded with the details. The appointment ran from 5:00 a.m. on 25 October (today—or at least Sheppard thought it was) to 31 December in the year 2999. The maximum the diary would allow. The appointment was titled in large block letters "4404." And the location? Sheppard scrolled down to see: TGH.

Sheppard dropped the phone to his side. 4404. This room? The room Winter had measured out. If this was 4404 (and it had to be), the location was The Great Hotel. It all lined up. What was Winter doing with the evil man? And why would he willingly come to this room if he knew what was going to happen to him? Unless he didn't. The appointment running until 2999. Winter was all booked up until the end of time.

"Sheppard." He looked up to see Mandy standing in front of him. How long had he been staring into space? Behind Mandy, Sheppard saw Alan trying to gain height by jumping up and down. It was almost funny. Almost. "There's nothing. No signal anywhere."

"No," Sheppard said.

"How is that possible?" Mandy said, turning her phone over in her hands.

"I don't know," he said, half-heartedly. "Maybe a blocker like Alan said. Maybe he did something to the phones." Tired of assumptions. Tired of shooting wildly in the dark. The running theme of all that had happened so far.

"That's not really how blockers work," Ryan said, coming forward. "Unless the horse man has a blocker taking out the entire floor. But someone would notice."

"What about—?" Mandy started.

"We don't have time for this," Sheppard said.

"I know," Mandy said, almost smiling. "I just thought you'd

want this." She held up a thin sliver of metal. It took Sheppard a moment to realize what it was. An army dog tag. It had been hanging off her phone. The name PHILLIPS pressed on it—a string of numbers underneath.

Sheppard looked confused. "I'm not sure why I..."

Ryan seemed to be on Mandy's wavelength. His eyes lit up. "Not a penny, but it'd do." Mandy nodded.

Sheppard got it, and smiled. He smiled—because after everything, there was finally something. He took the dog tag and looked at it. "The vent."

"Can I have the other one?" Ryan said.

"Why?"

Mandy gave it to him anyway. He held it up. It matched the other perfectly. "The bathroom. I'm not a plumber, but I know there's at least one way out of the room. The pipes."

Sheppard wondered why he hadn't thought of it before. There were at least two things traveling in and out the room. The air in the vents. And the water in the toilet.

"If I can jimmy the toilet off the wall, maybe there'll be some kind of opening."

"Yes," Sheppard said, looking down at the dog tag in his hand. It might just work.

"There's one problem," Mandy said, cutting into the hope. "What do you think the horse mask'll do when he sees what you're up to?"

That was true. One press of a button on the evil man's part and all this could be over. But Sheppard couldn't see any other way forward.

"I don't think the horse mask is done with us yet. I don't think he'd blow up his little game on a whim," Ryan said. He looked at Sheppard and they both nodded in turn.

"What if you're wrong?" Mandy said.

"This is the best chance we have," Sheppard said.

Mandy thought for a moment, growing quiet. Slowly she nodded. "Okay."

"After Ryan helps me get the grate off the wall, I'll go through the vents while he tries to find a way out in the bathroom. And I need you here. You need to keep the peace. Keep Constance quiet and keep Alan at bay and keep Headphones… I trust you."

"Okay," Mandy said. "Will you be okay? I would fit better in there."

"This is my problem," Sheppard said firmly. "It's only right that I go."

Mandy nodded and went to sit with Constance.

Ryan watched her go. He lowered his voice to a whisper. "She was right, you know. She would have fit better in the vents. Or Rhona, even."

Sheppard shook his head. "Rhona has claustrophobia and Mandy doesn't owe anyone anything. This is on me. I don't want it to be her fault if the horse mask takes this the wrong way. I don't want it to be her fault if we all die."

29

Ryan made his way down the right side of the bed and Sheppard followed, twirling the dog tag in his fingers. The name PHILLIPS shining in the light. Sheppard hadn't asked Mandy what the tags meant, but he assumed a family member. He resolved he would do it if...no, when he got back.

Ryan reached up to the vent, half above the bed and half above the bedside table where the countdown slowly ebbed away. Sheppard didn't look at it—if this worked, there would be no need. Getting out of here had never been so close.

"You'll have to take the whole unit off the wall. Behind the grate'll be a dehumidifier. It'll be heavy."

"You seem to know a lot about this," Sheppard said. Ryan smiled. "Perks of the job."

Even now, his mind wandered. An intricate knowledge of the room. The perfect profession to set this all up.

But why? What motive did he have? What motive did any of them have?

"Thanks," Sheppard said. "We get out of this and I owe you a beer."

Ryan laughed, for the first time. "We get out of this and you owe me a brewery." Ryan clapped Sheppard on the shoulder and turned. "I'm going to get started on the plumbing."

Sheppard nodded as the young man rounded the corner and opened the door to the bathroom. He paused. Being hit with the smell. He pushed past it and disappeared, the door shutting behind him.

Sheppard started unscrewing the grate. When he had got both of the top flatbed screws out, he felt the grate wane with the weight behind it. He kept one hand pressed on the grate, pushing it in as he undid the bottom screws. As he did so, he heard Alan somewhere behind him, finally giving up on his phone. "Bloody hell, this is a day and a half."

He slowed down, unscrewing so he could hear better. He stared straight forward at the grate. What would Alan be saying when he thought Sheppard was preoccupied?

Mandy stood up from the bed. As he felt the third screw come loose, Sheppard heard the muffled impact of shoes on carpet, then a little gasp and a shuffle. Like Alan had surprised Mandy somehow. Pulled her closer, maybe.

"We need to start thinking laterally here," Alan whispered. As if to prove his point. However, he himself had been correct when saying that no one could have a private conversation. Now on the other side of one, Sheppard realized that everyone did indeed hear everything.

"Laterally?" Mandy said, with a tone that would have matched Sheppard's at that moment.

What was Alan's endgame? He was still suspect number one after all.

"This game is rigged, I bet you," Alan whispered, harshly. "There is no answer, or at least no answer that was presented as such."

"What are you talking about?"

"Misdirection, Mandy. The oldest of tricks. The reason people think magic is real, or bombs were in Iraq. The simple art of misdirection."

"I suppose you know all about it. Being a sleazy lawyer and all."

"Of course. I use it all the time. And I'm seeing it here."

Sheppard took another screw out and the grate lurched again. How could a dehumidifier be this heavy?

Alan continued. "What if this isn't *his* game?"

"I have no idea what you're saying."

"Why is he the one who gets to call the shots? Because the TV said so, or because he's the one with the star power?"

"Hijinks." A new voice in the conversation.

Sheppard looked around. Constance Ahearn was looking right at him. "Even in your thoughts, do not curse the king, nor in your bedroom curse the rich, for a bird of the air will carry your voice, or some winged creature tell the matter."

Sheppard glared at her. What was that? The Bible. Sounded more like *The Hobbit*. But her outburst made the two behind him stop.

"Shut up, Ms. Ahearn, there's a good little lunatic," Alan said.

Sheppard looked back as the final screw came loose. The grate launched at him as it came free and he gripped it. It was too heavy. And he didn't have it. He pushed back with his legs, as he felt a body next to him.

Mandy had climbed onto the bed and quickly grabbed the left side of the grate, taking some of the weight. He smiled his thanks as he got a better grip. Between them, they managed to pull out the dehumidifier. They carefully leveraged it and put it down on the bed.

When Sheppard looked back up at the vent, he saw a long and narrow path. It carried on into darkness. "We're at the end of the corridor," he said. "There's no way it could carry on for that long if we weren't. I'll have to make my way around."

Mandy looked into the vent and frowned.

"I'll be back before you know it," Sheppard said, "hopefully having got someone's attention. Who knows, we could be ten minutes away from getting out of here."

"If you're sure," Mandy said.

Sheppard looked from the vent to Mandy. He wasn't sure about anything. But he wasn't about to say that.

"Keep the peace, okay. These people trust you."

Mandy nodded and got off the bed.

Sheppard stepped back and looked into the vent again. He took out Winter's BlackBerry and looked at it. No. "Does anyone have a flashlight on their phone?" he said and looked around. Mandy and Alan shook their heads, Ryan was gone and Constance had turned back into herself. But Headphones showed a glimmer of recognition.

The teenager slid out from the desk, dug into her hoodie pocket and took out her phone. She threw it to him.

He caught it and smiled at her. He thought that he caught her blushing before she went back to her burrow under the desk. There seemed to be a lighter air in the room. Everyone seemed to be happier. Except Alan.

Sheppard was happier. The bourbon in his pocket and escape just a short shuffle away. This nightmare—almost over. The cold, hard crash seemed to have gone away for a while. That itching feeling on the backs of his hands was sated. The ache behind his eyeballs diminished.

Sheppard turned the flashlight on, catching a glimpse of Headphones's dog again. He silently promised to bring the phone back safe.

He reached into the vent, hitching both his elbows into either side of the shaft. He placed a precarious foot onto the bedside table and the other foot on the bed, pulling himself up.

It took a few pushes with his elbows to fully get himself up into the small passageway. It was cramped. A small vent. His shoulders rubbing against the steel top. His legs flailing behind him. He wondered what the others were seeing in the room. Probably something comical. He took the smartphone and placed it in his top pocket. It illuminated enough for him to see ahead.

He felt the edges of the opening with his feet. The room behind him now. The room he thought he would die in. After this, he'd swear off hotels for life.

Because, finally, it was time to check out.

30

Sheppard shuffled forward, his knees already aching in response. More than ever, he felt like a mouse in a maze, chasing around to satisfy the horse mask, Mr. TV, the evil man. Although maybe this maze could lead to freedom. And maybe the evil man slipped up, maybe this was something he hadn't thought of. He started forward again. His back scraped against the top of the vent, igniting it in a rush of pain. He would just have to worry about that later, drowning the agony in thoughts of escape.

He shuffled for a while longer, the flashlight in his top pocket bobbing up and down with each sliver of progress. The light showed the first intersection rather quickly, bouncing the light back to him. There were two paths—left and right. Both were tight corners—but they both looked able to support Sheppard's size. Sheppard got to the intersection, shut his eyes and thought. If the window was looking north (he decided, just for orientation purposes), the wall with the bed against it was the east wall. So he could either go north or south. Whichever way he chose, he would be making his way around the room—skirting the walls.

He chose north for no particular reason, slowly edging around the corner. He got his torso around with little issue, leading with his arms, but when he tried to bring his legs around, the sharp corner of the vent dug into his shins. He briefly panicked, flailing with his arms and trying to pull himself around. He managed it and took a deep breath. He had never been a claustrophobic person, but he had never been in a situation like this before. It felt like the walls were closing in on him ever so slowly, as if he was going to get crushed in the slowest compactor ever.

The other thing he hadn't thought of was the smell. Not the smell of the vent, although it did slightly smell of burnt, hot air. The overpowering scent was his own—a sickly mix of severe body odor and recently jettisoned vomit.

Detectives don't smell.

He adjusted to the new direction. He got into a routine, slumping like a handicapped dog, moving his elbows and then his legs. Forward, back, forward, back.

The phone light was strong but only carried so far—he could only see a few feet in front of him. The air had an eerie feeling—the aluminum (or was it steel?) echoing conversations seemingly happening all around the building. Ghosts of voices seemed to come to him, although when he tried to focus on them, they disappeared.

Maybe you're just going crazy.

There were definitely a few voices he could hear. Alan and Mandy and another voice that sounded like Ryan's. It sounded underwater, the words impossible to decipher. The vent sloped down and Sheppard found himself gaining speed. He came to another turn—only one choice this time, left. He made his way around and saw that the vent grew visibly narrower, supposing it was running under the window. He had to flatten his stomach, flopping like a fish to get through the opening. It grew slightly larger—but only slightly. He was able to bend his arms again to gain some grip and propel himself forward. The phone light was no help here, as it was pointed downwards. The darkness ahead of him loomed large. He became adamant there was something there in the dark, just out of his field of view, taunting him. He almost heard the shuffling of something, something that wasn't him—not allowing him to think it was just his imagination. Which of course, it was.

Probably...right?

After a while, another decision. Forward or left. Left would follow the room so he decided forward. This would mean he would be heading toward the next room, and toward rescue.

He repositioned himself and fished Headphones's phone out of his shirt pocket. He angled it ahead. The vent seemed to go on forever, or at least as far as he could see.

"Morgan." A whisper in his ear.

He jumped, slamming his head on the top of the vent. The pain erupting before mixing in with all the rest. A voice. He had heard it. He had heard it, right? The hairs on his neck stood on end. Someone was right behind him. Someone had to be.

He realized the phone had a camera, and opened the camera app. He swapped to the front-facing camera. His face again. He could never escape it. He looked like he was dying. His skin, unreasonably pale, looking more like the scales of a snake than human skin. His hair seemed thin. His eyes, in the warm flashlight, almost looked yellow—the final curse of the alcoholic.

Get out of here, get to a doctor. Abridge the drinking history a bit.

Nothing behind him though. He tried to look over his shoulder to make sure, but couldn't manage it. The more he thought of it, the less he thought it had been real. Maybe it had just carried through the vents? Maybe someone in the room had said it?

No one calls you Morgan. Not anymore.

No one except him. He did. The masked man.

He started moving forward again, keeping the camera on just for peace of mind. But there was nothing behind him, and never had been—not really. He lowered the camera just in time to keep from slamming head first into the vent wall. Another corner? No, this wasn't a turn or an intersection. There were walls all around him. And there was something there, something white, on the vent wall.

He switched the flashlight back to front-facing. A sheet of metal was in front of him. And a piece of paper held up with a piece of tape. Sheppard looked at the words written on it, suppressing the sudden urge to retch up whatever was left in his stomach. No way forward. Air. There wasn't enough air. And all he could think of was the words on the paper.

THERE WAS AN OPENING HERE IT'S GONE NOW ☺ C

31

Sheppard stayed still. There was nothing else to be done. His eyes ran over and over the paper, reading the words again and again. A dead end? How could it be a dead end? The evil man blocked it off? He knew that they would get into the vents. All this time, he knew. And planned accordingly. Sheppard pulled his arms out in front of him and flattened his palms against the cold metal. He pushed. Nothing. No give. It had been blocked off.

Unless this had never been a way around. Maybe the evil man was just toying with him. Maybe he had got turned around somehow. Because how could someone block off a vent—make it look like there was never an opening to begin with? Maybe he had just chosen a wrong turn.

He shuffled backwards, replacing the phone in his top pocket. Soon, he was back at the previous turn. This time, he went left. This meant he should be running parallel to the west wall of the room and the east wall of the next room. Sheppard stopped for a moment, listening. He couldn't hear anything, apart from a low mutter of familiar voices that was surely coming from his left. Nothing from the next room.

What if no one was there? What if he couldn't get anyone's attention?

Then you keep going. You keep going until you do.

It was exhausting. Dragging himself along. And as he brought his knee up for another shuffle, he felt and heard the two bottles of single-serving bourbon in his trouser pocket. That would give him some more strength—a little pick-me-up. But he didn't think he could reach them even if he wanted to.

He pressed on, the dark closing around him and the pain coming in waves. Knees, back, shoulders. All feeling raw and tender. He continued until he thought he must be nearing the edge of the room.

Sure enough, he came to the edge. Left, right or up—straight up, vertical. He angled the torch and looked. Up seemed like a hard task to accomplish so he went right.

As he traveled down the passage, he tried to focus on the low voices he heard, just to distract him from the pain. Mandy and Alan. He wondered what they were talking about, and remembered what he had heard just before he went into the vent. It felt like hours ago. He severely hoped it wasn't.

Alan was clearly up to something, and even if he didn't murder Simon Winter, he was a dangerous man. Unscrupulous. Never thinking he's wrong. A talker.

Remind you of anyone?

Maybe that was why he was so wary of Alan. Because they were so alike.

He hoped Mandy was keeping him at bay.

About a minute later, the flashlight hit on something white ahead. He took the flashlight and almost dropped it. Another piece of paper, the same message…

THERE WAS AN OPENING HERE IT'S GONE NOW
☺ C

How? How was this happening? Another dead end, just as closed off as the last. He looked carefully at the sides of the vent but he saw no join or connection where the evil man (this C?) closed it off. It was just as if the vent ended here. But how was that possible? Was he turned around again? No, he was running along the south wall of the next room, he had to be. He retraced the route he'd taken in his mind. Yes, that was it.

He banged on the side of the vent with his right hand, the sound bouncing around him. "Hey. Hey. Anybody. Can anybody hear me?"

No sound apart from his own voice echoed back to him. No voices. No shuffling of movement beyond the vent. Nothing. What he had come to expect—the worst possible outcome.

"Hey. Anyone? Come on," he shouted. Trying to convince himself he had some optimism left.

He tried the left side too—facing the corridor. But nothing.

He looked back at the message on the piece of paper.

C. Was C the one who was doing this to him? Was C the man behind the horse mask? The man who had known he would go into the vents. The man who seemed to know him better than he knew himself. The smiley face seemed to broaden its grin, and then it winked.

He was sure it did.

But it didn't. He imagined it. He must have.

And all of a sudden, it drew closer. The feeling of it all getting too much. The cold, hard crash shuffling into him. He could feel his skin—all of it, itching, like thousands of spiders running over him. He could almost hear them—could almost see their silky webs in front of his eyes. He shut them. He was so tired. And it would be so easy to let them consume him.

He moved backwards. Had to move on. Had to get out of here. If not away, then at least back to the room. Because he wouldn't do this here. He wouldn't die in a vent—refused to.

He kept his eyes closed until he felt the pressure let up. He opened his eyes to see the pathway up. He decided to take it, panicking now. He steadied himself and brought his legs around to the front of him. Reaching out with his hands, he managed to slowly stand up. His legs howled with pain as they tried to support his weight. Looking around, he found another offshoot—only one, to the left. This meant he would be going back toward the room. He didn't care anymore. He clambered into it, pulling himself up and pushing off with his legs.

He tried to think about where he was. He had to be over the room. It had to be the ceiling. And as he finally got his full form into the vent, he looked ahead and saw light. Yellow strips of light.

He wondered if he was coming to another opening, but as he got closer, he realized it was a grate in the bottom of the vent. It looked down into the room. And as he reached it, the voices inside were easier to hear.

"…crazy."

"Am I? Or am I the only one who actually has a brain in this room?"

He looked down. To see the mess of covers on the bed.

Couldn't get an angle to see anything else.

"Let's hear him out, Mandy." Ryan. "At least then he might shut up."

"That man has the power of the Devil behind his eyes." Constance. Impossible to tell who she was talking about.

"Shut up." Alan.

He could see shadows of them. Could picture them all standing around talking about him. Alan. Mandy. Ryan. Constance. Maybe even Headphones.

When the cat's away…

"Are you hearing what I said?" Alan said. "That man cannot be trusted."

"He's trying to help," Mandy said.

"Help who? He's trying to help himself. Why do you think we're all still here and he's off gallivanting around in the vents? We don't even know if he'll come back."

"Of course he's going to come back. You're not making any sense."

"How's this then—we're not going to pretend we didn't hear everyone else's story, right? Everyone has a connection to either Simon Winter or this horse mask guy, everyone except him. Why hasn't he told us anything about that?"

"We don't know it's the horse mask guy. And why would Sheppard need to tell us? We already know who he is."

"Yes, Mandy," Ryan said, "but how much do we know, really? Maybe Alan has a point. An incredibly labored point, but a point. Anything could be going on here. This could be all some kind of weird setup."

"This man is not a detective. Not in any real sense of the word. He's a TV phony. They crave attention. Especially him. And I'm quite sure he'd do anything to stay in the limelight." Alan's voice.

A sigh. Sounded like Mandy. "Will you two listen to yourselves, please? Mr. Sheppard is stuck here just like the rest of us. Right now, he's trying to get us out of here. Why would he kill anyone? It doesn't make any sense."

Sheppard's stomach turned over. What? That was what they were talking about? How in the hell could they think… Alan. Alan was turning them against him. And it seemed like it had already worked on Ryan.

"Why is him killing Winter any weirder than one of us killing him? I know for a fact that I didn't, and I'm not sure anyone else here right now did. What did you say before—misdirection?"

No. No. No. This couldn't be happening. Not Ryan. "Exactly," Alan said, not bothering to hide the triumph in his voice. "What if this isn't his game at all? What if it's ours?"

Sheppard didn't want to hear any more. He had to get back in the room as quickly as possible. The vents were a washout—a dead end before they'd even started. And if he didn't get back, things could get a whole lot worse. He shrugged off the itching feeling and carried on, moving faster than he thought he could. Mandy could only fight his corner for so long.

Alan did it. He had to have done. This was his plan all along. Convince everyone else that Sheppard killed Winter. But why? What was in it for him?

And there it was. Another wrinkle in the plan. One so obvious he didn't know why he hadn't seen it before. Why was the murderer even going along with this? Why had no one just owned up to it? Because surely they were going to die too if Sheppard got it wrong. Unless he/she had been promised safety. But how would that work?

Alan killed Winter. The why didn't matter. Probably something to do with his precious case. Or maybe not even that. If he had been in on the plan from the start, it could have just been to set up the game. He would get back to the room, and declare Alan the murderer.

Before he knew it, he came to another turn. His head awash with theories.

Down or left? This layout made no sense—down would put him back to where he started and left would have him retreading the east wall albeit from higher up. He didn't know for sure, but he didn't think this was how vents worked. Why were there none going to any of the other rooms? It was almost as if this was all there was to the vent system. Did every room have their own system? But he knew better than that. The dead ends. C, the evil man, had done something to the vents. He had foreseen Sheppard's little expedition and planned it all out.

He probably rigged it all—the discovery of the phones, finding something to unscrew the grate. Maybe he even hoped it would happen. To waste time.

Oh God, *time*. How long had he been in here?

Ahead there was some kind of widening. He could see the vent turn but also carry on. As he got closer, he saw that it was a wide junction. He pushed himself into it and immediately stretched out. The phone light flailed and caught on something in the center of the junction.

A flicker of white.

He focused on it, crawling forward. Something else was there—something reflective, bouncing back the light. And then, as he moved forward arcing the flashlight, he saw it. The red—the blood that had dulled and dried on it. It was a knife, a wide knife—sharp, one that looked like it was to flake fish or something. The moment he saw it, he had no doubt that this was the knife that had killed Simon Winter. It had to be. And it had been hidden in the vents because that was always where Sheppard was going to go. This was just another part of the plan.

An unreasonable sadness burrowed into him. The knife sat in a pool of blood, which had dried and clotted and now looked more like jelly than something that came out of a human. Next to the knife, slightly stained in scarlet, was a message on another piece of paper.

THIS IS THE MURDER WEAPON ☺ C

That smiley face again. That signature—C. This was the knife that had killed his psychologist—the knife that had been thrust into his gut, pulled out and thrust in again. Who had put it here? The murderer or C himself? Maybe the murderer was C? Making his way through all the vents just to leave the knife here. C was guiding him—had been all this time. And time was ticking away.

C wants you to fail. The murderer wants you to fail. The masked man wants you to fail. He wants you to die. And he wants you to kill them all.

He had to get the knife back to the room. There could be a clue to it, but there was no way he could see well enough to notice it here. This wasn't over. With no exit, all he could do was carry on. With any luck, he hadn't been in the vents as long as it felt.

He reached forward and touched the knife. He ran a finger slowly down the blade. It was definitely sharp. Sharp enough to pierce skin, muscle, organs. Sharp enough to end a life. He grasped the knife's wooden handle with his thumb and forefinger and pulled it out of the mess of congealed blood. He tried to ignore the ripping squelch that accompanied it. He put the knife down now it was free of its trappings and wiped some Simon Winter on the breast of his shirt. He instantly regretted it.

As the situation seemed too much, he remembered the minute bottle of bourbon in his trouser pocket. As good a time as any, he thought. With some difficulty, he reached a hand into his pocket and brought out the bottle. It was even smaller than he remembered. He unscrewed the top and looked down at the knife. He gulped the liquid down and it was gone in less than a second.

The feeling of salvation was so fleeting that he had to question if he had felt it at all. It subsided the pain a little at least. But it couldn't touch the dejection. He had come into the vents with thoughts of escape.

But now he knew that this was far from over. C was nowhere near finished with him.

Silently, he placed the bottle down and picked up the knife instead. With one last look at the pool of blood and his bourbon bottle sitting next to it, he shuffled back toward the room.

32

Sheppard felt sunlight on his face as he stuck his head back into the room. He tried to climb out of the grate as gracefully as possible but ended up falling face first onto the bed. The knife fell down next to him, dangerously close to his eyes.

He scrabbled around and sat up. Alan was staring at him, arms crossed and face stern with focused rage. Next to him, on either side, were Ryan and Constance. Mandy stood off to the side, next to Headphones who was looking worried. Both of them were looking nervously at the knife, while the others seemed not to have noticed it.

"The Good Sheppard returns," Alan said, with all the triumph still in his voice.

Sheppard quickly got off the bed—the left side. The bed between him and everyone else.

Ryan looked down at the knife. "What is that?"

Sheppard spluttered. "It's the murder weapon. I found it in the vents."

"What about a way out?" Mandy said.

"There is no way out. He knew someone was going to go in there. He blocked it off."

Sheppard went to pick up the knife, but Ryan jumped forward.

Sheppard suppressed a groan. "Are you serious?"

"No sudden moves, Detective," Alan said.

He threw his hands up in disgust. "Are you hearing what I'm saying? There's no escape. You have to let me do what I can to get us out of here. The knife is the next clue. I'm closer to solving this thing."

"And how did you know where to find it?" Alan said.

There was a murmur from Constance, who seemed to be hiding behind Alan now.

"I didn't know where to find it. I was in the vents trying to get us all out of here. That's what I've been doing ever since we woke up here."

Alan smiled. "You were being reckless—endangering everyone in this room. And you were so adamant that it had to be you, weren't you? You had to be the one who went into the vents. See, we've decided something while you were gone. Because from the very beginning this was always about you—the big shot television man stroking his ego just a little bit more. Well maybe this was more about you than I cared to admit."

"No. No," Sheppard said, "it's you. I know it's you. And I'm going to prove it."

"Ramblings of a drunk and a drug addict and a piece of human waste. Don't try and confuse things now. Go out with a little dignity, huh?"

"You're insane," Sheppard said. Panicking. "This is insane. I'm trying to…" But he trailed off. Not knowing what else to say. He shot a look at Mandy. She looked away. Not her too. If she believed it, then that was it. It was over. Headphones's, Rhona's, eyes were shut, her face screwed up.

"Why did you go and get the knife?" Alan continued. "So you could off another one of us. Stab us in the back."

"If you just listened to yourself, you'd see that this makes no sense."

They were advancing now. Closing the gap between them and him.

"I think this actually makes perfect sense," Alan said. "You killed Simon Winter, didn't you? What secrets would he have told us if he were still alive?"

Ryan stepped around the bed. Sheppard looked at him pleadingly. "Ryan, please. We don't have time for this."

Ryan looked guilty, but not for long. "It does make sense. You being all secretive, keeping things from us. We don't even know anything about you. Not really."

"I'm being the detective," Sheppard said, in the same voice as a child playing dress-up. "I can't tell everyone everything. That's not how it works. And besides, the murderer is here with us."

"Yes," Alan said definitively. "He is."

Ryan put his hand around Sheppard's back and before he realized what he was doing, he felt something cold lock around his wrist.

Not again. No, not again.

Ryan forced Sheppard's other arm around and cuffed the other wrist. There was no point in struggling. There was nowhere to go.

"You're making a terrible mistake," Sheppard said, to anyone who'd meet his gaze. "I have to solve this murder or we're all going to die."

Ryan brought him around—still weak from the vent crawling—and pushed him in the back. Forcing him forward.

"Don't worry about that, Morgan," Alan said. "I've just solved this murder."

Morgan.

Sheppard looked into Alan's smug face. "What did you just call me, you bastard?"

Ryan pushed him again. Toward the bathroom.

This was all happening too fast. Ryan jabbed him again and Sheppard stumbled forward. He glanced around to the bedside before it disappeared from view.

The timer. 01:02:43. Ticking down and down.

"No, you can't do this," he shouted. "He's playing games with you." He couldn't fight it—too exhausted, too thirsty, too wanting. It was all he could do not to crumple in a heap. It was over. It was all over. Alan had brainwashed them all, and there was barely an hour left.

Ryan went around him and opened the bathroom door.

He nodded inside. "Make it easy, yeah."

"Ryan." A harsh whisper. "It's Alan. Alan killed him. I know he did. You have to trust me."

"I can't trust anything anymore," Ryan said. And he grabbed Sheppard by the wrists and shoved him into the bathroom. He tripped on the first tile and went barreling into the room, crashing into the sink. He turned to see Ryan staring dumbly at him.

"For what it's worth," Ryan said. "I didn't think it would be you."

He shut the door.

33

Before...

He was sitting on his hands—didn't know what else to do with them. He looked around the room. Winter was staring at him like a bespectacled praying mantis and he tried not to meet his eyes. There was only twenty minutes left on the clock and this meeting was cutting into his valuable drinking time. He was currently in the throes of a managed addiction—a day without drinking seemed like a wasted opportunity although he could hold off if he needed to.

Winter cleared his throat. Sheppard just tried to focus on the items on Winter's desk. In the twenty years he had been coming to this room he didn't think anything on the desk had ever moved—not even a millimeter—even down to the pile of papers and pen positioned neatly in the center.

Winter cleared his throat again. Sheppard finally gave in and looked at the old man sitting in the red armchair he always did for his sessions. "We're twenty-five minutes into the session, Morgan, and you don't seem to be as open as usual."

Not a question, a statement. *Just putting it out there.*

Nothing to really respond to—apart from calling him Morgan when he had very kindly asked Winter not to. Everyone called him Sheppard—to the point where when someone called him by his first name it took him a second to remember they were addressing him.

"How's work?" Winter said.

"Fine," Sheppard said. It was fine. The show had been picked up for another two series, which would see it run for at least another two years—another 120 episodes. If life were measured in content, he would have won a long time ago.

"I watch you on television when I don't have a session. There was a rather interesting one on yesterday."

"What do you think?" Sheppard said.

"It's…good."

He was lying. Sheppard didn't need a psych degree to tell that. "What do you like about it?" he said, just to have a little fun.

Winter seemed to visibly squirm for a second *(bluff called)* but then realized what Sheppard was doing and snapped out of it, straightening his glasses. "You've been doing a lot of work."

"Twelve hours a day. I have to be at the station in the morning for any live cuts to *Morning Coffee*…"

"Wait, your show is called *Resident Detective*, is it not?"

Sheppard sighed. "Yes, but it's on after *Morning Coffee*. Sometimes the presenters of *Morning Coffee* throw it over to me to do a 'Today on the show…' kind of thing."

"Why do you have to do that live? Could you not just record them?"

"I've been fighting the bosses over that one. Their response is they want to do it live so that it feels genuine. Like if *Morning Coffee* had just had a news story or a feature on socks for cats, I could comment on it." *I hate it. I hate it. I hate it.* Sheppard hated *Morning Coffee*. He hated the smug presenters. He hated his stupid live links. And what was worse, it meant he had to get up two hours earlier than he would have to normally. "We start filming the actual show at half ten. We usually run till about eight at night, four days a week and shoot about four, maybe five episodes in a day."

Winter looked visibly impressed, but then that could just be a trick. Over the years Sheppard had become wary of the old man. Winter understood human behavior very well and mimicking it for a cheap revelation was not above him. "That *is* a lot of work. How do you keep going?"

I pop pills like a lunatic and I wash them down with liquid only a few rungs down from paint thinner. "A positive attitude."

Winter laughed and then grew silent. He put his pen down on the notebook he always had in his lap—a sure sign that things were about to get serious. "I cannot lie—I am slightly concerned about you, Morgan."

Sheppard suppressed a sigh.

"Throwing yourself into your work is good, but you must achieve a balance between work and leisure time. You look like you haven't slept since our last session."

I have slept—if fragmented drunken dozing can be called sleep. Sheppard remembered a conversation with Douglas—ironically, over beers—where Douglas said that heavy drinkers pretty much forget what normal sleep is like, and what feeling truly awake is like. He could now confirm that. Sheppard drifted through life constantly half unconscious, just going from one scene to the next because there was nothing else—it was something to do.

"I just want to make sure that you are not doing yourself any harm by taking too much on. You have to stop sometime, Morgan. Why don't you take some time for yourself?"

It was Sheppard's turn to laugh. "Do you have any idea how television works? Hmm? You can't just take time off whenever you want. I'm at the forefront of one of the biggest morning shows in the country. I'm making money out my ass. And if nothing else, I'm contracted for two years. I can't drop everything for some spirit journey."

Winter inched forward in his chair—his usual stance when he was expecting a fight. "No one's talking about a 'spirit journey,' Morg—"

"Sheppard. Sheppard. Sheppard. My name is Sheppard," he shouted, and got up. He went toward the door. *This is over.* He reached for the door handle.

"You never talk about it anymore," Winter said, behind him. He willed his hand to clasp the handle, for his legs to carry him out the room, for his mind to give over to the pills and the drink so he couldn't go back. Back to that time.

For all Sheppard's willing, he found himself turning around and looking toward Winter, still sitting in his chair. *"It?"*

"You know what I mean," Winter said softly. Sheppard ran a hand down his face—sleek with sweat.

"What more do you want from me, old man? You want me to cry again? You want me to scream again? You want me to recount every detail of the nightmare again? I am not some broken machine to fix, some puzzle to solve. It happened— Mr. Jefferies happened. Not everything has to have some cosmic significance. Maybe I did what I did purely because I did what I did. Maybe all your psychology crap isn't worth a damn because humans are simply spontaneous. I did what I did and now I live with that. Chisel it on some stupid stone somewhere because it's never going to change. I am the person I made myself. And the world carries on. Just like it always does—always will." For some reason, his eyes were welling up with tears. He choked, cleared his throat and repeated finally, "I did what I did because I did what I did."

Winter got up at this. "You solved a murder. You caught a killer."

"Yes," Sheppard said, "and wasn't it amazing? But that doesn't mean I want to microanalyze it with you every week."

"I still feel we haven't fully explored..." Winter stepped toward him. Sheppard stepped back.

"You know what? I'll see you next week," Sheppard said, turning and opening the door.

"We have ten more minutes," Winter said.

"Take that ten minutes to think up a few more original questions for next time, yeah?" And Sheppard slammed the door behind him.

In Winter's front hall, he breathed. He didn't like to argue with Winter, but the drugs had made him impatient, and he needed to be out of this house. But that didn't excuse Winter's behavior. Talking about something, yet again, which he would never truly understand. Sheppard was trying to bury it down deep—forget all about it. The drink and drugs were helping with that—as if every night he was shoveling one more mound of dirt into the grave of his memory. Soon it would be all gone and he would be free of it. But for now, all he wanted to do was have some fun.

A quick thundering down the stairs surprised him and Abby Winter appeared in front of him. Sheppard had first met her after his first session with Winter; they were both children then. Now she was grown and beautiful. She blushed when she saw him. "Sheppard, sorry, I heard the door and I thought you would have gone by now."

He didn't know if it was his lingering resentment of what had just happened with Winter or the fact he just wanted to forget everything but he found himself saying, "Do you like cocktails? I know a good place not far from here that does amazing cocktails. Wanna go?"

"I..." Abby laughed uncomfortably, squirming slightly, "uh... yes of course. Of course, I'd love to."

Of course. Well of course of course. "Great."

"I should just tell…" Abby gestured toward Winter's office.

"Ah, don't bother him. He's busy doing paperwork anyway."

Abby looked unconvinced, but equally didn't seem to care. "Okay. I'll just go get ready." And Abby retraced her steps up the stairs.

Sheppard smiled to himself and took a pill. He sat down on the stairs and waited. This was going to be good—there was no way that this could be a bad idea. Sheppard didn't really care even if it was. Abby was beautiful and fun and he wouldn't sleep with her. He just needed a companion. Drinking alone was never fun in public, even for him. He tapped on the steps while he waited, making up a rhythm. And then for good measure, he took another pill.

Another shovelful of earth fell into the abyss.

Five weeks later…

It had been five weeks since he first asked Abby out. They had been out nearly every night since. He had no doubt Winter knew, but he didn't really care. Abby was worth it—she was a lot more fun than he thought a daughter of a stuffy psychologist could ever be. She fit in well on his arm as he showed her the best clubs in London. She could hold her drink, and she even tried some pills. She was great, charging forward with a youthful energy that sometimes made it hard to keep up with her. It was almost like she was trying to rebel against something—maybe a strict, rigid, old stickinthemud of a father (*just a guess*). He put his shaky arm around her and pulled her in for a kiss. She wrapped her arms around him, while also managing to rummage in her bag for her keys.

How long had they been standing here? He didn't know. It felt like forever and no time at all.

"I can't find them," she said, slurring slightly. She couldn't handle it as well as him. And, as if to prove the point, the bag sprang out of her hands and hit the floor, the contents spilling out over the welcome mat.

They both erupted into laughter. Until he realized they were being way too loud for this time of night. He held a finger to her lips, barely able to stifle his own laughs, let alone hers.

She bent down and picked up the keys, which had miraculously revealed themselves. She held them up in triumph, smiling that smile—the smile that made him forget about all the badness in the world, all the badness inside everyone. There was only her. And he wanted to be with her always.

She lurched forward, searching for the lock on the door. A fumbling as she failed to find it, scraping the door, leaving fresh scars on the metal, and then success.

But before she could turn the key, the door seemed to open of its own accord. He was amazed…until he saw the old man stood there in his dressing gown, with eyes like thunder, arms folded and a frown on his face that could sour wine. He looked at her and then at him.

"Go upstairs, Abby," he said.

She pouted. "But…"

"Go upstairs."

Abby took one long look at Sheppard, and went to hug him.

"Don't you touch him. Just go upstairs."

Abby passed her father and disappeared into the house without another word. Sheppard heard her taking the stairs two at a time, then slamming her bedroom door.

He looked at Winter and wondered how long he had stayed up just to make this little show. He wondered if it would be worth it.

"Simon," he started, after a long silence.

"Don't *Simon* me, son. Do you even care what I have been through tonight, waiting for my little girl to come home. You took her after our session didn't you? This afternoon. Where the bloody hell have you been for fourteen hours?"

Fourteen— So that meant the time was...? Wait, so the session this afternoon was... Nope he lost it. Instead he decided on, "Here and there. She came because she wanted to."

"She is too young for whatever you have on your mind."

"Last I checked, she was plenty old enough," he said, realizing when it was out there that he'd meant to keep that bit in his head.

Winter was silent. In response, he reached into his dressing gown pocket and brought out two little tubs. He held them up to the light, in his open palm. "You know what this is?"

Sheppard looked at them, really trying to concentrate. One looked like a capsule of some kind and the other looked like a pill bottle. That was all he could manage. "Should I know?"

"This is ketamine. Found in Abby's room, son."

"The horse tranquilizer?" he said, suddenly proud of himself for knowing that.

"No," Winter said, "a common misconception. Ketamine can be used to sedate animals but it is mainly used on humans." Sheppard turned a sudden laugh into a hiccup. Even in blind rage, Winter couldn't turn the doctor in him off. "What's important is Abby has been taking this."

"I don't do ketamine," Sheppard slurred.

"No, but you've taken and drunk everything else under the sun. And you introduced my daughter to the prospect, so you'll be okay if I go and blame you anyway. This life you're leading? It's not for my girl, son. I wouldn't wish it upon anyone, so not my little girl."

Sheppard snorted. "I get it."

"Good."

"No, not that," he said, holding the doorframe for support. "I get IT. You get to sit in your chair all day and lord yourself over other people's lives. Well, here's my turn. You love your daughter. You love her so much you want to wrap her up in cotton wool and keep her indoors away from the baddies, and the criminals, and the Disney villains. She's all you've got. Because your wife went to that hospital, all fat and busting, and only little Abby came back." Somewhere in his brain he knew the line was being crossed.

Winter let out a small wheezing sound, but was silent for a long time. Sheppard's eyes swam. A gust of wind threatened to upend Sheppard and he tried to grab the doorframe again. Winter smacked his hand away.

"I don't think I can treat you anymore, Morgan."

"What?" It caught him off guard. Punched him in the stomach. But what had he expected? Winter was the only constant in his life, and he had done nothing but abuse that fact. How could he say things like he did and expect Winter to take it? It wasn't the old man's fault.

That's how he felt the next morning when he found the fragmented memories of the night nestled in amongst the empties around his bed. At the time, however, he found Winter nothing but a selfish old coot.

"Oh shut up. Really?" Sheppard said, shouting a little too loud. "Because of Abby? You understand how stupid that sounds? You're going to stop seeing me, just because you're so anal about your daughter? You're supposed to be helping me."

"No, son, you're meant to be helping yourself. But you won't. You're simply refusing to change. You're the most stubborn boy I've ever met."

"I'm not a boy."

"I should have stopped this long ago. Our relationship has become volatile, and yes, part of it is your fraternizing with my girl. If we continue, my personal feelings will affect my job."

"And what are your personal feelings?"

"I've known you since you were eleven, Morgan. I've known you since before you knew yourself. That scared little boy sitting in my waiting room. I was always able to look past what you've become and see that little boy. But now—"

"Say what you have to say," Sheppard spat.

"You disgust me."

Sheppard didn't know what he had expected. He was suddenly frozen, an uncontrollable shivering taking over his whole body. Winter meant more to him than he had ever known, meant more to him than his own father. And now—he was disgusted by him?

"Wait," Sheppard said, wanting to rewind the last ten minutes and go about everything differently—the drunk version of him finally realizing the significance of what was happening. "I need you."

"I'm sorry, Morgan. But you can't be here anymore." Winter went to shut the door, but Sheppard slammed his palm against it.

"This...can't..." He couldn't even think.

"You know," Winter said, relenting the door, "a third party came to me, purely by coincidence. That was the final nail in the coffin for us. Just another patient, telling tales of what a man called Morgan Sheppard had done. I didn't believe it at first— part of me simply couldn't believe it. But over time—well—it all makes such perfect sense."

"Who came to you?"

"I'm a psychologist, Morgan. I know how people work. And I've always thought there was something deep down in the heart of you. And now I know. And I can't un-know. And that is why I can't possibly treat you anymore."

Winter tried to close the door again, but this time Sheppard thumped the wood with his fist. "No," he choked. Even drunk-Sheppard understood that when the door closed, it wasn't going to open again.

Winter stepped forward and wrenched Sheppard's fist off the door with a surprising amount of force and Sheppard toppled back. "You know the worst part?" Winter said, hissing. "You don't even remember, do you? All the substance abuse has just turned you rotten. You can't even remember who you really are. It's a coping mechanism, you know—you don't have to be a doctor to see that. You drink and take all that rubbish because you're running away from yourself. From what you did."

"And you're going to turn your back on me?" Sheppard said. He felt like crumpling to the floor.

Winter's face flamed, and he lunged at him. Sheppard dodged back, managing to keep his balance by stumbling down the porch steps.

"Get out of here," Winter said, almost sadly. "Before I call the police." And he shut the door.

The walk from the door to the gate seemed to stretch on. Sheppard's feet felt heavier with every step. This was it. He knew he would never come here again, forgetting Abby at that moment. Because Winter had been important to him. And for some reason, he had forgotten that. But now he had pushed him away. Just like everyone else.

He didn't want to look back, but as he opened the gate, he couldn't stop himself. The house was quiet and dark, as though nothing had ever happened. He knew every detail of this house. He could almost see the eleven-year-old Morgan standing there on the doorstep, shuffling his feet nervously. He had been coming to this house forever. But he couldn't quite remember why.

Forever and no time at all.

34

What was happening to him? Time was fluctuating all around him—rocking the bathroom back and forth. Things went in and out of focus at random. His mind dashed from thought to thought. The spiders had him now.

One thought—how long had he been here? Had he ever been anywhere else?

Another thought—the doctor said not to exceed the recommended dose. Unless you were awesome.

Another—he couldn't remember her name, the one from Paris. She was so pretty. He didn't even get her number. How would he find her again? After...

This brought on a bout of uncontrollable laughter. Going crazy, or maybe coming down from it. Something a little appropriate medication would fix. Nice and easy. One little pill. Or maybe two.

Treat yourself.

Did he say it or did he think it or both?

He wanted to laugh again, but stopped himself. Instead he

straightened up, trying to stretch his arms behind him. They had cramped up.

Just like before. Just like when it began.

He'd never been one for talking to himself. Whenever he had tried, he felt like one of those idiots talking to themselves in movies. The kind that only talked to themselves to make sure the audience knew what they were doing. The kind of bad writing Sheppard could not advocate even when he was alone.

"Sheppard is thinking of dying now," he said aloud.

And cackled.

Things were happening outside. In the room. Echoes. He couldn't focus on them enough to hear what they were saying. It was as if out there didn't exist—at least not in the same way as in here. Two separate realities connected by the greatest invention of mankind: the humble door.

He suppressed another laugh. Until he heard something. Shouting. His ears perked up slightly, like a lethargic meerkat. Someone was shouting really loudly, almost loud enough to penetrate the fog that had settled around him.

It was Alan, or at least he thought it was. Still couldn't make out what he was saying.

Something was wrong.

A sound. A horrible sound. How to even think of it? It was a grunt, but louder and more urgent, halfway between an acknowledgement and a scream. And then there was a scream. Not just one but two women's screams.

The sound startled him so much that he jammed his shoulder against the toilet trying to get up.

This game is not over.

No, no, he couldn't do it. He couldn't carry on. This was it. Had to be.

But Mandy and Headphones were in there.

He pushed on his palms until he was as high as he could go

and then tried to leverage himself up the toilet. Surprisingly, he managed it and before the screamers had even drawn breath, he was sitting on the toilet lid. He got up, feeling his head loll on his shoulders. He thought he would never get up again, but it hadn't been too hard, right?

His need for the things he desired had to be filed away.

The spiders had to go away. Come again another day.

NO. No laughing.

Another scream. By the same person. One of them at least. There was a commotion. Raised voices cursing and shouting.

He staggered around his small space. What was happening out there? Why were they shouting? His cuffed hands got caught around the towel rail and he face-planted the wall, his forehead erupting into pain.

He recovered. And looked at the bathroom door. He had to get out. He had to know what was happening. He stumbled forward and turned around, feeling with his hands for the door handle. Grasping it, he pushed it down.

Nothing. It didn't open. Even though the lock was on this side, they'd found a way to keep it shut.

"Hey," he tried to shout, but his throat was so dry it wasn't louder than a whisper. He forcefully cleared his throat and tried again. "Hey." Better this time. But the voices outside kept screaming and shouting.

"Hey. What's going on?" he said, slamming his shoulder into the door. He backed up and kicked the door repeatedly with an unsteady foot. "Hey. What's happening?" Bang. Bang. Bang.

The sick sense of humor that resided in his head punctuated these three bangs with three rings of a phone. *Press 6 for early checkout…*

"What's going on out there?" He raised his foot again. Bang.

They were being too loud. Something was very wrong. He could hear a scream that was not Mandy's, but was still youthful.

He thought it must have been Headphones. He could hear Mandy's incoherent sobs. He could hear Ryan shouting at someone, telling them to calm down, telling them to…put down the knife.

And Sheppard realized what had happened. He had brought a weapon into a room with a murderer. Alan had seized his chance and had obviously been backed into a corner where he had to do it again.

Another murder. No.

He had to get in there. He had to know.

With a renewed strength, he slammed his entire body weight into the bathroom door and continued to do it even as his right arm became numb. "Hey," he shouted, over and over again.

Finally, outside, the conversation subsided and someone moved, close enough to the door for him to feel it. There was someone standing right on the other side.

"Come on. Come on," he said, deciding to slam once more into the door. "Come on."

There was no response, and it seemed so long that Sheppard thought maybe the person had moved away again. Maybe he was still deemed the murderer even though something else had just very obviously happened. Maybe locking Sheppard up had been the best decision they ever made. No, Sheppard thought, that's Winter talking.

Sheppard backed up and slammed his entire side into the door one last time. Silence. And then…a click. And then the bathroom door opening very slowly.

He stepped back as it swung wide.

Ryan stood there, very pale and very uncertain. He didn't look at all like the cavalier guardsman he had played while throwing him in there earlier. "I'm… I'm sorry," the young man said, not daring to meet his eyes. "I thought it was you. I… He got into my head. You know…" Ryan was blaming himself as much as Sheppard was, and why not? At that moment, he wanted the young man to blame himself for everything. Because now Alan had killed again and Sheppard would have to clean up the mess.

Sober. Straight and clean. A miserable existence.

Sheppard stepped forward but couldn't manage a friendly look toward Ryan no matter how hard he tried. Sheppard turned around and showed Ryan his handcuffs. "Oh," Ryan said, patting himself down, "of course." A few seconds later, the cuffs were off. Sheppard made sure to keep hold of them and Ryan looked at him sadly. "We're going to need them," he said, and turned into the room.

More death in a room that needed none at all. Alan Hughes, the murderer. Sheppard walked out of the bathroom, picturing what the scene would look like when he turned clear in his mind.

He looked—and it was different.

As he expected, Ryan, Mandy and Headphones were all standing back, visibly shaken, trying not to look at the body that was making a mess on the carpet in front of the television.

Alan Hughes lay face down on the carpet, the knife protruding from his upper back, around about where the heart was. He looked rather pathetic, lying there—a molecule of his former self. Blood was slowly leaking out of the wound, on either side of the knife.

There was a trail of blood leading off to the window and Sheppard followed it with his eyes, not quite ready to believe who was going to be standing at the end of it. But it all made sense, in a kind of odd way. It all sort of added up.

Because at the end of the blood trail, with blood staining the torso of her dress and a big grin on her face, was Constance Ahearn.

35

Constance? How could it be Constance? But in some ways, it made sense—in an odd sort of way. It all added up. He had to act quickly. He threw the handcuffs to Ryan, who advanced on Constance. Sheppard went to Alan and checked his neck for a pulse. None. He checked his wrist. Nothing either. Alan was dead. The knife was sticking out from under his shoulder blades. Must have threaded through two ribs, pierced his heart. The big, bad lawyer didn't seem so scary anymore. As he looked up, he saw Mandy and Headphones, squashed into the farthest corner, holding each other.

Constance was moaning as Ryan tried to put the handcuffs on her. Sheppard helped him by grabbing one of Constance's flailing arms. She wasn't making any sense, spouting rubbish about Jesus and God and Hell. Pretty much par for the course there then.

"The promised land is filled with traitors. The promised land is here."

Ryan managed to slip on one handcuff and then stopped. "We should cuff her to a chair."

Sheppard nodded and took the chair that was slotted under the desk and held it as Ryan wrestled Constance down. Sheppard took the other handcuff as Ryan pushed Constance's right arm through the back of the chair so they could be sure she wasn't going to go anywhere. Not easily, at least.

Sheppard and Ryan straightened up and stepped back from Constance. She regarded them with those wide eyes of hers. The kind of eyes you could get lost in, that's what he had thought, right? Now those eyes looked like somewhere he was afraid he would get imprisoned.

"What happened?" Sheppard said, turning to the others. Mandy and Headphones seemed unable to respond. But Ryan cleared his throat and managed to speak, although it seemed like he was fighting himself the entire way.

"We were just talking. That's all. Just talking. We hadn't kept track of the knife—we should have done, but we didn't. Putting you in the bathroom, we were all a bit shaken up. Alan said that we had finally solved the puzzle. He was so sure, so adamant, that you had killed the man and that you were the answer to the question that the horse man asked. He kept saying that—over and over.

"So he just shouted for a while. Looking at the TV, looking all around. 'We've got him. Morgan Sheppard is the murderer.' All around the room. But there was no kind of answer. No kind of sign that the horse man had even noticed him. Alan said that he was playing games with us. So he got annoyed and shouted louder. Then he started screaming some incoherent rubbish, just venting you know?

"We were all just watching him. I admit that he got to me. He made me think it was you. But I wasn't happy about it. But Alan was almost gleeful. I sat on the bed, watching the TV. I mean, watching the letters flicker up and down. 'We hope you enjoy your stay.' I can't help but think it means something. Anyway, Rhona was where she always was and Mandy and Constance were sitting on the right side of the bed."

Sheppard looked to Mandy. She silently nodded.

"So nothing happened for a while. Alan calmed down for a bit. We all kept to ourselves. Me and Mandy had a talk and I understood maybe I was a bit hasty putting the cuffs on you and throwing you in the bathroom. I told this to Alan and obviously he wasn't best pleased. We had a talk; all of us gathered around and that was when it happened. She stabbed him, like it was nothing. She must have slid it in his back like she was cutting a cake. Alan gave out this kind of yowl and then keeled over. Dead."

Sheppard sighed. It wasn't as if Alan wasn't a thorn in his side the entire time he'd been in the room, but that didn't mean he should die. He looked from Alan to Constance, who was rocking the chair left and right, almost looking like she was enjoying it. Her own little fairground ride.

He looked down at what was once Alan Hughes.

"We need to move him," Sheppard said, "he's only going to make people uncomfortable here."

Sheppard stepped over Alan to get the man's feet while Ryan got his shoulders. On three, they hoisted him up. They slowly carried him to the bathroom, attempting to not drip too much blood on the carpet. They mostly succeeded, with only a small trail tracking to where he lay—Ryan backed into the bathroom, pushing the door open as he went and Sheppard followed. They lowered Alan onto the floor—blood dashed across the white tiles as they let go.

Two dead bodies. It didn't feel weird anymore. Being around all this death. That kind of day.

"Should we, you know," Ryan said, nodding to the knife, "take it out? Just doesn't seem right to leave it in there sticking out like that."

Sheppard didn't particularly want to touch it, but knew that it was probably the right thing to do. With one glance at Ryan, seeing that the young man had no intention of actually doing the deed, he stepped forward. He bent over the body. With a deep breath, he grasped the wooden handle of the knife, standing up to attention. The spiders were still there, on the back of his hand, but he tried to forget about them. He pressed down on either side of the wound with his other hand, knowing that this was how they did it on those Saturday evening hospital dramas. He yanked the knife. It didn't move. It was stuck in tight. Sheppard yanked again and it gave way slightly. On the third pull, it came free and in its place a fresh fountain of blood spattered Sheppard's shirt. He flinched away, but too late.

Ryan looked at him, freshly colored in Hughes. "That's gross."

"It was stuck in there tight," Sheppard said, trying to connect two dots that he couldn't see, at least not at first. But then he got it. The wounds in Winter's gut had been deep, really deep. That was why he thought that it was probably a male. But if Constance could manage to plunge a knife so far into Alan's back, she could easily have killed Winter.

"What?" Ryan said, reading his expression.

"Nothing, or maybe something." Sheppard went to the sink and washed off Alan's blood. It all blended in—Winter's, Alan's, creating a pinkish stain on his torso.

He studied the knife in the light, stuck it under the sink, and saw Ryan staring at him. "I'm going to hold on to this," Sheppard said. "Do we have a problem with that?"

Ryan shook his head.

"How long was I in here?" Sheppard said. "How long do we have left?"

"I'm sorry I put you in here."

"How long do we have left?"

"It's just Alan was so…"

"Ryan. How long?"

Ryan said nothing but walked out of the bathroom, holding the door open for him. Sheppard stepped forward, knowing that he had to look, but couldn't bring himself to do it. He managed by shutting his eyes and looking in the direction of the timer. He opened his eyes and felt his stomach lurch.

He had seventeen minutes left.

36

Constance Ahearn was humming some inconsequential tune as Sheppard turned back into the room. She looked at him and smiled. He did not smile back.

He barely registered that Mandy and Headphones were now sitting on the side of the bed in each other's arms. Ryan looked like he didn't know what to do with himself. The room suddenly seemed a lot more empty—Alan's ego had filled the room full of something, at least. Now everything was quiet. The horse man hadn't been around for a long time. It was only them now. Him and the young people and a killer. It had to be her. She had to have killed Winter too.

Sheppard walked up to her, got level with her, got up in her face like he was on his TV show. Like the lights had just come on and the audience was rabid.

Because you know why? NOTHING GETS PAST HIM.

He heard it, behind him. The audience shouting it out, prompted by some assistant holding up a card saying "Catch-phrase." Not real. He was still hallucinating. Needed to get more of a grip. He couldn't lose it now.

"What did you do?" Sheppard said to Constance, a lot sadder than he thought it was going to come out.

Constance's eyes snapped to his. There was madness there now. It wasn't there before, right? He would have seen it. She smiled. "I saved you. I saved you all."

"What do you mean?" Sheppard said. "You killed a man."

"He was a liar. He was an adulterer. He was a glutton."

Constance tensed up in the chair and the handcuffs rattled as she tried to move her hands. "No man resided there."

"How do you know all that?"

"I just know."

"You're crazy," Ryan said, beside him.

Constance's eyes shot to him. Then back to Sheppard. Sheppard held a hand up to Ryan. He was thinking exactly the same thing. But crazy people didn't know they were crazy.

"So you saved us," Sheppard said. "Is that because you thought Alan killed Simon Winter?" After all, he had thought the same himself.

"Yes and no."

"Did you kill him? Simon Winter."

Constance looked at him for too long. "No."

"You're religious. What happened to 'Thou shalt not kill'?"

"I don't need to be talked down to by you, Mr. Sheppard. I know what I've done, but He will see it differently. He will forgive me, when I am come to the kingdom of Heaven. He sent someone to tell me what to do."

"What are you talking about?"

"You could see it. You could see it in his eyes," Constance said, widening her own. "He had evil in them. And I was told that I must act. To save everyone in this room."

"Who told you to kill Hughes?"

Constance looked around, as though she was trying to avoid the question.

"Please, Constance," Mandy said, "just answer him."

Constance looked at Mandy and softened slightly. It seemed she trusted the young girl more than Sheppard. Obliging, she leaned forward on her chair and whispered, "The Mary Magdalene."

Sheppard chuckled and nodded. What else had he expected? "The Mary Magdalene. You're insane. You killed a man in cold blood. Do you understand that, Ms. Ahearn?"

"I saved the soul of the man the Devil resided in by setting him free. She told me to kill him. She told me to take the knife and plunge it into his back. She said only I had the power— because I had the Holy Spirit on my side."

Sheppard felt that fire. The fire he felt when he was on set, but this time he wasn't acting. This was a real burning anger. An emotion free of the drugs and the drink. He hadn't felt one of those in a long time. Apart from fear of course. "You killed a man. And that means you had it in you to kill Winter too."

"Why would I kill Simon Winter?" Constance said, defensively. As though her integrity was still something she could fight for.

"I honestly have no idea. Maybe because you saw him with your Evil Man. Maybe because he was one of the four horseman of the apocalypse. Maybe because he cut you off in a bike lane once? I don't know anymore."

"Demons, Mr. Sheppard. We are already enduring our punishment."

And that made him remember. Constance's initial outbursts in the room, when she had been running around and throwing herself into the walls. What had she been saying?

Is this the punishment I must endure?

We're all in Hell. And you're all here with me.

"You said things, when we first woke up in the room. You

said something about this being your punishment. What did you mean by that?"

"What?"

Sheppard looked around. Ryan was nodding, remembering it too. "She was talking rubbish about this being her atonement."

"I don't know what you're talking about," Constance squealed. A little too readily.

"Who are you, Ms. Ahearn? Who are you really? What's your secret?"

"We all have secrets. That doesn't make them relevant."

Sheppard sighed. "The first thing you said to me. You said you were being punished." Just two hours ago, but it might as well have been a lifetime. If Sheppard didn't work this out, it was indeed a lifetime.

"My family is strongly Catholic, Mr. Sheppard."

"Really? I hadn't noticed," he said, sensing the sarcasm would probably be lost on her.

"My daughter got pregnant, and she had an abortion. I disowned her and she moved halfway across the world to America. California. She tried to contact me but I never talked to her. One day, I got a call from her husband. My baby girl had been hit by a drunk driver, killed along with a new unborn child. I prayed for the safety of one child and ended up killing another."

Sheppard frowned. He didn't want to be cruel but the first thing that sprang into his head was *Is that it?* He was sure it was very horrible but he was expecting something a little more... All he found was a dead end.

"I told you I had nothing to do with your investigation," Constance said. Constance was crazy, but he couldn't help thinking that in some ways, it wasn't her fault. She obviously had some severe mental problems, but right here and right now, that didn't matter. Unfortunately for her, if Heaven and Hell did exist, Constance had earned herself an ensuite in the latter, hotter one.

Sheppard paused. "I'm sorry. But I think you have everything to do with it. I think you killed Simon Winter."

37

Sheppard turned to the rest of the room, and raised his voice, just as Alan had done an age ago. "Constance Ahearn. The murderer is Constance Ahearn."

He waited for a moment. Nothing happened. Ryan looked around, expectantly, while the two girls just looked on, bewildered. This had to be it. It had to be her. He was looking for something, maybe some kind of acknowledgement. Some kind of hope. A reason to keep going—if only for a few more seconds.

Constance Ahearn gave out a fresh splutter of laughter. "Not quite, Mr. Sheppard."

Sheppard wheeled around, looking toward the timer.

It was still counting down. Five minutes.

What had gone wrong? Constance was the murderer. She was the only one that made sense. But the game was still going. They were still dying one second at a time.

"Why didn't it work? How could it not work?" Ryan said.

This wasn't over. This couldn't be over. "Maybe we haven't worked it out right. Maybe she needs to say something." Sheppard kneeled down and was face-to-face again with Constance.

The woman looked normal, as if nothing was happening at all. She smiled at him and tilted her head to the side, as though she were greeting a family pet.

"You know something," Sheppard said, "I know you do."

"I know everything and I know nothing," Ahearn said, almost singing it in her tuneful voice. "It depends what type of everything you want to know."

"You killed a man. You killed a man like it was nothing. Like slicing butter. You've done it before. I know it's you."

"As I've already said, Mr. Sheppard, I didn't kill Dr. Winter. Why would I kill him? I have no motive." Constance winked at him. "But I do know who did."

"I knew it," Sheppard said, through clenched teeth. "Why didn't you say anything?"

"Because I cannot dishonor by telling."

Sheppard laughed in her face. "You understand we're dying, don't you? That when that timer runs down, we're all exploding? We're all going to die in a mess of fire."

Constance smiled. "Rapturous."

Sheppard stood up in annoyance and felt someone at his side. It was Ryan—anger flared in his eyes. "Why won't you tell us, you bitch?" Ryan said, and Constance smiled at him too. Ryan turned to Sheppard. "We can make her talk."

"What do you mean?" Sheppard said, but he thought he already knew. He could see it in Ryan's eyes. "No, we can't..."

"You said it yourself. We don't find out and we all die. I just have to hurt her a little bit. She'll crack easily."

Sheppard opened his mouth and closed it again—had he discounted Ryan so quickly?

Ryan made his way behind Constance. She tried to follow him with her eyes but he was in her blind spot. She looked back at Sheppard, with confused eyes.

"We can't do this," Sheppard said. *Could they?*

"Yes, we can," Ryan said, bending down behind Constance. "Just ask her the question."

"What is he doing behind there? Demon." Constance looked at Sheppard, as though she could see him entirely. She could see all his secrets, all his bad decisions, all his failed relationships. She could see *him*, the real *him*, beyond all the clutter and the bad blood.

Mandy stepped forward, seeing what Ryan intended to do. "No, you can't do this."

"We need to do this. Whether we want to or not. We don't do this and we're all going to die," Ryan said. He had clearly justified it to himself. He nodded with such a conviction, it was exciting.

"Sheppard," Mandy said, "please stop this."

"When are you going to see, Mandy?" Ryan said, "Sheppard failed. He doesn't know who did it, so now it falls to the rest of us."

"This is what he wants," Mandy cried. "This is exactly what the horse man wants. Don't make him turn you into this."

"I'm confused," Ryan said. "Are you saying this because of the well-being of Ms. Ahearn here, or because you're scared of what she'll say."

Silence. Ryan's gaze darting from Mandy to Sheppard and back.

"Ryan," Sheppard said, as Mandy gave an exasperated sigh, "come on, this is lunacy."

"Just ask the question."

"Ryan."

"Sheppard, ask the question."

"I..." Sheppard said, unsure how to start the sentence, let alone finish it. With a glance at Mandy, he got down in front of Constance again.

"Sheppard, no," Mandy said.

Sheppard looked at Constance and tried a sad smile. She smiled back. "Ms. Ahearn, I need to ask you, who killed Simon Winter?"

Constance looked at him, then at Mandy and Headphones, even trying to look at Ryan although she couldn't manage it. "I won't tell you. But God will forgive us in the kingdom of Heaven." She gave a yelp of surprise and struggled. "What are you doing back there? Don't you think about hurting me."

"Ryan," Sheppard said.

Ryan disappeared behind the chair for a few long moments. Sheppard could only see what was happening sketched on Constance's face. She looked slightly uncomfortable and he thought that maybe Ryan had a hold of her fingers. But her expression didn't change. And a moment almost became a minute, when a sorrow-filled yelp came from behind the chair, and not Constance.

Ryan stood up behind her, tears in his eyes. "I can't do it," he said, with all the defensiveness of a child who had been caught stealing pic 'n' mix. "I can't do it. It's over. We're all going to die."

Mandy let out a skittering breath, sounding as though she was holding back a cry. She sat on the bed with her back to them. Ryan wiped his nose with his hand and looked at Sheppard.

"I'm sorry," he said, before going to sit down as well. Sheppard got up, looking at Constance with one final, long glance. Their last hope. Not much of a hope anyway. It was indeed all over. *Time always runs out in the end.*

Sheppard walked over to the wall beside the TV and slid down it. As he hit the floor he was struck by one final opportunity. And the more he thought about it, the more it made sense. His heart rose in his chest, he had worked it out. It was all so simple, and he had finally worked it out. "Horse Mask," he shouted, almost sounding happy, "the murderer is Horse Mask." He waited a few seconds. Nothing. Nothing at all.

The timer slid to two minutes left.

38

Sheppard looked from Ryan to Headphones to Mandy. Behind him, Constance had started chuckling about something. Most likely, the prospect of dying. Looking at the others' faces, they were contemplating it too.

He had to try again. "Constance Ahearn. The murderer is Constance Ahearn."

He waited again. Nothing happened. The seconds slipping away too fast. This was it—it was over. They were really going to die.

Why not? He was already a joke. He couldn't protect himself, let alone the others.

"Rhona," Sheppard said, turning away from her as he said it. He couldn't look her in the face. "The murderer is Rhona."

Again, a few seconds wait yielded nothing. "Ryan Quinn, the murderer is Ryan Quinn." One, two, three. Nothing.

One name left. That meant…

"Amanda Phillips. The murderer is Amanda Phillips." One, two, three. Nothing.

Had he expected that to work? He had at least hoped for some kind of response. Maybe a comical uh–uh "No" noise? That sort of seemed like the horse man's style.

He looked up to the television. It was still showing the flickering, putrid-colored words "We Hope You Enjoy Your Stay."

Sheppard grabbed it by the corners and stared into it, as if he could summon up the horse man. "Hey, hey. You. I need to talk to you." The words flickered. "You. You bastard. Come on." Nothing.

Frustration welled from his stomach. In a swift move, Sheppard— not thinking—leapt up and picked up the television. He lifted it over his head and was poised to throw it on the floor, but at the last second, he felt a hand on his shoulder. He turned to see Mandy giving him a sad smile. He looked to Headphones and Ryan, and he saw something like acceptance in their eyes.

Sheppard sank to his knees, feeling the carpet rub against his sore knees. The timer slid down to one minute. He looked up to the ceiling as if to ask a higher power for help, but instead he just said, "Morgan Sheppard. The murderer is Morgan Sheppard."

39

"What's your biggest fear?" Winter had once said, sitting in his high-backed chair assuming his usual therapist pose. His legs crossed, his glasses down his nose, his notebook in his lap—there was no confusing the profession Winter was in.

"To be forgotten," Sheppard said, after a moment's deliberation.

Winter regarded him and leaned forward. "Most people say their greatest fear is death."

"Death is inevitable; being remembered is a courtesy."

Winter took off his glasses and tapped them against the arm of the chair. "You're an interesting man, Morgan."

Sheppard smiled. "Thank you."

Winter smiled too, albeit a bit too late. "I don't know if I meant that as a compliment."

The only thing Sheppard could take with him now was that he'd never be forgotten. No matter how this played out, he would go down as a tragic figure held hostage in a hotel room. But sitting there, looking into the faces of the people he had failed, he wished it could end any other way. He wished he could have saved them.

Saying his own name had done nothing. Had he really expected it to? Did he really think in some warped way that he had killed Winter, and forgotten it? No, he was clutching at straws.

But now there were none left.

Sheppard looked from his hands to Ryan. The young man who worked at the very hotel he would die in. Now, Ryan seemed a lot younger than he was. A scared child trying to put on a brave face, he peeked out from his hands occasionally to see that everything was still in its place. Ryan would never see his family again, the parents he was working to support.

Next to Ryan sat Mandy. The blonde who had stuck her head over the bed when he had only just woken up handcuffed to the bed. She had looked so scared then, but now she was wearing a stoic expression, almost resigned. Sheppard knew from the brief time he'd known her that she wouldn't be one to die crying and screaming. She was noble, someone with a set of morals to live by. And one of them was dying silently.

On the floor was Rhona, her headphones around her neck. She had her hands dug deep into her hoodie pockets. She was silently crying, tears falling down her cheeks erratically. She took a hand and jabbed at the tears sporadically, as if angry that she had even created them. When she had finished mopping them up, she quietly stood up and walked over to Constance Ahearn. She didn't even look at the woman cuffed to the chair but instead walked straight past her to the desk. She climbed under the desk and resumed the position she had been in for most of the three hours. She caught Sheppard's eye and hollowly looked at him. She took her headphones and slid them onto her head.

Constance Ahearn seemed to be all out of lunacy. She was finally quiet and looking down at the bloodstain on the lap of her dress. The woman had turned herself into a monster and

this was the first time that Sheppard thought she might have realized it. Her faith had got her nowhere in the end, a means to
facilitate her worst fears. Sheppard knew that faith was not always like that, but it only served to help Constance in her conviction. Gone was the woman whose biggest problem was her
estranged daughter, now she was a murderer. Maybe, if there
was a God, she could make up for it somewhere else.

Sheppard looked at his four roommates in turn, and still didn't
know which one did it. Maybe his first hunch had been true.
Maybe it was Alan Hughes who had killed Simon Winter, it
all being something to do with the MacArthur case. Somehow
though, this didn't really fit. This wasn't what it was about,
couldn't be. Because they weren't the biggest clues. And who
killed Simon Winter wasn't the biggest mystery.

Thirty seconds on the clock and how many people? How
many children and families would there be in this hotel? How
many around the building? What would the body count be?
Would they blame him? All the families who knew that the
building exploded just because he couldn't solve a simple puzzle?

The simple fact was one that he had been running from for
as long as he could remember—a fact that he was forever scared
that someone would find out. "I'm not a detective," he said into
the quiet room. No heads turned, no one acknowledged it. It
just hung there in the air. An epitaph of a nightmare.

Because that was what the horse man had wanted, wasn't it?
That's what this whole thing had been about.

Ten seconds, and Sheppard thought of his mother for the first
time in a long time. She was rotting in a care home in North
London. And he thought of his agent, who would probably la-
ment the loss of a revenue stream. The two people who might
possibly miss him. Yes, there may be fans who would weep for
him, but they would move on to bigger and better things, often

without even knowing it. The living were much more interesting than the dead.

Eight.

"I'm sorry," he said. Again, no one responded, but he knew he had to say it. He had failed them. He had failed them all. And now they were dead because of him.

Seven.

The Great Hotel becomes the Great Mess. Six.

A funny place to die. Five.

Would there be an investigation? Would they hunt the horse man down?

Four.

Or would they all dance on his grave and say "Good Riddance?"

Three.

He was so, so sorry.

Two.

Sometimes all we want is to be seen, said Winter, in his ear, and he told him to shut up. He wanted to die in peace.

One.

He closed his eyes. Would it be quick? Would it be painless?

Zero.

The sound of the explosion and the piercing white light was his only answer.

40

The body was hanging there in the center of the room. A strange mass in a strange place, almost like a specter of something impossible. It was ever-so-slightly moving, swaying. At first, he thought it was because of the breeze coming from the open window. Later, however, he would come to realize that it was probably from struggling.

He stood in the doorway, unable to move. The room was a mess: upturned desks, scattered papers, forgotten chairs. It was nothing like the neat and normal room it had been two hours before in Maths class. He could even still see the equation they had been working on, on the whiteboard. To step inside would be to step into a deeper, darker world—a world where he had no desire to be.

He was scatterbrained. His mother had always told him so. And this time, he had forgotten his notebook. He was halfway home when he realized and couldn't do without it. He had written down the Maths homework he had to do that night, and for the life of him, couldn't remember what it was.

The halls were quiet as he returned, the ghosts of laughter and shouting in the air. His classmates were long gone and it seemed that most of the teachers were too. The only person he saw was a caretaker, who didn't look familiar, who was unenthusiastically buffing the hall floor. The man looked up at him as he passed and smiled sadly, like he was apologizing for his mere existence.

The door to his Maths classroom had been ajar. Not wishing to appear impolite, he had knocked. There was no answer, apart from the door slowly creaking open.

Mr. Jefferies looked almost comical, like he was hung up on a coatrack—a discarded and empty anorak. His eyes were lifeless, his face a pale eggplant color, his arms hanging at his sides. The belt around Mr. Jefferies's neck was barely visible under his chins but he eventually saw it. The leather was strained, cracked and discolored. It was wrapped around an exposed pipe in the ceiling. The same pipe he had always complained about because it made a weird hissing sound whenever someone flushed the toilet on the second floor. Now that pipe was holding him up. Mr. Jefferies was dead.

At some point, he started to scream.

He heard footsteps behind him—running, and then someone clutched his shoulders tightly. He couldn't rip his eyes from the scene in front of him, but he smelled the familiar perfume of Miss Rain and heard his name in her soft voice.

"What in the heavens is wrong?" she said.

He couldn't speak; he just pointed into the room.

He saw the outline of Miss Rain turn and look. And then he heard her scream too.

The next few minutes were a rush of colors and lights.

He was so disorientated that he didn't know what was happening. He heard more people rushing around him and then he was picked up by someone and rushed away into the staff room. When he opened his eyes, Miss Rain was sitting across from him, smiling sadly, her eyes red with tears.

"Do you want a glass of water?"

Before he could reply, she got up and crossed over into the kitchen area. He looked down at his hands as he heard the tap—they were shaking. He tried to stop them but he couldn't.

Miss Rain put a glass of water down in front of him and then sat down again.

"Drink this. It'll help."

He picked up the glass of water. It sloshed around in the glass as he held it to his lips. Ever so slightly swaying in the glass. A wave of nausea as he took a sip. The water was cold and very real. Inviting. He took a sip and put it down again.

"How are you—feeling any better?"

A silly question, and from the sound of it Miss Rain knew it was. He didn't know. He couldn't know. There weren't enough words in the English language to explain how he felt, at least of the ones he knew. It wasn't fair. It wasn't fair to ask him that.

"Please, sweetie, can you talk to me? I need to know what you're feeling."

"I…" So many words—too many words. Why did the human race need so many words? "I've left my notebook in the Maths room."

"That's why you're back?"

"I just need to go get it and everything…"

"No…"

"…everything'll be okay."

He grew silent—his little brain was going too slowly.

He couldn't think. He couldn't even… "Mr. Jefferies…" he said slowly.

Miss Rain was crying now. He didn't understand. He didn't

understand why she was crying. She dabbed at her eyes with the sleeve of her cardigan. "Yes, I know. It'll all be okay. It'll all be fine. You just have to be strong now." Miss Rain moved round and sat next to him. He lay his head on her shoulder and she wrapped her arms around him. Soon they were both crying silently.

More people around him. He shut his eyes—screwed them up tight like they did in the movies. He heard bodies around him, he heard sharp whispering. Miss Rain was talking to the head teacher. Then there were sirens, slowly getting closer, and someone else ran into the staff room. He felt strong arms grasp him.

He opened his eyes. His father's face—very close. His father pulled him into a hug and he started crying more.

"I was outside waiting for you in the car. I saw the police cars. I'm so sorry."

His father hugged him for a long time, gripping him so tight that he found it hard to breathe. But at that moment, that was exactly what he needed. He felt safe there, he felt calm. He felt like a child being comforted by his father. But somewhere in the back of his mind, he knew that the child in him had died along with Mr. Jefferies. The child in him was hanging there in the Maths room with his teacher.

His father pulled away and looked him in the eye. "Talk to me, son. Are you okay?"

In his father's bright eyes, shadows glinting—the image of his teacher hanging from the ceiling. Would he see that everywhere now—forever and no time at all?

"Say something." His father looked worried. "Please say something, Eren."

41

The next few days passed in something of a fog. Before he went home that day, Eren had to talk to the police for what seemed like hours, although it was probably more like minutes. Time was not working like it usually did. His father held his hand in a tight grip throughout as he told of finding Mr. Jefferies's body. He left the details as fuzzy as the police allowed. He didn't want to think about it. And he could already feel his mind closing around the memory, like a chrysalis, protecting him from the horrors inside.

In the following days, the information started to come out. George Jefferies was dead. He hanged himself with his belt in the Maths room. Police said that Mr. Jefferies's mother had said her son had been unhappy for a long time. Eren had never even thought that Mr. Jefferies would have parents. They said that he had money troubles and he was very lonely.

The police visited Eren and told him this. They said that his teacher had taken his own life, not thinking that a student would find him. They said they were very sorry. Everyone apologized. "We're sorry this happened to you."

"I'm sorry you had to see that."

"The school is sorry for everything and understands if you need some time to collect your thoughts." He didn't understand why everyone was sorry. They hadn't done anything. When he told his father this, his father said that people just apologized when they didn't really know what to say, which was ironic as he was the one who said sorry the most.

He wasn't allowed to go to school for the next week and his TV privileges were gone. His father didn't want him seeing anything on the news. Eren learned from friends that it never reached the news though. It wasn't interesting enough. Mr. Jefferies, his kind, fun Maths teacher killed himself and the world didn't care.

His world had grown quieter. He no longer heard the birds in the trees or the traffic outside. He only heard silence. Colors were not as bright as they once were. His world was no longer exciting, no longer hopeful. Why bother with hope when one can just die, anytime or anywhere. He slept a lot. His father rang a psychologist—not telling him, but he snuck out of his room and listened on the stairs. Food didn't seem to be edible anymore.

On the Wednesday after the incident, he heard a knock at his bedroom door. He didn't answer, he just looked at his clock. It was 4:00 p.m.—when did it get to be 4:00 p.m.?

The door opened and his father stuck his head around the door.

"Eren, there's someone here to see you." Eren just turned his back. "I don't care."

His father ignored him. "It's your friend. Here he is." And Eren turned around to see Morgan standing there.

Morgan Sheppard with a big smile on his face. Morgan could

usually cheer him up, but today Eren could see that he was forcing that smile.

"I'll leave you two to it." The door shut.

Morgan dumped his backpack in the center of the floor and school textbooks spilled out. "How are you?"

"I'm fine," Eren said, never feeling further from fine. "You're the talk of the school," Morgan said. "Are all the rumors true? You found Mr. Jefferies in the Maths room?"

"Yes," Eren said, the image flashing through his mind quickly. "I found him."

"We've got a substitute for Maths. She's a real hard-ass. I also don't think she can count. And we have to have our lessons in the library which is annoying. No one's allowed in that room."

"Hmm," Eren said, not really listening.

"Sadie said that room's haunted now. She said that's why we can't go in," Morgan said, picking up one of Eren's action figures and sitting down at the edge of the bed. "She said that Eric said that Michael's sister saw Mr. Jefferies in the window last night. But I think she's lying just to get attention because…"

"Because he's dead," Eren said, sitting up.

Morgan fiddled with the action figure's arm, making it wave at Eren. "Yeah," he said, in a small voice.

"Do you…?" Eren started, sliding his bum to the edge of the bed so he was sat next to Morgan. "Why do you think he did it?"

Morgan was silent.

"What can be so bad that someone kills themselves?"

"Maybe he did something wrong," Morgan said, handing Eren the action figure. It was a knockoff superhero toy, a generic man in a cape with a big toothy grin and strong muscles.

"Everyone does wrong things—we don't all kill ourselves."

"Maybe he was just too sad."

Eren thought about this, but it didn't make any sense. Mr. Jefferies was always so happy. He was always smiling and joking with them. There was never a hint of sadness there. Maybe he was just good at hiding it.

"I'll miss him," Morgan said. "We all will. He was nice."

"Yes."

"And funny."

"Yes."

Morgan was quiet for a moment and then chuckled. "You remember the time he let us watch movies instead of do work…"

Eren's eyes were on the action figure. There was something at the back of his mind. Something gnawing at him. And it was only getting stronger when he looked at this stupid toy. But he had no idea what it was.

"…or when he told jokes all lesson. Even that dirty one, ha-ha."

Eren's eyes went down the action figure to the superhero's utility belt. Something…

"You remember when he lost all that weight a month ago? And he kept having to pull his trousers up all the time. He was a good teacher." Morgan looked at Eren and nudged him on the shoulder. "You want to play some SNES? It'll take your mind off it."

Eren looked up at Morgan, his eyes wide. "Say that again?"

Morgan smiled. "SNES. I've got really good at World 2." Morgan looked around. "Where'd your TV go?"

"No, no," Eren said, "say what you said before that."

Morgan looked confused. "What? About Mr. Jefferies? His trousers falling down. Surely you remember all that. He even made a joke of it."

Eren looked at Morgan, holding up the action figure. Morgan looked confused. "I remember," Eren said. "I didn't, but now I remember. I remember perfectly."

"What's wrong, Eren? You look like you've seen a ghost." Eren jumped off the bed.

"Okay," Morgan said, "poor choice of words."

"I'm going to need your help, Morgan," Eren said, picking up the other boy's backpack and throwing it at him.

Morgan caught it. "What are you doing?"

"I need to get back to school," Eren said, looking at Morgan. Somewhere in his mind, a spark lit. Memories of Mr. Jefferies came flooding back. He was happy. He was kind. He wasn't sad or miserable. He would never do what he did.

Colors and sounds flooded back into his world again. And also, in the darkest moment, a little bit of hope. Hope that his world was not entirely wrong.

Eren slung his backpack over his shoulder and turned back to Morgan, still looking bewildered on the bed. "Mr. Jefferies didn't kill himself. Someone murdered him."

Eren threw the action figure to the ground.

It took Morgan a few minutes to catch up with him, although he was on his bike and Eren was only walking. Eren didn't really know where he was going—he was walking toward school taking the back alleyways he knew so well.

Morgan rode up alongside him. "What are you doing?"

"I'm not sure," Eren said truthfully.

"Why did you say Mr. Jefferies was murdered?"

"Because he was."

"He killed himself, Eren." Morgan was half riding the bike and half walking to keep pace with him. They emerged from the alleyways onto a big football field.

"He didn't. He didn't kill himself. He wouldn't do that."

"Eren, you're freaking me out."

Eren stopped abruptly. Morgan hit the brakes and almost fell as the bike went crashing to the ground.

"The belt. He hanged himself with a belt. I saw it. But Mr. Jefferies didn't have a belt."

"Yes he did."

"No, he didn't because of his trousers."

Morgan's face showed a flash of understanding. The same understanding that was fueling Eren now. "But that was weeks ago. He could've got a belt since then. Was he wearing a belt that day?"

Eren tried to think. He couldn't remember. It was a detail that you wouldn't actively forget but also one you wouldn't think to keep. It was a detail that could slip through the cracks. Eren wondered if adults could make the same mistake. If it could slip through the cracks of an investigation.

"I can't remember if he was," Eren said, and Morgan was looking similarly perplexed, "but that doesn't matter because I know Mr. Jefferies didn't do it."

"How?" Morgan said.

Eren thought for a moment. That was a good question. But he had a strong feeling that Mr. Jefferies really didn't do it. He knew there was something else. Some clue that he was missing. Something had happened that was out of place. But he couldn't put his finger on it.

"We have to find out who killed Mr. Jefferies."

Morgan scratched his forehead. "Eren, I can't even reach high shelves. I'm pretty sure I can't solve a murder."

"We owe it to him."

"I dunno. Maybe if you really think something's up, we should go to the police."

Eren put a hand on Morgan's shoulder. Morgan looked at it ominously. "You're always talking about how you want to be famous. Cricket, video games, acting—what if those things don't matter. What if you're going to be famous for this instead? What if we actually do solve a murder?"

A moment was all it took and Morgan's eyes lit up with possibilities. The boy was easy to talk around. Ever since Eren had known him, Morgan had had a desire to be known for something. Quite what it was, it didn't seem to matter. Morgan just wanted to be someone. "Okay," the boy said, "but are you sure? What if we find out that Jefferies did really kill himself?"

Eren started walking again. "He didn't." There was no way. Because that would mean that the world wasn't what he thought it was. That would mean everything would be different. He couldn't have killed himself. Or more accurately, he mustn't have. And as Eren stomped across the field, it became apparent that a little boy's psyche depended on it.

Eren and Morgan walked around in circles for the rest of the evening. The school was shut—locked up. There wasn't really anywhere else to go. They walked in silence, Morgan peddling his bike alongside him. They returned to Eren's house around six o'clock and Eren's dad ordered pizza. They ate and played SNES until it was time for Morgan to go home. Neither of them mentioned Mr. Jefferies.

For the next few days, nothing much happened. Eren returned to school and was harassed by other kids wanting to hear all the gory details. The teachers tried their best to stop this, but Eren still found himself repeating the same brief story over and over— they seemed to be content with that. Soon it was old news.

But it wasn't old news for Eren—far from it. The death of Mr. Jefferies weighed on him even more than it had on the fateful day. More than ever, a single thought burned at the back of his mind—he didn't do it—and he still felt that niggling feeling that there was something obvious he was missing.

Nearly a week later, Eren and Morgan were in the park after school. It was the first time the two of them had been alone since Eren had made his assumption. Morgan was tightrope-walking on a small, short brick wall that belonged to a house that had been knocked down on the edge of the park. Eren was sitting on the grass, picking at the blades.

"You want to go to the cinema?" Morgan asked, putting his hands out to steady himself as he walked along the wall. "My cousin got a new job there. If I ask him really nicely, he might get us in to see *Reservoir Dogs*. Someone's ear gets cut off and you see everything."

Eren ignored him. He kept on picking at the grass. He was thinking about that day again. He was always thinking about it. There was something to be found there, in his memory.

"Eren. Eren. Eren. Eren. Eren," Morgan continued. "Eren. Eren. Eren."

"What?" Eren said, annoyed.

Morgan smiled. "What's wrong with you? You're superquiet."

"I'm just thinking. Thinking about when I found Mr. Jefferies."

Morgan jumped off the wall and slumped down on the grass splaying his arms out dramatically. "You're still talking about that? That was like—" Eren could almost see the gears whirring around in his little friend's head "—that was like two weeks ago."

Two weeks felt like a lifetime and Eren's memory was starting to fade. The chrysalis around the memory was destroyed. He didn't want to forget. Because he knew that was where the answer lay. It was the strongest feeling he'd ever had.

"I'm trying to remember," Eren said, pulling up a fresh clump of grass, "but it's hard."

"Why don't you say it out loud?" Morgan said, "Maybe that'd help."

Morgan was usually a rather simple boy but even Eren couldn't deny that this made a lot of sense.

"Okay," Eren said and for some reason, he stood up in front of Morgan, almost as if he was about to perform a play.

"So start at the beginning," Morgan said, "unless you're sure we can't just try and go see *Reservoir Dogs*."

"Morgan, focus."

"But the ear, dude. The ear."

Eren ignored him. "Okay, it started about halfway home. I looked in my bag trying to find the sweets we'd bought at the shop, and I knew I'd left my notebook behind. Me and Benny Masterson were playing tic-tac-toe with it in Maths, and I just knew that I didn't put it back in my bag. I don't know why. I just could see it lying there on the table. I don't know how but I always do it. I always manage to leave it somewhere."

"Like that time you left it at the aquarium," Morgan said, laughing.

"Yeah, I guess," Eren said, dismissing Morgan so he could continue. "So I doubled back, and went back to school. It was quiet. Quieter than I'd ever seen it really, even at parent's evening. There was no one there apart from this caretaker guy I didn't know. He was using that thing that shines the floor. Mr. Jefferies's room was open. And I went in.

"And there he was. Then I shouted—" Eren somehow didn't want to admit he screamed and cried, at least not to Morgan "—and Miss Rain came and other teachers too, although my eyes were closed so I don't know who. We went to the staff room, and then my dad was there. And then I had to talk to the police for ages."

"Hmm," Morgan said, scratching his chin, most likely to look intelligent.

"Yes?"

"I think maybe you need to take your mind off this," Morgan concluded.

"I don't need to do anything. Apart from find out who killed Mr. Jefferies," Eren shouted. It was so loud that a few boys playing football across the field looked over in their direction. Morgan shuffled around so he blocked Eren from view.

"Eren, dude, calm down. Maybe you just need some more time. Mr. Jefferies killed himself. And it was really sad. And we'll all miss him. And it was really messed up that you found him. But he did kill himself. And going around saying that he was killed maybe isn't the best thing."

"You still don't believe me?" Eren said, trying not to cry.

"I believe that you've seen something messed up. And maybe you need to take your mind off it. By seeing something equally messed up. Like an ear severed from a man's head. Where you see everything."

"Morgan, I'm not going to the cinema," Eren said defiantly, shuffling away from him. It wasn't fair. If he couldn't persuade his best friend that Mr. Jefferies was killed, then what hope did he have of convincing anyone else? "Do you not want to know what happened? Do you not feel it?"

"Feel what?" Morgan said.

"He didn't do this. He couldn't have."

"I dunno, I guess it's possible. But the police can't be wrong. They're never wrong. That's what my mum said."

"But what if they are? What if there's a killer out there free right now? And I know there's something I'm missing." Eren threw up his hands in disgust, soil and grass going everywhere.

"Maybe you need one of those cleaning machines for your mind. You know like that caretaker was using. You need to wash the memories away."

"That's dumb—" and Eren trailed off. That was it. That was what he was missing. He looked at Morgan intently.

"What?" the other boy said.

"The caretaker. I didn't recognize the caretaker."

"But the caretaker's Gerry," Morgan said. The caretaker at their school was referred to only as Gerry. He was a small mousy man with huge jam-jar glasses. He was often seen pottering around school during the day, fixing light fixtures or battling the demons inside interactive whiteboards. The school could only afford one caretaker, so he was always really busy.

"This wasn't Gerry," Eren said, the color draining from his face.

"Then," Morgan said slowly, as he matched Eren's expression, "who was it?"

They were both silent for a very long time.

42

"So this caretaker guy, you're sure you haven't seen him before?"

They were back in Eren's room sitting on his floor. Eren doodled on a piece of paper while Morgan watched. Downstairs, Eren's father was watching football. They could hear the chanting of the home team and various cheers as someone scored.

Eren had never been one for sports, much to the disappointment of his father. When his mother had died, his father tried to get him into football. Eren had seen it as some kind of attempt to get closer to him. They went to a couple of games, Eren pretending to be enthusiastic when Arsenal, the team his father supported, scored. But over time, he couldn't keep it up, and eventually he told his father he just wasn't interested.

"I didn't recognize him at all. I've never seen him around school before."

"What did he look like?" Morgan said.

"He had brown hair. He looked big, not like fat, but big like muscly. He had like a green overall thing on and he was using that thing to shine the floor of the hall."

"Couldn't he have just been a cleaner? Like someone who comes in when all us kids have gone home?"

Eren thought for a moment. He wished he could remember the man a little better. "I guess he could've been. But he looked more like a caretaker. And he definitely wasn't Gerry."

Morgan rubbed his eyes and sighed. "So what does this mean?"

"If this guy wasn't a caretaker, and he wasn't a cleaner, then what was he doing there?" Eren asked, with a degree of finality. He'd found it, that one strand of thread that didn't fit in the picture. He felt happy for the first time since he had gone into that room. He was getting somewhere.

There was a fresh cheer from downstairs and the sound of Eren's father shouting "Get in!" Arsenal had scored.

"You're saying that…" Morgan didn't finish, but Eren knew exactly what he meant.

"Yes. I think it was him. I think he killed Mr. Jefferies. I think he went into that room and he…he killed him. Made it look like Jefferies had killed himself to get away with it. Then he left the room, maybe heard people coming, and had to work out how to blend in. Maybe he found that shining machine and decided to pose as a caretaker. Then when I had passed by, he ran away." Eren put his pen down, in resolution. "What do you think?"

Morgan scoffed. "I don't— I mean it makes some kind of sense I suppose. And it sounds like it could've happened. But…"

"Yes?"

"…that doesn't mean it did."

Eren had known Morgan all his life. The two of them had met at kindergarten and had stayed together since. They'd never once fallen out. Even as an eleven-year-old, Eren had a basic understanding of how people worked, and he knew how Morgan worked more than anyone. If his friend was going to help him, he would have to appeal to his more exciting side. Eren needed to know what happened to Mr. Jefferies for his peace of mind, but Morgan had no such issue. Morgan was just a kid who wanted life to be more like it was in the movies.

"Morgan, imagine if Mr. Jefferies was murdered, and we caught the killer? Imagine how famous we would be? The two kids who caught a dangerous man, who had killed their own teacher. We could be better than everyone else. We could be better than the police. We would be superheroes."

Eren slid the action figure across the carpet, in front of Morgan. It had still been where he'd thrown it a week before.

Morgan looked at him, his eyes alight. He picked up the action figure. And smiled. "Okay. So what do we do?"

"We need to make sure that that guy wasn't just a cleaner."

"How do we do that?"

"There's a book with pictures of all the staff at the school. I saw it once—it was out at parents' evening. They probably have it in the office. We need that book to see if that guy's in there. I'll know it if I see him, I just can't describe him."

"And what if he is in there? Hell, what if he isn't in there? What then?"

"We'll work that out when we've found out."

Morgan nodded, not looking entirely convinced. "Okay, I guess."

"One more thing, we have to keep this totally quiet. Only you and I can know we're doing this. We could be in danger if it gets out that we're investigating."

Morgan looked insanely happy about this. The more danger, the more exciting it was to him, no doubt. "Okay."

Eren put a fist out. "Pard'ner," he said, in an old-timey voice.

"Pard'ner," Morgan said, bumping his fist with his own.

Downstairs, Eren's father howled. The other team had scored.

★ ★ ★

The next day during break, Eren and Morgan went to the school office, and were confronted with a rather crotchety Miss Erthwhile. She was an old woman who had worked at the school since the dawn of time, and famously hated children. She was always in the office, dunking biscuits into her coffee and typing slowly on the computer. She was also the qualified nurse for the sick room, and since she had taken up that particular job, the number of children who went to the sick room had gone down by more than half. No one wanted to be faced with her.

Eren and Morgan walked up to the desk slowly as if approaching an almighty dragon. Similarly to a dragon, Miss Erthwhile could be defeated if you knew her weaknesses.

"Hello, Miss Erthwhile," Eren said sunnily.

Miss Erthwhile peered down at the both of them. Her face was just a pile of wrinkles. Many scholars had died attempting to figure out how old she was. "Yes?" she said.

"Me and Morgan here were wondering if maybe you had a book with pictures of all the staff at the school?"

Miss Erthwhile regarded them with her small squirrelly eyes. "The alumni book? Now, why would you want that?"

Eren and Morgan looked at each other. "We, uh, we're doing a project," Morgan said—he was always far quicker with the excuses. He'd had plenty of practice.

"Project for what?"

"Geography. We're doing a map of the city, and the teacher says we can get pictures of everyone to stick on the map. Like which areas they live in."

Eren looked at his friend, with something like admiration. Even he had to admit that that wasn't a bad save.

"Hmm." Erthwhile thought, while looking down her nose at them. "If you bring me a note from the teacher, I'll let you have a look."

Morgan smiled. "We don't really have time for that, Miss Erthwhile. Our project's due tomorrow and we really wanted to do the project now."

"Sorry, but you can't see it without a note," Erthwhile said, not even attempting to hide her happiness that she had disrupted someone's day. "That book is not for children to see."

Morgan and Eren looked at each other again. Eren shrugged, not knowing what else to do. Morgan got in close and whispered in Eren's ear, "Watch this. I saw this thing called reverse psychology on a TV show." Morgan straightened up again and cleared his throat. Erthwhile watched him, bemused.

"Don't give us the alumni book," Morgan said, confidently.

Erthwhile chuckled, "Righto." She went back to typing very slowly on the computer.

Morgan looked confused. He leaned in to Eren again. "Okay, there may have been more elements to it."

The two boys walked out of the office, dejected. Eren needed that book, it was the only way he could know for sure if the man he had seen worked at the school or not.

Out in the corridor, Eren slammed his fist into a locker. "Ouch," he said, instantly regretting it. "We need that book."

"Is there no other way?"

"No," Eren said, rubbing his hand.

"Okay then," Morgan said, "then there's only one thing for it."

"What?"

"One of us has to go to the sick room."

During English, Morgan suffered an intense and concentrated stomachache. The teacher rushed him off to the sick room, telling the class to reread the opening of *Of Mice and Men*. Eren waited as long as he could, which was about two minutes, and then snuck out the back of the class.

The corridors were quiet, reminding him of that fateful day, but this time he could hear the muffled sounds of classrooms full of children all around him. He took the shortcut through the courtyard, nodding to Gerry, who was clipping a bush, as he passed. He emerged into the office corridor. The sick room was just down the hall from Erthwhile's office and Eren could hear the howls of his friend. He was either overacting his stomach-ache or Erthwhile was torturing him. No one knew the horrors of the sick room.

Eren stuck his head around the office door. It was empty. He went round Erthwhile's desk and started rummaging. The top drawer had packs of sweets in.

The next drawer down had random papers all heaped together. They all seemed to be spreadsheets filled with more letters and numbers than Eren knew existed.

To Eren's dismay, the final drawer was locked. He tried pulling on it three or four times before he noticed that there was a sticky note on the upper right corner of the drawer. In Erthwhile's unmistakable scrawl, it said "Key on monitor."

Eren looked up at the bulky computer monitor but couldn't see a key. All he found was another Post-it note, this time reading "Cactus."

Eren almost laughed as he realized that this was Erthwhile's version of enhanced security. He reached across the desk and picked up the small potted cactus in the corner. Just below a layer of soil was the key.

Eren unlocked the drawer and opened it. Piles of books were in there—big luxury embossed books. Most of them were yearbooks, dating back as far as 1985. But under them all, he found what he was looking for. A large leather book with "Alumni" embossed on it in gold lettering.

Eren opened it, flipping through the pages of staff. He saw Miss Rain smiling out at him and next to her, he saw the kind face of Mr. Jefferies. He looked so alive. But now he was dead. He turned the page quickly, and finally found the Cleaning Staff section. No one was smiling here, just a bunch of older women looking stern and very unhappy about having their photo taken. They were all women, not a man amongst them. Eren turned over the page, but saw that that was the only page for cleaning staff. The man wasn't there. He wasn't there.

Eren calmed down. He decided to go through the entire book, looking at every picture. He realized for the first time that he almost wanted to see the man. Because the alternative would be horrifying. He looked through the entire book, but he wasn't there.

Eren shut the book and put his head in his hands. Who was that man? How could he be there, in the hall, when he had walked past. Was this man the murderer? It was the only lead he had.

Eren put the book back in the drawer, locked it and replaced the key in the cactus. He didn't know what to think anymore. This was too real.

He looked up and almost jumped out of his skin. Miss Rain was in the doorway, watching him.

Miss Rain was nice—she didn't even really ask what Eren had been doing. She said that all the teachers were worried about him. He'd been acting distant, not been working very well. That was mostly because he had been drawing diagrams of the Maths room and thinking about how someone could stage a murder to look like a suicide, but Eren didn't tell her that.

"I understand, Eren. It's horrible. It really is. And no one would blame you if you needed to take some more time off."

"No," Eren said firmly, "I can't just sit around and do nothing." He was talking about his investigation, but Miss Rain obviously took it to mean schoolwork.

She smiled sadly. "You're very strong and intelligent, Eren. More than most eleven-year-olds. You could achieve such great things."

Eren smiled at her, trying to ignore Morgan, who was standing outside the window, pulling funny faces.

"So this mystery man is our guy," Morgan said, at lunch.

It was a nice day and Eren and Morgan had walked all the way down to the far side of the field, where no one ever bothered to go, so they could have a conversation in peace.

"Maybe. Possibly," Eren said, thinking. He was thinking about what had happened after he screamed on that day. After he had reached the edge of his sanity and just howled. Who had come for him?

"What?"

"We have to consider…other possibilities."

"Other possibilities? What other possibilities? You see a mysterious guy on the day Mr. Jefferies is killed? That seems pretty good to me. He's our guy." Morgan was climbing the fence and stopped about halfway up, perching precariously on an iron bar. Eren was always impressed by Morgan's energy—he could never stay still.

"We need to look at every possible avenue. We don't want to make a mistake."

"Eren, if the police couldn't solve this, what makes you think we can? What are we actually doing? Even if this guy did kill Mr. Jefferies—or someone else, or whoever—what do we do then?"

"Then we go to the police. If we don't have concrete proof, they'll never believe us. It's just like you said, we're eleven. We can't even reach high shelves."

"Exactly," Morgan said, jumping off the fence and stumbling

on the landing. He put his arms out anyway, like the gymnasts you saw on TV. "We're eleven. We can't figure this out."

"Why not?" Eren said. "Eleven-year-olds solving a murder. Maybe we'd be the first."

"It sounds great, Eren. But can we do it?"

Eren thought for a long time. "I have to try."

"Okay, so what now?"

"We have to get into the Maths room."

"More rooms, huh?"

Eren and Morgan stayed behind after school, pretending to study in the library. They waited until five o'clock, when they made their way down the quiet corridors toward the Maths department.

They found the door to Mr. Jefferies's classroom closed—a wrapping of police tape around it. POLICE LINE—DO NOT CROSS.

"I heard the head talking," Morgan said. "They're just keeping the tape there to stop kids wandering in. The police are long gone."

Eren nodded. He looked at the door, suddenly unable to move.

Morgan nudged him. "C'mon, it's just a room."

"I know, it's just…" Eren trailed off, not knowing what it was just.

Morgan pushed the handle. The door creaked open wide of its own free will, revealing the perfect classroom behind. Someone had tidied up, of course. The chairs and tables were all set out in an immaculate symmetrical pattern. It was all ready for learning.

Morgan ducked under the tape and walked into the room. He stopped in the center, right under the exposed pipe, and looked back.

Eren was watching wide-eyed.

"Come on then," Morgan said, and seeing Eren's horrified face looked up to the pipe. He sidestepped quickly. Eren shook himself out of his paralysis and ducked under the tape. He shivered as he entered the room. It was as cold as it had been on that day. Someone had left the window open again.

"So what are we looking for?" Morgan said, picking up an exercise book that had been left on one of the desks and flipping through it.

Eren looked around. It was like nothing had ever happened in here. No one had died. No one had even lived. There was no hint that Mr. Jefferies had ever been here at all. His desk was scrubbed of any character.

Eren walked around it and expected to see the framed photo of his dog, or the weathered copy of *The Catcher in the Rye*. People used to ask him why he had become a Maths teacher if he loved books so much. Eren remembered his answer word for word.

"Maths is mechanics. You can work at it and get better, until you are the greatest mathematician to ever live. To write like Salinger is a gift, a gift you cannot teach, and one which I sadly do not possess."

It wasn't there. The book wasn't there. It was always there, at the end of the desk, perfectly lined up to the edges. But it wasn't there. It became imperative that Eren found it. Why would someone take it? Why was it not where it belonged?

Eren yanked open the desk drawers. They were all empty. There was nothing left. There was nothing of him. He slammed them shut.

"Careful," Morgan said, stepping toward Eren, "we don't want to make too much noise."

Eren's eyes were filling up with tears, and he didn't think he could stop them this time. He buried his head in the sleeves of his school sweater. "He's gone, Morgan. They got rid of him. All of them. All the grown-ups."

"Turn around, Eren."

"It's like he never even existed."

"Eren, turn around."

"He's gone. He's all gone."

"Eren," Morgan said, in a sharp whisper, "he's not gone, not quite."

Eren finally heard his friend, looking up from his sleeves. He looked around.

Although the room was spotless, the whiteboard had remained untouched. It seemed whoever had cleaned the room had not been able to wipe away the last things Mr. Jefferies ever did. Eren saw the equations that his class had been working on, Mr. Jefferies's convoluted explanation of Pythagoras, and in the upper right corner his name, which he had written the very first day they had met him and never erased. Eren looked at it and smiled sadly. It was almost like a mural to the forgotten.

Morgan stood next to Eren as they both looked at the diagrams and the numbers.

"I still don't bloody understand it," Morgan said, and started laughing.

Eren laughed too, as his eyes scanned the equations. His eyes fell to the bottom left corner of the board where, in Mr. Jefferies's scrawl, there was a three-digit number.

"Wait," Eren said, "what's that?" He pointed to the number. 391.

"That?" Morgan said, confused. "It's just a number, Eren."

"But it's not got anything to do with the other stuff. It's not connected at all."

"It's a number. He was a Maths teacher."

"Do you remember him writing this in the lesson?" Eren said, examining the number closer.

Morgan chuckled and threw his arms up at the whole board. "I don't remember him writing any of this. I wasn't paying attention."

"I don't remember him writing this," Eren said, taking a step back and looking behind him at where he was sitting in that lesson. "And it's in the bottom corner. None of us could've seen it."

"So he didn't write it in the lesson. So it was already there. Or so it wasn't. Eren, you're starting to sound a little crazy."

Eren rounded on him, suddenly angry. "What if this is Mr. Jefferies's last message? What if it's a clue to who murdered him?"

"Seriously?" Morgan said, reverting to harsh whispers as the boys heard someone pass the room. The footsteps didn't stop and then they were gone. "So Mr. Jefferies's last words were 391. Three, nine, one. What does that even mean? It means nothing, Eren. And no one would ever think it did. You have to stop obsessing over this."

"No. No, I don't," Eren said, feeling the prick of tears in his eyes again. "Everyone else needs to start obsessing over it. Someone killed Mr. Jefferies and they're going to get away with it."

Morgan was silent for a moment and stepped back from Eren shaking his head. "I thought maybe being in here would help you."

"What are you talking about?"

"He killed himself, Eren. Mr. Jefferies killed himself and he left the rest of us behind. He is not coming back. We just need to forget him." Morgan was stone-faced, but Eren could read the sadness on his face.

Eren saw red. "You don't believe me. You've never believed me. You're just like everyone else. You're an idiot." Before he could stop himself, Eren pushed Morgan hard. The boy fell back into a desk, and took a moment to regain his composure.

He went to his backpack, unzipped it and pulled out something. He held it up to Eren.

It was a photo. A photo of the man—the man Eren had seen that day cleaning the hall floor.

"Is this him?" Morgan said.

Eren couldn't talk, he couldn't manage a word.

"I saw him the other day in the PE department. His name's Martin. He's the new caretaker."

He threw the photo at Eren. It bounced off his chest and fell on the floor. The man's face stared up at Eren. He couldn't take his eyes from it.

Morgan picked up his bag and slung it over his shoulder. He went to leave and then turned back, looking at Eren with a seething anger in his eyes. "You know what, I am an idiot. And so are you. We're kids. We're allowed to be."

Morgan left.

Eren fell to his knees, picking up the photo. He looked at it and he cried—he didn't know for how long.

43

1992

The investigation, as short-lived as it was, was officially over. Eren and Morgan kept their distance from each other. Morgan didn't even look at him. Eren felt as though the only friend he had had betrayed him. No one believed him and maybe he didn't even believe himself anymore. After all, he had no suspects—not now. He started to believe that maybe Mr. Jefferies was just a sad, sad man who couldn't think of anything else to do but kill himself. Eren threw himself into his schoolwork, having a lot to catch up on, since he had spent all his free time on an investigation that went nowhere. He felt stupid, he felt embarrassed.

He didn't talk to anyone at school. From afar, he watched Morgan's new scheme to get famous. The boy had started a band. All the other kids and teachers carried on as normal, like nothing had ever happened.

The school and Eren's father agreed that Eren should go to see a therapist, which he did without any argument. He talked more in the sessions than he did anywhere else, but he never brought up what he thought had happened to Mr. Jefferies. He actually liked his therapist a lot—a young man called Simon who the school had recommended. It was funny—the tricks he pulled to make Eren explore himself. Eren often looked back on the sessions fondly.

Christmas went by without much consequence. Eren sat at a table with his father, his aunt's family and his grandmother. He laughed and joked with his cousins, who were his age. There was still nothing from Morgan, and Eren began to be glad. Maybe this was just a fresh start. He had extra helpings of turkey and sprouts. He liked sprouts.

1993 came around and Eren and his father ate chips on the beach, watching the New Year wake up. It was bitterly cold and the sea lapped against the sand like water on velvet. They walked five miles, tracing the coastline.

At the end of January, Eren started working a paper route. It had been a freezing month, and he trod out in the snow every morning and delivered people's papers. He had fifty-five papers on his route. He passed the time thinking to himself.

He never thought of *that* anymore. Simon said that the mind was a magical thing and although it hurt now, there would be a time when he didn't have to actively *not* think about it. *He would just forget?* Not really, it would always be there, but for all intents and purposes, day to day he would forget.

And he was starting to feel like maybe he could carry on. The rest of the world was, so why couldn't he? The morning sun in the January air was so strong, why couldn't it wipe away the past? That was why, when he went into the newsagents on the first Saturday in February, he was shocked when Mr. Perkins told him he had a new house to deliver to. He knew the address well. It was Mr. Jefferies's old house.

Eren didn't think much of it as he went on his round, but when he rounded the corner to Mr. Jefferies's house, he found that his legs had grown heavier. Every step he took toward the house was slow and lumbering. He had to fight himself to get there, and after he had put the newspaper through the letter box, he just stood there and looked at the house sadly.

There was a sharp sound at the door, as the newspaper got pulled through the letter box. A dog barked and an elderly lady shushed it. Before Eren could turn away, she had opened the door.

"Hello, dear," she said, not appearing the slightest bit confused as to why he was standing there in the snow.

"Sorry, ma'am," Eren said, "I… I just used to know someone who lived in this house. My teacher."

The old woman smiled at him. "You mean George?"

Eren was taken aback. "Um…yes, ma'am. Sorry, but how do you know him?"

"Oh, poor child, I'm his sodding mother," the old woman said, laughing as a cocker spaniel poked its head around the doorframe with the bundled-up newspaper in its chops. "Come on, you'd better come in for a nice cup of tea. You look like you're much about to catch your death."

"I really can't, ma'am. I've got more papers." He nodded to his sack full of undelivered newspapers.

The old woman shook her head. "Nonsense. No one ever missed a bit of bad news. They can wait for their papers."

And before Eren knew it, he was ushered into the small house. It smelled odd—not unpleasant but strange and the place looked like a traditional old person's house. It was very compact and there was a putrid red carpet running throughout the place. Eren spotted a tiny kitchen branching off from the living room—the sideboards cluttered with things all stacked on top of each other. The living room was equally small, with two hideous brown fabric sofas and a chair. Eren perched on one of the sofas, putting his bag down. *What am I doing here?*

"There you go," the old woman said. "So a tea yes?"

"I don't drink tea, ma'am," Eren said, apologetically.

The woman laughed and went into the kitchen. "You will," she said.

Eren looked around the room. It was hard to believe that Mr. Jefferies used to live here. It all looked so—old. He stared at his reflection in the small television. He looked uncomfortable. Most likely because he was. He couldn't meet his own eyes, so looked down to the glass coffee table. There were a few gossip magazines, along with a paper with an unfinished crossword.

The clock was very loud.

A few minutes later, the old woman came back. She carried one cup and saucer very shakily, handing it to Eren. The tan liquid slopped over the side as it changed hands and pooled in the saucer. Eren smiled at her as she went back into the kitchen to get her own.

"What did you say your name was, my dear?" she said as she came back, and slowly lowered herself into the armchair.

Eren's mouth worked faster than his brain. "Morgan Sheppard," he said. If this was Mr. Jefferies's mother, it was possible that she knew Eren's name. It wasn't likely, but Eren was already uncomfortable enough—he didn't want her knowing he was the one who found her son.

"Morgan. Now that's a nice name. And you were George's student?" the old woman asked, raising the cup to her lips and slurping.

"Yes. I was in his Maths class. I… I just want to say how sorry I am, about everything."

The woman put the cup down on the table and smiled at him. "We can't change what happened, dear. It's no one's fault—let alone yours. I'm sure it's harder for you than anyone else. I mean, all you children. To be faced with something like that at your age. How old are you, dear?"

"Eleven," Eren said, taking a sip from the cup, swallowing and then promptly putting the cup down reminding himself never to touch it again. He coughed. "Twelve in two months."

"You're just a baby," the old woman said, and her voice cracked with sadness. "Oh dear, what a mess. But we all must carry on. That's all there is to do."

"Do you mind if I ask a question?" Eren said.

"No, dear. You must have so many."

Eren spoke slowly, picking his words very carefully. "Do you... Do you know why Mr. Je—George—did what he did?"

The woman pursed her lips and picked up her cup again. "None of us can really know, dear. That's the curse—the curse of the ones left behind. I can tell you why I think he did it. I think he did it because he saw no other way out. There're two types of people in this world and you don't know what type you are until it's too late."

"Two types of people?"

"Yes. Say you're running through the forest. It's dark and you don't know exactly where you are. All you know is you're far from home, far from everyone you've ever loved. And you're running. You're running because things are chasing you. The most ferocious and hideous monsters you can think of are right behind you. So you run. You run and run because you won't let them get you. The trees start to thin and suddenly, you find yourself at the edge of the forest. You come to a rise and beyond it, you find you are at the peak of a cliff. You turn back but the monsters are coming out of the tree line. You are cornered. There is no way past them. You look down and hundreds of feet below you are jagged rocks and the unkempt sea. The monsters are creeping up on you slowly but they are gaining ground. You have two clear choices placed in front of you—you submit, let the monsters get you and do whatever they want with you or you jump off the cliff, giving yourself to the rocks and the sea."

"And Mr. Jefferies jumped?"

The woman looked at him, with her old eyes. He thought she was about to cry. But then she snapped out of it and slurped at her tea again. "Yes. George jumped. Figuratively, of course. That was a metaphor—you know about metaphors?"

"Yes. Saying something *is* something else."

"Yes, you are a smart child. George taught you well."

Eren didn't remind her that Mr. Jefferies taught Maths and it was in fact another teacher who had taught him about metaphors.

"George had monsters?"

The woman chuckled, an almost entirely humorless sound but still kindly. "We all have monsters, dear. Even me. Even you. There's always something chasing us in the forest, even if we don't want to admit it. But to answer your question, yes, George had monsters. They just caught up with him."

"What were they?" Eren saw the old woman physically recoil. "I'm sorry if that's rude," he said quickly, "but I think I need to know why. I just need to know why someone would do that."

The old woman settled back into her chair and looked at him. "I forget what it's like to be eleven. I've lived your life eight times over. There's a thought. I was once inquisitive. Life'll beat it out of you though.

"The truth was, George was always a very lonely man. He lived here with me his whole life. He kept saying that it was be-cause he wanted to look after me, wanted to make sure I had a good life. Along the way, he forgot to have his own. He never had any partners. He used to say that he didn't need anyone, but I could see the loneliness in his eyes—always there.

"He loved his job. He had always wanted to be a teacher. He put everything into his work. When he came home, he did all his marking and then watched sports. That's how it started, you see. He started to bet on all kinds of sport—football, rugby, cricket. He didn't even know how cricket worked, but he still bet on it. And then there were the horses. He went down the betting shop of a Sunday. That was where he fell in with the wrong crowd. Before long, he was betting too much. Addiction, dear, is a cancer, but it's a cancer that tricks you into thinking you want it. I tried to talk George around, but the addiction talked back.

"He borrowed money—money from the wrong people—thinking he would make it back. But of course he didn't. He lost it. He lost it all. People started coming round, to this house. Unsavory types, you know. People who looked like they were right out of the movies—shady people. They threatened George, they manhandled him and I couldn't do a thing. There was one man who came around a lot—he used to be as nice as nice could be with me. I even thought he might be different from the rest of them. But one night when it was very late, I heard him come over and assault my George. George wouldn't do anything of course, and I'm not stupid, I knew that something had to be done, but done in the right way.

"The next time this man came round, I had George sitting at the table with me. I told this man to sit down and we would civilly talk things out. He sat down, but he didn't seem happy about it. Neither of them did. And I said, 'Now look, George, Martin, you have to sort this out—'"

Eren froze. He suddenly had shivers down his spine. It took him a moment to realize why but when he focused, it came down on him like an anvil. The woman was still talking, but he couldn't hear her anymore. What had she said—? She couldn't have—?

"I'm sorry, ma'am." He wrenched the words out of him through tingling lips. "What did you say this man's name was?"

"What? Oh, um, Martin. Yes. I thought he was a nice boy, different from the rest of them. Turns out he was the worst of the lot though."

Eren's head swam. The man. The man cleaning the floor, with that stupid machine. The man in the caretaker uniform. The new caretaker. Martin.

Before he knew it, he was standing. The old woman was still talking. "I have to go," he interrupted.

The old woman looked at him, confused. "Alright then, dear, it was nice to meet you."

Eren was out of the room and down the short hall, before she could even get up.

"Please come back anytime," she called after him. "Morgan is such a nice name."

And he was out the door, slinging his coat on as the cold bit at him.

He made it around the corner before he vomited into the snow.

Eren found Morgan in the main hall at lunch. He was onstage with his band, a mismatched group of kids who had no business being anywhere. There was a fat boy on guitar, and a nerdy-looking girl on drums. Morgan, of course, was the lead singer.

They had just been making a terrible racket, but Morgan stopped them. He walked over to the fat kid with the guitar in his podgy hands.

"Eric, you were totally off."

"Sorry, Morgan," Eric said nasally.

"You remember how it goes right?"

"I think so."

"Okay, I'm sorry, Eric, but I think you might actually have to learn how to play guitar."

"Do I have to?" Eric said.

"I'm sorry, mate. You should have picked drums. You just hit them and it's fine." Morgan turned his attention to the girl on drums, and gave her a wink. "You're doing fabulous, Clarice."

Eren cleared his throat. Morgan and the others looked around. Morgan grimaced when he saw it was Eren. Eren had expected as much.

Morgan seemed to resign himself to it and clapped his hands. "Okay, take five. That's five minutes, not five chocolate bars, Eric."

The other two mumbled and grumbled and made their way offstage into the wings. Morgan jumped down from the stage and walked up to Eren.

"Well, it's Eren," he said, looking him up and down.

"Yes," Eren said.

"You like my band? This is going to take me straight to the top. We're going to be the next big thing. We're called The Future in Italics."

"You mean *The Future*?"

"No, I mean The Future in Italics," Morgan said, like it was the most obvious thing in the world. "You need an edgy band name if you're going to go places. Edgy like Blur…or ABBA. Actually, maybe not ABBA…or Blur now I think about it."

Eren smiled, and was surprised to find it was genuine. He'd forgotten how much he'd missed Morgan's schemes, and just the boy in general.

"What'd you want?" Morgan said. "As you can see, I'm super-busy."

"I need to talk to you," said Eren and he quickly relayed what he'd learned from Mr. Jefferies's mother. To his surprise, Morgan was actually intrigued by it, but he was still skeptical.

"I thought you'd forgotten all this, Eren."

"But you have to admit it's weird."

"Martin's a common name."

"But that guy was there. That day. That Martin."

Morgan scratched the back of his neck. "Yeah, I suppose it's a bit weird."

Eren smiled. "I just need you one last time. And then if I'm wrong, I'll drop the whole entire thing forever. I'll accept it and move on. But we just need to do one thing. One last thing."

Morgan looked around at the stage with all his band equipment. He looked back at Eren.

"Okay."

The plan was simple—watch for Martin when he left school and follow him home. There, there had to be some incriminating evidence proving that he'd killed Mr. Jefferies. Eren hadn't even considered the possibility that he didn't have any. There must be something linking him to the murder. Eren was more confident than ever that he had found the man who'd done the deed, and with Morgan's help, he could finally catch him.

Morgan didn't seem quite so convinced, but he was excited to break into someone's house. Maybe a little too excited.

They were in Eren's room the night before they planned to follow Martin. Morgan was playing SNES, while Eren was rummaging around under his bed.

"I know I saw them around here somewhere," Eren said. He was looking for a pair of walkie-talkies that his aunt had got him for Christmas. At the time, he hadn't really thought much of them—he'd had no one to call—but now they seemed essential. What was a tailing mission without the right tech?

"Have you checked in the cupboard?" Morgan said, with no attempt to actually help his friend.

"Yeah," Eren said, sliding out from under the bed and slumping down on it. "I think they might be in the attic." Eren watched Morgan play Mario until he heard his father go out to the pub. He always did on a Thursday night, every week since his mother had died. Eight o'clock on the dot.

"Morgan, come on, I need help."

Morgan moaned all the way to the garage as Eren enlisted

him in helping to carry the ladder up the stairs. Five minutes and a few future bruises later, Eren propped the ladder on the landing in front of the attic hatch.

He went into his father's room and found two flashlights in his tool cupboard. He threw one to Morgan. "The walkie-talkies should be in a blue plastic box."

Morgan smiled. "Right you are, guv'nur." He raised his hand in a little salute.

Eren laughed. He had definitely missed Morgan's special brand of immaturity.

Eren climbed the ladder and pushed on the attic hatch until it gave way. The attic was pitch-black, and Eren shone his flashlight inside. A shaft of light etched out a few boxes near the hatch, as though they were only there when the flashlight was on. There was no blue box nearby. He looked down to Morgan.

"I'm going to have to go up there. You stay here and hold the ladder."

Morgan laughed. "You really think I'm going to stay down here, while you have the time of your life up there?"

"It's just an attic, Morgan."

But Morgan followed him up into the attic anyway. The ladder was not quite tall enough for Eren to easily get up. He had to push hard with his elbows to fling the rest of him inside. He helped Morgan up into the attic.

The two beams of light explored the room as Morgan and Eren looked around. The attic was incredibly cluttered, with piles upon piles of cardboard removal boxes stacked on top of each other. Eren had no idea that his father and he had so much stuff, and he couldn't see his blue box anywhere. He walked over to a mound of boxes, careful to pick his way over the wooden beams.

Morgan's flashlight lay on a clutter of loose items. He went over to a big monitor and started poking at it. "Whoa, computer monitors are tiny now compared to this monster."

Eren ignored him, putting the flashlight in his mouth as he shifted boxes over in his great pile to see what was behind them. There he found the blue box, depressingly, at the bottom of the biggest pile of boxes he had ever seen.

As Morgan looked around, his flashlight dancing around on the edges of Eren's vision, Eren started to shuffle boxes around so he could get to the pile he wanted. It took him ten minutes to finally lift all the boxes down and get to his blue box. He breathed out with exhaustion—his arms ached with the ghost of how they would feel in the morning. He opened the lid and there was the pack of two walkie-talkies still in their impenetrable plastic womb. Eren picked them up, and expected some sort of fanfare for all the trouble he'd gone to. Instead he got one word.

"Eren."

Morgan's voice, but not like before, not excited or enthusiastic. It almost sounded...worried.

Eren looked around, but Morgan was nowhere to be seen. There was a crest of light coming from over a sea of boxes.

"Eren, come here."

Eren started to pick his way around the attic, getting worried himself, until he found Morgan at the very back of the dark space, with his flashlight fixed on an old wooden chest.

"What?" Eren said, trying to laugh it off.

Morgan looked at him and then looked back at the chest.

Eren looked too.

The chest looked old and rather rickety. Painted across the front of the chest in chipped and weathered letters was the name "Lillith."

"That's your mother's name, right?" Morgan said.

Eren nodded silently. He had never seen this chest before,

didn't even know it existed. His father had never told him about it, but had in fact said that all his mother's things had been left behind when they moved. His father said all the things were just too heartbreaking so he got rid of them. But here was something. A chest with his mother's name on it.

Eren kneeled in front of the chest, running his hands over the top. Just touching it made him think of her, her warm touch, her soft hugs. It made him feel closer to her, this wooden thing he didn't even know was here. He remembered the day she left, walked out of the house. She said she'd be back—she never was. Not that she could've known. Not that she could've predicted that car would barrel off the road and hit her. They said she had died almost instantly. His father comforted himself with the *instantly*, but Eren horrified himself with the *almost*.

Now, in the darkness of the attic, illuminated by Morgan's flashlight as well as his own, he felt more like a child than he ever had. A child who just wanted his mother.

He went to open the chest, but the lid was stuck. He moved his flashlight along the seam of the lid to find a padlock.

There was no keyhole, but instead three tumblers with the digits 0 to 9. He sighed.

"It's locked," he said, looking past the flashlight beam to where he thought Morgan's face was. "A three-digit number."

"Can we just guess it? Or try every combination?" Morgan said. Eren knew he was trying to be helpful, but that didn't offset how dumb it sounded.

"Three numbers. Ten digits on each. That's a thousand combinations."

"Whoa," Morgan said, briefly moving the flashlight to his face to show his impressed look. "How did you do that?"

Eren sighed. "We literally did that in Maths this morning."

"Oh, I—"

"—wasn't listening," Eren finished. "Yeah, no surprise there."

He waved his flashlight around. "There must be something around here we can use to break the lock." He got up and went over to the pile of stuff that Morgan had been looking in previously.

"But if we break it open, your dad'll know we've been up here," Morgan said.

"I don't care." Eren moved the bulky monitor aside, looking for something sharp and strong.

"But maybe it's not something you should see. Maybe he kept it from you for a reason."

"I don't care," Eren shouted, rounding on Morgan, pointing the flashlight in his face so it made his eyes squint. "This is my mother's. And I'm her son. And I deserve to know what's in here."

"Okay, okay," Morgan said, pushing Eren's flashlight down. "It would just be easier if we knew the three-digit number. I mean, maybe your father wrote it down somewhere. I have to write stuff down or else I forget it."

"Write it down?" Eren said, something in his brain clicking into gear.

"Yeah. Like passwords for SNES and stuff."

Eren rushed back to the chest. He kneeled down in front of it again and fiddled with the padlock. "Shine the light here again."

Morgan did.

Eren moved the tumblers quickly. It couldn't be—? This couldn't work. It made no sense. But it was the only three-digit number in his head. He finished. The padlock clicked open.

Morgan looked confused. "What the—? Did you just—?"

"Think, Morgan. You have to write stuff down to remember it. What's the only three-digit number we've seen out of place these past few months?"

"I don't know what you're talking about."

"Yes you do. 391. On the board. In Mr. Jefferies's classroom. The code for this padlock was 391."

"Wait, what?" Morgan said. "That doesn't make any sense. Why would a code for a chest in your attic be on Mr. Jefferies's board?"

"I don't know," Eren said, touching the lid of the chest as a tingle prickled his spine. "I don't know."

Eren remained motionless, feeling the edges of the chest lid with his fingers. What was this? How could this even be possible? This couldn't be a coincidence.

A thousand combinations and it just so happened to be that one. That one number written on the board by his dead teacher— the answers to all the questions swarming around in his head must be inside this chest, which was why he couldn't open it.

A shuffling beside him. Morgan sat next to him and put his hands on the lid too. He started to open the chest, and Eren found himself pushing too. The chest opened, the lid springing back. Inside was darkness.

The two children shone their flashlights into the box, at first afraid that it was completely empty. But the chest was not. It was about half full with scraps of paper all bundled together with paperclips. There were also a few photos of Eren's mother, smiling out at them.

Eren picked up one of the bundles of papers and took off the paperclip. He looked through them slowly. They were letters from his mother to his father. They were love letters. They all started *My love* and were signed *Your Lillith*. They were long, all over a page and some spanning two or three. They talked of how much his mother loved his father, detailing their encounters in minute detail.

Do you remember the café on the lake? one read. *We fed the ducks, and ate carrot cake until the sun set behind the trees. I don't think I've ever been as happy as you make me. When I'm with you, my soul is peaceful. Life is drowned out with how much I love you. Why do I have to keep you secret? I hide our love in a chest in the attic. The combination is the room number of the hotel we stayed in that first night, you remember—you can't not.*

Eren blushed, and he put up his hand to mask his face from Morgan even though it was probably indecipherable in the dark of the attic. He felt like he was intruding on something private, but he couldn't stop himself. He had never felt that his mother and father shared this level of affection although they must have at some point.

He shuffled the letters and read another.

My love, how much this mundane existence can be ignited by just the mere chance of meeting you. My life would be so boring if not for you, and I know I have made some choices I am not proud of. If only we could be together. But one day, we will be. We'll be together forever. I promise I will do it soon.

This one seemed odd. Do what? What choices? He scanned the rest of the letter, but there was nothing more of any interest. He went on to the next.

My love, I'm sorry. I just need more time. Please you have to allow me time. I'm stuck, I'm stuck in this place and I don't know how to get out. But knowing you are there at the end of the road is what will give me the strength to break out. I promise you, I will tell him soon.

Eren's stomach knotted, although he didn't know quite why. This letter was strange, weirdly urgent. And what was his mother talking about? He read the rest and came to the bottom of the page. She signed off in her usual way, but added a PS.

Your Lillith. P.S. I have included our photo overleaf. Look how happy we are, let's be this happy forever.

Eren saw a little sketched arrow in the corner of the page and he turned the paper over. Paper-clipped to the top of the page was the photo.

Eren dropped the letter in plain shock and scampered backwards, hitting a pile of boxes so the top one fell off causing a small avalanche of boxes.

Morgan looked up from some of the letters and looked at Eren. "What?"

Eren was too busy processing what he'd seen in the photo. And now things were slotting into place. Things were becoming clear—for the first time in a long time. For the first time in forever.

That feeling he had had on that day, that terrible day when he had found Mr. Jefferies—that feeling that he had missed something, an important detail. He thought it had been the caretaker. He really thought it had been the caretaker. But it hadn't been, not at all. He had spent the last few months chasing the wrong man.

Morgan picked up the letter with the photo on it and shone his light at it. His face dropped, his trademark smugness falling away. "Oh," was all he could say. "What the hell does this mean?"

He turned the photo to Eren and Eren saw it again. A photo taken in a park, by a pond. His mother smiling, looking happier than she ever had when she was at home. And with his arm around her, smiling too, was Mr. Jefferies.

It was so simple. What he had been missing. But sometimes

the simplest things were the things that got lost. He'd been walking home when he realized he'd forgotten his notebook, so he went back to school, back to the Maths room where he found Mr. Jefferies hanging from the ceiling. Miss Rain took him to the staff room where he cried and cried. And then his father came in. His father, who said he had been waiting for him outside. But his father wasn't meant to be picking him up. Eren was walking home.

391. His mother's chest where she hid her love for Mr. Jefferies. The number on the board was Mr. Jefferies's last clue. The number was his final declaration—to get justice.

Silent tears fell down Eren's face.

Morgan looked at him. "Eren, what does this mean?" The boy was almost pleading.

Eren opened his mouth and only a raw cry of anguish came out. It was all so simple. So real. "I don't think Martin killed Mr. Jefferies," he said, amidst sobs, "because my father did."

"I still don't understand," Morgan said. They were still in the attic and both of them had been quiet for a very long time.

"My father," Eren said, his voice devoid of any emotion, as though he were answering a question in class, "my father killed Mr. Jefferies."

"But how do you know that?"

"He was there, that day. But he shouldn't have been. That's what I'd been missing. It was nothing to do with the caretaker, but someone else who was there that shouldn't have been. My father."

"But surely there's some other explanation for all this," Morgan said, staring at the photo as though trying to find another secret that wasn't there.

"My mother was in love with Mr. Jefferies, this is their chest. The code, Morgan, the code on the board."

"What does this mean, look?" Morgan said, holding up the letter with the photo. *"See you on the 24th?"*

But Eren didn't even need to hear it. He had worked it out. He was clever. He was cleverer than anyone knew. Mr. Jefferies, his father, his mother, even Morgan. They didn't know. Because it was all laid out in front of him. And he knew with a burning certainty that his father killed his teacher.

"My father told me what happened. She said she was going to a conference at Bank in the City. I kinda remember it—I remember my father was annoyed and they fought about it. It was Sunday 24th October."

Eren looked at him. The world was warped and wrangled through his tears. He thought it might never look right again.

"She wasn't going to a conference. She was going to see him. And that was how she died. Got run over by a car, while going to him."

Eren wiped his eyes and sniffed.

Morgan looked down at the picture again. "But..."

Eren gathered together all the papers on the attic floor, suddenly spurting into life. He threw them back into the chest and snatched the piece of paper out of Morgan's hand. He took one last look at the smiling faces of Jefferies and his mother and threw that in the chest as well.

Morgan got up. "Eren, I..."

"Shut up."

"Did he really do this?"

"The window was open wide. The Maths room window. He could have easily got out, snuck around to the car and waited there."

"How did the police not find out?"

"I don't know," Eren said, hating how his voice sounded as it came out. He sounded...broken.

"But the police are supposed to know everything?"

"I don't know. It all lined up. He was a sad man. He had problems. It looked like he killed himself." Eren shut the lid of the chest. It felt more final than it should have. It felt like the whole world had been contained in that chest, and he was trapping it. His father's guilt, all locked up.

Eren replaced the padlock, spinning the numbers around to some random combination. After that, he made his way downstairs like a zombie, not really understanding what he was doing.

Before he knew it, he was back in his room. He threw the flashlight down and sat, leaning against the bed. Burying his head in his knees, he cried. He cried and cried for his mother, for Mr. Jefferies, for his father and for himself.

When he finally looked up, the light in the room had dimmed. It was dark out and Morgan was sitting in his desk chair staring at him.

"He killed Mr. Jefferies," Eren said, somewhere between a statement and a question.

Eren sat with his head in his hands. The revelation hung in the air—he could feel it. His own father—a murderer. He knew it was true, but willed it not to be. His father wrapping that belt around Mr. Jefferies's neck, stringing him up on the pipe in the middle of the room, disappearing out the window. His own father.

"Imagine how famous we're going to be," Morgan said, softly.

Eren looked at him. "What?"

"I mean, your own dad. We're going to be famous, Eren, the talk of the city. The Kid Detectives."

"What the hell are you saying?" Eren said.

"We solved the murder. That's what it was all about, right, finding out who killed Mr. Jefferies and getting famous?"

Eren found another emotion nestled amongst the despair, a white-hot rage. "What the hell are you saying?" he hissed.

"When we tell people, we'll be famous."

"What is wrong with you? I was doing this because it was the right thing to do."

"Oh." Morgan seemed genuinely surprised—like it had all been fun and games.

"I guess I knew that at the start, but after Christmas? I thought you were just doing it for the same reasons." And Eren saw the real Morgan for the first time. A horrible, vapid creature, so immature and careless. The kind of creature who would see the tearing apart of his friend's world as an opportunity. Morgan was not his friend.

"No one can know about this," Eren said, through clenched teeth.

"What?"

"No one can ever know what my father did."

"But, Eren…"

"No one. You understand? No one. My mother's gone. I can't lose my father too."

"But, Eren…"

And there it was—a moment. A moment Eren would remember for the rest of his life. He remembered how lonely he felt, how small he was in relation to everything else in the world, how far anger governed everything. He remembered his hot tears splash against the navy of his jeans creating dark blue spots, he remembered Morgan's childish face. But most of all he would come to remember the next five words out of the idiot's mouth.

"…I want to be famous."

Eren's vision crackled blood red, as he launched himself at his former friend. Morgan jumped out of the desk chair sending it careening backwards into the wall. Eren connected with the desk, banging his head and shrieking in pain.

Morgan looked down at him, dumbfounded, as he propped himself up with his arms.

"Get out," Eren said, in a voice that was not his own. Morgan looked down at him.

"Get out," he shouted, launching himself once again. Morgan ran out of the room and Eren slammed the door. He heard the boy rushing down the stairs and the front door bang.

Eren fell to his knees and wailed, a strange and painful sound. He crawled into his bed and put the covers over himself—protecting him. He lay there, as still as he could, the tears pooling on his cream-colored sheets.

Mr. Jefferies was dead and his father had killed him.

The evidence was all there, in the attic. Why had he done it? Because he blamed Jefferies for Eren's mother's death? How could his father do it? How could anyone do it? Kill someone? These past few months felt like an endless stream of questions.

"I'm sorry, Eren. I'm so sorry," his father had said that day. Now he knew what it really meant.

Over and over and over he had said it. At the time, he didn't know why—not really. But now he did. And he wished he didn't. He wished he had dropped the whole investigation thing. What was it all to achieve anyway? But he knew why. It was to prove that his teacher wouldn't have killed himself, to prove that the world wasn't a certain shade of dark. But now it was darker than ever.

As he lay there, he wondered how he was going to carry on. He wondered that if he tried really hard, if he willed it, he could just die, lying there in the warmth of his bed. If he wanted so much to die, could he will it so? Probably not, and anyway he knew that it was not to be. He had to carry on. He had to find some kind of strength, even if it felt like he couldn't. No one could know what he had found, least of all his father. He would put the information away, in his brain—lock it up and throw away the key. He would force himself to forget. His father was still his father because he had to be. For Eren to survive, he had to be.

He lay there for longer than seemed possible, his breathing becoming more regular, his tears drying. He was staring at his hands, thinking of them wrapping a belt around Mr. Jefferies's neck, tying it to the pipe in the ceiling. And after a while, he thought of his mother. He thought of how happy she looked with Jefferies, how kind she was. And with his mother's face in his mind, he found enough peace to lapse into a gentle sleep.

And at about 1:00 a.m., he heard the front door open and shut as his father returned.

He had bad dreams, so bad that he thought the sirens were in his head. But when he opened his eyes, they were still there. He sat up, the covers falling away from him. It was light in the room, the sun shining in through the window and stinging his eyes. He jumped up and looked out the window, and his stomach immediately turned.

The scene was abhorrent. Two police cars parked on the curb—two officers standing by the cars, talking to each other. Over the road, Eren's neighbors peered from their windows, watching. The old couple directly opposite had even come to the front door, not even disguising the fact they were being nosy.

Maybe it was something unrelated. Maybe this was just a co-incidence. But as the police officers reached into their respective cars to turn their sirens and lights off, he knew it couldn't be for anything else. They knew. And the police officers started walking down the drive to his house.

He panicked but couldn't move. He didn't know what was happening. The fog of sleep was still wrapped around him but he knew that his father was in trouble.

He watched out the window as the two police officers went to their door. Eren heard it open. His father's voice.

And then shouting. And then they had him. They cuffed him. What were they doing? They cuffed him and he tried to struggle, but one of the officers pinned him down on the grass.

More neighbors were coming out of their houses to see what was going on. He wanted to scream at them to go away. He didn't want them to see. But he was still frozen there. At the window.

The other police officer disappeared, and Eren heard him inside the house. What was happening? How—how was this happening? How did they know? How did they find out?

And as Eren heard the other police officer come up the stairs, taking each step one by one, the answer came to him, fully formed and crystal clear. Two words. One name.

Morgan Sheppard.

44

Sheppard took a breath—in and out. Curious—he shouldn't be doing that. Because he was dead. Breathing stopped when you were dead—that was how it worked. And there was no way he was still alive. He'd been blown up.

Although, he had to admit, it hadn't hurt a bit. Dying.

But it was meant to, right? It had to. But it hadn't.

And now he thought about it, something about that explosion sound had been strange too. It had been almost tinny, like it wasn't actually happening. Like it was being played through a speaker.

He opened his eyes. The room was still there. The same as it had always been. Mandy, Headphones, Ryan and Constance all still there—looking as confused as he felt.

Could they really be still alive? Was that possible? Or was death very similar to life? He held up a shaky hand and looked at his palm, just to check it was still there. It was—he was. He felt fine—better than fine. Alive.

He looked toward the bed. Toward the timer. It was flashing 00:00:00.

"What happened?" Ryan said, pale and small.

"It didn't work," Mandy said.

Nothing had happened. The explosion sound, the lights, they had both gone off at the exact moment the timer had hit zero. An illusion? The illusion of death?

Sheppard got to his feet, on legs that thought they were never going to stand again. Even the fact that he was still breathing air was joyous—a cause for celebration. But there would be time for that later. The explosion had failed—the horse mask man had finally shown his hand. They were alive. They were blissfully alive. And now, it was time to make a break for it.

They had been played—all of them.

"There was never going to be any explosion," Sheppard said, fighting back his sheer glee. "Mandy was right all along."

The others seemed to be two steps behind. Headphones's eyes were still shut. Constance was abnormally still. Ryan was staring at him with wide eyes. Mandy cleared her throat of sadness. "That this was all for television?"

"Yes," Sheppard said, "or no. Maybe not TV, maybe the internet or something like that. I'm betting this was all staged. I'm betting the horse man has been filming this entire thing. And now he's got what he wanted, we can leave."

"But what did he want?"

Sheppard looked into the corners of the room, seeing if he could see anything that looked like a camera. He knew the horse man was watching. It didn't take a leap in logic to think he was recording it. "He wanted to watch me squirm. He wanted to show the world I couldn't solve a murder. Well—" he threw his arms up "—you got me. You've done it. I don't care. I refuse to care. Whoever you are. Because now the bell's rung. And it's home-time."

Mandy got up and Ryan wasn't far behind. They both stepped around the bed as though wading through treacle.

"Has it stopped?" Mandy said.

"It's over," Ryan said.

Sheppard turned to them. "He got what he wanted. The ending he assumed. Reality 101, no one actually likes a happy ending. The horse man's story ended with us dying."

"But we didn't," Mandy said.

"It doesn't matter. It never did. In the narrative of the thing, we die and we fail. That's what the cameras got. Just a game."

"This still doesn't feel right," Ryan said taking a step back and observing the room.

Mandy looked from Ryan to Sheppard as if wondering who to believe. She seemed to settle on Sheppard and smiled. "Then what are we waiting for?"

Headphones got out from under the desk and joined them. Even behind them, Ahearn seemed to be happy—she sang some kind of upbeat hymn. Sheppard almost joined her.

Sheppard went to the door, followed by the others. It was all over. Finally. And how stupid of them all to go along with it anyway. A murder in a hotel room—a body in the bathtub. Blowing up the building. A setup—all an elaborate way of stringing them along. Sheppard fell for it—feared for his life and everyone else's. Exploding in a bout of fire. But what kind of work would that have been to orchestrate? Committing mass murder just to get back at one man? That would have been too much, no matter who the horse man was.

But Winter? Winter was dead. There was no doubt about that. Winter had died for what? A sham. A joke. Some things still didn't add up—but it was hard to think about them when there was an overwhelming feeling of relief. Once Sheppard got out of here, he would not rest until he found Winter's killer, but he had to get out first. Sheppard reached for the door handle. The light was green now. Just as he knew it would be. Go down the corridor, down to the lobby. Call the police. They had to know what was going on. And then get some fresh air, go outside and live. "Who's ready to go home?" he said, with more hope than he had ever felt.

There was a positive response behind him. Everyone. Sheppard depressed the handle.

He took a deep breath in and out. Still alive. And swung the door open.

To reveal a wall of concrete on the other side.

45

They were silent—not quiet, but completely and utterly silent, as though they had been frozen in place. On the other side of the hotel room was a wall of gray concrete. Nothing else. Directly on the other side. He didn't understand—couldn't wrap his head around it.

No.

"No," he said, out loud this time—breaking the silence. He reached out to touch the concrete. It was cold and rough against his fingers. It was real—very, very real. He pushed on it, hoping it might give way to something—but it didn't. It stayed strong and steadfast. "No, no, no, no, no, no, no, no." He hit the concrete with his fist and sharp pain erupted in his hand. "Ah…"

"What is this?" Mandy said—it seemed to be all she could manage. "How is this possible?"

"I told you," Ryan said. "I told you something wasn't right."

Mandy shook her head. "How is this in a hotel? Why would a fake door be in a hotel? Sheppard, please, what does this mean?"

"We're not in a hotel," Sheppard said. "Everything was made to trick us. To…keep us busy."

"But I saw the corridor. I saw the corridor in the peephole," Mandy said, questioning reality—questioning what was right in front of her.

Sheppard swung the door back and looked through the peephole. Surprisingly, he could see a hotel corridor, distorted and odd in the way a fisheye lens was. He looked away and looked back a few times just to make sure he wasn't seeing things. "It must be a small screen showing a corridor somewhere. The corridor is there—it just isn't here."

A small sound emanated from Headphones and she backed up.

"What is this?" Ryan said, angry this time. "You said the game was over."

"I thought it was." Sheppard touched the concrete again, searching for anything—any little bit of hope. But he didn't find any. The wall seemed strong and steadfast—no way there was another side.

"How is this in a hotel?" Mandy said again, as if they were all stuck in a bewildered time loop.

"We're not in a hotel," he said again, softer this time, and turned to Mandy and the others. "We never were. It's the phones." Mandy looked confused. "That's why he gave us them. He wanted to give us a clue. None of us got any signal even though we're high up in the center of London. Or at least we're supposed to be.

"And the vents. The vents didn't lead anywhere. Because there's nowhere else to go. Maybe everything we know was wrong. We were led down the garden path. Maybe we're not in London at all."

Mandy and Ryan looked at him, their faces looking more desperate.

"The timer," a voice behind them. Headphones. "The timer's restarting."

Sheppard's mind raced. "The thing Headp— The thing

Rhona saw in Winter's office. The whole reason she's here. The land deed. We're not in The Great Hotel. We're where…"

"Sheppard," Mandy said, touching his shoulder. He jumped, but gave her a sad smile. "Where are we?"

"We're where we've always been," he said. "Underground."

46

Underground. Trapped in a box. With a killer. Maybe with two killers.

"Underground?" Mandy said. "How is that possible? How can we be underground? London's out there." She pointed to the window. Constance Ahearn followed her finger and laughed.

Sheppard looked to the window as well. And went over to it. He gazed out of the glass. Central London at the peak of day. Nothing out of place. He could almost feel it—the city all around him. The electricity of being part of something bigger than you could possibly imagine. But it couldn't be real. And the closer Sheppard looked, the more he could see it. It was only very slight—you couldn't see it if you weren't looking for it—but the image looked grainy. Made up of pixels. The highest quality he had ever seen, but fake nonetheless. How had he done it? Sheppard looked down as much as he could. It really looked like he was looking down from a hotel room window. The perspective was perfect.

"I should have realized," Sheppard said, putting a hand on the window. He reached up to the edge of the window and ran his finger along the seam where the glass met the frame. "There were enough clues. He didn't even hide it sometimes. But I didn't get it. Of course I didn't. We never were in a hotel room."

"But…" Mandy started and Ryan put a hand on her shoulder to stop her.

"He's right. I didn't understand it until now, but…the toilet's locally plumbed in. It's not hooked up to a bigger pipe system like it would be in the hotel. I didn't think much of it at the time…but it all makes sense."

"This is insane. You two are insane," Mandy said.

"Insane, yes, but that doesn't mean wrong," Sheppard said, slapping the window when he couldn't find a way through. It gave a soft clink. "If this isn't a hotel window, I wonder if we can break it."

"Can someone please explain what is going on?" Mandy shouted.

And the familiar sound of feedback. A sound that he had heard once before in the room, but couldn't place it. He didn't remember until he heard the voice.

"Hello, everyone," the horse man said.

Sheppard wheeled around. Headphones jumped out of the way in surprise. They were all looking at the television, showing the same shot of the man wearing his horse mask.

Who is he? The horse mask, the horse man, C, the evil man. So many names—but none that count.

It looked like he hadn't moved for three hours, had probably been watching everything. No doubt enjoying the show. Making them think they were getting out, then flipping the script.

We're all in danger. More danger than we ever were before.

Now the killer knew there was no way out, what was to stop them killing again? Killing them all? Maybe the masked man wasn't the main enemy anymore.

"Where are we?" Sheppard said, stepping forward.

"You're underground, as you said. Exactly where really doesn't matter for your current predicament, does it?" the horse man said, in that familiar muffled voice.

"Why are you keeping us here? You've got what you wanted," Sheppard said, pointing to the corners of the room where he presumed the cameras were. "Your little game went exactly as you planned. I failed."

Mandy stepped forward, slightly unsure of herself. "We named everyone in the room. How did we fail exactly?"

The horse man shifted his never-ending gaze from left to right, plastic eyes glinting in the light—Sheppard to Mandy and back. "It's not enough just to name everyone. You could have done that at the start, for God's sake. You had to *know* who killed Simon Winter and why. Captivity seems to have made you all brain-dead. Maybe I should have done this experiment somewhere more airy, more public."

"Who killed Simon Winter?" Sheppard said.

The horse man laughed. "Well, I'm not going to tell you, am I? That's the whole point."

"The game is over. And I'm done with you. So just tell me."

The horse man seemed to actually consider it. "Hmmm. No. You see your problem at the moment, Morgan, is that you're not looking on the bright side. You're still alive, ergo you still have time to find out."

"What do you mean? You're not going to blow up somewhere underground. I doubt that you even ever planned to. What's the point in us cooperating now?"

"Because you haven't exactly found an exit, have you? And because for about three hours now, I've been pumping air into your little room—at great expense I might add. So about two minutes ago, I stopped."

Quiet—processing the information. "Wait…what?" Ryan said.

Unease settled over Sheppard again—control slipping away. "What do you mean?"

"I mean just that. I stopped. I cut off the air supply. If you look at the timer, it should be showing you your new countdown. Courtesy of the Great Fake Hotel."

Just as Headphones had said. Sheppard looked to the bedside table. The timer displaying a new number—counting down again. Twenty-four minutes.

"It should be somewhere around twenty-five minutes until there's no air left in the room. That's an extra twenty-five minutes. You should all be thanking me. Although after about fifteen minutes, areas of brain function will probably start to shut down, so…"

"Liar," Sheppard shouted at the television.

The horse man stopped. "You don't have to take my word for it. Just listen. I've been circulating air in the room for the past three hours—that makes a sound. That sound you thought was the air conditioning? Is it there anymore?"

Everyone was silent. Sheppard strained to hear—anything. But he couldn't.

"You're sealed up all tight now."

Mandy gave out a squeaking sound—suppressing a scream. Ryan looked like he was about to vomit, and Rhona clutched her headphones around her neck, as though for comfort. Only Constance seemed unperturbed.

Suffocating. Worse than being incinerated.

This had been part of the plan all along. Another step in breaking him down.

"You know, I think I'm done here," Sheppard said, saying the exact opposite of what he was thinking. Inside, he was wondering how to get out of this. He was still wondering who killed Winter. But even if he worked it out, who was to say the horse mask would let him go? Maybe this was all for naught. "Who are you?"

"You still haven't worked it out? Even after all this time, you still don't know. That's one of the reasons you're here in the first place. You've bewitched everyone—most of all yourself. That's exactly why I did this."

"What?" Sheppard said.

"You don't even know. I bet now you're thinking and thinking about who I could be, but you'll never work it out. Because you don't function like a normal person. You don't think, or feel, how normal people do. You're a disgrace."

His mind flitted from person to person—the protective shell around which he'd put his deepest, darkest memories finally chipping away. But it still wasn't enough. His memory had fused a long time ago. All the drugs and drink had made him forget things. Especially things he repressed. Or, no, it couldn't be called repressed when you forced it down to the back of your memory and left it there to rot.

"I told you right at the start, Morgan. I'm your best friend," the horse man said, reaching up to grasp the mask. And Sheppard didn't even get it then. That was who he was—he didn't live in the past, couldn't bring himself to. People came and went within him. It wasn't strange to think he'd lose track of them all.

The horse man reached back behind his head. And pulled the mask away.

A man he didn't even know he remembered. But he did. It was unmistakable. He was twenty-five years older than when Sheppard had last seen him. Now he was a man, his piercing eyes, wrinkles, his big smile. It was the smile that made him so familiar. That smile hadn't changed. In a quarter of a century, that smile had not changed a bit. Sheppard found himself speechless, rasping for words to come out. The man on the television just smiled that smile.

The smile of Eren Carver.

47

"Hello again, Morgan," Eren said.

What? How...?

Sheppard's knees buckled. He fell to the ground—mouth wide.

How is this possible? And the more pertinent question—*how did I not know?*

Twenty-five years—it had been twenty-five years. And now he was here. How could he have forgotten him—how had he not known straight away who it was? Could he really be so naïve? All the memories he had buried deep with booze and pills suddenly surfaced. Mr. Jefferies. Eren's dad being taken away by the police. It had made little Morgan Sheppard famous (what he had always wanted) but it had left Eren without a father. Eren was the only person the masked man could have ever been— and he hadn't thought once about him.

Calling him Morgan. That was the first clue. No one ever called him by his first name anymore. His publicist, his agent, even his array of girlfriends—everyone just called him Sheppard. He had talked to his agent about it—it wasn't like he hated his first name, but rather fell back on his last one. *Sheppard is a good strong name, it's a name you can hang your hat on. Biblical—if with a few typos.*

The glasses. That had been the next thing. Sheppard hadn't worn glasses in public, probably since his school days. He hated having them, so didn't wear them much, preferring to strain his eyes. He was badly shortsighted, but he had learned to live with it. When he got older, he got contact lenses, but always had his glasses for around his flat where no one else would see. He remembered the first time he'd got glasses. His mother forced him to wear them every day, which he did. But he always took them off by first period—sick of them. He'd put them in his back pocket—joking (but not joking) that he hoped he would sit on them and break them.

It all made sense, but even now, as he looked at Eren's face on the television screen, he couldn't bring himself to believe it. Even with all the clues there in front of him and the truth staring him in the face.

"Eren?" he said, his face incredibly close to the television screen.

"Hello, old friend," Eren said, smiling, "but it's not Eren anymore. I found Eren a bit too homely, and a bit too ingrained in bad memories. It's Kace now. Kace Carver. You like it?"

"Kace? What is that?"

"That's my name."

"No, it's not. Your name's Eren."

Eren frowned. "We may have a history, you and me. But, I'll warn you now, Morgan, do not attempt to pretend you know me. You left me all that time ago, and I have changed since then. So have you, although in your case it's rather for the worse, I'm afraid, if that was even possible. Who would think that this is the way it would work out?"

"Wait…" Ryan. At least he thought it was. All he heard were

the words. Couldn't discern who it was anymore. "What is he talking about? Who is that?"

How to explain...

"Sheppard."

"It's come to the point in proceedings that I've been looking forward to the most," Carver said. "It's time for our hero, our protagonist, to explain himself."

"Eren," Sheppard said, holding his hand out to the screen, "stop this, let us out. Please."

"No. I won't. Because it seems throughout this whole charade, you haven't learned a thing. You didn't even know who I was."

"But I know you now, Eren. I know you. I remember you. I remember everything we did together. And I'm sorry. I'm so sorry. We were best friends. I remember everything. Just please— let us go." A tear rolled down Sheppard's cheek. Crying—he hadn't cried, he could never remember crying. Crying wasn't something he did—that was for other people. "Please, Eren."

"Don't call me Eren," Eren said. "I am not Eren."

"Please let everyone else go. Please, this is between you and me. These people have nothing to do with it," Sheppard said, sweeping his arm across the rest of the room.

Eren faltered slightly, peered closer at the screen. "That is un-characteristically selfless of you. Are you okay? Do you have in-digestion? I can only assume it's to save some kind of face. You still think you're getting out of this, don't you?"

He didn't anymore. He didn't know anything.

"But no, I will not be letting any of you go. At first, I just thought I'd put you in there. Plop you all in there like flies in a jar and watch you buzzing around, not knowing what to do. But now I have the bite, the bite of curiosity. I want to see if you can do it. And more than that, I want to see you die. So keeping you in there to rot sounds good to me. But if you do it, if you manage it, I'll let the others go free."

The others...

"So I solve this and you let everyone else go?"

Eren looked frustrated. "Is your brain already that starved? I just said that, didn't I?"

"Can someone tell me what is going on?" Mandy this time. But he couldn't think about anyone else. Not right now.

"And what happens to me?" Sheppard said.

"I think we need a nice little chat," Eren said, smiling again. Sheppard didn't move except to nod. "Okay."

"Solve it Morgan, or die with your roommates. It's your decision. But can you please do something for me?" Carver said.

"Yes—of course." What a sniveling little hermit he'd become. He knew that Eren was his only way out. Didn't Eren see that? Didn't Eren see that he would do anything? "Tell the truth, Morgan," Eren said. "Just for once in your life, tell the truth."

Sheppard collapsed on the floor, finally admitting to himself he was crying. Eren Carver. The boy who had been his best— his only—friend.

But something was different. Something had happened to him.

And as his eyes stung with tears, he realized that what had happened to Eren was Morgan Sheppard.

48

"Sheppard. Sheppard." Who was it?

The air felt thicker. Was that a real thing or was it just because he knew the air was in short supply—the oxygen decreasing by the second? He and his roommates were dying one breath at a time. He didn't need a timer, he didn't need a countdown to know that they were in trouble—more trouble than they had ever been in. Death by suffocation—death worming its way around your body, gripping the heart and squeezing the life out of it.

"Sheppard. Damn it."

It was the image of himself choking in a corner, his eyes becoming redder, which made him get up. He pushed himself up by his hands and then tested his legs. They seemed okay and he got up on them.

Eren Carver. He had been right.

Sheppard had forgotten all about him. He had turned the memory of Mr. Jefferies's death into a little ball and stuffed it at the back of his mind. He had written his own narrative of how those few months in 1992 played out—and started to believe it. And that made it all the worse. Sheppard held out a hand to skirt the bed as he got his balance back. Ryan and Mandy were still standing around, Headphones had somehow got back to her place under the desk and Constance had resumed rocking on the chair. It wasn't enough to fail them once, or even twice. Eren was going to humiliate him as many times as he could.

"Sheppard?" Ryan said. The young man was halfway between anger and panic. Didn't seem to appreciate being kept out of the loop. "What the hell is going on? Who was that? And what did he mean by telling the truth?"

"Please, Sheppard," Mandy said. Looking at her, he realized there was no more hope in her eyes.

Headphones stared across the room, watching the timer. She appeared to be breathing through the sleeve of her hoodie, as though that might use less air.

Constance had shut her eyes and even looked asleep.

She obviously didn't care anymore.

Sheppard looked at them all. All he had been running from, his entire life, etched across their faces. He remembered how he had been back then. He had just wanted to be famous. He smiled when he thought that that was no different to how he was now. All he wanted was to be known. *Sometimes all we want is to be seen.* An old thing Winter said once. He remembered it because when it got stripped down, that was all he ever wanted. To be seen.

Was this it? And as he thought about it, he was relieved. It was more than time. "I'm a liar. A fraud. That's the simplest way of putting it."

"What?" Ryan said.

"I am known as the Child Detective. But that's not true. I did not solve the murder of George Jefferies in 1992, didn't even have much of a part in it. The person who solved the murder was Eren Carver, the son of the man who did it. He was brilliant and fantastic in all the ways I could never be. He was my friend. And I betrayed him. And, for all intents and purposes, I assumed his identity. For twenty-five years. I told everyone I solved it. And Eren didn't come forward because it had gone too far. Everyone truly believed it was me. Morgan Sheppard means nothing.

"That's the reason we're all here. That man on the TV is Eren, or whatever he calls himself now. He's torturing me, proving to everyone else that I'm not who I say I am. And he's right."

His eyes fell, not able to hold anyone else's gaze anymore. Eren was watching, and for all he knew, so were others. He hoped they were. It was time for Morgan Sheppard to die, or at least what Morgan Sheppard had become. The man was gone, cast away like a snake's shed skin. It wasn't by choice, but by need. And Sheppard didn't know if that kind of made it forego the point.

No one moved around him, but he had one last job to do. If he'd never done anything selfless in his entire life, let him do this. He had to rescue three of the four people in the room— one of them killed a friend of his, and the other three deserved to live. Hell, they all deserved to live.

The killer. We're in here with a killer.

Sheppard had gone too far—he knew that too. He had gone beyond the bounds of his particular abyss to something bigger than killing and something bigger than mere deceiving. He was the man who fooled the world. And he guessed that he'd at least have that accolade right up until the very end.

Atonement was on a timer and dependent on shallow breaths.

"What the hell are you talking about?" Ryan said.

"It's all true." He breathed in and out—savoring it. And promised it was the last time he would do it. From now on, he would only breathe slightly. To give them enough time to maybe get out of this.

Mandy still looked like she was trying to process everything. But it seemed to have finally clicked for everyone else. Headphones was watching him with shifty eyes. Constance had regained a little bit of interest too, staring around. Ryan seemed like he was about to explode, going a reddish color.

"Are you serious?" he said, striding forward, like a peacock showing his feathers. "That's what all this is about? I'm going to die because of you? Ever since the beginning, this has all been about you. Me, Mandy, Rhona, even Constance and Alan. We've all been nothing. Just things to get in your way."

"I'm sorry," Sheppard said. It was all he could say.

"You're a joke," Ryan said. "A sick, sick joke. How did you live with yourself?"

Very easily. "Ryan, I'm sorry. I didn't want any of this to happen."

"Well, yeah, of course you didn't. But still…"

"Ryan, I need all of you. I need you to help me. I'm going to save you. I'm going to save you and Mandy and Headphones and Ahearn. Hell, I'm even going to save Alan's body so he can have a proper burial. I know it's the end for me. I know I'm a dead man walking. Eren isn't going to let me walk out of here."

"How do you know that?"

"Because I know Eren and he is resolute—but he's something more than that. He's just. You see that?"

"Why would any of us listen to you anymore? Why would we trust you?"

"Because this is not over. You can hate me all you want— later."

"He's right," Mandy said, dully.

"Thank you," Sheppard said to her. He tried a smile. It felt like lifting weights piled on the ends of his mouth. He didn't get very far. Not when he was interrupted.

Mandy slapped him straight in the face. It was stronger than he

ever thought would be possible from such a small girl. His face
flew to the side and he felt a hand mark developing on his cheek.

Mandy, the sweet girl who had always been by his side, now
looking so angry. "Why would you do that? Why would you
do that?" and again, just because it seemed she couldn't think
of anything else, "Why would you do that?"

Sheppard looked at her, his tears drying on his right cheek
and his left cheek stinging.

The air definitely felt thicker now—it drooped around them
almost visibly. Sheppard could see it in the corner of his eye.
Like reflections of a time never lived. His cravings kept on a
shelf in the back of his mind with the other lives.

And some kind of new feeling manifested itself. He mistook
it for the need to vomit again.

"I just need some water," Sheppard said, still watching Mandy
intently. She was watching him, as though he was the devil, but
he thought he detected an element of softness coming through.
"I need some water. And then I'll get you all to safety."

He started toward the bathroom, but a hand shot out from
under the desk to grab his leg. He looked down. Headphones
looked at him and pointed. To the timer. It seemed to be going
faster than before. Accelerating.

Fifteen minutes.

Sheppard looked back to Headphones and nodded.

Smiled.

Headphones lowered her sleeve. "Also, my name's Rhona…
dick. Who the hell calls someone Headphones?"

Sheppard dropped the smile and nodded dutifully. He passed
Ryan without looking.

"You better know what you're doing," Ryan called after him
as he walked toward the bathroom. He pushed the door open,
and chanced a look back at them. They were all watching him—
of course they were.

Behind the others, Constance was still shackled to her chair—she wasn't smiling, or rocking back and forth. She was actually looking scared—the first time Sheppard had ever seen her look scared in all her time in the room.

Sheppard stumbled through the bathroom door—no closer to knowing how to rescue them all.

49

Sheppard almost forgot where Alan had been placed. He walked into the bathroom and felt something squish under his feet. He looked down to see one of Alan's hands. He jumped back against the door.

When he had regained some kind of composure, he maneuvered around the lawyer, trying not to step in any of the blood, and went to the sink. He turned the hot tap on. Winter's body was still there in the tub—he saw it in the mirror. Winter, a pawn in Eren's plan. He felt even sorrier for the old man now, being manipulated so easily. Sheppard cupped water into his hands and splashed it on his face. It felt good. He had to stay awake, and stay alert. All his sordid addictions would have to be kept at bay. He had to save everyone else—that was all that mattered now.

He leaned over the sink and shut his eyes as the steam rose— overriding the cold, slick sweat on his clammy skin.

He opened his eyes.

The mirror had steamed over. As if nothing behind him existed anymore. But he could feel Winter.

Winter had always been such a strong figure in his life. He remembered going to his house on Saturday afternoons for his therapy sessions. He had protested to start with, but after a while, he relied on them. Winter always had a way of explaining things to him, making them seem more entertaining than they actually were. He taught Sheppard how to deal with his increasing fame, told him which thoughts were harmful and which were beneficial. He taught Sheppard how to be a better man.

If only I had listened.

Sheppard reached into his pocket and took out Winter's notebook. He still had no idea why the old man was carrying it—an old notebook with old session notes. He flipped to his own notes—looking at the underlined words. Was this what Winter really thought of him? Aggressive? Muddled? Important words, he guessed—but then why had Winter also underlined "A new dream about..."? Not even a full sentence. He read on: "A new dream about a field of corn. Out in the distance there is a farmhouse—a farmyard. It's on fire and it's burning down. Morgan is out in the field looking at it. As he watches, a scarecrow rises up out of the field of corn. Morgan just knows that it was the scarecrow who set the fire. The scarecrow smiles at him. And that's when he wakes up." Sheppard read this, enraptured. He'd forgotten all about the nightmare. He used to have it every night—waking up in cold sweats, sometimes even having wet himself. It began just after—just after he did what he did.

But the painting on the wall? The painting on the wall was depicting the dream almost to the letter. Such a strange painting to have in a hotel room—he had thought that when he saw it. Now even just thinking about it made his skin crawl. And Mandy had said it looked creepy too. He read on: "I need more information to really understand this nightmare. It sounds like a classic 'created destroys creator' thought stream, but I don't know how that pertains to Morgan exactly. Also—NB—

IMPORTANT POINT Morgan says that the worst part of the nightmare is he knows the children upstairs are burning alive."

Sheppard almost dropped the notebook. Children upstairs? Why was that so shocking? Had someone... He looked at the page—at the underlined words, at the wording of the dream.

Sheppard looked at the words. What did they mean? How could they mean anything? He traced his finger over them. Too broad. Too— He stared at the words. And he thought. And suddenly, it all clicked.

No.

It all came back. The air was solid now. He couldn't breathe.

No. Not— But it all made sense.

50

Before…

She clutched the invite tightly, making the card crease down the middle. She had arrived far too early—couldn't just sit around at home. Besides, she knew she would have to scan the entrance and pick the opportune time to make a move.

Her brain was already trying to convince her this was a bad idea. *Suppose the bouncers know this woman? Suppose they know what she looks like? What then? Will they call the police?* What would she do then? Hold up her hands, call "guilty" and walk away? There was too much riding on this for that.

They wouldn't know her. She had to get in.

It was simple. She was going to wait for the time when it was busiest. Then even if people did know the woman, no one would notice. The bouncers would be flustered—more capable of making mistakes. She would slip through the cracks. And through the door.

She checked her watch. Far too early indeed. So she propped herself up in a café across the street. It was just gone five—

the party didn't start till eight. Party rules dictated that people wouldn't be arriving until about ten.

She ordered a coffee and waited.

She checked her Dictaphone was working—switching it on and off. Full battery. When that was done, she spent most of her time thinking, or gazing unenthusiastically at YouTube videos on her laptop. For a while, they were on-topic—watching his smug face on that damn show, watching him lord himself over everyone else, watching an audience lap it up, but soon they just became whatever came up on the sidebar: Top 10 English Haunted Hotels, Nyan Cat Remixes, the funniest things babies have ever done, the stuff that kept the internet rolling on its endless journey to ruin the world. Still, she was part of the problem—she was hypnotized by this crap just as much as everyone else. She looked through the window to see no one had arrived at the club yet.

At seven, the café closed. She asked to stay a little longer, but seeing as she had only ordered one small coffee in two hours, she knew she wasn't going to win. She moved to a pub down the road, opting for a window seat. She could still see the club, although not as well.

She ordered a Diet Coke at the bar and got the Dictaphone out of her pocket again. Off and on. Light flashing. It was still fine.

The internet was to blame for him. He could've been a daytime television anomaly—a person that most of the population weren't even aware of because they all turned their televisions off at nine when they went to work. But it was the age of the internet, where every show could be chopped up and put online and farmed out for millions and millions of views. This was his home and he wasn't even the one who made it. The television channel made him his own website, where clips of his show were put up. His YouTube channel quickly flooded with ten-minute segments—Celebrity Cuckold, The Truth About You, Sleepin'

Around and Around. Eight million subscribers were the audience, a pack that grew incredibly quickly as they enjoyed his brand of Sherlockian hilarity. If Sherlock had been an idiot, that is. Most of what he deduced wasn't even true. He was a detective who couldn't really detect anything. But above that he was a personality—a television personality, an internet personality, it didn't really matter. He was right even though he was wrong.

As the light in the sky dimmed, she put her laptop away and made sure the external mic on the Dictaphone was working. She recorded herself reading the fact on a beer mat—*A blind chameleon still changes color to match the environment.* She played it back. It sounded fine. It was going to be far noisier in the club, but she thought it would still pick voices up if she held it close enough. And she would. Because too much was riding on this to make a simple little mistake like that.

It had only been two weeks since…since… People were calling it the tragedy. The tragedy—so cold and distant. Maybe that's why people called it that, to put space between themselves and what happened. But that wasn't what she wanted. She wanted to understand why. And she was ready. Her anger fueled her most—it was what got her out of bed in the morning, what saw her through the day. Her brother had always hated when she was angry, could see in her eyes how it wrapped around her and consumed her. Her brother had always said that she could never let her anger control her—put a lid on it while there was still a lid. Because if she didn't, there would be nothing else.

But she was alive and he was dead. And it was all Morgan Sheppard's fault.

And, now, sitting in the pub, she was angry. She was so very angry. But she was also resourceful. Her journalism degree was almost over and she had signed the recorder and mic out at the desk. She was ready.

Because she was alive and she didn't understand why he had to be dead.

She watched out the window and by eight thirty, a slow trickle of people started entering the club. Brickwork was an underground nightclub just around from Leicester Square tube station. It was notoriously expensive and notoriously exclusive. She had never set foot in there before, and by all account, had no right to set foot in there now. This was a private party for television people and their high-class friends. The invite she had swiped had been from a low-level employee working on his show. She watched as the gaggle of women who walked up to the door pulled out their invites. They were all stopped at the door by a burly bald man dressed in black. The bouncer had a list. The women were checked off and disappeared inside.

At nine, a limousine pulled up and she saw him get out. He had a tuxedo on and was already swaying. The bouncers didn't ask him his name.

She wondered if she should go in, but there was no queue and she didn't want to risk it. She waited another thirty minutes, until she couldn't wait any longer. A queue of about thirty people had built up and she swallowed the rest of her Diet Coke, checked her hair in the bathroom and went out. She joined the queue and noticed the crease on her invite. She tried to straighten it out but only made it worse.

The queue moved slowly and she tried to blend in with the women waiting in line. She noticed that there was only one man in the queue, a straightened-up button-down type who seemed rather stoic and out of place. He didn't say a word as the women around him laughed and joked, sometimes about him. The women were the usual glamorous, 2-D type—the kind of women you couldn't see from side-on. They were what her brother would've called "Extras from *The OC*," a dumb program they used to watch together when they were younger about pretty people with pretty problems.

When the woman ahead got to the door, the group became very flustered and high-pitched. There were three of them and the one in charge of the invites had not brought them, instead electing to bring more drink. They were stupidly drunk, considering they hadn't yet entered the club. It seemed like their names were on the list though as they were allowed inside— probably nothing at all to do with how slutty they looked. Self-doubt seeped in.

What was she doing? Really? Starring in her own little espionage thriller? This was stupid. She turned and saw a wall of sexy young women coming down the stairs, blocking her exit. She felt the recorder in her hand.

You're a lot more than you think. You're strong, stronger than him. And you've read the papers—he'll be worse for wear, you just wait and see. You're cleverer than he could ever dream of being. It was her brother's voice. Her thoughts often came to her in his voice. He was always more confident than her.

A fresh pang of anger flared in her mind.

You've come this far.

See it through.

Without another thought, she entered the club—the doors spitting her out onto a bustling, dark dance floor. The place seemed to be far more crowded than she expected, given she had watched everyone enter. People were everywhere, blocking her view of the rest of the club. She made her way over to where she presumed the bar was, dodging all the featureless silhouettes of people, lit up occasionally by a flash of multicolored light. The dance floor was densely packed and progress was slow. Getting through it was like an impossible version of *Frogger*, sometimes having to double back on herself to avoid people swooping by with drinks. Finally, she made her way through and got to the bar.

She ordered a gin and tonic. She often thought nightclubs were intolerable without at least something coating your judgment. A sober her could see the absolute insanity of a penned-in drinking factory. She got her drink and paid an astronomical amount for it. The price of being thirsty in London.

She looked around. The dance floor was the majority of the club but there were booths to the left and right sides. She scanned around and found what she was looking for—the booth nearest to her on the left-hand side had a partition around it. It was the VIP area. And behind the theater-esque ribbon, was him. She watched him smiling and talking, swaying even though he was sitting down. He had this look of joyful bewilderment. He was drop-dead drunk. The others in the VIP area she didn't recognize, apart from one person who she thought might be a host of *Morning Coffee*. The rest of the men looked like business types and they were peppered with scantily clad women, who looked as though they had won a prize just by being there. Add smug, subtract self-respect.

Propping herself up against the bar, she watched him. She hated him. It was red, raw, unbridled hate. She had never felt anything like it before. She understood why people equated hate to love. It felt the same. Wherever you were, whatever you were doing—it was there. Love pulled you to someone else, and so did hate. But for the exact opposite reasons. You looked at someone you loved, and saw a whole life spread ahead of you—a life that could be. But in hate, you just looked at someone and saw devastation—a life that once was. But both could drive people to terrible things.

Anger is not you. Her brother had been able to see it within her, before she had herself. And he had seen the dangers of it.

Three gin and tonics later and the world was shifting, as

though a wave lapping against an unknown beach. He was still in the VIP area, drinking amounts that seemed illogical. She hadn't stopped watching him but no one seemed to notice. The music was deafening and the lights were low, so the chances of someone even seeing her were slim. She wondered if this was it. If he wouldn't leave the VIP area at all, and she had gone to all this effort just to spend a night staring at him… Would it all be for nothing?

The middle of the fourth drink and someone tried to talk to her. A young man who looked too confident for his own good. Bad news.

"Wow, I love your outfit," he said, with the enthusiasm of a self-help coach. "You seem quiet. You haven't talked to anyone all night. Are you on your own?"

This made her shiver slightly. The idea that he had been watching her all night was not particularly enticing. "I'm here with some people," she said. "I'm just waiting for them."

"What's your name?"

"Zoe," she said, without hesitation.

"I'm Tim," the man said. Tim was a boring name even if you made it up. "I work with a Zoe. She's not here though." He seemed lost as he looked around.

She didn't notice. She was watching as he, him not Tim, stood up on two unsteady feet. He whispered something into one of the women's ears and she laughed for an unreasonable amount of time. He stepped over the cordon, tripping as he brought up his right foot. A fresh bout of laughter came from the VIP area and he turned to them and gave them a thumbs-up. He staggered off and got swallowed by the crowd of dancers.

"I wonder if I could buy you a drink?" Tim was saying, as she slid off her stool and left the bar. She didn't really care for Tim's feelings—leave it for the other Zoe to clean up.

She followed the dark mass she thought was him through the

dance floor. It didn't really matter if it wasn't him. She knew where he was going. The only place a man who had spent an hour heavydrinking in a nightclub would go. The toilets.

She tore her eyes from the mass to look up at the walls. There were two neon signs. One said "John" and she didn't really understand until she saw the other at the other end of the large area—"Yoko." She started toward the "John" arrow, but a dark figure appeared in front of her. In the next flash of lights, she saw it was the guy from the bar—Tim. The stalking creep— but she had underestimated him at least. "I would really like to buy you a drink."

"I'm not interested," she said, sharply. She tried to step around him, but he stepped too. She didn't have time for this— Sheppard would be in and out quickly, he was a man after all. She was going to miss her chance.

"It's weird, 'Zoe.' I only know one 'Zoe' on the set." Tim was slurring—he was drunk.

"I'm new," she hissed, and pushed past him. Tim responded in kind by grabbing her arm. She turned. "Let. Me. Go."

"I will, if you have a drink with me," Tim said happily— probably thinking all of this was flirty sparring.

"Don't take this the wrong way, but I'd rather kill myself."

"Don't be like that." Tim grabbed her other arm—he had her now. This was bad. And the opportunity she wanted was slowly slipping away. Her anger suddenly flared—she thought in that moment, she could kill this little minnow just to get her chance at the big fish. "Aren't you here to have fun?"

"You want to know why I'm here?" she said, before she could stop herself. "I'm here to have a little word with your lord and savior Morgan Sheppard. You're all pathetic little idiots party- ing with that monster, latching onto him just because he can get you to the top. You don't care what he's done, do you? In fact, you probably helped him do it."

Tim was struggling to comprehend what she was saying, and his grip on her arms was loosening. What she wanted to say—what she came here to do—was spilling out, and she couldn't stop it now. The fact that Tim was not her intended target didn't seem to matter anymore.

She started to cry. "Morgan Sheppard ruins people's lives. And you all stand there, and film it for television. For what? Personal gain. Do you remember him? Do any of you remember my brother? Sean Phillips? He was on Mr. Sheppard's, on your, show. Three years ago. He was on with his wife, the mother of his child. Morgan Sheppard proved that Sean was having an affair. When he wasn't. I can prove it—I have solid proof that he was not having an affair. And Morgan Sheppard ruined his life."

Tim was looking uncomfortable. She was screaming now but the volume of the music meant everyone else around them was oblivious.

"He killed himself," she shrieked. "My brother killed himself."

Tim let go of her.

"He killed himself," she said, finally. She buried her face in her hands and cried. She hated it. How he got to her. She hated the tears.

Sean was quiet in her mind. Had nothing to say. Was that it? Was she alone?

Tim was still staring at her. "Okay then," he said. "You know what, I prefer my girls a little less—you know—psycho. So I'm going to go have a drink alone and you have a nice night." And with that, Tim disappeared—becoming another black mass in the room.

She dried her eyes and thought she still may have a chance to catch Sheppard. She turned toward the bathrooms, and her heart stopped.

There he was, in front of her. The smug bastard, looking

glazed and happy. He was walking through the crowd toward her. She had missed him at the toilets but now he was coming for her. This was her chance. So why would her voice not work? She had seconds. He got to her—they were centimeters from each other—and then he passed her. She could almost feel the smugness coming off him like steam.

She wheeled around. He was disappearing into the anonymous crowd. This was it. Her last shot.

"Sheppard," she found herself shouting.

Sheppard stopped—he had heard her—and turned around. He didn't know it was her of course, and his eyes moved around the room as he tried to find out who shouted.

She held her breath as his eyes fell on her. How long was it? It couldn't have been for more than a second, but for her it felt like an hour. All that time, all she had to do was open her mouth—open her mouth and say what she came here to say. But she couldn't. Whether it was her exhaustion, or Tim, or seeing Sheppard's face, she just found she couldn't do it. It suddenly became real.

And then it was over. He looked for another moment and then turned. He got swallowed up by the dark. And just like that it was all over. She suddenly felt dizzy, and staggered to the wall. She slid down and buried her face in her knees, becoming as small as possible. And the tears began. And they carried on.

Sometime later, she looked up to see two men laughing at her. She ignored them and got up, pushing past them with a force that stopped them laughing. She pushed her way across the dance floor. Not looking to the VIP area, not looking for him. She couldn't.

She got to the bar and ordered another gin and tonic. Just another to add to the collection. Sean used to say that their family was born with iron livers.

She toasted to nothing, and everything. Drank it in two gulps.

She stared at the empty glass, thinking about how she had failed. Maybe she would just get drunk—that seemed like a good way to forget. It was working for his holiness Morgan Sheppard.

"Can I buy you another?" said a voice. Had Tim lucked out with every other woman in the club and decided the crazy one was better than nothing? But when she looked up, she saw a different man. The smart man she had seen in the queue to get in.

"Gin and tonic," she said. Abruptly.

The man didn't seem to mind. He flagged down the barman and ordered. She regarded him a bit more. He was young, but not as young as her. Thirty, maybe thirty-five. He wore rectangular glasses and had on a suit with a red tie. He looked stern, but inviting. To most people, he would be disregarded as normal. But there was something about him. Something that she had noticed before in the queue—a sort of presence.

He slid her her drink—he had ordered a pint. "You seem distraught," he said.

"I'm fine," she said.

"These things are always despicable," he said, throwing his hands up all around him. "A monument for the self-involved."

"Then why are you here?" She sipped at her drink.

"Because it's always good to keep tabs on people. Otherwise you just get left behind," he said, and she totally understood. And everything he said seemed to make perfect sense. "Why are you here?"

She smiled sadly. "I had to get some answers."

"And did you get them?"

"I had my chance to get them. And I didn't take it." And he must have read her sad face, because he said, "Well, you mustn't take it out on yourself—answers aren't always the end. Sometimes they're just not worth the wait. Bad things happen to good people. That's the way of the world."

He was right. She touched his glass with hers, not loud enough to make a sound but enough to show the sentiment.

There was a loud commotion over in the VIP area. Sheppard's colleague had passed out and the man himself was creating quite a fuss about it. He gestured to the DJ and the music cut out.

Sheppard got up onto a table, liquid sloshing visibly off as if he'd landed in a puddle, and produced a microphone. "Three cheers for dopey Rogers!"

She didn't know who that was, but assumed it was the passed-out colleague. The entire club erupted into hip-hip-hoorahs. She did not join in and neither did the man.

When it was all over and the music turned back on, the man said, "Now, that Morgan Sheppard, that's a man who needs taking down a peg or two."

She looked at him and he looked back. "Kace Carver," he said, putting out his hand.

She started to say "Zoe" and stopped herself. She cleared her throat and said "Mandy," shaking his hand.

She smiled for the first time all evening.

51

The red string connections in Sheppard's mind were working overtime. Winter had made it so simple for him—and he still hadn't seen. But now it all made sense. It was all clear. The only possible conclusion. Winter laid a trap—maybe he saw the situation going south and decided to make a breadcrumb trail for Sheppard. If he was a better man, he would've seen it earlier.

He staggered out of the bathroom and looked up at them all. The notebook in his hand. A finger still marking the page, where the underlined words were—and where the description of the nightmare was. "Aggressive, Muddled, A dream about…" The answer he was searching for. And even if Sheppard didn't understand what Winter was getting at, he spelled it out too. A word puzzle—an incredibly easy one.

"It was you," he said quietly, not wanting it to be true. Ryan looked around.

The first letters…spelling it out…spelling out AMANDA. The trap that Winter set for Mandy, telling her about the dream no doubt—hoping that she would let something slip. And she did.

Headphones jumped up. But she jumped up too late.

Mandy had realized and grabbed the teenager, restraining her. To his surprise, Mandy brandished the knife—she must have slipped it from his back pocket—and held it to Headphones's throat. The teenager didn't make a sound—just looked at Sheppard with eyes that didn't fully understand.

"No one move," Mandy said, looking at them each in turn. "Move and I'll cut this emo's throat."

Movement didn't seem to be an option. He was too busy processing it. Mandy, the sweet young girl who'd always had his back.

Ryan seemed to be in a similar state of bewilderment, holding his hands up in surrender.

Mandy started backing to Ahearn, who screamed gleefully. Mandy took no notice of the mad old woman, sidling past her and resting her back against the window so Sheppard or Ryan couldn't get behind her.

"Mandy, what are you doing?" Ryan said.

"Go ahead, Sheppard," Mandy said. She didn't even sound like the same person anymore. She sounded cold and hard and inhuman. "Explain it to him." She waved the knife in front of Headphones's neck as if impatient for blood.

"What? You?" Ryan said, to Mandy.

"I was wrong," Sheppard said, wondering how to manage to get to Mandy before she did something insane. He tried a short step forward, holding his hands up too. Mandy didn't seem to notice, too focused on his eyes. "Ever since the start, this has been designed to fool me.

"It was the wounds—the wounds in Winter's gut that were so deep. I didn't think it could have been Mandy because of that. But there were some things that I missed, at least not enough for me to notice at the time, but she was more than capable of plunging a knife deep into the body of Simon Winter."

She pulled me up, one of the first things she did. I remember thinking she was strong.

"Right at the start—you pulled me up off the floor. If I had been a proper detective, I would have seen it, I would have noticed straight away." Another step forward.

She slapped me. My face flew to the side, because it was so strong. Anger. The anger in her eyes when she had done that. Like anger she had had to keep pent up for days, months, years even. Setting her eyes on fire.

"Somehow I just know there's a family in that house, children burning." The ultimate slipup that she wouldn't even know she was making. Winter was clever—he was very clever—and Sheppard had almost missed it entirely.

Ryan was incapable of helping—he still didn't understand. It would make him slow and unsure—not useful. Headphones was squirming in Mandy's grip, her eyes following the edge of the knife hovering at her throat. He couldn't be sure Mandy wouldn't do it. He didn't know her—not anymore. Another small step.

"You're strong, but that doesn't mean you're a murderer. But then there were more clues, weren't there? More reasons to suspect you," he said, edging closer. "Like how you woke up first and seemed to know information about everyone. You probably would have told me more if I'd asked, but you told me just few enough details to get away with it."

She knew plenty about Constance. Her name, where she worked. She got away with it because Constance was famous. But he was betting she had known about everyone in the room.

Step, a small breath, Mandy looked from him to Ryan, smiling to herself, as if she was pleased at what she had accomplished. Sheppard had never expected to see her face look that way.

He was level with the television now. Headphones watched him—she saw everything, she always did. She was the silent observer. She had said about ten sentences in the past three-something hours. She'd be able to see things others didn't, just by virtue of being silent. Sheppard gave her the quickest and smallest nod he was able to manage. His head hardly moved, tilting forward maybe a few centimeters. She watched him for a few moments after and then mimicked the motion.

Mandy was too busy, probably feeling proud of herself, to notice.

"I don't understand," Ryan said. "That doesn't explain what she did?"

"She's been playing us off against each other, Ryan. When Alan was stabbed, Constance was behind him, right? And who was next to her?"

Ryan didn't answer. He didn't have to.

"Constance here killed Alan, seemingly unprovoked. At least at first."

He chanced a look at Ryan. Finally, something in his eyes.

"All that rubbish Constance spouted wasn't rubbish at all. She *was* told. I looked her in the eyes and I knew she believed it herself, but I just thought she was mad. Sorry, Ms. Ahearn, but you have been lied to. We all have."

"How could Mandy get someone to kill someone? I saw—Ahearn did it."

"Do you want to field that one?" Sheppard said to Mandy, and when she shook her head, he continued, "Have you said two words to Constance, Ryan? No, there was only one person who spoke to Constance in the entire time we've been in here—whispering so no one else could hear."

Sheppard looked to Mandy, to make sure he was getting it alright. It appeared he was.

"You knew about her religion, and you used it against her. Mary Magdalene—really?"

Mandy smiled, an ugly-looking thing that reeked of positivity. "I embellished it a bit. Gave myself a nice title."

"You used a poor woman. You made her into a murderer," Sheppard said.

Mandy tilted her head and gave a pout. "Try and say that like you're not proud of me."

"All for what? Just to make things a bit more interesting?"

"Oh come on," Mandy sighed. "Hughes was eternally boring. Walking around like he was king of the world. He had to go."

Sheppard ignored the ease with which she dismissed a human life. "You set this whole thing up, didn't you? You and Eren and Winter. You lured Winter down here and killed him. Used him too. You're sick."

Mandy laughed. "Winter was in it all along, Sheppard. He knew what he was getting into. Winter hated you as much as we do. You ruined his life, just as you ruined ours, remember?"

"I don't know you. I've never seen you before today."

"No, but you knew my brother. You probably don't remember him, do you? You don't even remember Sean Phillips? How you drove him to kill himself?"

Sheppard faltered, stepping back a bit defensively. The name rang a bell, he thought he might have been briefed about the situation in some production meeting or something. But he couldn't remember Mandy at all. But that didn't say much when you couldn't remember what happened yesterday. "Whatever I did, it's not a reason to kill an innocent man."

"Sean Phillips was innocent. Winter was different. He had a darkness inside him—the burn for revenge. Just like me and Kace. Winter walked down here of his own accord. He was so very wanting to see your face when you woke up. When you realized what we'd done. Unfortunately for him though, his time came before then."

"You used him."

"Yes," Mandy said. "Rather stupid for a psychologist, don't you think?"

"I think he was more intelligent than you gave him credit for. I think he worked it all out. Albeit too late. He left me a message. Telling me exactly who killed him. I don't think you're as perfect as you think you are."

"Fantastic, wonderful," Mandy said, "you worked it out all too late. You really are pathetic, Sheppard, and now the whole world knows it. You are a fake, and you have blood on your hands that will never wash off. We've beaten you."

"Eren knew how to play into my hand," Sheppard said. "He knew I would never expect the young blonde. He knew you were just my type."

Mandy frowned at this. "What? Don't be disgusting. Kace and I are in love. There's no way he would use me like that. My reason for hating you is just as valid as his. Why don't you think I'm the mastermind of this whole thing, huh?"

"You're not the mastermind because you're here in the room. I almost feel sorry for you." Sheppard stopped. Mandy had to notice he'd moved now. He was almost within an arm span of her. He could probably reach out to grab Headphones. At least he hoped he could.

If Mandy had noticed him, she didn't show it. "You don't get to feel sorry for me. Why do you feel sorry for me? Stop it." The knife was quivering in anger in front of Headphones's throat.

Sheppard poised himself, ready. "I feel sorry for you because we got played—" he locked eyes with Headphones and did the small nod they had communicated before "—and so did you."

Headphones didn't falter—she sank her teeth into Mandy's wrist.

52

Mandy howled with pain, pulling her wrist free. Sheppard ducked forward, just avoiding Mandy's blind swing of the knife and grabbed Headphones, pushing her onto the bed and free from harm. Ryan had reacted to the move as well, jumping over the bed and moving up toward Mandy.

Mandy had other ideas, however, as she clutched her wrist which was blossoming with color, and with a primal scream, she launched herself at Sheppard. Sheppard dodged too late, and the two went sprawling into the alcove near the main door.

They both fell to the floor, Mandy on top of him. He grabbed her wounded wrist and she growled in pain, losing grip of the knife. It clattered off to the side and as Sheppard followed it with his eyes, he saw Ryan at the other end of the room, taking Constance's handcuffs off. Headphones was still on the bed, stunned.

A second later, Mandy was back, her hands around his neck. Her grip was strong and he rasped for the thick air that had enveloped the room, but her frame was still light. He forced her off him and she went flying into the closet, which stood open. She slammed against the wall and he lunged for her. She dodged and her nails plunged into his leg. Sheppard went careening forward. His fist struck the wall and kept going. It was plasterboard, thin and slight, a weakness in the walls of the room. His motion stopped as a shard of board dug into his wrist. It was stuck.

Mandy panted behind him. She reached behind her, no doubt picking up the knife. He pulled at his wrist, but the more he pulled, the more it seemed to get stuck. He looked over his shoulder as Mandy advanced toward him, knife in hand.

"Mandy," Sheppard said, pulling and pulling but getting nowhere.

"You don't know how long I've waited to hear you beg, to hear you scream," Mandy said, lifting the knife.

"No," Ryan shouted and lunged at Mandy.

Mandy was surprised by the noise and turned as Ryan collided into her. Sheppard saw what was going to happen before he heard the scream. Mandy turned the knife on Ryan, sweeping it around. Ryan grabbed Mandy, as the knife plunged into his stomach.

Ryan howled.

Mandy looked shocked. "I—I…"

Ryan clutched at his stomach, blood pouring out from between his fingers. He sank down to his knees.

Mandy held the knife up—now decorated with Ryan's blood. Her eyes seemed to be processing what she had done.

Sheppard took his chance pulling as hard as he could on his wrist. It came free, along with half of the plasterboard. He lunged at Mandy, bending down to pick up the cuffs, and he barreled into her. Mandy yelped and raised the knife again. Not caring anymore, Sheppard ignored it and as the knife came down, he just got to her other wrist first. The knife lurched back up as Sheppard got the handcuff around her wrist. *Click*—as it locked into place.

Mandy squawked. She slashed at him, but wasn't able to reach him. Even so, the blade ripped through the shoulder of his shirt, grazing his skin. He lunged at Mandy's free arm between slashes, forcing it around the back of her to meet the other. Even as he closed the second cuff, she tried to slash at him. But when the cuff touched her bitten wrist, she dropped the knife through pain. It clattered off the wall and fell to the floor.

"No," Mandy screamed, over Ryan's grunts.

"Is he okay?" Sheppard said, looking round to Ryan's fallen body. His head was propped up by the bed box spring, looking down at his stomach. Headphones had taken the edge of the duvet and was pressing it to his stomach. It was already turning red, even through the thick layer.

"He's losing blood," Headphones said.

Mandy had given up any discernible language and snarled at Sheppard, alternating whoops and growls.

What to do? What to do?

Sheppard opened the bathroom door, trying to push Mandy toward it. She didn't budge, obviously seeing the dead bodies of Simon Winter and Alan Hughes. He pushed her harder and she went careening into the room, her hands locked behind her back.

"Sheppard," Mandy shouted, and he would never forget the cold, murderous way she said it—she really wanted him dead. Was she like that before, or was this what Eren did to people? "I might not have done it, but you know he will. Kace is going to kill you. And then he'll come back for me."

Sheppard slammed the bathroom door and almost instantly there was hammering on the other side. He held his foot against the bottom of the door, ignoring the screams. Until they subsided. He took his foot away. There was nothing—she was stuck in there.

He went to Ryan. "Ryan, are you okay?"

He looked up at Sheppard and moved his mouth but no sound came out.

"He's dying, Sheppard," Headphones said, her hands slicked red. "We need to stop the bleeding. We need to get help."

Sheppard pressed his hands down around the area too. "We can't do that. There's no way out."

"We know who murdered Winter. Isn't it over?" Headphones said.

"I don't know."

But as he said that, he heard something. Where there was nothing before, there was a small whirring sound.

Sheppard slowly released his hands and got up. He went around Ryan and Headphones to look at the timer.

Three minutes. Twelve seconds.

He watched it. It didn't change. It had stopped.

Sheppard breathed out forcefully, expelling all the panic. "I think it's stopped. I think the air came back on." He looked down at Headphones and Ryan, his head lolling from side to side, a hum escaping his lips. Headphones wasn't looking at him. She was looking into the cupboard. He went around to her, looked her in the face. "What?" Inside the cupboard, the fake plasterboard wall had crumbled away to reveal a brick wall behind it. One of the bricks had come free, and in the gap, Sheppard saw an opening. "I think it's loose," he said, peering at it. He lifted his leg and kicked at the brick wall. The dust of old concrete and brick showered down, but nothing moved.

He ignored the slight jolt of pain in his foot and did it again. Still nothing.

Ryan's moans drove him to carry on, kicking the wall again and again until finally the wall collapsed in a satisfying *thud*.

There was a small opening behind the wall, an opening with a ladder. He stuck his head into the hole he'd made and looked up. It was dark, but the ladder seemed to carry on climbing into the darkness. He turned back to Headphones.

"It's a ladder. I think it's a way out."

Headphones couldn't look happy—a ghost of relief was barely there, but he saw it. She moved the segment of duvet down so she could press on Ryan's wound with a fresh piece. "You need to go," she said. "Get help. Ryan's not going to last much longer."

"But I can't leave you..."

"Sheppard," Headphones snapped, looking older than she ever had, "you have to go. You wanted to save us. So save us."

Sheppard reluctantly nodded. He took one more look at Ryan, who met his gaze only briefly. He might have imagined it but he thought he saw the young man nod too.

"I'll be as quick as I can," Sheppard said. "I'll be back for you."

"Go," Headphones said, impatiently.

Sheppard turned away. He walked into the cupboard, fitting into the dark section behind the wall. He grasped the first rungs of the ladder—feeling cold and strong. This was it—the end. So why wasn't he more relieved?

As he started to climb, the overwhelming feeling was one of fear.

53

Before…

Kace Carver entered the lobby of HMP Pentonville at 9:00 a.m. The place had become too familiar to him. He knew the drab walls, the stained carpets, the weathered fabric of the chairs as if this were his own home. The lobby was small and cramped, with a reception desk masked in a sheet of thick plastic. Kace went up to the desk and slipped his visitor's permit through the small slot on the desk.

"I'm here to see Ian Carver," he said, not bothering to look at the specimen behind the desk and behind the plastic. This always played out the same. He had no need for pleasantries. Next, there would be a spell where the pass was verified and then the great charade would begin. Kace would be searched, his belongings scanned and then he would be ushered into a room even shabbier than this one. A room filled with tables and chairs and hopeful prisoners looking for their loved ones. He hated it. It was pitiful and it was weak. The lack of hope sealed them all in a vacuum.

"Hmm…" the woman behind the plastic said. A new sound. That wasn't the sound they usually made. Kace looked at her. Through the plastic, she looked slightly distorted, but she was an elderly woman, wearing a drab dress. She had a peacock brooch above her left breast. Probably against code. "I'm sorry, Mr. Carver, can you wait a second?"

She gestured to the seating area and Carver drifted off. He didn't sit. He wondered what that "Hmm" was all about.

The woman behind the plastic picked up the telephone and dialed. Kace couldn't hear what she was saying and she'd brought her hand up to mask her mouth.

He stood still, not lifting his eyes from the woman, as she had her silent conversation. She put the phone down and smiled to him.

"Just a few minutes, Mr. Carver."

"Can I go through?"

"One of the officers on duty is coming to meet you, Mr. Carver. Have a seat."

Kace didn't sit. He stared at the receptionist for a number of minutes before a short skinny man in a suit came around the corner. He looked uncomfortable, as though he may spontaneously combust at any second. There was no way that he was a guard—this man couldn't police a slice of toast.

"Mr. Carver," the man said, holding out a shaky hand.

Kace took it. It was cold and clammy. Something was very wrong.

"I am Evan Wright, the family liaison officer for Pentonville. Would you follow me to my office?"

"I'd rather like to see my father instead."

Evan Wright offered a short smile. "Please." And he gestured down the hallway.

Without any real alternative, Kace followed the officer into a small office, filled with filing cabinets and stacks of paperwork.

The man slid behind the desk and sat down, instantly seeming to calm down. Now there was a desk between them, everything was okay. Kace sat.

"When was the last time you saw your father, Ian Carver?" Mr. Wright said.

"Last week. During weekend visiting. Has something happened?"

"How did he seem to you?" Mr. Wright said, ignoring Kace's question.

"He was fine. He was in prison. He was as fine as he could be. Can you tell me what is going on?" Kace was starting to get agitated, and he knew what he got like when he was angry. Dr. Winter's voice echoed in his head, "Use the anger. Don't let it control you. *You* control *it*."

Wright held up a hand, as if predicting Kace's outburst. He put it down and smiled that short sad smile again. "Your father seemed very odd this past week. He is usually obedient. He usually keeps his distance from the, let's say, more colorful characters we have here at Pentonville. But suddenly, he started getting on the wrong side of those very same people.

"Prisons are weird places. There's no real concept of time. Things can change at the drop of a hat. Your father started to make enemies. Powerful enemies."

"Why?"

"We were hoping you knew."

"No. He. He…" Kace said, trying to grasp words just out of reach, "he was fine."

"As far as we can tell, he was going through some kind of psychological crisis."

"As far as you can tell? You run the prison. Just ask him, for God's sake," Kace said.

That smile again. That was the moment Kace knew. They hadn't asked Ian Carver because there was no Ian Carver to ask.

Mr. Wright cleared his throat. His eyes flitted away from Kace every few seconds, as if looking at an invisible checklist of things to tick off. "We are to understand that this is around the anniversary of your mother's death? Maybe that was why Mr. Carver was…unpredictable. I'm afraid he was involved in an altercation."

"An altercation?" Kace said, almost laughing. How cowardly this man was, this Mr. Wright. Wright couldn't even look him in the eyes, let alone put a name to what had happened to his father.

"Yes," Wright said. "Your father and some other prisoners fought, and…"

"He's dead," Kace finished, begging for the other man to correct him.

Instead, Wright just looked at him. "I'm very sorry."

"Sorry?" Kace said, expecting to shout but instead whispering. "Sorry? Where were the guards?"

"There will be a full investigation into how this was possible."

"Who did it?"

"I'm sorry?"

"Who killed my father?"

"I'm afraid I can't tell you that."

"I want you to tell me who killed my father." Something uncurled inside Kace, some creature which had been asleep for a long, long time. An insatiable anger. And he wanted to laugh. He wanted to howl. And now his father was dead.

"We will do everything in our power to work out what and how this happened. On behalf of HMP Pentonville, you have our condolences. Everything will be done to support you at this difficult time."

Kace got up. "My father is dead," he said, tucking his chair in to the desk. "I have no further business here."

He walked out of the office, ignoring the fact that Mr. Wright was shouting to him about details and follow-ups and inquests.

He walked out of the reception, even as the receptionist begged him back to sign some forms and check out. He walked across the parking lot and made it to his car, as other visitors were arriving to see their, no doubt living, loved ones.

He sat in his car for a long time. He sat there in silence, barely moving, barely even breathing. It was a cold day but it felt even colder now. His father was dead. He was a thirty-three-year-old orphan. Why did that bother him as much as it did? He was alone. He sat in his car for a long time.

He just sat there.

And at some point, he started to laugh.

54

It went on forever. Up and up and up, like he was climbing out of Hell itself. His calf throbbed with pain every time he put his left leg down on one of the steel bars of the ladder. His leg ached where Mandy had dug her nails into him. Somewhere below him, he could hear Ryan and Headphones. It felt wrong to leave them, but what could he do?

It felt like he was back in the vents. The air was thinner here than it had been in the room. It took a lot of effort to heave himself up the ladder.

He had just got used to the cycle of effort and pain when he almost slammed headfirst into the hatch. It seemed invisible in the darkness—a nondescript lid on all the terrors happening below.

He sensed it just in time and stopped, putting a hand out to feel above him. It felt cold and strong. He ran his fingers across it and found a steel wheel in the center. He redistributed his weight, making sure he wouldn't fall, and grasped the wheel with both hands. It was stiff but after a few seconds it started to turn. He steadied himself and turned until he felt the seal open. He pushed on the wheel and it started to come free.

He felt the hatch move—start to open above him. It was heavier than he expected—requiring all the strength he had left to push it. Finally, he wrenched it up and over the hinge. It made a dull scraping sound as it rested open against something.

He took a deep breath of cold fresh air and stuck his head out. He was in what looked like a small stone outhouse. Tight and narrow, and somewhat hastily built. He could see sunlight through the gaps between the wonkily placed stones of the four walls.

He pulled himself out of the hatch and finally set his feet on solid ground, a sigh escaping him. He ran his hand over the stones of one of the walls, cold and rough against his fingers. They felt real, more real than anything he'd experienced today.

The door was wooden and rotten, hanging slightly off its hinges. On the back of it was a moldy poster of a soldier talking to someone. "They talked...this happened. Careless talk costs lives."

World War II. A World War II bunker. That must have been where he was—what the place was built for. A repurposed World War II bunker made up to look like a room in The Great Hotel. He had been fooled, hell, even the man who worked at the hotel had. The level of detail was astonishing. It really had been a hotel room in Central London. A very public place. But it wasn't. Really, it was just some nondescript bunker in the ground. Sheppard wondered how long it had taken to make something up like that and kept coming back to how much effort it had all been. The repurposing of the bunker, orchestrating everyone's kidnappings, keeping them all under until it was ready for them to wake up, placing the clues.

The one, horrible thought.

Eren must really hate me.

Hate didn't seem an adequate word.

Sheppard reached the door and slowly pushed it open. Sunlight flooded the outhouse. So bright, it blew out his vision for a few seconds. He shielded his eyes and looked out. A field— lush and green. Not quite the bright, airy summer's day he now knew to be manufactured down in the bunker. More dull and cold. The wind greeted him, whipping across his face as he stepped out. Seagulls cawed and he smelled salt in the air. He looked toward the noise as a couple of seagulls emerged from beyond the field. There, the grass grew longer and more disparate. Were they near the sea?

He looked the other way and saw only more fields. He decided the hill was the way to go and started walking. Following a hunch. Although he couldn't really rely on hunches anymore. He was a fool, and everyone knew it. Especially Eren.

But where was he?

He knew he was in Britain. He could feel it, smell it, sense it in the way you can do when you are home. But quite where he was, he had no idea.

More seagulls and as he climbed the hill, he looked up to see the birds making their way across a sky plagued with dark clouds. Two of the birds dipped and swirled through the sky, keeping pace with each other. Free. Together.

He was at the top of the hill before he knew it, the ground becoming more uneven and unstable. He looked down to see it was sand.

What he expected. The land cascaded into a beach that stretched as far as the eye could see. The tide was coming in, making the beach narrow, quickly dipping and getting swallowed by the sea. Even in the dingy light, Sheppard didn't think he'd seen anything more beautiful or ever felt so alive.

The scene was perfect. Until...

There was someone. A small figure standing on the beach. Possibly about a mile away. He knew who it was.

And he knew the figure was waiting for him.

55

Before…

Winter didn't like them in his house. Eren had obviously been there before, but it was something about him and the girl together. They were sitting around his kitchen table, with documents spread out all over it. In front of Eren, there was a large hand-drawn diagram of the hotel room that he himself had drawn when he had stayed in The Great Hotel.

In front of him and Phillips were fanned-out profiles of people—real people—that were candidates. A couple of them were about to become players in a game they could never hope to understand. Winter had been sorting through the profiles for the last five hours.

"Are we done?" Phillips said, sounding bored.

Eren smiled. "I think so. Simon, you want to run down the list of England's luckiest?"

There was a bad taste in Winter's mouth. "I'll let you do the honors," he said, and slid the pile over to Eren.

"I was secretly hoping you'd say that." Eren laughed and

picked up the first sheet of paper. He turned it round and showed it to the other two as though he was showcasing it in front of a class. The sheet had a picture of Phillips clipped to it. The rest detailed her backstory—like some crib sheet for a fantasy game.

Phillips smiled.

"Here we have our very own Amanda Phillips, our snake in the rough. Her task is to keep the game going along its intended path. You, Mandy, are the most important piece of the puzzle. You have to become Morgan's ally, he has to believe you are his friend. He'll like you—you're young and pretty. And he's stupid. As long as you don't do anything to reveal your position, there's no way he'll ever suspect you."

"I won't let you down," Phillips said, and she put a hand on Eren's arm. Winter had noticed this happening more and more. They had tried to keep it from him but he knew. They had entered a romantic relationship—maybe it had been going on for weeks. He was sure that at the start they had probably been using each other for their own ends. But now it wasn't hard to see that Phillips had become truthfully infatuated. Eren saw it too.

"Up next," Eren said, picking up the next piece of paper. "Ryan Quinn. The boy that works at The Great Hotel, so it's going to be hardest to convince him. But he is an important player—he will provide legitimacy if anyone else starts to question if they are in a hotel. We need to fool Ryan Quinn and if we fool him, we've fooled everyone else.

"Next is Constance Ahearn. Me and Simon were on the lookout for someone who could incite some trouble in the room. We might be able to bring out Morgan's dark side if he's faced with lunacy. Ahearn will be desperate and that'll bring everyone in the room down with her. For you Mandy, this will be a tricky one. Ahearn is massively unstable, which means that you should be able to lean on her and make her do things if things get a bit too quiet. One of your priorities is to stick to Ahearn, be the little angel on her shoulder whispering into her ear. Whispering whatever you want. Sheppard doesn't like instability and he sure as hell doesn't like dealing with problems himself. If he trusts you, he'll surely palm off Ahearn to you."

Eren and Phillips laughed. Winter tried to smile too.

But he couldn't. This was all becoming very real.

"Next, we have Alan Hughes." Winter held his breath—he had put Hughes's name into the mix to throw a spanner in the works. Hughes was a dedicated lawyer, he had seen that through his involvement with the MacArthur case. Hughes could solve the murder, even if Sheppard couldn't. *And that's what you want now, is it? You want Sheppard to win?* He didn't know anymore. But this was all going too fast, and he was starting to foresee this whole thing spiraling out of control. Yes, it looked like Eren had a handle on it. But...

Go on, think it.

But Eren was insane.

He had seen it too late. The man was a good playactor, maybe even better than Morgan. He was not surprised they had been friends at school. They were two sides of the same coin.

"...Hughes is going to be a pillar of strength in the room. He's undoubtedly going to be an antagonist to Sheppard. It sounds like a lot of fun." Eren looked at Winter and beamed. "Good shout, Simon."

Winter scraped his chair back and got up. "I need to get the land deed documents from upstairs." A worthless lie as everyone knew why he had to leave the room. The next piece of paper hovering in Eren's hand. *Rhona Michel...its all your fault its all your fault.* Why had he told Eren?

"Fair enough, Simon," Eren said. "You know we have to do it though. She's the one who's seen the most. If only you had locked the door, huh? Poor little Rhona..."

"Don't say her name," Winter said quickly. "Just don't." And he stepped around the table and got out of the kitchen as quickly as possible. Out in the hall, he shut the kitchen door and leaned against it, as silent tears started rolling down his cheeks.

What had he got himself into? What had he got them all into? Those poor people were going to go through hell because of him. What could he do? Did he really have the power to stop this? He was in far too deep to go to the police—he couldn't reveal Eren's plan without revealing his own part in it. And he couldn't go to prison.

"Is he gone?" Phillips's voice. Very quiet. Through the door. "I think I heard him go upstairs."

"He won't be back for a while." Eren. "All because of this Michel girl. He can't deal with the consequences of his actions. I think he's faltering. We need to deal with it."

Phillips. "Do we need to remind him why he's here?"

Eren cleared his throat and lowered his voice even more, so Winter had to strain to hear. "No. He's working against us now. I'm not sure why he chose this Hughes man as a candidate."

"So we just take Hughes out the room."

"I'm afraid we're a little too far along for that. Besides, we can spin this Hughes situation to our advantage, I think. What we can't spin…is Simon's mindset."

"So what do we do?" Phillips said.

"I think you know really," Eren said, and Winter could tell he was smiling. "After all, we still haven't picked a body."

Winter started uncontrollably shaking, so hard he had to step away from the door. They were going to kill him. His part in the game had changed. He had to get out, he had to leave, he had to be anywhere but here. He was going to die.

But where would he go? They knew where he lived—they were sitting in his kitchen, for God's sake. The wrath Eren was bringing down upon Morgan—did Winter really think it would be any less for him? Winter had known Eren for years, knew his deepest, darkest secrets. Eren would find Winter wherever he went. And if he couldn't, he would find Abby. Hell, he already had. He'd already overheard that Phillips had scored a job at Abby's coffee shop.

Eren had him.

Winter's silent tears were now ones of fear. How was he going to get out of this? How was he going to stop Eren doing this to these poor people? And then—a thought, an almost impossibly warped thought. He couldn't do both—but he could help Morgan. Yes, because no matter how much he knew Eren, he knew Morgan more. He could get a message to him somehow.

But that means— Yes. It did. *That means you have to die.* And maybe that was his sacrifice—no—not sacrifice. Maybe that was his reward. For being so consumed by anger. For being molded into something despicable. A monster of his own. Eren and that insipid Mandy Phillips. He wanted to say they used him, but really he had been with them. Running so fast his conscience had to catch up. Maybe this was how it ended.

Abby would be safe. That was the main thing. And, at long last, he would have done the right thing.

But can you do it? Can you go down there knowing you're going to die. No. But he could go down there knowing it was right.

Winter wiped his eyes with his handkerchief and felt a light finality drape over him like a thin bedsheet on a summer's night. This was it.

All he needed was a plan.

And by the time he was ready to reenter the kitchen and rejoin the people who were going to kill him, he had one.

Carver straightened the pad of paper slightly closer to the bedside lamp. Impressions were the most important thing, and anything out of place would ruin the whole thing. That was why he had been extra careful. He had been to The Great Hotel many times, taken thousands upon thousands of photos that would seem dull to even the most enthusiastic photographer. He had even measured everything: the space between the pad and the lamp, the space between the television and the room service menu, banal things that wouldn't matter to anyone in isolation. But together, they might matter—they might spoil the whole illusion.

Amanda was "outside" positioning one of the screens that would show the center of London out the window. She hadn't believed it would work, but Carver had convinced her when he'd created a scale model. Now she was back to being skeptical. A large screen curved down around the window creating a sense of depth. Amanda was positioning a screen adjacent to that which would pipe in the exact same image but would create an illusion of depth. It was like those old TV sets—say a kitchen with a window looking out to the garden—you had to account for every possible way an audience member could view that window and create enough garden to accommodate that. It would give the illusion there was a garden beyond the window—just as his creation gave the illusion of the London skyline. It was a live feed and they were piping in the high-quality audio feed from the real room in The Great Hotel so all the faint traffic sounds, airplanes and city hum was there. It was all smoke and mirrors but it looked good—more than passable.

"Are you sure about this?" Mandy said, hopping over the "window" and taking a look at her handiwork. "All I see is a bunch of screens of London. Yes, they all join up and they all look and sound alright. But it's just screens."

"You see screens because you know they're screens," Carver said. "These people will be stressed, as stressed as they've ever been in their lives—their brains will work against them, fill in the blanks. And you're going to have to pretend." Carver went over to Mandy and carefully put his hands over her eyes. She giggled like a schoolgirl (it made his skin crawl). "Now think," he said, before taking his hands away. "What do you see?"

"London," she said, altogether too triumphantly. She jumped up and kissed Carver on the cheek.

He forced a smile. Of course he wasn't sure about this—not any of it really. Any part of the plan could fail at any moment. The screens. The body. The knife. The phones. And Mandy. He trusted Mandy—no matter how much he despised her—and he thought she could pull it off. That first night they had met in Brickwork he had known she was the right person for the job—but he would be lying if he said he wasn't a little worried.

Dr. Winter was hammering a nail into the wall. He picked up a painting he had specifically asked for himself and hooked it on the wall. Carver had signed off on it of course—it appealed to his warped sense of macabre. Dr. Winter had said that the real painting in the room he had visited was one of a peaceful stream on a summer's day. This one was far more apt.

Mandy looked at it. "Where the hell did you find this?"

"Yard sale," Winter shrugged. "Thought it looked a bit weird."

Mandy reached up her hand and ran her fingers over the dried paint. "You're right there, Doc."

Dr. Winter laughed. "I can't help but keep looking at it. I'm not sure what I find more horrible—the scarecrow's smile or the fact there are probably children upstairs in that house, burning alive as the scarecrow just watches."

Carver raised an eyebrow. Mandy seemed similarly affected. "You know, I might nick that," she said.

"Be my guest," Dr. Winter smiled.

Carver cleared his throat. "Simon, can you go into the bathroom and double-check everything again?"

"Eren, I've already done that three times over. Everything's fine. It's going to be fine."

"Please, just do it."

Winter frowned but scuttled off to the bathroom. He heard the door open and close. Winter was not wrong—he had already been in that small bathroom for about six hours. The man had proven himself to be rather adept at plumbing, believe it or not. Carver had always known that he would need a flushing toilet and working sink. The bathtub was fine, as no one was going to want to get in there. But the other luxuries had to be plumbed. Even if no one actually needed the toilet, Sheppard would be suffering from alcohol and drug withdrawal. So, odds said he was going to throw his guts up.

Carver centered the pad of paper and took the pen out of his pocket, resting it next to the pad. Next to the Holy Bible. Because that was the one staple of all hotels, no matter what the star rating. Every hotel presumed Christianity. Carver always thought how disgustingly offensive that was. Hopefully the Bible would at least help trigger Constance Ahearn's lunacy. Just to help things along.

"It looks like we're all set," Mandy said, looking around and checking everything.

"Yes," Carver said, "just one last thing."

Silently, he pulled the knife out from under one of the pillows on the bed. He handed it to her—handle out.

"This is it then," Mandy said. Carver thought she sounded almost excited. "After all we've planned." She took the knife and looked at it in the light.

"You don't have to be the one who does this, you know. I can do it and make it look like you." She looked at him and he saw her mistake his concern over the plan going awry as concern for her—just as intended.

"I can do this," Mandy said. "You believe in me, don't you?"

"Of course I do," Carver said, and kissed her.

"Everything seems fine in here," Dr. Winter's muffled voice came through the wall.

Mandy and Carver just looked at each other. He nodded. She nodded back.

No more words were needed.

56

Sheppard thought of turning away; walking in the opposite direction. But he knew that he couldn't. He knew that he had to face the man at the end of the beach—he knew that that was the ending to this story.

He made his way down the dunes onto the beach below. Sand kicked up under his feet and he almost fell, moving faster to get to solid ground. The sand on the beach was firmer and easier to walk on than on the dunes, but it was no less inviting. Exhaustion was lapping at him like the waves on the beach, but he knew he would be able to make it to the figure in the distance.

Sheppard took Winter's phone out of his pocket—no signal. He swore under his breath—still no signal even though he was finally out of that hole. He dialed 999 anyway—but nothing. Where was he? He needed to find a phone quickly or Ryan was going to die. And the best chance of a working phone was Eren himself—so Sheppard started walking toward him. Because he knew that, in some way, he deserved this. No one else would have to suffer because of him.

He'd hidden Eren away in his mind for so long. Hiding what

he did under all the good memories, all the substances, all the late nights and later mornings, all the television episodes. Eren was a ghost in the machine of his mind.

If he survived this, could he recover? Bury the fake hotel room like he buried Eren? Everything that happened on this day was a nightmare, buried deep inside him. The people there—like figments of a troubled imagination, fractures of a subconscious. Did he think that, in time, he would come to believe that? Just like, in some way, he had truly believed he solved Mr. Jefferies's murder? What life was there left for Morgan Sheppard after this?

Maybe dying here, in the sand, would be a fitting end. A footnote on a life. He dragged his legs along. They seemed to want him to stop—lie down in the sand. Lie there and die. This was it and this was always where it was going to end.

He was just happy to have been able to get out of the room. To come outside and see the sky again. He had always liked to be outside—needing freedom. Most likely because he loved an exit strategy. But now, he wasn't going to run away. Quite the contrary.

He thought of all the mistakes he made. The parties, the painkillers, the drink and all the bits in between. Every single day was incredibly hazy. The last few years just melded into each other—the same things over and over again. And nothing of any consequence. Not remembering much of anything. And it all began that day he went to the police about Eren's dad.

But everyone would remember this. The Lying Detective. A hell of a headline—one that would no doubt sell a few copies. The tabloids finally taking him down.

The figure was slightly closer now, yet still far enough for him not to be able to make out any features. A black sliver against the dull yellow sand. The only thing Sheppard knew for certain was that the figure was watching him, and had probably been waiting for him for quite some time.

Just keep on walking.

What would happen at the television studio? Would they all weep for him, or would they cry not really knowing why, mistaking grief for their jobs as grief for him? Someone would probably organize an expensive funeral and wake. It would be high profile—good publicity for the network. An open casket with a side of caviar. Lobster toast. Champagne to toast the great brute off.

The show would probably go on without him. It would be stupid not to use the publicity to their advantage. A fresh face would be ushered in. Hell, maybe even Eren himself or someone like him. Someone who deserved it. There would be a memorial episode before handing over—a changing of the guard—to a random, a nonentity. The entertainment business stopped for no one—cash the checks and move on. He'd be forgotten in a week.

He didn't have many friends. Couldn't think of a single person he would call one. There was Douglas, but that was different. It was in Douglas's best interests to get along with him—he was getting paid through the nose for it after all. There were a few people at the television studio he talked to. He didn't know them well enough to put a name to them. And as he thought more about it, he didn't know if he hadn't made those names up as well.

There were a few ex-girlfriends. Michelle, from university, was a plucky young English student. Sheppard had dumped her the minute he signed the TV. Last time he'd Googled her, she was happily married and pregnant. Her Facebook photos were bright and airy and she wore a smile that he'd never seen on her. He pictured her at a breakfast table with her husband, and a baby in a high chair, reading the paper. "Huh, I used to go out with him." And that would be it. Next came Suzie, a woman who didn't respect anything, least of all herself. She wasn't interested in the world, and the world wasn't particularly interested in her. She was a celebrity chaser, which Sheppard found out when he found her in bed with a boy band—all five of them. Sheppard dumped her and she took what little self-respect she had left with her. He fell down a hole of unnamed rendezvous, the ones of which he could remember being particularly sordid and fueled by drink or drugs or both. There were so many, it was a blink-andyoumissit type of life. All of them had names like Crystal, Saffron, Rouge—things that could be adjectives. None would mourn him, unless it garnered them some attention.

No, the person who would probably miss him most was his dealer. He had plunged a lot of capital into the ventures of a certain young druggie (who just so happened to be a bad medical student) with an eye for business etiquette. When the prescriptions ran out, he had had to rethink. He didn't know how many pills he had bought over the years—probably enough to kill a small army—but he was sure he was the reason that that dealer had kept afloat. What was his name? Sheppard could remember his face, but his name escaped him. He was always hyperactive, his medical degree very obviously in the toilet, and wanted Sheppard to stay and play *Call of Duty* with him. Sheppard always appreciated that he had never just upped and sold him out to a newspaper. That's what he would have done.

Sheppard looked up to see that he had covered a lot of ground. The man in front of him was wearing a suit, with a red tie. When Sheppard saw this, he knew it was impossible that he could have been wearing anything else. The elusive man with the red tie from Constance's story. The evil man.

The man was holding a pair of black, shiny, pointed shoes—his feet were buried in the sand. He wasn't looking at Sheppard but out to sea, with a glazed expression of wonder on his face. Sheppard had seen that expression many times on him when he was younger. It was a look of excitement.

Sheppard walked up to him, keeping his slow and plodding pace, and only when he was directly beside him did the man turn his head.

Kace Carver smiled, not horribly or wickedly, but genuinely as if he was indeed happy to see his old friend. "Hello, Morgan," he said.

57

He said it as if nothing had happened—as if they'd bumped into each other on the street years later.

"Eren," Sheppard said, feeling the fresh air gush down his throat, drying it up. The name came out as a small rasping sound.

He didn't respond—not at first, but his smile dipped slightly. His eyes became less kind. He broke eye contact and looked back out to sea. "No one's called me that in a long time. I'd really prefer it if you didn't either. It's Kace now."

"Why?" Sheppard said.

"Because the boy you knew is gone. This is the new me. The Carver that you created. So, what do you think?" Carver held his hands up and spun around, like someone trying on clothes in a shop, primed for inspection.

Sheppard wanted to punch him, smash his handsome face in, mash it into something unrecognizable. "You're a monster," he settled on instead.

Carver chuckled. "Well, you've looked better as well." Carver looked him up and down. "You really are a state. I didn't think you'd look this bad. I mean, Jesus. You're pathetic."

"You locked me in a bunker to die," Sheppard said, resenting himself at how much it sounded like an excuse.

"Yes I did, but here you are. Isn't it a marvel—the human being's resilience, the need to survive? Or, of course, maybe this was all part of the plan." Carver winked.

Sheppard looked out to sea. He couldn't bring himself to look at that face anymore. "Where are we?"

Carver looked around. "We're on Luskentyre, a beach in the Outer Hebrides. You're in Scotland, Morgan."

"How is that possible? How was I in Paris and now I'm in Scotland? How was everyone else in London and now they're here?"

"Nothing supernatural, Morgan. No magic. Just a matter of science. Science and a private jet."

Sheppard genuinely laughed at this, looking back at Carver, but quickly saw that Carver was not joking. "A private jet?"

Carver cleared his throat. "Seeing as you are going to ask me all these questions, I might as well just tell you. I think I owe you an explanation before you leave."

Before you leave.

Sheppard had no fight left in him. He had no will to run away screaming. He just nodded. He wanted to know. "Okay."

Carver nodded too. "You don't know how long I've waited for this moment. I have been harboring a special kind of resentment for you, Morgan Sheppard, and if you have to ask why, then you really haven't been paying attention. I've been watching you, watching all your feeble relationships, your vapid television program, all your enigmatic substance abuse. Sometimes I have been right behind you, so much so I could whisper in your ear—but you never noticed me. I'd been content being the observer, but something changed.

"Three years ago, my father died in prison. I visited him every week, ever since my aunt let me. I never missed a visit—and then one day I went and he wasn't there. He was never built for prison. In some ways, I'm shocked he lasted as long as he did. Two guys blinded him with sharpened plastic cutlery, cut his throat. When the guards found him, half of him was spread out on the floor. Some people say the guards were in on it. You see, I think my father was killed because he was too nice.

"That's the first time I really knew the extent of my hatred. That was when it was over and when it had just begun. I knew the one man who had ruined my life was out there, popping pills like Tic Tacs and barreling through lives like they're nothing. I knew I had to stop you. I knew it was my duty.

"My father left behind not an unreasonable estate. But it wouldn't have been enough to support me. I sold everything. Even...no, *especially*...the family house. It gave me enough to start anew. I bought a small flat in Milton Keynes. Not very grand, but enough.

"I used the rest of the money to invest in stocks. A risky venture, you might say. But it was easy enough for me. As you remember, or don't, as the case may be, I've always been gifted with a rather special mind. I treated the stock market like I would, say, a murder. I analyzed every inch, every eventuality, every outcome. It was almost fun. But it was also too easy. I still do it—but I've lost interest.

"Once you have so much money—well, even that seems boring.

"So I needed a new venture. And that is when I got the idea. To finally find you. And make you see what you'd done. I had the capital, all I needed was the plan."

"What about the others? Mandy and Winter," Sheppard said.

"I knew very quickly that I would need help on this venture of mine. It was a lot of work. I found one of my helpers at one of your God-awful parties. She had snuck in to try and get you to confess to killing her brother. Not directly killing, of course.

You never do anything that could actually get you in trouble, do you? You prefer the indirect route.

"Amanda Phillips seemed keen—she was almost as eager for revenge as me. You have probably seen it—that fire behind her eyes. Did you know that you could do that to people? Anyway, Amanda was on board almost immediately, but I couldn't let there be a slight chance that she would disappear. So I let her fall in love with me. It was pretty easy—she was vulnerable, and I've always been blessed with a certain charisma. We bonded over you. Soon enough, she would do anything for me. Even kill, and even die. Of course, she never actually thought I would let her die down there. Even when we were planting the explosives, she thought I would somehow swoop in to save her, in the event of us blowing the place sky-high. She was so clever, but what is it they say? Ah yes—love makes fools of us all. I didn't ever believe that, but it turns out it's true.

"Dr. Winter was a little harder to bewitch. Even though you messed up his daughter and he knew the truth…"

"It was you," Sheppard said, "it was you who told him. That's what he was talking about that night."

"I'll let you into a little secret, Morgan," Carver said. "I was there that night." He laughed. "In the kitchen. It was quite a show."

Sheppard felt a shiver go down his spine. Eren had been there—had really only been one step behind him.

"Anyway, even after all that, Winter was still reluctant. The old man had a code. The terrible thing about codes though—the wording's always terrible, no one really knows how far they can go before they get to their breaking point, so how is one to know when to stop? Winter was a fragile soul. Eventually, he snapped. It was that night—you remember it. He was very useful in providing information about drugs that could knock someone out for long periods of time, for instance. And he was good at doing the things I didn't want to do. Like going to the hotel and buying the land on which the bunker is based. It's always nice to have a partner after all. Well half partner, half scapegoat.

"See, I had to make sure that things went how I wanted. So we had to make sure anyone who could possibly rumble us was taken care of. Luckily we needed people inside the room so that worked out well. We didn't have to choose random people. In a way, they chose themselves. And Mandy fit in perfectly as one of them—and after all, she could easily play the pretty young thing. The girl that just so happened to be entirely your type. It was perfect—almost like it was destined to be.

"There was one person who was never in my plan though. One person who was never meant to be in the room. Alan Hughes. Dr. Winter went off script, used my plans for himself. So I changed mine.

"See, we knew Mandy was going to be in the room as your temptress, but the body was never meant to be Dr. Winter. I wanted him with me, watching everything, providing his professional opinion. But he decided to get personal, do things he didn't tell us about. He got very angry toward the end—not just toward you but toward the world. It was about his daughter—he found out I had Mandy take a job where she worked, just to check on her. I knew that he might lash out again at a point I couldn't predetermine. So I knew we had to get rid of him—and we did need a body for the bathtub. Of course he didn't know—the old fool."

No, Sheppard thought, *Winter was worth more than you gave him credit for. He worked it out straight away. He knew he was going to his death—and decided to tell me exactly who killed him.* This was what he thought, but he found he still couldn't speak.

"Of course, with Winter being in the bathtub, I knew the whole structure of your investigation would change. People would recognize Winter and you would start to piece together some kind of truth. I thought about it for a long time, but in the end I knew you wouldn't have enough of the facts to get to me, and even if you did figure it out, you couldn't do anything. In a way, having Winter there was better. I could see the look in your eyes when you saw him."

Carver smiled. Sheppard felt sick. An old man died and the only way his friend could think of it was as a cog in his machine.

"I was planning to pick the corpse at random so it would be more difficult. So really, you were playing my game on Easy mode. And you still couldn't do it."

A gust of wind threatened to blow him over. Carver stood steadfast.

"Far less easy was actually getting everyone into the room. The stage was set, but we needed the players. We extracted most people without incident—we used the gas to knock a person out and then got them into a van where we gave a general anesthetic that could be applied at regular intervals on the trip. We used my private jet to get here, transferring you first and then all the London people. Mandy stayed with you to make sure you didn't wake up while we got everyone else. You think that it has only been a matter of hours since you fell asleep in Paris. But in truth it's been two days."

"Two days," Sheppard said. "How is that possible?"

Carver smiled. "People seem so astounded at this, but hospitals keep patients asleep for hours upon hours, sometimes days. You know that the longest surgery ever was four whole days. The human body is a wonderful thing, Morgan. You should know that. How much alcohol have you poured into that liver of yours? And you're still standing. The body adapts, repairs itself, forgives and forgets."

They were quiet for a moment. Sheppard didn't know what to say—there was nothing left.

Carver seemed to agree. "I think that's it," he said. "I know it's probably not what you had dreamed up in that head of yours, but there it is. The cruel hard truth I have found over the last three years is that money really can buy anything. But anything isn't enough for me. No, I just want one little thing in particular." Carver put his hand into the waistband of his suit trousers and brought out a small compact pistol. Sheppard had never seen a gun in real life before, but even the sight of it sent him into uncontrollable shivers. "Do you have any more questions?" He clicked the safety off, and held the gun at his side. "Or shall we begin?"

He had to force the words out. "Begin? What have we been doing up to this point?"

"Playing."

"Playing? People died, Eren." Fear in his voice, impossible to mask. "What else do you want? You wanted to hear me say it? I said it. You deserve everything that I have. I admit it. I am nothing. I never was—not without you."

Carver's face suddenly turned a shade of red. However, when he spoke, his voice was still calm. "You know you're only here because of yourself. You have waded through life without even the slightest sniff of consequences. I am the man at the end of the road. This is the path that you set us on twenty-five years ago, Morgan. And you have to be held accountable for that."

Sheppard opened his mouth and found that he could talk again, or that he was allowed. "I was a child. I was eleven years old."

"And it seems like you still are. I guess I have to give you a bit of credit. Not many eleven-year-olds manage to deceive the world. All these years, you could have owned up, come clean, but you never did. You're pathetic. You just wrapped yourself up in all your rubbish and started to believe it yourself. You—a detective? You can't even save yourself. How are you meant to protect other people?"

"I've saved people…"

Carver laughed. "You're talking about those people down in the bunker? Ahearn and Quinn and Michel. You saved them from what exactly? You?"

"No. I saved them from you."

"You didn't save Hughes. You didn't save Winter. Ahearn is going to prison now, for the rest of her life. So will my little helper, Amanda. And Quinn—he's down there dying right now. Because you couldn't protect them."

"How could I have stopped it? I was locked in…"

"Oh shut up. Hughes and Winter are dead because of you. Ahearn and Amanda are killers because of you. What part of that don't you understand? This was all because of you."

Sheppard's strength was low, and Eren's accusations hit him harder than the gusts of wind. He found himself looking down. Because of him—that was undeniable. But this had all happened because of Eren too, and somehow his old friend was blind to that fact.

"So this is the end of your plan? The ending of your story? You're going to kill me?" Sheppard said, meeting Eren's eyes.

Carver looked at the gun in his hand and waved it at him. "Yeah. Kind of poetic. I was thinking about drowning you, but even I have limits."

For some reason, this made Sheppard smile. Was this even happening? The delirium, the withdrawal, the exhaustion. It was all making it seem like a dream. Maybe he was still stuck down in the bunker, gasping for air as the timer ticked down to zero. Was this just all the final brain gasp of a dying man? He wasn't sure which prospect was better, but it seemed that the outcome was going to be the same.

Maybe it was for the best.

People had died. Alan Hughes. Simon Winter. Mandy's brother. He'd messed up Winter's daughter. He just took from the world—take and take and take. Maybe it was time to give back—a debt repaid.

"So," Carver said, "are you ready, old friend?" He held the pistol to Sheppard's head.

58

"Get on your knees," he said, placing his shoes down on the sand, so he could hold the gun up with both hands.

Sheppard did what he was told.

Why fight it?

"Why didn't you just kill me? Why didn't you just do it at the start? Why all this? Why all this theater...?"

Carver laughed, standing over him, holding the barrel of the gun to Sheppard's forehead, death just a millimeter away. "Do you remember back in school? You were always so sure of yourself? Just like you were all your life. Just like you aren't now. See, I had to show you what it felt like to fail. You were always such a bastard," Carver said. "I should have known you would do something like this. Like all this. Your entire life has just been one big joke. I needed to make you understand that."

"What happened to you, Eren?"

"You happened to me. And don't call me that."

"Your father was guilty, Eren."

"Never call me that. My father was guilty of protecting his family."

Sheppard almost laughed at that—somehow. "Protecting his family? Really? Did you ever ask yourself why your father waited so long to kill Jefferies? He wasn't protecting anyone; he was just a time bomb that went off. The only person he did it for was himself."

"That doesn't matter," Carver hissed.

"No, Eren, it's the only thing that matters. This wasn't a crime of passion. It was a well-thought-out and coordinated plan. Your father just plucked up the courage one day to do it. Pathetic. Looks like you really take after him."

"My whore of a mother was going to see Jefferies the night she died. My father was devastated. He took an acceptable measure."

"He took a measure six years later," Sheppard said. "I pity him."

"Shut up," Carver shouted.

Sheppard looked at him, into his eyes—and saw that Eren Carver was indeed gone. This was something new—someone new. The person standing over him was so sure of himself he hadn't even thought about what he, himself, had done. And yes, maybe Morgan Sheppard was the beginning of the path, but the trail he followed had been his own—that of Kace, not Eren.

Maybe Carver saw this flash of realization in Sheppard's face because he spat at him. "You did this," Carver said, standing over him, waving the gun around as though it were a conductor's baton. "You. Did. This. And as you lie there dying, your blood flowing out onto the sand, you just remember you wanted this. This is the end of the path you started us on. This is on you."

Sheppard breathed, spluttered. "No, Kace, this is on both of us."

Carver stopped, rested the barrel of the gun in the center of Sheppard's forehead. "Morgan, it's over."

"You think…" Sheppard said, stopping to splutter, "you think I stole your shot at being a hero. You think I ruined your life.

But I can't have done both. You were never a hero. You were always a monster. You would have ruined your own family, or you would have condoned a murderer. Which would it have been? You're the villain."

"Say that again and I swear to God..."

"You're the villain. And I'm a terrible excuse for a human being. I've sat back and wreaked havoc with other people's lives. I've done some, no, a lot of things that I am deeply ashamed of. But I can change. You, you'll always be a monster."

The butt of the gun came hurtling toward Sheppard. His nose plumed into a mess of blood and hurt. He howled.

Carver was laughing. "You are the parasite. You think the world will miss you?"

"No," Sheppard said, nasally, spitting blood this time. "Not in the slightest."

He saw his parents, his ex-girlfriends, his colleagues. All people he had driven away. The only real friend he'd ever had was moments away from putting a bullet in his brain.

This isn't the end.

With the last of his strength, Sheppard charged forward, taking Carver by surprise. He collided with the man's legs just as the gun went off. The bullet passed millimeters from Sheppard's right ear, ripping into the top of it. Carver went sprawling on the ground. The gun fell an arm's stretch away from both of them.

Sheppard reached out for the gun, but Carver punched him in the face. His vision blurred and he scrabbled around in the sand with one hand. With the other, he slammed Carver's head into the sand.

Carver yowled as Sheppard pressed the man's nose into his face.

Sheppard blinked away the blur and grasped the gun. He pinned Carver down and his friend roared with unbridled hatred. Without thinking twice, Sheppard threw the gun into the sea. It sailed through the air and landed in the water with a plop. Sheppard watched it and Carver took his chance to send his fist ramming up into Sheppard's chin.

Sheppard went sprawling and Carver got up, going over to Sheppard and grabbing him by the scruff of the neck of his shirt. He pulled him over to where the water was coming up against the beach. Carver bent down and gripped Sheppard by the neck. "I don't need a gun to kill you."

Sheppard realized what was going to happen too late. Carver forced his head up then plunged it down into the cold, cold water. Sheppard didn't have time to breathe before water filled his lungs. He struggled—his life draining out of him. How many seconds could he last? How long did he have?

Carver wrenched him out of the sea. "These are consequences, Morgan."

Sheppard swung around at Carver blindly. It was nowhere near connecting but it was enough for Carver to lose his grip around Sheppard's neck. His face planted into the sand and he kicked out with his legs. They connected with Carver's shins, and the man groaned.

Now. You have to get away now.

Sheppard fell into an oncoming wave and scrabbled around to get up. Carver was staggering away from him, sinking down onto all fours. Sheppard got to him and grabbed him by the shoulders, pulling him up by his tie. Carver choked and snarled at him through clenched teeth. He'd cut his lip, so it was a bloody scowl.

"Thank you, Kace, for showing me people can change," Sheppard said, spitting seawater at him. "Maybe there's hope for me after all."

Carver looked at him, an unwavering gaze. "This isn't over, Morgan. If it's not today, it'll be another. Wherever you go, I'll be there. No matter how much you feel protected. I would burn the world down to get to you. So, kill me now." An animal voice that didn't even sound human.

Sheppard smiled. "No, I don't think so. It's not my style," he said.

He headbutted Carver as hard as he could.

59

Before everything…

"You know, when you convinced me to skip class I thought it was for a reason," Eren said. He and Morgan had been walking around Central London for about two hours. It was two thirty on a Friday and Eren was missing Maths with Mr. Jefferies. He liked Mr. Jefferies and was already building up a guilty conscience for missing it.

Eleven years old and they were out on their own in London. Morgan had got them out of school by saying that his mum was taking them to a science exhibit. Morgan's mum hadn't ever taken them anywhere, so Eren agreed only because he thought it wouldn't work. But, it did and here they were.

Morgan was giddily skipping along the pavement, ducking and weaving through the crowds of tourists. They had found their way to Leicester Square and beyond, and Eren was starting to believe that there wasn't actually an intended destination.

"You feel that, Eren," Morgan said, turning to him. "That's what freedom feels like."

Eren was still hung up on the Maths class issue. "I just think—like, what if we get homework? We're going to be behind and everything. Maybe we should just go back."

Morgan stopped. "Just chill, Eren, okay. It's one Maths class. School isn't everything."

"It kinda is," Eren said.

Morgan sighed and turned to Eren holding him by the arms. "Eren, mate, we're gonna be fine. I have a foolproof plan to success."

"What is it this time? Olympic gymnast? Writer? Weatherman?"

"I don't know what it is yet, but I just know, Eren, that one day you and me are going to be famous."

"Mmhmm."

"Look," Morgan spun Eren around. "Look at this place." They were standing in front of a hotel. It looked like a pretty expensive one too. There were men at the large glass doors. One of them opened a door to let in a man in a business suit and Eren saw a flash of the lobby. Beautiful clean marble floors and people in crisp uniforms.

"You see this place? All fancy and stuff. Someday we'll be able to stay somewhere like this, Eren."

Eren looked around at his friend. "Okay, but how?"

"Because we'll be able to afford it. We'll be able to get rooms in cool places and actually be able to use minibars and drink beer at ten in the morning and say stuff like 'It's five o'clock somewhere.'"

"You hate beer. You had that bottle you stole from your mum's fridge and you threw up."

"Yes, but I'll drink it till I like it," Morgan said.

Eren sighed. "I'm a little confused what we're doing here."

"We're living in the moment, Eren," Morgan said. "You always act so…old. You're always thinking things through too much. Can't we just for once go 'We're going to be awesome' without having to plan out our entire future. I'm just being… in the moment…that thing that Miss Rain said?"

"Spontaneous?" Eren said.

Morgan clapped his hands and beamed. "Yes, I'm being spontaneous."

"Okay." Eren smiled too. "I'll make a deal with you. You use your spontaneity and I'll use my thinking and we'll see where it gets us. The winner is the one who gets the furthest. The loser has to get the winner a room in that dumb hotel." He nodded to the entrance of the building.

"That, my friend," Morgan laughed, "is a deal. Now, c'mon, I think there's a good noodle place round here." And he started off walking again, so fast that Eren had to jog to keep up. "My mum took me once when she was feeling guilty for leaving me at the supermarket that one time."

"Is that why we skipped class? For noodles?"

"Nope," Morgan said, nudging Eren, "we just so happened to be here. See, Eren, spontaneousity."

"That's not how you say it. You know what, never mind." Eren dodged a large clump of tourists who were crowding around a map. "You never did tell me your new big success plan."

Morgan jumped and laughed. "What do you think about being in a band?"

"I think that's the dumbest thing I've ever heard," Eren said, and they both burst out laughing.

Once they had finished, Morgan skipped across the road (without waiting for the green man of course) and beckoned to Eren. "It's through an alley up here."

Eren crossed the road when it was safe, and as Morgan disappeared around a corner, he looked back at the hotel they had been standing in front of. It looked even more intimidating at a distance—a sleek, rectangular building stretching up into the sky. On the front, the name "The Great Hotel" shone in muted gold.

Eren made a mental note and followed Morgan to the noodle place.

How would Morgan put it?

Ah yes—he followed Morgan to the future.

60

Sheppard screamed with pain as Carver went sprawling on the sand and lay still, his head bleeding. Unconscious. That had been a lot more painful than it looked in the movies. He dipped his hand into the sea and wiped his forehead. His legs gave out and he fell backwards into a wave.

Crawling out of the sea, he vomited—the same purple sludge as before.

Was it over? The nightmare? He couldn't bring himself to think that. Maybe this was all just another step in the plan. Maybe Carver was pretending.

But no. His old friend was lying still, breathing shallowly, eyes closed. The cut on his forehead oozing blood at intervals. Now, he was still and quiet, Sheppard could see Eren in there. The little boy who played SNES and snuck into movies with him—the boy who was the kindest and the smartest person he'd ever known.

How did this happen? How did we get here?

Blink. He was back in Eren's room. Back in time. The children, them, sitting there. He wanted to tell them.

Just don't go in the attic.

Blink. He was back on the beach. And the sky started to spit out rain. Drops fell on his face.

Ryan and Headphones. They need help.

He held himself up by his elbows and looked over to Carver. With some trepidation, he reached over and checked his trouser pockets. Nothing. But in the right pocket of his jacket was a smartphone.

He pulled it out and unlocked it. Falling back into a lying position. He had to sleep—had to rest. But not before…

He pressed the 9 button three times and held the phone to his ear.

It took a while to connect and he thought it wasn't going to work, just like the one he had brought out of the room. But eventually, faintly, it rang.

Beside him, Carver expelled a deep breath. But he was still out. And the sky gave a loud clap of thunder.

As Sheppard listened to the ringing, he saw one lone seagull traveling across the sky, trailing behind the others. Probably on his way home. Sheppard breathed in, feeling the air hitch in his abdomen. He had never felt worse. Or better.

The ringing stopped. He heard a voice. "Hello?" Sheppard said, and closed his eyes.

61

Three Months Later...

Paris was hot in the summer, but not insufferably so. He strolled through the city, regarding the crowds of tourists and locals mixing together. This time, he didn't bother with the tourist locations but instead enjoyed walking around the back alleyways and roads, finding obscure cafés and shops. Fractured discussions in French and English came to him on the breeze. He even understood some of it.

His leg was much better now, and although his slight limp was still noticeable, he barely paid attention to it. People here didn't recognize him as much as they did in London, for which he was thankful. Besides, he didn't really look the same anymore. He'd changed.

He made his way to La Maison around twelve. She was already there, sitting at the bar. He recognized her immediately. His memory of her was blurred, as fractured as the conversations he heard around him. When he looked back, she was not there, not fully, in his memory, in his mind. But he had spent a long time thinking about her. So much so that now, she seemed so familiar. Her brown hair tucked behind her ears, her kind, youthful face. The very things that had attracted him to her in the first place. *"Bonjour,"* she said, with a smile.

"Bonjour." He sat on the stool next to her.

The same place they had first met—almost exactly. "You look different," she said, regarding him with a very precise stare—those wistful eyes. "Yes," he said. "And you look captivating."

"Can I get you a drink?" she said, gesturing to her cocktail.

He could smell it. Alcoholic—sweet yet sharp. He wanted nothing else.

"Soda water," he said, and when she looked at him strangely, he added, "I'm trying to quit." One day at a time.

"Vous allez faire une boisson de femme seule?"

"Je le crains," he said, after a moment of thinking. She was surprised.

"Vous parles français?"

"Just a little. I'm taking a class."

She gestured to the barman and he came over instantly. She wasn't the kind of woman you kept waiting. *"L'eau petillante s'il vous plait."* The barman quickly put a bottle of chilled sparkling water in front of him with a glass. The man waved off the offer of her money. It looked like he was smitten. Hard not to be.

"Why are you learning French?"

"Doctor says it helps to keep the mind busy. Also, there's this girl I like who inconsistently lapses into French, so I thought it might be useful."

"How gallant of you. She must be a lucky woman."

She took a sip of her cocktail. "I'm surprised you found me. We didn't really know that much about each other when…you know…"

He chuckled. "Yeah well… I had a few favors to call in from the television show."

"I looked you up—heard you quit."

He poured a glass of water. "Yeah. I guess I did. Just didn't seem right to carry on, you know. They wanted me to stay—turns out any publicity really is good publicity—but I couldn't. You heard everything?"

"Yes."

"And you don't mind."

"My grandmother used to say *'Un homme sans demons n'est pas un homme du tout.'* A man with no demons is no man at all."

"Yeah. No, I got that one. It was pretty easy."

She laughed. "So what are you going to do now?"

"For the first time in my life, I have no idea."

"Scary," she said, smiling at him.

"Yes." He cleared his throat, took a drink. The bar was filling up with afternoon tourists, and the temperature was rising. "I need to ask you something—why I needed to find you."

"Yes."

He looked at her—looked into her deep blue eyes and wondered if he wanted to know what secrets lurked there. "Did you know what was going to happen? Did you know Eren—Kace Carver?" The name still fell heavy on his lips. He was back on the beach, the salty water in his stubble. Wiping blood off on his shirt. "I just keep thinking—maybe he had got someone to get me back to my room."

"*Non.* The last I saw of you was when I went to get ice. I came back and knocked on your door but there was no answer. I stayed there for about thirty minutes—just knocking. I thought you must have gone—or fallen asleep. It was not the first time someone had run out on me, I'll have you know. But there was nothing to be done. So…"

"So you forgot it ever happened."

"Yes. Until I saw the news. And then I knew."

"You could have come forward, you know. Sold your story."

"I could have. I didn't."

He nodded. She was telling the truth—didn't seem like the type of person who didn't.

"How are the others?" she asked. "The people you were with?"

He thought for a moment. He hadn't seen any of them in a while. Anytime he had, it had been awkward. He'd gone to see Ryan in the hospital a few times, but it was strange. Like their story together was over. They would always be bound by what happened in the Room. But that was done. "They're okay, as far as I know," he decided on. "Hughes's funeral is next week. I don't know if I'm going to go though."

"You should go," she said. "You owe him that."

What he had been wrestling with. Spoken aloud. He knew he had to go.

"Is he in prison?" she asked. He knew who she was talking about.

"He's going to trial soon. Amanda—I mean Phillips—" (they were all referred to by their last names in the newspapers) "—has already been sentenced. And Ahearn got sent to Broadmoor. Turns out she'd been skipping out on a lot of medication."

"The *mechants* are behind bars. *Une fin heureuse?*"

"No, I think my *fin* will not terribly be *heureuse*."

"That doesn't make any sense."

He took another sip of water. Nervous, for some reason. He thought maybe it was some kind of PTSD. His doctor said it was a side effect of being normal and sober. He decided to go for it. "Have you eaten? I know a good place."

"Are you asking me out on a date?"

"I guess I am."

She mused for a moment. "Okay. *J'adorerais.*"

"Good. Great," he said, and then chuckled. "It occurs to me that I still don't know your name."

She laughed, and put out her hand. "I'm Audrey."

He shook it. "Morgan Sheppard."

She laughed. "I know."

★ ★ ★ ★ ★

Acknowledgements

Firstly, I wouldn't be a writer without my grandfather who encouraged my love of books and inspired me to start writing my own. Given that this novel was written as my thesis for the MA in Creative Writing (Crime/Thriller) at City University London, the number of people who have been part of it is rather astronomical. Firstly, I would like to thank Claire McGowan, the course leader, who was always there when I needed a helping hand, and my personal "celebrity guest" tutor A.K. Benedict, who believed in me from the very start, even when I didn't believe in myself. Without the guidance of these two people, this book would not be in your hands today. They were always there to pick me up when I was down (one time, literally). To William Ryan, who offered help in the early stages of the novel's life. Of course, to all the wonderful people I met throughout the MA course and helped me along the way. I couldn't have asked for better classmates. To the #SauvLife crew (simply put, we're a crew and we like sauvignon blanc), Fran Dorricott, Jenny Lewin and Lizzie Curle, some of the most talented and kind people I have ever met. To my wonderful agent Hannah Sheppard, who is incredibly dedicated and didn't mind having to explain incredibly simple things to me about business. To my amazing editor Francesca Pathak, who was behind this book from the second she read it and sourced a horsehead mask in record time to attempt (and succeed) to wow me. And finally, to all the people at Orion, who have made me feel perfectly at home. An incredible thank you to everyone. I would also love to thank everyone at Hanover Square Press who have supported *Guess Who*—Peter Joseph, Natalie Hallak and all others, who have made Hanover a real home away from home!